The Joy Of Christmas

Betty Neels
Margaret Way
Helen Brooks

Harlequin Mills & Boon™

First Published 2007
Second Australian Paperback Edition 2007
ISBN 978 0 733 58252 3

Published by
Harlequin Mills & Boon
Level 5
15 Help Street
CHATSWOOD NSW 2067
AUSTRALIA

Printed and bound in Australia by
McPherson's Printing Group

CONTENTS

THE MISTLETOE KISS

BY
BETTY NEELS

CHAPTER ONE

IT WAS a blustery October evening, and the mean little wind was blowing old newspapers, tin cans and empty wrapping papers to and fro along the narrow, shabby streets of London's East End. It had blown these through the wide entrance to the massive old hospital towering over the rows of houses and shops around it, but its doors were shut against them, and inside the building it was quiet, very clean and tidy. In place of the wind there was warm air, carrying with it a whiff of disinfectant tinged with floor polish and the patients' suppers, something not experienced by those attending the splendid new hospitals now replacing the old ones. There they were welcomed by flowers, a café, signposts even the most foolish could read and follow…

St Luke's had none of these—two hundred years old and condemned to be closed, there was no point in wasting money. Besides, the people who frequented its dim corridors weren't there to look at flowers, they followed the painted pointed finger on its walls telling them to go to Casualty, X-Ray, the wards or Out Patients, and, when they got there, settled onto the wooden benches in the waiting rooms and had a good gossip with whoever was next to them. It was their hospital, they felt at home in it; its lengthy corridors held no worries for them, nor did the elderly lifts and endless staircases.

They held no worries for Ermentrude Foster, skimming up to the top floor of the hospital, intent on delivering the message which had been entrusted to her as quickly as possible before joining the throng of people queuing for buses on their way home. The message had nothing to do with her, actually; Professor ter Mennolt's secretary had come out of her office as Ermentrude had been getting into her outdoor things, her hours of duty at the hospital telephone switchboard finished for the day, and had asked her to run up to his office with some papers he needed.

'I'm late,' said the secretary urgently. 'And my boyfriend's waiting for me. We're going to see that new film…'

Ermentrude, with no prospect of a boyfriend or a film, obliged.

Professor ter Mennolt, spectacles perched on his magnificent nose, was immersed in the papers before him on his desk. A neurologist of some renown, he was at St Luke's by invitation, reading a paper on muscular dystrophies, lecturing students, lending his knowledge on the treatment of those patients suffering from diseases of the nervous system. Deep in the study of a case of myasthenia gravis, his, 'Come,' was absent-minded in answer to a knock on the door, and he didn't look up for a few moments.

Ermentrude, uncertain whether to go in or not, had poked her head round the door, and he studied it for a moment. A pleasant enough face, not pretty, but the nose was slightly tip-tilted, the eyes large and the wide mouth was smiling.

Ermentrude bore his scrutiny with composure, opened the door and crossed the room to his desk.

'Miss Crowther asked me to bring you this,' she told him cheerfully. 'She had a date and wanted to get home...'

The professor eyed her small, slightly plump person and looked again at her face, wondering what colour her hair was; a scarf covered the whole of it, and since she was wearing a plastic mac he deduced that it was raining.

'And you, Miss...?' He paused, his eyebrows raised.

'Foster, Ermentrude Foster.' She smiled at him. 'Almost as bad as yours, isn't it?' Undeterred by the cold blue eyes staring at her, she explained, 'Our names,' just in case he hadn't understood. 'Awkward, aren't they?'

He had put down his pen. 'You work here in the hospital?'

'Me? Yes, I'm a telephonist. Are you going to be here for a long time?'

'I can hardly see why the length of my stay should interest you, Miss Foster.'

'Well, no, it doesn't, really.' She gave him a kind smile. 'I thought you might be a bit lonely up here all by yourself. Besides I rather wanted to see you—I'd heard about you, of course.'

'Should I feel gratified at your interest?' he asked coldly.

'No, no, of course not. But they all said how handsome you were, and not a bit like a Dutchman.' She paused then, because his eyes weren't cold any more, they were like blue ice.

He said levelly, 'Miss Foster, I think it might be a good idea if you were to leave this room. I have work to do, and interruptions, especially such as yours, can be annoying. Be good enough to tell Miss Crowther on no account to send you here again.'

He bent over his work and didn't watch her go.

Ermentrude went slowly back through the hospital and out into the wet October evening to join the queue at the nearest bus stop, thinking about the professor. A handsome man, she conceded; fair hair going grey, a splendid nose, heavy-lidded eyes and a firm mouth—which was a bit thin, perhaps. Even sitting at his desk it was easy to see that he was a very large man. Still quite young, too. The hospital grapevine knew very little about him, though.

She glanced back over her shoulder; there were still lighted windows on the top floor of the hospital; one of them would be his. She sighed. He hadn't liked her and, of course, that was to be understood. She had been ticked off on several occasions for not being respectful enough with those senior to her—and they were many—but that hadn't cured her from wanting to be friends with everyone.

Born and brought up in a rural part of Somerset, where everyone knew everyone else, she had never quite got used to the Londoners' disregard for those around them. Oblivious of the impatient prod from the woman behind her, she thought of the professor sitting up there, so far from anyone… And he was a foreigner, too.

Professor ter Mennolt, unaware of her concern, adjusted his spectacles on his nose and addressed himself to the pile of work on his desk, perfectly content with his lot, careless of the fact that he was alone and a foreigner. He had quite forgotten Ermentrude.

The bus, by the time Ermentrude got onto it, was packed, and, since it was raining, the smell of wet raincoats was overpowering. She twitched her small nose and wondered what was for supper, and, after a ten-minute ride squashed between two stout women, got off with relief.

Five minutes' walk brought her to her home, midway down a terrace of small, neat houses in a vaguely shabby street, their front doors opening onto the pavement. She unlocked the door, calling, 'It's me,' as she did so, and opened a door in the narrow hallway. Her mother was there, sitting at a small table, knitting. Still knitting, she looked up and smiled.

'emmy—hello, love. Supper's in the oven, but would you like a cup of tea first?'

'I'll make it, Mother. Was there a letter from Father?'

'Yes, dear, it's on the mantelpiece. Have you had a busy day?'

'So-so. I'll get the tea.'

Emmy took off her raincoat and scarf,, hung them on a peg in the hall and went into the kitchen, a small, old-fashioned place with cheerful, cheap curtains and some rather nice china on the dresser shelves. About all there was left of her old home, thought Emmy, gathering cups and saucers and opening the cake tin.

Her father had taught at a large school in Somerset, and they had lived in a nearby village in a nice old house with a large garden and heavenly views. But he had been made redundant and been unable to find another post! Since an elderly aunt had recently died and left him this small house, and a colleague had told him of a post in London, they had come here to live. The post wasn't as well paid, and Mrs Foster found that living in London was quite a different matter from living in a small village with a garden which supplied her with vegetables all the year round and hens who laid fresh eggs each day.

Emmy, watching her mother coping with household

bills, had given up her hopes of doing something artistic. She drew and painted and embroidered exquisitely, and had set her sights on attending a school of needlework and then starting up on her own—she wasn't sure as what. There had been an advertisement in the paper for a switchboard operator at St Luke's, and she had gone along and got the job.

She had no experience of course, but she had a pleasant voice, a nice manner and she'd been keen to have work. She'd been given a week's training, a month's trial and then had been taken on permanently. It wasn't what she wanted to do, but the money was a great help, and one day her father would find a better post. Indeed, he was already well thought of and there was a chance of promotion.

She made the tea, offered a saucer of milk to Snoodles the cat, handed a biscuit to George the elderly dachshund, and carried the tray into the sitting room.

Over tea she read her father's letter. He had been standing in for a school inspector, and had been away from home for a week. He would be coming home for the weekend, he wrote, but he had been asked to continue covering for his colleague for the next month or so. If he accepted, then it would be possible for Mrs Foster to be with him when it was necessary for him to go further afield.

'Mother, that's wonderful—Father hates being away from home, but if you're with him he won't mind as much, and if they're pleased with him he'll get a better job.'

'I can't leave you here on your own.'

'Of course you can, Mother. I've Snoodles and George for company, and we know the neighbours well enough if I should need anything. I can come home for my lunch hour and take George for a quick walk. I'm sure Father will agree to that. Besides, Father gets moved from one school to the other, doesn't he? When he is nearer home you can be here.'

'I'm sure I don't know, love. The idea of you being on your own…'

Emmy refilled their cups. 'If I had a job in another town, I'd be on my own in some bedsitter, wouldn't I? But I'm at home. And I'm twenty-three…'

'Well, I know your father would like me to be with him. We'll talk about it at the weekend.'

By breakfast time the next morning Mrs Foster was ready to concede that there was really no reason why she shouldn't join her husband, at least for short periods. 'For you're home by six o'clock most evenings, when it's still quite light, and I dare say we'll be home most weekends.'

Emmy agreed cheerfully. She was due to go on night duty in a week's time, but there was no need to remind her mother of that. She went off to catch a bus to the hospital, glad that the rain had ceased and it was a nice autumn day.

The switchboard was busy; it always was on Fridays. Last-minute plans for the weekend, she supposed, on the part of the hospital medical staff—people phoning home, making appointments to play golf, arranging to meet to discuss some case or other—and all these over and above the outside calls, anxious family wanting news of a patient, doctors' wives with urgent messages, other hospitals wanting to contact one or other of the consulting staff. It was almost time for her midday dinner when a woman's voice, speaking English with a strong accent, asked to speak to Professor ter Mennolt.

'Hold the line while I get him for you,' said Emmy. His wife, she supposed, and decided that she didn't much like the voice—very haughty. The voice became a person in her mind's eye, tall and slim and beautiful—because the professor wouldn't look at anything less—and well used to having her own way.

He wasn't in his room, and he wasn't on any of the wards she rang. She paused in her search to reassure the voice that she was still trying, and was rewarded by being told to be quick. He wasn't in Theatre, but he was in the Pathology Lab.

'There you are,' said Emmy, quite forgetting to add 'sir'. 'I've a call for you; will you take it there?'

'Only if it's urgent; I'm occupied at the moment.'

'It's a lady,' Emmy told him. 'She told me to hurry. She speaks English with an accent.'

'Put the call through here.' He sounded impatient.

It wouldn't hurt him to say thank you, reflected Emmy as she assured his caller that she was being put through at once. She got no thanks from her either. 'They must suit each other admirably,' said Emmy under her breath, aware that the bossy woman who went around with a clipboard was coming towards her. As usual she was full of questions—had there been delayed calls? Had Ermentrude connected callers immediately? Had she noted the times?

Emmy said yes to everything. She was a conscientious worker, and although it wasn't a job she would have chosen she realised that she was lucky to have it, and it wasn't boring. She was relieved for her dinner hour presently, and went along to the canteen to eat it in the company of the ward clerks and typists. She got on well with them, and they for their part liked her, though considering her hopelessly out of date, and pitying her in a friendly way because she had been born and brought up in the country and had lacked the pleasures of London. She lacked boyfriends, too, despite their efforts to get her to join them for a visit to a cinema or a pub.

They didn't hold it against her; she was always good-natured, ready to help, willing to cover a relief telephonist if she had a date, listening to emotional outbursts about boyfriends with a sympathetic ear. They agreed among themselves that she was all right—never mind the posh voice; she couldn't help that, could she, with a father who was a schoolmaster? Besides, it sounded OK on the phone, and that was what her job was all about, wasn't it?

Home for the weekend, Mr Foster agreed with Emmy that there was no reason why she shouldn't be at home on her own for a while.

'I'll be at Coventry for a week or ten days, and then several schools in and around London. You don't mind, Emmy?'

She saw her mother and father off on Sunday evening, took George for a walk and went to bed. She wasn't a nervous girl and there were reassuringly familiar noises all around her: Mr Grant next door practising the flute, the teenager across the street playing his stereo, old Mrs Grimes, her other neighbour, shouting at her husband who was deaf. She slept soundly.

She was to go on night duty the next day, which meant that she would be relieved at dinner time and go back to work at eight o'clock that evening. Which gave her time in the afternoon to do some shopping at the row of small shops at the end of the street, take George for a good walk and sit down to a leisurely meal.

There was no phone in the house, so she didn't have to worry about her mother ringing up later in the evening. She cut sandwiches, put *Sense and Sensibility* and a much thumbed *Anthology of English Verse* in her shoulder bag with the sandwiches, and presently went back through the dark evening to catch her bus.

When she reached the hospital the noise and bustle of the day had subsided into subdued footsteps, the distant clang of the lifts and the occasional squeak of a trolley's wheels. The relief telephonist was waiting for her, an elderly woman who manned the switchboard between night and day duties.

'Nice and quiet so far,' she told Emmy. 'Hope you have a quiet night.'

Emmy settled herself in her chair, made sure that everything was as it should be and got out the knitting she had pushed in with the books at the last minute. She would knit until one of the night porters brought her coffee.

There were a number of calls: enquiries about patients, anxious voices asking advice as to whether they should bring a sick child to the hospital, calls to the medical staff on duty.

Later, when she had drunk her cooling coffee and picked up her neglected knitting once again, Professor ter Mennolt, on his way home, presumably, paused by her.

He eyed the knitting. 'A pleasant change from the daytime rush,' he remarked. 'And an opportunity to indulge your womanly skills.'

'Well, I don't know about that,' said Emmy sensibly. 'It keeps me awake in between calls! It's very late; oughtn't you to be in your bed?'

'My dear young lady, surely that is no concern of yours?'

'Oh, I'm not being nosy,' she assured him. 'But everyone needs a good night's sleep, especially people like you—people who use their brains a lot.'

'That is your opinion, Ermentrude? It is Ermentrude, isn't it?'

'Yes, and yes. At least, it's my father's opinion.'

'Your father is a medical man, perhaps?' he asked smoothly.

'No, a schoolmaster.'

'Indeed? Then why are you not following in his footsteps?'

'I'm not clever. Besides, I like sewing and embroidery.'

'And you are a switchboard operator.' His tone was dry.

'It's a nice, steady job,' said Emmy, and picked up her knitting. 'Goodnight, Professor ter Mennolt.'

'Goodnight, Ermentrude.' He had gone several paces when he turned on his heel. 'You have an old-fashioned name. I am put in mind of a demure young lady with ringlets and a crinoline, downcast eyes and a soft and gentle voice.'

She looked at him, her mouth half-open.

'You have a charming voice, but I do not consider you demure, nor do you cast down your eyes—indeed their gaze is excessively lively.'

He went away then, leaving her wondering what on earth he had been talking about.

'Of course, he's foreign,' reflected Emmy out loud. 'And besides that he's one of those clever people whose feet aren't quite on the ground, always bothering about people's insides.'

A muddled statement which nonetheless satisfied her.

Audrey, relieving her at eight o'clock the next morning, yawned widely and offered the information that she hated day duty, hated the hospital, hated having to work. 'Lucky you,' she observed. 'All day to do nothing…'

'I shall go to bed,' said Emmy mildly, and took herself off home.

It was a slow business, with the buses crammed with

people going to work, and then she had to stop at the shops at the end of the street and buy bread, eggs, bacon, food for Snoodles and more food for George. Once home, with the door firmly shut behind her, she put on the kettle, fed the animals and let George into the garden. Snoodles tailed him, warned not to go far.

She had her breakfast, tidied up, undressed and had a shower and, with George and Snoodles safely indoors, went to her bed. The teenager across the street hadn't made a sound so far; hopefully he had a job or had gone off with his pals. If Mr Grant and Mrs Grimes kept quiet, she would have a good sleep… She had barely had time to form the thought before her eyes shut.

It was two o'clock when she was woken by a hideous mixture of sound: Mr Grant's flute—played, from the sound of it, at an open window—Mrs Grimes bellowing at her husband in the background and, almost drowning these, the teenager enjoying a musical session.

Emmy turned over and buried her head in the pillow, but it was no use; she was wide awake now and likely to stay so. She got up and showered and dressed, had a cup of tea and a sandwich, made sure that Snoodles was asleep, put a lead on George's collar and left the house.

She had several hours of leisure still; she boarded an almost empty bus and sat with George on her lap as it bore them away from Stepney, along Holborn and into the Marylebone Road. She got off here and crossed the street to Regent's Park.

It was pleasant here, green and open with the strong scent of autumn in the air. Emmy walked briskly, with George trotting beside her.

'We'll come out each day,' she promised him. 'A pity the parks are all so far away, but a bus ride's nice enough, isn't it? And you shall have a good tea when we get home.'

The afternoon was sliding into dusk as they went back home. George gobbled his tea and curled up on his chair in the kitchen while Snoodles went out. Mrs Grimes had stopped shouting, but Mr Grant was still playing the flute, rivalling the din from across the street. Emmy ate her tea, stuffed things into her bag and went to work.

Audrey had had a busy day and was peevish. 'I spent the whole of my two hours off looking for some decent tights—the shops around here are useless.'

'There's that shop in Commercial Road…' began Emmy.

'There?' Audrey was scornful. 'I wouldn't be seen dead in anything from there.' She took a last look at her face, added more lipstick and patted her blonde head. 'I'm going out this evening. So long.'

Until almost midnight Emmy was kept busy. From time to time someone passing through from the entrance hall stopped for a word, and one of the porters brought her coffee around eleven o'clock with the news that there had been a pile-up down at the docks and the accident room was up to its eyes.

'They phoned,' said Emmy, 'but didn't say how bad it was—not to me, that is. I switched them straight through. I hope they're not too bad.'

'Couple of boys, an old lady, the drivers—one of them's had a stroke.'

Soon she was busy again, with families phoning with anxious enquiries. She was eating her sandwiches in the early hours of the morning when Professor ter Mennolt's voice, close to her ear, made her jump.

'I am relieved to see that you are awake and alert, Ermentrude.'

She said, round the sandwich. 'Well, of course I am. That's not a nice thing to say, sir.'

'What were you doing in a bus on the Marylebone Road when you should have been in bed asleep, recruiting strength for the night's work?'

'I was going to Regent's Park with George. He had a good walk.' She added crossly, 'And *you* should try to sleep with someone playing the flute on one side of the house, Mrs Grimes shouting on the other and that wretched boy with his stereo across the street.'

The professor was leaning against the wall, his hands in the pockets of his beautifully tailored jacket. 'I have misjudged you, Ermentrude. I am sorry. Ear plugs, perhaps?' And, when she shook her head, 'Could you not beg a bed from a friend? Or your mother have a word with the neighbours?'

'Mother's with Father,' said Emmy, and took a bite of sandwich. 'I can't leave the house because of George and Snoodles.'

'George?'

'Our dog, and Snoodles is the cat.'

'So you are alone in the house?' He stared down at her. 'You are not nervous?'

'No, sir.'

'You live close by?'

What a man for asking questions, thought Emmy, and wished he didn't stare so. She stared back and said 'Yes,' and wished that he would go away; she found him unsettling. She remembered something. 'I didn't see you on the bus...'

He smiled. 'I was in the car, waiting for the traffic lights.'

She turned to the switchboard, then, and put through two calls, and he watched her. She had pretty hands, nicely well-cared for, and though her hair was mouse-brown there seemed to be a great deal of it, piled neatly in a coil at the back of her head. Not in the least pretty, but with eyes like hers that didn't matter.

He bade her goodnight, and went out to his car and forgot her, driving to his charming little house in Chelsea where Beaker, who ran it for him, would have left coffee and sandwiches for him in his study, his desk light on and a discreet lamp burning in the hall.

Although it was almost two o'clock he sat down to go through his letters and messages while he drank the coffee, hot and fragrant in the Thermos. There was a note, too, written in Beaker's spidery hand: Juffrouw Anneliese van Moule had phoned at eight o'clock and again at ten. The professor frowned and glanced over to the answering machine. It showed the red light, and he went and switched it on.

In a moment a petulant voice, speaking in Dutch, wanted to know where he was. 'Surely you should be home by ten o'clock in the evening. I asked you specially to be home, did I not? Well, I suppose I must forgive you and give you good news. I am coming to London in three days' time—Friday. I shall stay at Brown's Hotel, since you are unlikely to be home for most of the day, but I expect to be taken out in the evenings—and there will be time for us to discuss the future.

'I wish to see your house; I think it will not do for us when we are married, for I shall live with you in London when you are working there, but I hope you will give up your work in England and live at Huis ter Mennolt—'

The professor switched off. Anneliese's voice had sounded loud as well as peevish, and she was reiterating an argument they had had on several occasions. He had no intention of leaving his house; it was large enough. He had some friends to dine, but his entertaining was for those whom he knew well. Anneliese would wish to entertain on a grand scale, fill the house with acquaintances; he would return home each evening to a drawing room full of people he neither knew nor wished to know.

He reminded himself that she would be a most suitable wife; in Holland they had a similar circle of friends and acquaintances, and they liked the same things—the theatre, concerts, art exhibitions—and she was ambitious.

At first he had been amused and rather touched by that, until he had realised that her ambition wasn't for his success in his profession but for a place in London society. She already had that in Holland, and she had been careful never to admit to him that that was her goal… He reminded himself that she was the woman he had chosen to marry and once she had understood that he had no intention of altering his way of life when they were married she would understand how he felt.

After all, when they were in Holland she could have all the social life she wanted; Huis ter Mennolt was vast, and there were servants enough and lovely gardens. While he was working she could entertain as many of her friends as she liked—give dinner parties if she wished, since the house was large enough to do that with ease. Here at the Chelsea house, though, with only Beaker and a daily woman to run the place, entertaining on such a scale would be out of the question. The house, roomy though it was, was too small.

He went to bed then, and, since he had a list the following day, he had no time to think about anything but his work.

He left the hospital soon after ten o'clock the next evening. Ermentrude was at her switchboard, her back towards him. He gave her a brief glance as he passed.

Anneliese had phoned again, Beaker informed him, but would leave no message. 'And, since I needed some groceries, I switched on the answering machine, sir,' he said, 'since Mrs Thrupp, splendid cleaner though she is, is hardly up to answering the telephone.'

The professor went to his study and switched on the machine, and stood listening to Anneliese. Her voice was no longer petulant, but it was still loud. 'My plane gets in at half past ten on Friday—Heathrow,' she told him. 'I'll look out for you. Don't keep me waiting, will you, Ruerd? Shall we dine at Brown's? I shall be too tired to talk much, and I'll stay for several days, anyway.'

He went to look at his appointments book on his desk. He would be free to meet her, although he would have to go back to his consulting rooms for a couple of hours before joining her at Brown's Hotel.

He sat down at his desk, took his glasses from his breast pocket, put them on and picked up the pile of letters before him. He was aware that there was a lack of lover-like anticipation at the thought of seeing Anneliese. Probably because he hadn't seen her for some weeks. Moreover, he had been absorbed in his patients. In about a month's time he would be going back to Holland for a month or more; he would make a point of seeing as much of Anneliese as possible.

He ate his solitary dinner, and went back to his study to write a paper on spina bifida, an exercise which kept him engrossed until well after midnight.

Past the middle of the week already, thought Emmy with satisfaction, getting ready for bed the next morning—three more nights and she would have two days off. Her mother would be home too, until she rejoined her father later in the week, and then he would be working in and around London. Emmy heaved a tired, satisfied sigh and went to sleep until, inevitably, the strains of the flute woke her. It was no use lying there and hoping they would stop; she got up, had a cup of tea and took George for a walk.

It was raining when she went to work that evening, and she had to wait for a long time for a bus. The elderly relief telephonist was off sick, and Audrey was waiting for her when she got there, already dressed to leave, tapping her feet with impatience.

'I thought you'd never get here…'

'It's still only two minutes to eight,' said Emmy mildly. 'Is there anything I should know?'

She was taking off her mac and headscarf as she spoke, and when Audrey said no, there wasn't, Emmy sat down before the switchboard, suddenly hating the sight of it. The night stretched ahead of her, endless hours of staying alert. The thought of the countless days and nights ahead in the years to come wasn't to be borne.

She adjusted her headpiece and arranged everything just so, promising herself that she would find another job, something where she could be out of doors for at least part of the day. And meet people…a man who would fall in love with her and want to marry her. A house in the country, mused Emmy, dogs and cats and chickens and children, of course…

She was roused from this pleasant dream by an outside call, followed by more of them; it was always at this time of the evening that people phoned to make enquiries.

She was kept busy throughout the night. By six o'clock she was tired, thankful that in another couple of hours she would be free. Only three more nights; she thought sleepily of what she would do. Window shopping with her mother? And if the weather was good enough they could take a bus to Hampstead Heath...

A great blast of sound sent her upright in her chair, followed almost at once by a call from the police—there had been a bomb close to Fenchurch Street Station. Too soon to know how many were injured, but they would be coming to St Luke's!

Emmy, very wide awake now, began notifying everyone—the accident room, the house doctors' rooms, the wards, X-Ray, the path lab. And within minutes she was kept busy, ringing the consultants on call, theatre staff, technicians, ward sisters on day duty. She had called the professor, but hadn't spared him a thought, nor had she seen him as he came to the hospital, for there was a great deal of orderly coming and going as the ambulances began to arrive.

She had been busy; now she was even more so. Anxious relatives were making frantic calls, wanting to know where the injured were and how they were doing. But it was too soon to know anything. The accident room was crowded; names were sent to her as they were given, but beyond letting callers know that they had that particular person in the hospital there was no more information to pass on.

Emmy went on answering yet more calls, putting through outside calls too—to other hospitals, the police, someone from a foreign embassy who had heard that one of the staff had been injured. She answered them all in her quiet voice, trying to ignore a threatening headache.

It seemed a very long time before order emerged from the controlled chaos. There were no more ambulances now, and patients who needed admission were being taken to the wards. The accident room, still busy, was dealing with the lesser injured; the hospital was returning to its normal day's work.

It was now ten o'clock. Emmy, looking at her watch for the first time in hours, blinked. Where was Audrey? Most of the receptionists had come in, for they had rung to tell her so, but not Audrey. Emmy was aware that she was hungry, thirsty and very tired, and wondered what to do about it. She would have to let someone know…

Audrey tapped on her shoulder. She said airily, 'Sorry I'm late. I didn't fancy coming sooner; I bet the place was a shambles. I knew you wouldn't mind…'

'I do mind, though,' said Emmy. 'I mind very much. I've had a busy time, and I should have been off duty two hours ago.'

'Well, you were here, weren't you? Did you expect me to come tearing in in the middle of all the fuss just so's you could go off duty? Besides, you're not doing anything; you only go to bed…'

The professor, on his way home, paused to listen to this with interest. Ermentrude, he could see, was looking very much the worse for wear; she had undoubtedly had a busy time of it, and she had been up all night, whereas the rest of them had merely got out of their beds earlier than usual.

He said now pleasantly, 'Put on your coat, Ermentrude; I'll drive you home. We can take up the matter of the extra hours you have worked later on. Leave it to me.'

Emmy goggled at him, but he gave her no chance to speak. He said, still pleasantly, to Audrey, 'I'm sure you have a good reason for not coming on duty at the usual time.' He smiled thinly. 'It will have to be a good one, will it not?'

He swept Emmy along, away from a pale Audrey, out of the doors and into his Bentley. 'Tell me where you live,' he commanded.

'There is no need to take me home, I'm quite able—'

'Don't waste my time. We're both tired, and I for one am feeling short-tempered.'

'So am I,' snapped Emmy. 'I want a cup of tea, and I'm hungry.'

'That makes two of us. Now, where do you live, Ermentrude?'

CHAPTER TWO

EMMY told him her address in a cross voice, sitting silently until he stopped before her home. She said gruffly, 'Thank you, Professor. Good morning,' and made to open her door. He shook her hand and released it, and she put it in her lap. Then he got out, opened the door, crossed the pavement with her, took the key from her and opened the house door. George rushed to meet them while Snoodles, a cat not to be easily disturbed, sat on the bottom step of the stairs, watching.

Emmy stood awkwardly in the doorway with George, who was making much of her. She said again, 'Thank you, Professor,' and peered up at his face.

'The least you can do is offer me a cup of tea,' he told her, and came into the hall, taking her with him and closing the door. 'You get that coat off and do whatever you usually do while I put on the kettle.'

He studied her face. Really, the girl was very plain; for a moment he regretted the impulse which had urged him to bring her home. She had been quite capable of getting herself there; he had formed the opinion after their first meeting that she was more than capable of dealing with any situation—and with a sharp tongue, too. She looked at him then, though, and he saw how tired she was. He said in a placid voice, 'I make a very good cup of tea.'

She smiled. 'Thank you. The kitchen's here.'

She opened a door and ushered him into the small room at the back of the house, which was, he saw, neat and very clean, with old-fashioned shelves and a small dresser. There was a gas stove against one wall—an elderly model, almost a museum piece, but still functioning, he was relieved to find.

Emmy went away and he found tea, milk and sugar while the kettle boiled, took mugs and a brown teapot from the dresser and set them on the table while Emmy fed Snoodles and George.

They drank their tea presently, sitting opposite each other saying little, and when the professor got to his feet Emmy made no effort to detain him. She thanked him again, saw him to the door and shut it the moment he had driven away, intent on getting to her bed as quickly as possible. She took a slice of bread and butter and a slab of cheese with her, and George and Snoodles, who had sidled upstairs with her, got onto the bed too—which was a comfort for she was feeling hard done by and put upon.

'It's all very well,' she told them peevishly. 'He'll go home to a doting wife—slippers in one hand and bacon and eggs in the other.'

She swallowed the last of the cheese and went to sleep, and not even the flute or Mrs Grimes' loud voice could wake her.

The professor got into his car, and as he drove away his bleep sounded. He was wanted back at St Luke's; one of the injured had developed signs of a blood clot on the brain. So instead of going home he went back and spent the next few hours doing everything in his power to keep his patient alive—something which proved successful, so that in the early afternoon he was at last able to go home.

He let himself into his house, put his bag down and trod into the sitting room, to come to a halt just inside the door.

'Anneliese—I forgot…'

She was a beautiful girl with thick fair hair cut short by an expert hand, perfect features and big blue eyes, and she was exquisitely made-up. She was dressed in the height of fashion and very expensively, too. She made a charming picture, marred by the ill-temper on her face.

She spoke in Dutch, not attempting to hide her bad temper.

'Really, Ruerd, what am I to suppose you mean by that? That man of yours, Beaker—who, by the way, I shall discharge as soon as we are married—refused to phone the hospital—said you would be too busy to answer. Since when has a consultant not been free to answer the telephone when he wishes?'

He examined several answers to that and discarded them. 'I am sorry, my dear. There was a bomb; it exploded close to St Luke's early this morning. It was necessary for me to be there—there were casualties. Beaker was quite right; I shouldn't have answered the phone.'

He crossed the room and bent to kiss her cheek. 'He is an excellent servant; I have no intention of discharging him.' He spoke lightly, but she gave him a questioning look. They had been engaged for some months now, and she was still not sure that she knew him. She wasn't sure if she loved him either, but he could offer her everything she wanted in life; they knew the same people and came from similar backgrounds. Their marriage would be entirely suitable.

She decided to change her tactics. 'I'm sorry for being cross. But I was disappointed. Are you free for the rest of the day?'

'I shall have to go back to the hospital late this evening. Shall we dine somewhere? You're quite comfortable at Brown's?'

'Very comfortable. Could we dine at Claridge's? I've a dress I bought specially for you...'

'I'll see if I can get a table.' He turned round as Beaker came in.

'You had lunch, sir?' Beaker didn't look at Anneliese. When the professor said that, yes, he'd had something, Beaker went on, 'Then I shall bring tea here, sir. A little early, but you may be glad of it.'

'Splendid, Beaker. As soon as you like.' And, when Beaker had gone, the professor said, 'I'll go and phone now...'

He took his bag to his study and pressed the button on the answering machine. There were several calls from when Beaker had been out of the house; the rest he had noted down and put with the letters. The professor leafed through them, listened to the answering machine and booked a table for dinner. He would have liked to dine quietly at home.

They talked trivialities over tea—news from home and friends, places Anneliese had visited. She had no interest in his work save in his successes; his social advancement was all-important to her, although she was careful not to let him see that.

He drove her to Brown's presently, and went back to work at his desk until it was time to dress. Immaculate in black tie, he went to the garage at the end of the mews to get his car, and drove himself to the hotel.

Anneliese wasn't ready. He cooled his heels for fifteen minutes or so before she joined him.

'I've kept you waiting, Ruerd,' she said laughingly. 'But I hope you think it is worth it.'

He assured her that it was, and indeed she made a magnificent picture in a slim sheath of cerise silk, her hair piled high, sandals with four-inch heels and an arm loaded with gold bangles. His ring, a large diamond, glittered on her finger. A ring which she had chosen and which he disliked.

Certainly she was a woman any man would be proud to escort, he told himself. He supposed that he was tired; a good night's sleep was all that was needed. Anneliese looked lovely, and dinner at Claridge's was the very least he could offer her. Tomorrow, he reflected, he would somehow find time to take her out again—dancing, perhaps, at one of the nightclubs. And there was that exhibition of paintings at a gallery in Bond Street if he could manage to find time to take her.

He listened to her chatter as they drove to Claridge's and gave her his full attention. Dinner was entirely satisfactory: admiring looks followed Anneliese as they went to their table, the food was delicious and the surroundings luxurious. As he drove her back she put a hand on his arm.

'A lovely dinner, darling, thank you. I shall do some shopping tomorrow; can you meet me for lunch? And could we go dancing in the evening? We must talk; I've so many plans…'

At the hotel she offered a cheek for his kiss. 'I shall go straight to bed. See you tomorrow.'

The professor got back into his car and drove to the hospital. He wasn't entirely satisfied with the condition of the patient he had seen that afternoon, and he wanted to be sure…

* * *

Emmy, sitting before her switchboard, knitting, knew that the professor was there, standing behind her, although he had made no sound. Why is that? she wondered; why should I know that?

His, 'Good evening, Ermentrude,' was uttered quietly. 'You slept well?' he added.

He came to stand beside her now, strikingly handsome in black tie and quite unconscious of it.

'Good evening, sir. Yes, thank you. I hope you had time to rest.'

His mouth twitched. 'I have been dining out. Making conversation, talking of things which don't interest me. If I sound a bad-tempered man who doesn't know when he is lucky, then that is exactly what I am.'

'No, you're not,' said Emmy reasonably. 'You've had a busy day, much busier than anyone else because you've had to make important decisions about your patients. All that's the matter with you is that you are tired. You must go home and have a good night's sleep.'

She had quite forgotten to whom she was speaking. 'I suppose you've come to see that man with the blood clot on the brain?'

He asked with interest, 'Do you know about him?'

'Well, of course I do. I hear things, don't I? And I'm interested.'

She took an incoming telephone call and, when she had dealt with it the professor had gone.

He didn't stop on his way out, nor did he speak, but she was conscious of his passing. She found that disconcerting.

Audrey was punctual and in a peevish mood. 'I had a ticking off,' she told Emmy sourly. 'I don't know why they had to make such a fuss—after all, you were here. No one would have known if it hadn't been for that Professor ter Mennolt being here. Who does he think he is, anyway?'

'He's rather nice,' said Emmy mildly. 'He gave me a lift home.'

'In that great car of his? Filthy rich, so I've heard. Going to marry some Dutch beauty—I was talking to his secretary…'

'I hope they'll be very happy,' said Emmy. A flicker of unhappiness made her frown. She knew very little about the professor and she found him disturbing; a difficult man, a man who went his own way. All the same, she would like him to live happily ever after…

If he came into the hospital during the last nights of her duty, she didn't see him. It wasn't until Sunday morning, when the relief had come to take over and she was free at last to enjoy her two days off, that she met him again as she stood for a moment outside the hospital entrance, taking blissful breaths of morning air, her eyes closed. She was imagining that she was back in the country, despite the petrol fumes.

She opened her eyes, feeling foolish, when the professor observed, 'I am surprised that you should linger, Ermentrude. Surely you must be hellbent on getting away from the hospital as quickly as possible?'

'Good morning, sir,' said Ermentrude politely. 'It's just nice to be outside.' She saw his sweater and casual trousers. 'Have you been here all night?'

'No, no—only for an hour or so.' He smiled down at her. She looked pale with tiredness. Her small nose shone, her hair had been ruthlessly pinned into a bun, very neat and totally without charm. She reminded him of a kitten who had been out all night in the rain. 'I'll drop you off on my way.'

'You're going past my home? Really? Thank you.'

He didn't find it necessary to answer her, but popped her into the car and drove through the almost empty streets. At her door, he said, 'No, don't get out. Give me your key.'

He went and opened the door, and then opened the car door, took her bag from her and followed her inside. George was delighted to see them, weaving round their feet, pushing Snoodles away, giving small, excited barks.

The professor went to open the kitchen door to let both animals out into the garden, and he put the kettle on. For all the world as though he lived here, thought Emmy, and if she hadn't been so tired she would have said so. Instead she stood in the kitchen and yawned.

The professor glanced at her. 'Breakfast,' he said briskly and unbuttoned his coat and threw it over a chair. 'If you'll feed the animals, I'll boil a couple of eggs.'

She did as she was told without demur; she couldn't be bothered to argue with him. She didn't remember asking him to stay for breakfast, but perhaps he was very hungry. She fed the animals and by then he had laid the table after a fashion, made toast and dished up the eggs.

They sat at the table eating their breakfast for all the world like an old married couple. The professor kept up a gentle meandering conversation which required little or no reply, and Emmy, gobbling toast, made very little effort to do so. She was still tired, but the tea and the food had revived her so that presently she said, 'It was very kind of you to get breakfast. I'm very grateful. I was a bit tired.'

'You had a busy week. Will your mother and father return soon?'

'Tomorrow morning.' She gave him an owl-like look. 'I expect you want to go home, sir...'

'Presently. Go upstairs, Ermentrude, take a shower and get into bed. I will tidy up here. When you are in bed I will go home.'

'You can't do the washing up.'

'Indeed I can.' Not quite a lie; he had very occasionally needed to rinse a cup or glass if Beaker hadn't been there.

He made a good job of it, attended to the animals, locked the kitchen door and hung the tea towel to dry, taking his time about it. It was quiet in the house, and presently he went upstairs. He got no answer from his quiet, 'Ermentrude?' but one of the doors on the landing was half-open.

The room was small, nicely furnished and very tidy. Emmy was asleep in her bed, her mouth slightly open, her hair all over the pillow. He thought that nothing short of a brass band giving a concert by her bedside would waken her. He went downstairs again and out of the house, shutting the door behind him.

Driving to Chelsea, he looked at his watch. It would be eleven o'clock before he was home. He was taking Anneliese to lunch with friends, and he suspected that when they returned she would want to make plans for their future. There had been no time so far, and he would be at the hospital for a great deal of the days ahead. He was tired now; Anneliese wasn't content to dine quietly and spend the evening at home and yesterday his day had been full. A day in the country would be delightful…

Beaker came to meet him as he opened his front door. His, 'Good morning, sir,' held faint reproach. 'You were detained at the hospital? I prepared breakfast at the usual time. I can have it on the table in ten minutes.'

'No need, Beaker, thanks. I've had breakfast. I'll

have a shower and change, and then perhaps a cup of coffee before Juffrouw van Moule gets here.'

'You breakfasted at the hospital, sir?'

'No, no. I boiled an egg and made some toast and had a pot of strong tea. I took someone home. We were both hungry—it seemed a sensible thing to do.'

Beaker inclined his head gravely. A boiled egg, he reflected—no bacon, mushrooms, scrambled eggs, as only he, Beaker, could cook them—and strong tea… He suppressed a shudder. A small plate of his home-made savoury biscuits, he decided, and perhaps a sandwich with Gentlemen's Relish on the coffee tray.

It was gratifying to see the professor eating the lot when he came downstairs again. He looked as though he could do with a quiet day, reflected his faithful servant, instead of gallivanting off with that Juffrouw van Moule. Beaker hadn't taken to her—a haughty piece, and critical of him. He wished his master a pleasant day in a voice which hinted otherwise. He was informed that Juffrouw van Moule would be returning for tea, and would probably stay for dinner.

Beaker took himself to the kitchen where he unburdened himself to his cat, Humphrey, while he set about making the little queen cakes usually appreciated by the professor's lady visitors.

Anneliese looked ravishing, exquisitely made-up, not a hair of her head out of place and wearing a stone-coloured crêpe de chine outfit of deceptive simplicity which screamed money from every seam.

She greeted the professor with a charming smile, offered a cheek with the warning not to disarrange her hair and settled herself in the car.

'At last we have a day together,' she observed. 'I'll

come back with you after lunch. That man of yours will give us a decent tea, I suppose. I might even stay for dinner.'

She glanced at his profile. 'We must discuss the future, Ruerd. Where we are to live—we shall have to engage more servants in a larger house, of course, and I suppose you can arrange to give up some of your consultant posts, concentrate on private patients. You have plenty of friends, haven't you? Influential people?'

He didn't look at her. 'I have a great many friends and even more acquaintances,' he told her. 'I have no intention of using them. Indeed, I have no need. Do not expect me to give up my hospital work, though, Anneliese.'

She put a hand on his knee. 'Of course not, Ruerd. I promise I won't say any more about that. But please let us at least discuss finding a larger house where we can entertain. I shall have friends, I hope, and I shall need to return their hospitality.'

She was wise enough to stop then. 'These people we are lunching with—they are old friends?'

'Yes. I knew Guy Bowers-Bentinck before he married. We still see a good deal of each other; he has a charming little wife, Suzannah, and twins—five years old—and a baby on the way.'

'Does she live here, in this village—Great Chisbourne? Does she not find it full? I mean, does she not miss theatres and evenings out and meeting people?'

He said evenly, 'No. She has a husband who loves her, two beautiful children, a delightful home and countless friends. She is content.'

Something in his voice made Anneliese say quickly, 'She sounds delightful; I'm sure I shall like her.'

Which was unfortunately not true. Beneath their

socially pleasant manner, they disliked each other heartily—Anneliese because she considered Suzannah to be not worth bothering about, Suzannah because she saw at once that Anneliese wouldn't do for Ruerd at all. She would make him unhappy; surely he could see that for himself?

Lunch was pleasant, Suzannah saw to that—making small talk while the two men discussed some knotty problem about their work. Anneliese showed signs of boredom after a time; she was used to being the centre of attention and she wasn't getting it. When the men did join in the talk it was about the children eating their meal with them, behaving beautifully.

'Do you have a nursery?' asked Anneliese.

'Oh, yes, and a marvellous old nanny. But the children eat with us unless we're entertaining in the evening. We enjoy their company, and they see more of their father.'

Suzannah smiled across the table at her husband, and Anneliese, looking at him, wondered how such a plain girl could inspire the devoted look he gave her.

She remarked upon it as they drove back to Chelsea. 'Quite charming,' she commented in a voice which lacked sincerity. 'Guy seems devoted to her.'

'Surely that is to be expected of a husband?' the professor observed quietly.

Anneliese gave a little trill of laughter. 'Oh, I suppose so. Not quite my idea of marriage, though. Children should be in the nursery until they go to school, don't you agree?'

He didn't answer that. 'They are delightful, aren't they? And so well behaved.' He sounded remote.

He was going fast on the motorway as the October day faded into dusk. In a few days it would be

November, and at the end of that month he would go back to Holland for several weeks, where already a formidable list of consultations awaited him. He would see Anneliese again, of course; she would want to plan their wedding.

When they had first become engaged he had expressed a wish for a quiet wedding and she had agreed. But over the months she had hinted more and more strongly that a big wedding was absolutely necessary: so many friends and family, and she wanted bridesmaids. Besides, a quiet wedding would mean she couldn't wear the gorgeous wedding dress she fully intended to have.

Anneliese began to talk then; she could be very amusing and she was intelligent. Ruerd wasn't giving her his full attention, but she was confident that she could alter that. She embarked on a series of anecdotes about mutual friends in Holland, taking care not to be critical or spiteful, only amusing. She knew how to be a charming companion, and felt smug satisfaction when he responded, unaware that it was only good manners which prompted his replies.

He was tired, he told himself, and Anneliese's chatter jarred on his thoughts. To talk to her about his work would have been a relief, to tell her of his busy week at the hospital, the patients he had seen. But the cursory interest she had shown when they'd become engaged had evaporated. Not her fault, of course, but his. He had thought that her interest in his work was a wish to understand it, but it hadn't been that—her interest was a social one. To be married to a well-known medical man with boundless possibilities for advancement.

He slowed the car's speed as they were engulfed in London's suburbs. She would be a suitable wife—good looks, a charming manner, clever and always beautifully turned out.

On aiming back he said, 'We'll have tea round the fire, shall we? Beaker will have it ready.' He glanced at his watch. 'Rather on the late side, but there's no hurry, is there?'

The sitting room looked warm and welcoming as they went indoors. Humphrey was sitting before the fire, a small furry statue, staring at the flames. Anneliese paused halfway across the room. 'Oh, Ruerd, please get that cat out of the room. I dislike them, you know—I'm sure they're not clean, and they shed hairs everywhere.'

The professor scooped Humphrey into his arms. 'He's a well-loved member of my household, Anneliese. He keeps himself cleaner than many humans, and he is brushed so regularly that I doubt if there is a single loose hair.'

He took the cat to the kitchen and sat him down in front of the Aga.

'Juffrouw van Moule doesn't like cats,' he told Beaker in an expressionless voice. 'He'd better stay here until she goes back to the hotel. Could you give us supper about half past eight? Something light; if we're going to have tea now we shan't have much appetite.'

When he went back to the sitting room Anneliese was sitting by the fire. She made a lovely picture in its light, and he paused to look at her as he went in. Any man would be proud to have her as his wife, he reflected, so why was it that he felt no quickening of his pulse at the sight of her?

He brushed the thought aside and sat down opposite her, and watched her pour their tea. She had beautiful hands, exquisitely cared for, and they showed to great advantage as she presided over the tea tray. She looked at him and smiled, aware of the charming picture she made, and presently, confident that she had his attention once more, she began to talk about their future.

'I know we shall see a good deal of each other when you come back to Holland in December,' she began. 'But at least we can make tentative plans.' She didn't wait for his comment but went on, 'I think a summer wedding, don't you? That gives you plenty of time to arrange a long holiday. We might go somewhere for a month or so before settling down.

'Can you arrange it so that you're working in Holland for a few months? You can always fly over here if you're wanted, and surely you can give up your consultancies here after awhile? Private patients, by all means, and, of course, we mustn't lose sight of your friends and colleagues.' She gave him a brilliant smile. 'You're famous here, are you not? It is so important to know all the right people…'

When he didn't reply, she added, 'I am going to be very unselfish and agree to using this house as a London base. Later on perhaps we can find something larger.'

He asked quietly, 'What kind of place had you in mind, Anneliese?'

'I looked in at an estate agent—somewhere near Harrods; I can't remember the name. There were some most suitable flats. Large enough for entertaining. We would need at least five bedrooms—guests, you know—and good servants' quarters.'

Her head on one side, she gave him another brilliant smile. 'Say yes, Ruerd.'

'I have commitments for the next four months here,' he told her, 'and they will be added to in the meantime. In March I've been asked to lecture at a seminar in Leiden, examine students at Groningen and read a paper in Vienna. I cannot give you a definite answer at the moment.'

She pouted. 'Oh, Ruerd, why must you work so hard? At least I shall see something of you when you come back to Holland. Shall you give a party at Christmas?'

'Yes, I believe so. We can talk about that later. Have your family any plans?'

She was still telling him about them when Beaker came to tell them that supper was ready.

Later that evening, as she prepared to go, Anneliese asked, 'Tomorrow, Ruerd? You will be free? We might go to an art exhibition…?'

He shook his head. 'I'm working all day. I doubt if I shall be free before the evening. I'll phone the hotel and leave a message. It will probably be too late for dinner, but we might have a drink.'

She had to be content with that. She would shop, she decided, and dine at the hotel. She was careful not to let him see how vexed she was.

The next morning as the professor made his way through the hospital he looked, as had become his habit, to where Ermentrude sat. She wasn't there, of course.

She was up and dressed, getting the house just so, ready for her mother and father. She had slept long and soundly, and had gone downstairs to find that the professor had left everything clean and tidy in the kitchen. He had left a tea tray ready, too; all she'd needed to do was put on the kettle and make toast.

'Very thoughtful of him,' said Emmy now, to George, who was hovering hopefully for a biscuit. 'You wouldn't think to look at him that he'd know one end of a tea towel from the other. He must have a helpless fiancée…'

She frowned. Even if his fiancée was helpless he could obviously afford to have a housekeeper or at least a daily woman. She fell to wondering about him. When would he be married, have children? Where did he live while he was working in London? And where was his home in Holland? Since neither George nor Snoodles could answer, she put these questions to the back of her mind and turned her thoughts to the shopping she must do before her parents came home.

They knew about the bomb, of course; it had been on TV and in the papers. But when Emmy had phoned her parents she had told them very little about it, and had remained guiltily silent when her mother had expressed her relief that Emmy had been on day duty and hadn't been there. Now that they were home, exchanging news over coffee and biscuits, the talk turned naturally enough to the bomb outrage. 'So fortunate that you weren't there,' said Mrs Foster.

'Well, as a matter of fact, I was,' said Emmy. 'But I was quite all right...' She found herself explaining about Professor ter Mennolt bringing her home and him making tea.

'We are in his debt,' observed her father. 'Although he did only what any decent-thinking person would have done.'

Her mother said artlessly, 'He sounds a very nice man. Is he elderly? I suppose so if he's a professor.'

'Not elderly—not even middle-aged,' said Emmy. 'They say at the hospital that he's going to marry soon. No one knows much about him, and one wouldn't dare ask him.'

She thought privately that one day, if the opportunity occurred, she might do just that. For some reason it was important to her that he should settle down and be happy. He didn't strike her as being happy enough. He ought to be; he was top of his profession, with a girl waiting for him, and presumably enough to live on in comfort.

Her two days went much too quickly. Never mind if it rained for almost all of the time. Her father was away in the day, and she and her mother spent a morning window shopping in Oxford Street, and long hours sitting by the fire—her mother knitting, Emmy busy with the delicate embroidery which she loved to do.

They talked—the chances of her father getting a teaching post near their old home were remote; all the same they discussed it unendingly. 'We don't need a big house,' said her mother. 'And you could come with us, of course, Emmy—there's bound to be some job for you. Or you might meet someone and marry.' She peered at her daughter. 'There isn't anyone here, is there, love?'

'No, Mother, and not likely to be. It would be lovely if Father could get a teaching post and we could sell this house.'

Her mother smiled. 'No neighbours, darling. Wouldn't it be heaven? No rows of little houses all exactly alike. Who knows what is round the corner?'

It was still raining when Emmy set off to work the following morning. The buses were packed and tempers were short. She got off before the hospital stop was reached, tired of being squeezed between wet raincoats and having her feet poked at with umbrellas. A few minutes' walk even on a London street was preferable to strap-hanging.

She was taking a short cut through a narrow lane where most of the houses were boarded up or just plain derelict, when she saw the kitten. It was very small and very wet, sitting by a boarded-up door, and when she went nearer she saw that it had been tied by a piece of string to the door handle. It looked at her and shivered, opened its tiny mouth and mewed almost without sound.

Emmy knelt down, picked it up carefully, held it close and rooted around in her shoulder bag for the scissors she always carried. It was the work of a moment to cut the string, tuck the kitten into her jacket and be on her way once more. She had no idea what she was going to do with the small creature, but to leave it there was unthinkable.

She was early at the hospital; there was time to beg a cardboard box from one of the porters, line it with yesterday's newspaper and her scarf and beg some milk from the head porter.

'You won't 'arf cop it,' he told her, offering a mugful. 'I wouldn't do it for anyone else, Emmy, and mum's the word.' He nodded and winked. She was a nice young lady, he considered, always willing to listen to him telling her about his wife's diabetes.

Emmy tucked the box away at her feet, dried the small creature with her handkerchief, offered it milk and saw with satisfaction that it fell instantly into a refreshing sleep. It woke briefly from time to time, scoffed more milk and dropped off again. Very much to her relief, Emmy got to the end of her shift with the kitten undetected.

She was waiting for her relief when the supervisor bore down upon her, intent on checking and finding fault if she could. It was just bad luck that the kitten should wake at that moment, and, since it was feeling better, it mewed quite loudly.

Meeting the lady's outraged gaze, Emmy said, 'I

found him tied to a doorway. In the rain. I'm going to take him home...'

'He has been here all day?' The supervisor's bosom swelled to alarming proportions. 'No animal is allowed inside the hospital. You are aware of that, are you not, Miss Foster? I shall report this, and in the meantime the animal can be taken away by one of the porters.'

'Don't you dare,' said Emmy fiercely. 'I'll not allow it. You are—'

It was unfortunate that she was interrupted before she could finish.

'Ah,' said Professor ter Mennolt, looming behind the supervisor. 'My kitten. Good of you to look after it for me, Ermentrude.' He gave the supervisor a bland smile. 'I am breaking the rules, am I not? But this seemed the best place for it to be until I could come and collect it.'

'Miss Foster has just told me...' began the woman.

'Out of the kindness of her heart,' said the professor outrageously. 'She had no wish to get me into trouble. Isn't that correct, Ermentrude?'

She nodded, and watched while he soothed the supervisor's feelings with a bedside manner which she couldn't have faulted.

'I will overlook your rudeness, Miss Foster,' she said finally, and sailed away.

'Where on earth did you find it?' asked the professor with interest.

She told him, then went on, 'I'll take him home. He'll be nice company for Snoodles and George.'

'An excellent idea. Here is your relief. I shall be outside when you are ready.'

'Why?' asked Emmy.

'You sometimes ask silly questions, Ermentrude. To take you both home.'

Emmy made short work of handing over, got into her mac, picked up the box and went to the entrance. The Bentley was outside, and the professor bundled her and her box into it and drove away in the streaming rain.

The kitten sat up on wobbly legs and mewed. It was bedraggled and thin, and Emmy said anxiously, 'I do hope he'll be all right.'

'Probably a she. I'll look the beast over.'

'Would you? Thank you. Then if it's necessary I'll take him—her—to the vet.' She added uncertainly, 'That's if it's not interfering with whatever you're doing?'

'I can spare half an hour.' He sounded impatient. She unlocked the door and ushered him into the hall, where he took up so much room she had to sidle past him to open the sitting-room door.

'You're so large,' she told him, and ushered him into the room.

Mrs Foster was sitting reading with Snoodles on her lap. She looked up as they went in and got to her feet.

'I'm sure you're the professor who was so kind to Emmy,' she said, and offered a hand. 'I'm her mother. Emmy, take off that wet mac and put the kettle on, please. What's in the box?'

'A kitten.'

Mrs Foster offered a chair. 'Just like Emmy—always finding birds with broken wings and stray animals.' She smiled from a plain face very like her daughter's, and he thought what a charming woman she was.

'I offered to look at the little beast,' he explained. 'It was tied to a door handle…'

'People are so cruel. But how kind of you. I'll get a clean towel so that we can put the little creature on it while you look. Have a cup of tea first, won't you?'

Emmy came in then, with the tea tray, and they drank

their tea while the kitten, still in its box, was put before the fire to warm up. George sat beside it, prepared to be friendly. Snoodles had gone to sit on top of the bookcase, looking suspicious.

Presently, when the kitten had been carefully examined by the professor and pronounced as well as could be expected, he thanked Mrs Foster for his tea with charming good manners, smiled at Emmy and drove himself away.

'I like him,' observed Mrs Foster, shutting the front door.

Emmy, feeding the kitten bread and milk, didn't say anything.

CHAPTER THREE

ANNELIESE found Ruerd absent-minded when they met on the following day—something which secretly annoyed her. No man, she considered, should be that while he was in her company. He was taking her out to dinner, and she had gone to great pains to look her best. Indeed, heads turned as they entered the restaurant; they made a striking couple, and she was aware of that.

She realised very soon that he had no intention of talking about their future. She had a splendid conceit of herself—it never entered her head that the lack of interest could be anything else but a temporary worry about his work—but she had the sense to say no more about her plans for the future, and laid herself out to be an amusing companion.

She considered that she had succeeded too, for as he drove her back to the hotel she suggested that she might stay for several more days, adding prettily, 'I miss you, Ruerd.'

All he said was, 'Why not stay? Perhaps I can get tickets for that show you want to see. I'll do my best to keep my evenings free.'

He drew up before the hotel and turned to look at

her. She looked lovely in the semi-shadows, and he bent to kiss her.

She put up a protesting hand. 'Oh, darling, not now. You always disarrange my hair.'

He got out, opened her door, went with her into the foyer, bade her goodnight with his beautiful manners and drove himself back home, reminding himself that Anneliese was the ideal wife for him. Her coolness was something he would overcome in time. She was beautiful, he told himself, and she knew how to dress, how to manage his large household in Holland, how to be an amusing and charming companion…

He let himself into his house and Beaker and Humphrey came into the hall.

'A pleasant evening, I trust, sir?' asked Beaker smoothly.

The professor nodded absently. Humphrey had reminded him about the kitten and Ermentrude. He frowned; the girl had a habit of popping into his thoughts for no reason. He must remember to ask about the kitten if he saw her in the morning.

Emmy, still refreshed by her days off, was a little early. She settled down before the switchboard, arranged everything just as she liked it and took out her knitting. She was halfway through the first row when she became aware that the professor was there. She turned to look at him and, since it was a crisp autumn morning and the sun was shining and she was pleased to see him, she smiled widely and wished him good morning.

His reply was cool. He took his spectacles out of his pocket, polished them and put them on his commanding nose in order to read the variety of notes left for him at the desk.

Emmy's smile dwindled. She turned back and picked up her knitting and wished that she were busy. Perhaps she shouldn't have spoken to him. She was only being civil.

'It's Friday morning,' she said in a reasonable voice, 'and the sun's shining.'

He took his specs off, the better to stare down at her. 'The kitten—is it thriving?'

'Yes. Oh, yes, and Snoodles and George are so kind to it. Snoodles washes it and it goes to sleep with them. It's a bit of a squash in their basket.' She beamed at him. 'How nice of you to ask, sir.'

He said testily, 'Nice, nice...a useless word. You would do well to enlarge your knowledge of the English language, Ermentrude.'

'That is very rude, Professor,' said Emmy coldly, and was glad that there was a call which kept her busy for a few moments. Presently she turned her head cautiously. The professor had gone.

I shall probably get the sack, she reflected. The idea hung like a shadow over her for the rest of the day. By the time she was relieved, Authority hadn't said anything, but probably in the morning there would be a letter waiting for her, giving her a month's notice.

She went slowly to the entrance, wondering if a written apology to the professor would be a good idea. She began to compose it in her head, pausing on her way to get the words right so that the professor had plenty of time to overtake her as she crossed the entrance hall. He came to a halt in front of her so that she bounced against his waistcoat. Emmy, being Emmy, said at once, 'I'm composing a letter of apology to you, sir, although I really don't see why I should.'

'I don't see why you should either,' he told her. 'What were you going to put in it?'

'Well—"Dear sir", of course, to start with, and then something about being sorry for my impertinence.'

'You consider that you were impertinent?' he wanted to know.

'Good heavens, no, but if I don't apologise I dare say I'll get the sack for being rude or familiar or something.'

She received an icy stare. 'You have a poor opinion of me, Ermentrude.'

She made haste to put things right. 'No, no, I think you are very nice…' She paused. 'Oh, dear, I'll have to think of another word, won't I?' She smiled at him, ignoring the cold eyes. 'But you are nice! I suppose I could call you handsome or sexy…'

He held up a large hand. 'Spare my blushes, Ermentrude. Let us agree, if possible, on nice. I can assure you, though, that you are in no danger of being dismissed.'

'Oh, good. The money's useful at home, you know.'

Which presumably was why she was dressed in less than eye-catching fashion.

'The matter being cleared up, I'll drive you home. It's on my way.'

'No, it's not. Thank you very much, though; I can catch a bus…'

The professor, not in the habit of being thwarted, took her arm and walked her through the door.

In the car he asked, 'What are you doing with your evening? Meeting the boyfriend, going to a cinema, having a meal?'

She glanced at him. He was looking ahead, not smiling.

'Me? Well, I haven't got a boyfriend, so I won't be going to the cinema or out for a meal. Mother and Father are home, so we'll have supper and take George for a walk and see to Snoodles and the kitten. And we'll talk…' She added, 'We like talking.'

When he didn't answer she asked, 'Are you going to have a pleasant evening, Professor?'

'I am taking my finacée to Covent Garden to the ballet, and afterwards we shall have supper somewhere. I do not care for the ballet.'

'Well, no, I dare say men don't. But supper will be fun—especially as it's with your fiancée. Somewhere nice—I mean, fashionable…'

'Indeed, yes.'

Something in his voice made her ask, 'Don't you like going out to supper, either?' She wanted to ask about his fiancée but she didn't dare—besides, the thought of him getting married made her feel vaguely unhappy.

'It depends where it is eaten and with whom. I would enjoy taking a dog for a long walk in one of the parks and eating my supper…' He paused. 'Afterwards.' Which hadn't been what he had wanted to say.

'That's easy. Get a dog. You could both take it for a walk in the evenings and then go home and have a cosy supper together.'

The professor envisaged Anneliese tramping round Hyde Park and then returning to eat her supper in his company. No dressing up, no waiters, no other diners to admire her—his mind boggled.

He said slowly, 'I will get a dog. From Battersea Dogs Home. Will you come with me and help me choose him, Ermentrude?'

'Me? I'd love to, but what about your fiancée?'

'She returns to Holland in a few days.'

'Oh, well, all right. It'll be a lovely surprise for her when she comes back to see you again.'

'It will certainly be a surprise,' said the professor.

He dropped her off at her house with a casual nod and a goodnight, and began to drive to his own home. I must be out of my mind, he reflected. Anneliese will never agree to a dog, and certainly not to long walks with it. What is it about Ermentrude which makes me behave with such a lack of good sense? And why do I enjoy being with her when I have Anneliese?

Later that evening, after the ballet, while they were having supper, he deliberately talked about Ermentrude, telling Anneliese something of the bomb scare, mentioning the kitten.

Anneliese listened smilingly. 'Darling, how like you to bother about some little girl just because she got scared with that bomb. She sounds very dull. Is she pretty?'

'No.'

'I can just imagine her—plain and mousy and badly dressed. Am I right?'

'Yes. She has a pretty voice, though. A useful attribute in her particular job.'

'I hope she's grateful to you. I mean, for a girl like that it must be a great uplift to be spoken to by you.'

The professor said nothing to that. He thought it unlikely that Ermentrude had experienced any such feeling. Her conversation had been invariably matter-of-fact and full of advice. As far as she was concerned he was just another man.

He smiled at the thought, and Anneliese said, 'Shall we talk about something else? I find this girl a bit boring.'

Never that, thought the professor. Though unable to hold a candle to Anneliese's beauty. If circumstances had not thrown them together briefly, he would never have noticed her. All the same he smiled a little, and Anneliese, despite feeling quite confident of Ruerd's regard for her, decided there and then to do something about it.

* * *

Emmy told her mother and father about going to Battersea Dogs Home with the professor.

'When does the professor intend to marry?' asked her mother.

'I've no idea. He doesn't talk about it, and I couldn't ask him. We only talk about things which don't matter.' She sighed. 'I expect he'll tell me when he's got the time to choose a dog.'

But although he wished her good morning and good evening each day, that was all. He didn't ask after the kitten either.

It was towards the end of the next week when Emmy came back from her dinner break and found someone waiting for her. After one look she knew who it was: the professor's fiancée; she had to be. He would, she thought, decide for nothing less than this beautiful creature with the perfect hairdo and the kind of clothes any woman could see at a glance had cost a small fortune.

She said, 'Can I help? Do you want the professor?'

'You know who I am?'

Emmy said diffidently, 'Well, not exactly, but Professor ter Mennolt mentioned that his fiancée was staying in London and—and you're exactly how I imagined you would be.'

'And what was that?' Anneliese sounded amused.

'Quite beautiful and splendidly dressed.' Emmy smiled. 'I'll show you where you can wait while I try and get him for you.'

'Oh, I don't wish to see him. He was telling me about the bomb scare here and what an unpleasant experience it was for everyone. He told me about you, too.' She gave a little laugh. 'I would have known you anywhere from his description—plain and mousy and badly dressed. Oh, dear, I shouldn't have said that. Forgive me—my silly tongue.'

Emmy said quietly, 'Yes, that's a very good description of me, isn't it? Are you enjoying your visit? London in the autumn is rather special.'

'The shopping is good, and we enjoy going out in the evenings. Do you go out much?'

Her voice, too loud and with a strong accent, grated on Emmy's ears.

'Not very much. It's quite a long day here. When I do go home I walk our dog…'

'You have a dog? I do not like them, and certainly not in the house. I dislike cats also—their hairs…'

Emmy's relief telephonist was showing signs of impatience, which made it easy for her to say that she had to return to her switchboard.

'It's been nice meeting you,' said Emmy mendaciously. For once she agreed with the professor that 'nice' was a useless word and quite inappropriate. She hoped that she would never see the girl again.

'I won't keep you from your work. It was most satisfying to find that Ruerd's description of you was so accurate.'

Anneliese didn't offer a hand, nor did she say goodbye. Emmy and the relief watched her go.

'Who's she?'

'Professor ter Mennolt's financée.'

'The poor man. She'll lead him a dance; you see if she doesn't.'

'She's very beautiful,' said Emmy, in a voice which conveyed nothing of her feelings. Though her goodnight in reply to the professor's passing greeting was austere in the extreme.

The following evening, after a wakeful night, and a different day, it held all the hauteur of royalty in a rage.

Not that the professor appeared to notice. 'I'm free on Sunday. Will you help me choose a dog—some time in the morning—or afternoon if you prefer?'

He didn't sound friendly; he sounded like someone performing an obligation with reluctance. 'My fiancée has gone back to Holland this morning,' he added inconsequentially.

'No,' said Emmy coldly. 'I'm afraid I can't.'

He eyed her narrowly. 'Ah, of course—you consider it very incorrect of me to spend a few hours with someone other than Anneliese. The moment she sets foot in the plane, too.'

'No. At least partly.' She frowned. 'It was the bomb which…' she sought for the right words '…was the reason for you speaking to me. In such circumstances that was natural. There is no need—'

He said silkily, 'My dear Emmy, you do not for one moment imagine that you are a serious rival to Anneliese? For God's sake, all I have asked of you is to help me choose a dog.'

'What a silly thing to say,' said Emmy roundly. 'It is the last thing I would think. I am, as you so clearly described me, plain and mousy and badly dressed. Certainly no companion for you, even at a dogs' home!'

He said slowly, 'When did you meet Anneliese?'

'She came here to see me. She wanted to see if you had described me accurately.' Emmy added stonily, 'You had.'

The professor stood looking at her for a long minute. He said, 'I'm sorry, Ermentrude, it was unpardonable of me to discuss you with Anneliese and I had no idea that she had come here to see you.'

'Well,' said Emmy matter-of-factly, 'it's what any

woman would do—you could have been lying about me.' She gave a rueful smile. 'I might have been a gorgeous blonde.'

'I do not lie, Ermentrude. I will not lie to you now and tell you that you are neither mousy nor plain nor badly dressed. You are a very nice—and I use the word in its correct sense—person, and I apologise for hurting you. One day someone—a man—will look at you and love you. He won't notice the clothes; he will see only your lovely eyes and the kindness in your face. He will find you beautiful and tell you so.'

Emmy said, 'Pigs might fly, but it's kind of you to say so. It doesn't matter, you know. I've known since I was a little girl that I had no looks to speak of. It's not as though I'm surprised.' She gave a very small sigh. 'Your Anneliese is very beautiful, and I hope you'll be very happy with her.'

The professor remained silent and she put through an outside call. He was still there when she had done it.

He was not a man in the habit of asking a favour twice, but he did so now.

'Will you help me choose a dog, Ermentrude?'

She turned to look at him. 'Very well, Professor. In the afternoon, if you don't mind. About two o'clock?'

'Thank you. I'll call for you then.'

He went away, and just for a while she was too busy to reflect over their conversation. Which was a good thing, she decided, for her bottled up feelings might spill over. She would go with him on Sunday, but after that good morning and good evening would be sufficient.

Later, when she considered she had cooled down enough to think about it, she thought that it wasn't that he had discussed her with Anneliese so much as the fact that he hadn't denied calling her plain which had made her angry. On the other hand, supposing he had denied it—and she'd known that he was lying? Would she have been just as angry? In all fairness to him she thought that she would. She liked him even if there was no reason to do so.

Her mother and father, when she told them on Sunday, answered exactly as she had known they would. Her mother said, 'Wear a warm coat, dear, it gets chilly in the afternoons.'

Her father said, 'Good idea—enjoy yourself, Emmy!'

Her parents were going to Coventry on the following day—the last week away from home, her mother assured her, for her father would be round and about London after that. 'You're sure you don't mind?' she asked anxiously. 'I know you're busy all day, but it's lonely for you, especially in the evenings.'

'Mother, I've heaps to do, honestly, and I'll get the garden tidied up for the winter.' Though the garden was a miserably small patch of grass surrounded by narrow flowerbeds which Emmy would hopefully plant.

The professor arrived punctually, exchanged suitable and civil remarks with her mother and father and ushered Emmy into the car. She had gone to great pains to improve her appearance. True, her jacket and skirt were off the peg, bought to last, and therefore a useful brown—a colour which didn't suit her. But the cream blouse under the jacket was crisp, and her gloves and shoulder bag were leather, elderly but well cared for. Since her brown shoes were well-worn loafers, she had borrowed a pair of her mother's. Court shoes with quite high heels. They pinched a bit, but they looked all right.

The professor, eyeing her unobtrusively, was surprised to find himself wishing that some fairy godmother would wave a wand over Emmy and transform the brown outfit into something pretty. He was surprised, too, that she wore her clothes with an air—when he had thought about it, and that hadn't been often, he had supposed that she had little interest in clothes. He saw now that he was wrong.

He made casual conversation as he drove, and Emmy replied cautiously, not at all at her ease, wishing she hadn't come. Once they had reached the dogs' home she forgot all about that. She had never seen so many dogs, nor heard such a concert of barking.

They went to and fro looking at doggy faces, some pressed up to the front of their shelters, eager for attention, others sitting indifferently at the back. 'They're pretending that they don't mind if no one wants them,' said Emmy. 'I wish we could have them all.'

The professor smiled down at her. Her face was alight with interest and compassion and, rather to his surprise, didn't look in the least plain.

'I'm afraid one is the best I can do. Have you seen a dog which you think might suit me? There are so many, I have no preference at the moment.'

They had stopped in front of a shelter to watch the antics of an overgrown puppy, chosen by a family of children and expressing his delight. There were a lot of dogs; Emmy looked at them all and caught the eye of a large woolly dog with the kindly face of a Labrador and a tremendous sweeping tail. He was sitting in the corner, and it was obvious to her that he was too proud to attract attention. Only his eyes begged her…

'That one,' said Emmy. 'There.'

The professor studied the dog. 'Yes,' he said. 'That's the one.'

The dog couldn't have heard them, but he came slowly to the front of the shelter and wagged his tail, staring up at them. When, after the necessary formalities had been gone through, the professor fastened a new collar round the dog's powerful neck, he gave a small, happy bark.

'You see?' said Emmy. 'He knew you'd have him. He's so lovely. Did they say what breed he was?'

'Well, no. There is some uncertainty. He was left to fend for himself until some kind soul brought him here. He's been here for some time. He's rather on the large side for the average household.'

They got into the car, and the dog settled warily on a blanket on the back seat.

'You do like him?' Emmy asked anxiously.

'Yes. An instant rapport. I can only hope that Beaker will feel the same way.'

'Beaker?'

'Yes, my man. He runs the house for me. Did I mention him when I told you about Humphrey? He's a splendid fellow.'

He drew up in front of his house and Emmy said, 'Oh, is this where you live? It's not like London at all, is it? Is there a garden?'

'Yes—come and see it?'

'I'd like to, but you'll have a lot to do with the dog, and you have a day off today, too, haven't you?'

He said gravely that, yes, he had, but he was doing nothing else with it. 'So please come in and meet Beaker and Humphrey and help me to get this beast settled in.'

Beaker, opening the door, did no more than lift a dignified eyebrow at the sight of the dog. He bowed gravely to Emmy and shook the hand she offered. 'A handsome beast,' he pronounced. 'Straight into the garden, sir?'

'Yes, Beaker. He's been at the home for a long time

so he's a bit uncertain about everything. Ten minutes in the garden may help. Then tea, if you please.'

Beaker slid away and the professor led Emmy across the hall, into the sitting room and out of the French window into the garden. For London it was quite large, with a high brick wall and one or two trees—a mountain ash, a small silver birch, bare of leaves now, and a very old apple tree.

The dog needed no urging to explore, and Emmy said, 'Oh, how delightful. It must look lovely in the spring—lots of bulbs?'

When he nodded, watching her face, she added, 'And an apple tree. We used to have several…'

'You had a large garden?' he asked gently.

'Yes. A bit rambling, but everything grew. It was heaven to go out in the morning. And the air—there isn't much air here, is there? Well, not around St Luke's.' She turned away, annoyed with herself for saying so much, as though she had asked to be pitied. 'What will you call him?'

'I was hoping you would think of a name.'

'Something dignified and a bit regal to make up for his unhappy life.' She thought about it. 'No, it should be a name that sounds as though he's one of the family. Charlie—when I was a little girl I wanted a brother called Charlie.'

'Charlie it shall be.' The professor called the dog, and he came at once, lolloping across the lawn, his tongue hanging out, his preposterous tail waving.

'You see?' said Emmy happily. 'He knows.'

The professor put a gentle hand on Charlie's woolly head. 'I think he has earned his tea, don't you? Let us go indoors; we've earned ours, too.'

'Oh, well,' said Emmy. 'I didn't mean to stay, only to see your garden.'

'Charlie and I will be deeply offended if you don't stay for tea. What is more, Beaker will think his efforts aren't sufficiently tempting.'

Not meaning to, she smiled at him. 'Tea would be very nice.'

They had it in the sitting room, sitting by the fire with Beaker's efforts on a low table between them. Tiny sandwiches, fairy cakes, a chocolate cake and miniature macaroons, flanked by a silver teapot and paper-thin china cups and saucers.

Charlie, mindful of his manners, sat himself carefully down before the fire, hopeful eyes on the cake. Presently Beaker opened the door and Humphrey came in, circled the room slowly and finally sat down beside Charlie. He ignored the dog and stared into the flames, and Emmy said anxiously, 'Will they get on, do you think?'

'Yes. Humphrey has no intention of losing face, though. Charlie will have to play second fiddle.'

'Oh, well, I don't suppose he'll mind now he has a family of his own. Will your fiancée like him?'

The professor bit into some cake. 'No. I'm afraid not.'

When Emmy looked concerned he added, 'I spend a good deal of the year in Holland and, of course, Charlie will stay here with Beaker.'

She poured second cups. 'Do you have a dog in Holland?'

'Two. A Jack Russell and an Irish wolfhound.'

She wanted to ask him about his home in Holland, but although he was friendly he was also aloof. Emmy, willing and eager to be friends with everyone, found that daunting. Besides, she wasn't sure what to make of him. In his company she was happy even when they weren't on the best of terms, but away from him, looking at him from a distance as it were, she told herself that there was no point in continuing their friendship—if it could be called that.

Tea finished, she said a little shyly, 'I think I had better go home, Professor. Mother and Father are going to Coventry in the morning. It will be Father's last job away from home.'

'He enjoys his work?' the professor asked idly.

'He'd rather be a schoolmaster, and not in London.'

'If he were to get a post in the country, you would go with your parents?'

'Yes, oh, yes. I expect I'd have to look for another kind of job. I like needlework and sewing. I expect I could find work in a shop or helping a dressmaker.' She added defiantly, 'I like clothes…'

He prudently kept silent about that. He had a brief memory of Anneliese, exquisitely turned out in clothes which must have cost what to Emmy would have been a small fortune. Emmy, he reflected, would look almost pretty if she were to dress in the same way as Anneliese dressed.

He didn't ask her to stay, but waited while she said goodbye to Charlie and Humphrey and thanked Beaker for her tea, and then went with her to the car.

The streets were almost empty on a late Sunday afternoon and the journey didn't take long. At the house he declined her hesitant offer to go in. He opened her door, thanked her for her help, still standing on the pavement in the dull little street, and waited while she opened the house door and went inside.

Driving back home, he reflected that he had enjoyed his afternoon with Emmy. She was a good companion; she didn't chat and she was a good listener, and when she did have something to say it was worth listening to. He must remember to let her know from time to time how Charlie progressed.

A pleasant afternoon, Emmy told her parents, and the dog, Charlie, was just what she would have chosen for herself. 'And I had a lovely tea,' she told them. 'The professor has a man who runs his home for him and makes the most delicious cakes.'

'A nice house?' asked her mother.

Emmy described it—what she had seen of it—and the garden as well.

'It's not like London,' she told them. 'In the garden you might be miles away in the country.'

'You miss our old home, don't you, Emmy?' her father asked.

'Yes, I do, but we're quite cosy here.' Empty words which neither of them believed.

'I dare say the professor will tell you how the dog settles down,' observed her mother.

'Perhaps.' Emmy sounded doubtful.

She didn't see him for several days, and when he at length stopped to speak to her on his way home one evening, it was only to tell her that Charlie was nicely settled in.

'A very biddable animal,' he told her. 'Goes everywhere with me.'

He bade her good evening in a frosty voice and went away, leaving her wondering why he was so aloof.

He's had a busy day, reflected Emmy, he'll be more friendly in the morning.

Only in the morning he wasn't there. Audrey, who always knew the latest gossip, told her as she took over that he had gone to Birmingham.

'Gets around, doesn't he? Going back to Holland for Christmas too. Shan't see much of him—not that he's exactly friendly. Well, what do you expect? He's a senior consultant and no end of a big noise.'

Which was, Emmy conceded, quite true. And a good reason for remembering that next time he might pause for a chat. He was beginning to loom rather large on the edge of her dull, humdrum life, which wouldn't do at all. Sitting there at her switchboard, she reminded herself that they had nothing in common— Well, Charlie perhaps, and being in the hospital when the bomb went off.

Besides, she reminded herself bitterly, he considered her plain and dowdy. If I could spend half as much on myself as that Anneliese of his, reflected Emmy waspishly, I'd show him that I'm not in the least dowdy, and a visit to a beauty salon would work wonders even with a face like mine.

Since neither of their wishes were likely to be fulfilled, she told herself to forget the professor; there were plenty of other things to think about.

It was a pity that she couldn't think of a single one of them—within minutes he was back in her thoughts, making havoc of her good resolutions.

She was in the professor's thoughts too, much to his annoyance. The tiresome girl, he reflected, and why do I have this urge to do something to improve her life? For all I know she is perfectly content with the way she lives. She is young; she could get a job wherever she wishes, buy herself some decent clothes, meet people, find a boyfriend. All of which was nonsense, and he knew it. She deserved better, he considered, a home and work away from London and that pokey little house.

But even if she had the chance to change he knew that she wouldn't leave her home. He had liked her parents; they had fallen on bad times through no fault of her father. Of course, if he could get a post as a schoolmaster again away from London that would solve the problem. Ermentrude could leave St Luke's and shake the dust of London from her well-polished but well-worn shoes.

The professor put down the notes he was studying, took off his spectacles, polished them and put them back onto his nose. He would miss her.

'This is ridiculous,' he said to himself. 'I don't even know the girl.'

He forbore from adding that he knew Ermentrude as if she were himself, had done since he had first seen her. He was going to marry Anneliese, he reminded himself, and Ermentrude had demonstrated often enough that she had no interest in him. He was too old for her, and she regarded him in a guarded manner which made it plain that in her eyes he was no more than someone she met occasionally at work…

The professor was an honourable man; he had asked Anneliese to marry him—not loving her but knowing that she would make a suitable wife—and there was no possible reason to break his word. Even if Ermentrude loved him, something which was so unlikely that it was laughable.

He gave his lectures, dealt with patients he had been asked to see, arranged appointments for the future and always at the back of his mind was Ermentrude. She would never be his wife but there was a good deal he could do to make her life happier, and, when he got back once more to Chelsea, he set about doing it.

CHAPTER FOUR

DESPITE her resolutions, Emmy missed the professor. She had looked forward to seeing him going to and fro at St Luke's, even if he took no notice of her. He was there, as it were, and she felt content just to know that he was. Of course, she thought about him. She thought about Anneliese too, doubtless getting ready for a grand wedding, spending money like water, secure in the knowledge that she was going to marry a man who could give her everything she could want.

'I only hope she deserves it,' said Emmy, talking to herself and surprising the porter who had brought her coffee.

'If it's women you're talking about, love, you can take it from me they don't deserve nothing. Take my word for it; I'm a married man.'

'Go on with you!' said Emmy. 'I've seen your wife, she's pretty, and you've got that darling baby.'

'I could have done worse.' He grinned at her. 'There's always an exception to every rule, so they say.'

'No sign of our handsome professor,' said Audrey when she came on duty. 'Having fun in Birmingham, I shouldn't wonder. Won't be able to do that once he's a married man, will he? Perhaps he's going straight over to Holland and not coming back here until after Christmas.'

'Christmas is still six weeks away.'

'Don't tell me that he can't do what he chooses when he wants to.'

'I think that if he has patients and work here he'll stay until he's no longer needed. I know you don't like him, but everyone else does.'

'Including you,' said Audrey with a snigger.

'Including me,' said Emmy soberly.

Emmy was on night duty again. Her mother was home and so was her father, now inspecting various schools in outer London and coming home tired each evening. He didn't complain, but the days were long and often unsatisfactory. He had been told that the man he had replaced would be returning to work within a week or ten days, which meant that he would be returning to his badly paid teaching post. Thank heaven, he thought, that Emmy had her job too. Somehow they would manage.

Emmy had dealt with the usual early enquiries, and except for internal calls the evening was quiet. She took out her knitting—a pullover for her father's Christmas present—and began the complicated business of picking up stitches around the neck. She was halfway round it when she became aware of the professor standing behind her. Her hand jerked and she dropped a clutch of stitches.

'There, look what you've made me do!' she said, and turned round to look at him.

'You knew that I was here?' He sounded amused. 'But I hadn't spoken…'

'No, well—I knew there was someone.' She was

mumbling, not looking at him now, remembering all at once that what was fast becoming friendship must be nipped in the bud.

She began to pick up the dropped stitches, and wished that the silent switchboard would come alive. Since he just stood there, apparently content with the silence, she asked in a polite voice, 'I hope that Charlie is well, sir?'

The professor, equally polite, assured her that his dog was in excellent health, and registered the 'sir' with a rueful lift of the eyebrows.

'Your kitten?' he asked in his turn.

'Oh, he's splendid, and George and Snoodles take such care of him.'

The professor persevered. 'Has he a name?'

'Enoch. Mother had a cat when she was a little girl called Enoch, and now he's clean and brushed he's the same colour. Ginger with a white waistcoat.' She added, 'Sir.'

The professor saw that he was making no headway; Ermentrude was making it plain that she was being polite for politeness' sake. Apparently she had decided that their friendship, such as it was, was to go no further. Just as well, he reflected, I'm getting far too interested in the girl. He bade her a cool good-night and went away, and Emmy picked up her knitting once more.

A most unsatisfactory meeting, she reflected. On the other hand it had been satisfactory, hadn't it? She had let him see that their casual camaraderie had been just that—casual, engendered by circumstances. He was shortly going to be married, she reminded herself; he would become immersed in plans for his wedding with Anneliese.

* * *

She was mistaken in this. The professor was immersed in plans, but not to do with his future. The wish to transform Emmy's dull life into one with which she would be happy had driven him to do something about it.

He had friends everywhere; it wasn't too difficult to meet a man he had known at Cambridge and who was now headmaster of a boys' prep school in Dorset. The professor was lucky: a schoolmaster had been forced to leave owing to ill health and there was, he was told cautiously, a vacancy. 'But for the right man. I've only your word for it that this Foster's OK.'

The headmaster wrote in his notebook and tore out the page. 'He can give me a ring…'

The professor shook his head. 'That wouldn't do. If he or his daughter discovered that I was behind it, he'd refuse at once.'

'Got a daughter, has he? Thought you were getting married.'

The professor smiled. 'You can rule out any romantic thoughts, but I would like to help her get out of a life she isn't enjoying; away from London. To do that her father must get a post somewhere in the country, for that's where she belongs.'

His friend sighed. 'Tell you what I'll do. I'll concoct a tale, you know the kind of thing—I'd met someone who knew someone who knew this Foster, and as there was a vacancy et cetera… Will that do? But remember, Ruerd, if I contract any one of these horrible conditions you're so famous for treating, I shall expect the very best treatment—free!'

'A promise I hope I shall never need to keep.' They shook hands, and his friend went home and told his wife that Ruerd ter Mennolt seemed to be putting himself to a great deal of trouble for some girl or other at St Luke's.

'I thought he was marrying that Anneliese of his?'

'And still is, it seems. He was always a man to help lame dogs over stiles.'

'Anneliese doesn't like dogs,' said his wife.

It was the very next day when the letter arrived, inviting Mr Foster to present himself for an interview. And it couldn't have come at a better time, for with the same post came a notice making him redundant from his teaching post on the first of December. They sat over their supper, discussing this marvellous stroke of luck.

'Though we mustn't count our chickens before they are hatched,' said Mr Foster. 'How fortunate that I have Thursday free; I'll have to go by train.'

Emmy went into the kitchen and took the biscuit tin down from the dresser-shelf and counted the money inside. It was money kept for emergencies, and this was an emergency of the best kind.

'Will there be a house with the job?' she asked. 'Littleton Mangate—that's a small village, isn't it? Somewhere in the Blackmore Vale.' She smiled widely. 'Oh, Father, it's almost too good to be true…'

'So we mustn't bank on it until I've had my interview, Emmy. Once that's over and I've been appointed we can make plans.'

The next day, replying sedately to the professor's grave greeting, Emmy almost choked in her efforts not to tell him about the good news. Time enough, she told herself, when her father had got the job. Only then, too, if he asked her.

'Which he won't,' she told George as she brushed him before taking him on his evening trot.

The professor, it seemed, was reluctant as she was to resume their brief conversations. He never failed to greet her if he should pass the switchboard, but that was all. She felt bereft and vaguely resentful, which, seeing that she had wanted it that way, seemed rather hard on him. But at least it boosted her resolve to forget him. Something not easily done since she saw him willy-nilly on most days.

Her father, in his best suit, a neatly typed CV in his coat pocket, left on Thursday morning on an early train, leaving Emmy to fidget through her day's work, alternately positive that her father would get the post and then plunged into despair because he had been made redundant, and finding a job would be difficult, perhaps impossible. In a moment of rare self-pity she saw herself sitting in front of the switchboard for the rest of her working life.

The professor, catching sight of her dejected back view, was tempted to stop and speak to her, but he didn't. A helping hand was one thing, getting involved with her spelt danger. It was a good thing, he reflected, that he would be going over to Holland shortly. He must see as much of Anneliese as possible.

The bus ride home that evening took twice as long as usual, or so it seemed to Emmy. She burst into the house at length and rushed into the kitchen.

Her mother and father were there, turning to look at her with happy faces. 'You've got it,' said Emmy. 'I knew you would, Father. I can't believe it.'

She flung her coat onto a chair, poured herself a cup of tea from the pot and said, 'Tell me all about it. Is there a house? When do you start? Did you like the headmaster?'

'I've been accepted,' said Mr Foster. 'But my references still have to be checked. There's a house, a very nice one, a converted lodge in the school grounds. I am to take over as soon as possible as they are short of a form master. There are still three weeks or so of the term.'

'So you'll be going in a day or two? And Mother? Is the house furnished?'

'No. Curtains and carpets...'

Mr Foster added slowly, 'Your Mother and I have been talking it over. You will have to give a month's notice, will you not? Supposing we have as much furniture as possible sent to Dorset, would you stay on for the last month, Emmy? Could you bear to do that? We'll take George and Snoodles and Enoch with us. The house can be put up for sale at once. There's little chance of it selling quickly, but one never knows. Could you do that? In the meantime your mother will get the house at Littleton Mangate habitable. We can spend Christmas together...'

Emmy agreed at once. She didn't much like the idea of living alone in a half-empty house, but it would be for a few weeks, no more. The idea of leaving St Luke's gave her a lovely feeling of freedom.

'Money?' she asked.

'The bank will give me a loan against this house.' Her father frowned. 'This isn't an ideal arrangement, Emmy, but we really haven't much choice. If you give a month's notice you'll be free by Christmas, and in the meantime there is always the chance that the house will sell.'

'I think that's a splendid idea, Father. When do you start? Almost at once? Mother and I can start packing up and she can join you in a few days. I'll only need a bed and a table and chairs. There's that man—Mr Stokes—at the end of the street. He does removals.'

'I'm not sure that we should leave you,' said her

mother worriedly. 'You're sure you don't mind? We can't think what else to do. There's so little time.'

'I'll be quite all right, Mother. It's for such a short time anyway. It's all so exciting...'

They spent the rest of the evening making lists, deciding what to take and what to leave. Tired and excited by the time she got to her bed, Emmy's last waking thought was that once she had left St Luke's she would never see the professor again.

Going to work the next morning, she thought that perhaps she would tell him of the unexpected change in her life.

However, he didn't give her the chance. Beyond an austere good morning he had nothing to say to her, and later, when he left the hospital, he had a colleague with him.

Oh, well, said Emmy to herself, I can always tell him tomorrow.

Only he wasn't there in the morning; it wasn't until the day was half-done that she heard that he had gone to Holland.

She told herself that it didn't matter at all, that there was no reason to expect him to be interested in her future. She had already given in her notice and would not tell anyone about it.

Back home that evening, she found her mother already busy, turning out drawers and cupboards. 'Your father's arranged for Mr Stokes to collect the furniture in three days' time.' She beamed at Emmy. 'Oh, darling, it's all so wonderful. I don't believe it. Your father is so happy; so am I. It is a great pity that you can't come with us. I hate the idea of you being here on your own.'

Emmy, wrapping up the best china in newspaper and stowing it carefully in a tea chest, paused to say, 'Don't worry, Mother. I'll be working all day, and by the time I get back here and have a meal it'll be time to go to bed—the days will fly by. Won't it be lovely having Christmas away from here?'

Her mother paused in stacking books. 'You've hated it here, haven't you, darling? So have I—so has your father. But we can forget all this once we're at Littleton Mangate. Just think, too, when we've sold this house there'll be some money to spend. Enough for you to go to a school of embroidery or whatever else you want to do. You'll meet people of your own age, too.'

Emmy nodded and smiled and, much against her will, thought about the professor.

He, too, was thinking about her, not wishing to but unable to prevent his thoughts going their own way. It was easier to put her to the back of his head while he was at the various hospitals—Leiden, the Hague, Amsterdam, Rotterdam. There were patients for him in all of these, and he was able to dismiss any thoughts other than those to do with his work while he was in the hospitals consulting, examining, deciding on treatment, seeing, in some cases, anxious relations and reassuring patients.

His days were long and busy but when he drove himself home each evening he had time to think. Anneliese was in France, but she would be back soon and he would spend his leisure with her. But in the meantime his time was his own.

Each evening he turned into the drive leading to his house and sighed with content at the sight of it. It was on the edge of a village, a stately old house behind the dunes, the North sea stretching away to the horizon, magnificent stretch of sand sweeping into the distance, north and south. The house had been built by his great-great-grandfather, and was a solid edifice, secure against the bitter winter winds, its rooms large, the windows tall and narrow, and the front door solid enough to withstand a siege.

Ruerd had been born there, and between schools, universities and hospital appointments went back to it as often as he could. His two sisters and younger brother—the former married, the latter still at medical school—were free to come and go as they wished, but the house was his now that his father, a retired surgeon, and his mother, lived in den Haag.

He had had a tiring day in Rotterdam, and the lighted windows welcomed him as he got out of the car. They were not the only welcome either—the door was opened and the dogs dashed out to greet him, the wolfhound and the Jack Russell pushing and jostling to get near their master. They all went into the house together, into the large square hall with its black and white marble floor, its plain plastered walls hung with paintings in ornate gilded frames.

They were halfway across it when they were joined by an elderly man, small and rotund, who trotted ahead of them to open double doors to one side of the hall.

The room the professor entered was large and high-ceilinged, with a great hooded fireplace on either side of which were vast sofas with a Regency mahogany centre table between them. There were two tub wing armchairs with a walnut card table between them, and a couple of Dutch mahogany and marquetry armchairs on either side of a Georgian breakfast table set between two of the long windows overlooking the grounds at the back of the house.

Against the walls there were walnut display cabinets, their shelves filled with silver and porcelain, reflecting the light from the cut-glass chandelier and the ormolu wall lights. It was a beautiful room, and magnificent; it was also lived in. There were bowls of flowers here and there, a pile of newspapers and magazines on one of the tables, a dog basket to the side of the fireplace.

The professor settled his vast frame in one of the armchairs, allowed the Jack Russell to scramble onto his knee and the wolfhound to drape himself over his feet, and poured himself a drink from the tray on the table beside him. A quiet evening, he thought with satisfaction, and, since he wasn't due anywhere until the following afternoon, a long walk with the dogs in the morning.

He was disturbed by his manservant, who came bearing letters on a salver, looking apologetic.

The professor picked them up idly. 'No phone calls, Cokker?'

'Juffrouw van Moule telephoned, to remind you that you will be dining with her family tomorrow evening.'

'Oh, Lord, I had forgotten…thank you, Cokker.'

'Anna wishes to know if half an hour is sufficient for you before dinner, *mijnheer*.'

'As soon as she likes, Cokker. It's good to be home…'

'And good to have you here,' said Cokker. They smiled at each other, for Cokker had been with the family when the professor had been born and now, a sprightly sixty-year-old, had become part and parcel of it.

The professor took the dogs for a walk after dinner, across several acres of his own grounds and into the country lane beyond. It was a chilly night, but there was a moon and stars and later there would be a frost.

He strolled along, thinking about Ermentrude. By now her father would know if he had the post he had collocated. No doubt Ermentrude would tell him all about it when he got back to St Luke's. She would give in her notice, of course, and go to Dorset with her parents and he wouldn't see her again. Which was just as well. It was, he told himself, merely a passing attraction—not even that. All he had done was to take the opportunity to improve her life.

'She will be quite happy in the country again,' he told Solly, the wolfhound. He stooped to pick up Tip, who was getting tired, and tucked the little dog under one arm. He turned for home, dismissed Ermentrude from his mind and steered his thoughts to his future bride.

Later, lying in his great four-poster bed, Ermentrude was there again, buried beneath his thoughts and contriving to upset them.

'The girl's a nuisance,' said the professor to the empty room. 'I hope that by the time I get back to St Luke's she will be gone.'

His well-ordered life, he reflected, was being torn in shreds by a plain-faced girl who made no bones about letting him see that she had no interest in him. He slept badly and awoke in an ill humour which he had difficulty in shaking off during the day.

It was only that evening, sitting beside Anneliese at her parents' dining table, joining in the talk with the other guests, aware that Anneliese was looking particularly beautiful, that he managed to dismiss Ermentrude from his mind.

Anneliese was at her best. She knew that she looked delightful, and she exerted all her charm. She was intelligent, asking him all the right questions about his work at the hospitals he was visiting, talking knowledgeably about the health service in Holland, listening with apparent interest when he outlined the same service in England.

'Such a pity you have to go back there before Christmas. But of course you'll be back here then, won't you? Mother and I will come and stay for a while; we can discuss the wedding.'

She was clever enough not to say more than that, but went on lightly, 'Do you see any more of that funny little thing you befriended at St Luke's?'

Before he could answer, she said, 'Ruerd got involved in a bomb explosion in London.' She addressed the table at large. 'It must have been very exciting, and there was this girl who works there whom he took home—I suppose she was in shock. I saw her when I was staying in London. So plain, my dears, and all the wrong clothes. Not at all his type. Was she, Ruerd?' She turned to smile at him.

The professor had his anger nicely in check. 'Miss Foster is a brave young lady. I think perhaps none of us know enough of her to discuss her. It is quite difficult to keep calm and do whatever it is you have to do when there's an emergency, and to keep on doing it until you're fit to drop. In such circumstances, it hardly matters whether one is plain or pretty, old or young.'

Anneliese gave a little laugh. 'Oh, Ruerd, I didn't mean to be unkind. The poor girl. And we, all sitting here in comfort talking about something we know very little about.' She touched his arm. 'Forgive me and tell us what you think of the new hospital. You were there yesterday, weren't you?'

The rest of the evening passed off pleasantly enough, but, driving himself home, the professor reflected that he hadn't enjoyed it. He had never liked Anneliese's family and friends overmuch, supposing vaguely that once they were married she would welcome his more serious friends, live the quiet life he enjoyed. He tried to imagine them married and found it impossible.

She had seemed so suitable when he'd asked her to

marry him—interested in his work, anxious to meet his friends, telling him how she loved to live in the country. 'With children, of course, and dogs and horses,' she had added, and he had believed her.

Yet that very evening he had stood by, while she talked to some of her friends, and listened to her complaining sharply about the nuisance of having to visit a cousin with young children. 'They're such a bore,' she had said.

Her mother, a formidable matron who enjoyed dictating to everyone around her, had chimed in, saying, 'Children should stay in the nursery until they're fit to mix with their elders. I have always advised young girls of my acquaintance that that is the best for them. Besides, they can hamper one's life so. A good nanny is the answer.' She had smiled around at her listeners, saying, 'And I have given Anneliese the same advice, have I not, my dear?'

Her words, echoing in his head, filled him with disquiet.

Emmy meanwhile was busy. She was happy too. At least she told herself that she was several times a day. To live in the country again would be heaven—only would it be quite heaven if she was never to see the professor again? It wouldn't, but there was nothing to be done about that, and it was, after all, something she had wanted badly. Besides that, her mother and father were over the moon. She applied herself to the packing up with a cheerful energy which wasn't quite genuine, buoyed up by her mother's obvious delight.

Mr Stokes, with his rather decrepit van, and an old man and a young boy to help him, stowed the furniture tidily, leaving Emmy's bedroom intact, and a table and two chairs in the kitchen, as well as the bare necessities for living.

'It won't be for long,' said Emmy cheerfully. 'There

are two lots of people coming to view the house tomorrow; I'm sure it will be sold by the time I leave.'

Her mother said anxiously, 'You will get a hot meal at the hospital, Emmy? And do keep the electric fire on while you are in the house. Empty houses are so cold.' She frowned. 'I do wonder if there might have been some other way…'

'Stop worrying, Mother. I only need a bed and somewhere to have breakfast.' She didn't mention the long evenings alone and the solitary suppers. After all, it was for such a short time.

She was on night duty again, so she was there to see her mother, sitting beside Mr Stokes, leave for their new home. After they had gone she went into the kitchen and made herself some coffee. The house looked shabbier than ever now that it was almost empty, and without the animals it was so quiet. She put everything ready for an evening meal and went to bed. She was already some days into her notice. It was a satisfying thought as she dropped off. Everything was going according to plan, she thought with satisfaction.

Only she was wrong. Audrey hardly gave her time to get her coat off the following evening before bursting into furious speech.

'The nerve,' she cried. 'And there's nothing to be done about it—or so I'm told. Reorganisation, indeed, necessary amalgamation to cut expenses…'

Emmy took the envelope Audrey was offering her. 'What's the matter? What are you talking about?'

'Read it for yourself. I'm going home—and don't expect to see me tomorrow.'

She stomped away and Emmy sat down and read the letter in the envelope.

There were to be changes, she read, and regretfully her services would no longer be required. With the opening of the new hospital across the river, St Luke's and Bennett's hospitals would amalgamate and the clerical staff from Bennett's would take over various functions, of which the switchboard was one. The letter pointed out that she would be given a reference, and the likelihood of her getting a new job was high. It ended with a mealy-mouthed paragraph thanking her for her loyal services which as she had already given notice, would terminate on Friday next.

She read it through again, carefully, in case she had missed something. But it was clear enough—in two days' time she would be jobless.

She could, of course, join her mother and father. On the other hand there was far more chance of the house being sold if there was someone there to keep the estate agents on their toes and show people around. By the end of the night she had decided to say nothing to her parents. She would be able to manage on her own and she would have a week's salary, and surely an extra month's money, since she had been given barely two days' notice.

It would have been nice to have had someone to have talked things over with. The professor would have been ideal…

As it was, when the porter brought her coffee she forgot her own troubles when he told her that he was to go too. 'They've offered me a job in that new place across the river—less money, and takes me much longer to get to work. Haven't got much choice, though, have I? With a wife and baby to look after?' He glanced at her. 'What'll you do, Emmy?'

'Me? Oh, I'll be all right. Audrey was very angry…'

'You bet she was. Proper blew her top, she did. Didn't do no good. Wrongful dismissal, she said, but it seems it isn't. It's like when a firm goes bankrupt and everyone just goes home. If there's no money, see? What else is there to do?'

'Well, good luck with your job, anyway, and thanks for the coffee.'

Emmy hadn't believed Audrey when she had said that she wouldn't be there in the morning, but she had meant it. Emmy, going off duty late because a relief telephonist had had to be called in, was too tired to notice the icy rain and the leaden sky. Home, she thought, even if it is only my bedroom and a table and chairs.

Only they didn't look very welcoming when she let herself into the empty house. She boiled an egg, made toast and a pot of tea and took herself off to bed. When she had had a sleep she would mull over the turn of events and see how best to deal with it. One thing was certain: there was no way of changing it. And, being a sensible girl, she put her head on the pillow and slept.

She had time enough to think when she got up in the late afternoon. It was still raining and almost dark, and she was glad they had left the curtains hanging and some of the carpets. She showered, made tea and sat down in the kitchen to think. She would call into the estate agents on her way home in the morning and spur them on a bit. The market was slow, they had told her father, but the house was small, in fairly good order and soundly built, like all the other houses in the row. Its selling price was modest, well within the reach of anyone prudent enough to have saved a little capital and who could get a mortgage.

She allowed herself to dream a bit. There would be

a little money—not much, but perhaps enough for all of them to have new clothes, perhaps have a holiday—although being in Dorset would be like a holiday itself. She would get a chance to go to a needlework school—night classes, perhaps? Start a small arts and crafts shop on her own? The possibilities were endless. She got her supper presently, and went to work for the last time.

It was a busy night, and when it was over she bade goodbye to those she had worked with and left the hospital for the last time. She had her pay packet in her purse, and an extra month in lieu of notice, and she handed over to her older colleague, who told her that she had been working for the NHS for more than twenty years.

'I don't know what I would have done if I had been made redundant,' she said. 'I've an elderly mother and father who live with me. We make ends meet, but only just—to be out of work would have been a catastrophe.'

It was heartening to find on her way home that there had been several enquiries about the house. The agent, a weasel-faced young man she didn't much like, had arranged for them to inspect the house at any time they wished.

'You'll be there,' he told her airily. 'So it really doesn't matter when they call, if they do.'

'I can't be there all day,' Emmy told him, and was silenced by him.

'You're not on the phone—stands to reason, doesn't it? Someone will have to be there.'

'Will you ask anyone who wants to look round the house to come after one o'clock? I will stay at home for the rest of the day.'

'Suit yourself, Miss Foster. The two parties interested said they'd call in some time today.'

To go to bed was impossible; one never knew,

whoever was coming might decide to buy the house. Emmy had her breakfast, tidied away the dishes and sat down on the one comfortable chair in the kitchen. Of course she went to sleep almost at once, and woke to the sound of someone thumping the door knocker and ringing the bell.

The middle-aged couple she admitted looked sour.

'Took your time, didn't you?' observed the man grumpily, and pushed past her into the hall. He and his meek-looking wife spent the next ten minutes looking round and returned to Emmy, who was waiting in the kitchen after taking them on their first survey.

'Pokey, that's what it is,' declared the man. 'You'll be lucky to sell the place at half the asking price.'

He went away, taking his wife, who hadn't said a word, with him. Emmy hadn't said anything either. There seemed to be no point in annoying the man more than necessary. There would be several more like him, she guessed.

The second couple came late in the afternoon. They made a leisurely tour and Emmy began to feel hopeful, until the woman remarked, 'It's a lot better than some we've seen. Not that we can buy a house, but it gives us some idea of what we could get if we had the money.' She smiled at Emmy. 'Nice meeting you.'

Not a very promising start, decided Emmy, locking the door behind them. Better luck tomorrow. Though perhaps people didn't come on a Saturday.

She felt more hopeful after a good night's sleep. After all, it was early days; houses didn't sell all that fast. Only it would be splendid if someone decided to buy the place before she joined her parents.

No one came. Not the next day. She had gone for a

walk in the morning and then spent the rest of the day in the kitchen, listening to her small radio and knitting. Monday, she felt sure, would bring more possible buyers.

No one came, nor did they come on Tuesday, Wednesday or Thursday. She wrote a cheerful letter to her parents on Friday, did her morning's shopping and spent the rest of the day waiting for the doorbell to ring. Only it didn't.

The professor, back in London, striding into St Luke's ready for a day's work, paused on his way. While not admitting it, he was looking forward to seeing Emmy again. He hoped that all had gone according to his plan and that her father had got the job the professor's friend had found for him. Emmy would have given her notice by now. He would miss her. And a good thing that she was going, he reminded himself.

He was brought up short by the sight of the older woman sitting in Emmy's chair. He wished her a civil good morning, and asked, 'Miss Foster? Is she ill?'

'Ill? No, sir. Left. Made redundant with several others. There's been a cutting down of staff.'

He thanked her and went on his way, not unduly worried. Ermentrude would have gone to Dorset with her father and mother. He must find time to phone his friend and make sure that all had gone according to plan. She would be happy there, he reflected. And she would forget him. Only he wouldn't forget her…

He left the hospital rather earlier than usual, and on a sudden impulse, instead of going home, drove through the crowded streets and turned into the street where Emmy lived. Outside the house he stopped the car. There was a FOR SALE board fastened to the wall by the door, and the downstairs curtains were drawn across.

There was a glimmer of light showing, so he got out of the car and knocked on the door.

Emmy put down the can of beans she was opening. At last here was someone come to see the house. She turned on the light in the hall and went to open the door, and, being a prudent girl, left the safety chain on. Peering round it, recognising the vast expanse of waistcoat visible, her heart did a happy little somersault.

'It is I,' said the professor impatiently, and, when she had slid back the chain, came into the narrow hall, squashing her against a wall.

Emmy wormed her way into a more dignified stance. 'Hello, sir,' she said. 'Are you back in England?' She caught his eye. 'What I mean is, I'm surprised to see you. I didn't expect to…'

He had seen the empty room and the almost bare kitchen beyond. He took her arm and bustled her into the kitchen, sat her in a chair and said, 'Tell me why you are here alone in an empty house. Your parents?'

'Well, it's a long story…'

'I have plenty of time,' he told her. 'And I am listening.'

CHAPTER FIVE

EMMY told him without embellishments. 'So you see it's all turned out marvellously. We just have to sell this house—that's why I'm here. We thought I'd have to give a month's notice, and it seemed a splendid idea for me to stay on until I could leave and try and sell the house at the same time. Only being made redundant was a surprise. I've not told Father, of course.'

'You are here alone, with no furniture, no comforts?'

'Oh, I've got my bed upstairs, and a cupboard, and I don't need much. Of course, we thought I'd be at the hospital all day or all night. Actually,' she told him, wanting to put a good light on things, 'It's worked out very well, for I stay at home each day from one o'clock so that I can show people round…'

'You get many prospective buyers?'

'Well, not many, not every day. It isn't a very attractive house.'

The professor agreed silently to this. 'You will join your parents for Christmas? Have you a job in mind to go to?'

'Yes. Well, I've hardly had time, have I?' she asked reasonably. Then added, 'Perhaps I'll be able to take a course in embroidery and needlework…'

She didn't go on; he didn't want to know her plans. She asked instead, 'Did you have a pleasant time in Holland?'

'Yes. I'll wait here while you put a few things into a bag, Ermentrude. You will come back with me.'

'Indeed, I won't. Whatever next? I'm quite all right here, thank you. Besides, I must be here to show people round.' She added on a sudden thought, 'Whatever would your fiancée think? I mean, she's not to know that we don't like each other.' Emmy went bright pink. 'I haven't put that very well...'

'No, you haven't. You have, however, made it quite plain that you do not need my help.'

The professor got to his feet. He said coldly, 'Goodbye, Ermentrude.' And, while she was still searching for the right reply, let himself out of the house.

Emmy listened to the car going away down the street; she made almost no sound. She sat where she was for quite some time, doing her best not to cry.

Presently she got up and got her supper, and since there was nothing to do she went to bed.

She wasn't sure what woke her up. She sat up in bed, listening; the walls were thin, it could have been Mr Grant or Mrs Grimes dropping something or banging a door. She lay down again and then shot up once more. The noise, a stealthy shuffling, was downstairs.

She didn't give herself time to feel frightened. She got out of bed quietly, put on her dressing gown and slippers and, seizing the only weapon handy—her father's umbrella which had somehow got left behind—she opened her door and peered out onto the landing. Someone was there, someone with a torch, and they had left the front door open too.

The nerve, reflected Emmy, in a rage, and swept

downstairs, switching on the landing light as she did so. The man was in the empty sitting room, but he came out fast and reached the hall. He was young, his face half hidden by a scarf, a cap pulled down over his eyes and, after his first shock, he gave a nasty little laugh.

'Cor, lummy— An empty 'ouse an' a girl. Alone, are you? Well, let's 'ave yer purse, and make it quick.'

Emmy poked him with the umbrella. 'You get out of this house and you make it quick,' she told him. She gave him another prod. 'Go on…'

He made to take the umbrella from her, but this time she whacked him smartly over the head so that he howled with pain.

'Out,' said Emmy in a loud voice which she hoped hid her fright. She switched on the hall light now, hoping that someone, even at two o'clock in the morning, would see it. But the man, she was glad to see, had retreated to the door. She followed him, umbrella at the ready, and he walked backwards into the street.

Rather puffed up with her success at getting rid of him, she followed him, unaware that the man's mate was standing beside the door, out of sight. She heard him call out before something hard hit her on the head and she keeled over.

She didn't hear them running away since for the moment she had been knocked out. But Mr Grant, trotting to the window to see why there was a light shining into the street, saw them. Old though he was, he made his way downstairs and out of his house to where Emmy lay. Emmy didn't answer when he spoke to her, and she was very pale. He crossed the road and rang the bell of the house opposite. It sounded very loud at that time of the night. He rang again, and presently a window was opened and the teenager hung his head out.

'Come down, oh, do come down—Ermentrude has been hurt.'

The head disappeared and a moment later the boy, in his coat and boots, came out. 'Thieves? Take anything, did they? Not that there's anything to take.' He bent over Emmy. 'I'll get her inside and the door shut.'

He was a big lad, and strong; he picked Emmy up and carried her into the kitchen and set her in a chair. 'Put the kettle on,' he suggested. 'I'll be back in a tick; I'll get my phone.'

As he came back into the kitchen Emmy opened her eyes. She said crossly, 'I've got the most awful headache. Someone hit me.'

'You're right there. Who shall I ring? You'd better have a doctor—and the police.' He stood looking at her for a moment, and was joined by Mr Grant. 'You can't stay here, that's for certain. Got any friends? Someone to look after you?'

Mr Grant had brought her a wet towel, and she was holding it to her head. She felt sick and frightened and there was no one… Yes, there was. He might not like her, but he would help and she remembered his number; she had rung it time and again from the hospital.

She said muzzily, 'Yes, there's someone, if you'd tell him. Ask him if he would come.' She gave the boy the number and closed her eyes.

'He'll be along in fifteen minutes,' said the boy. 'Lucky the streets are empty at this time of night. Did they take anything?'

Emmy shook her head, and then wished she hadn't. 'No. There's nothing to take; my purse and bag are upstairs and they didn't get that far.' She said tiredly, 'Thank you both for coming to help me; I'm very grateful.'

As far as she was concerned, she thought, they can

make all the noise they like and I'll never even think of complaining.

Mr Grant gave her a cup of tea and she tried to drink it, holding it with both shaky hands while the boy phoned the police. Then there was nothing to do but wait. The boy and Mr Grant stood drinking tea, looking rather helplessly at her.

'I'm going to be sick,' said Emmy suddenly, and lurched to the sink.

Which was how the professor found her a couple of minutes later.

The boy had let him in. 'You the bloke she told me to phone?' he asked suspiciously.

'Yes. I'm a doctor. Have you called the police?'

'Yes. She's in the kitchen being sick.'

Emmy was past caring about anyone or anything. When she felt the professor's large, cool hand on her wrist, she mumbled, 'I knew you'd come. I feel sick, and I've got a headache.'

He opened his bag. 'I'm not surprised; you have a bump the size of a hen's egg on your head.' His hands were very gentle. 'Keep still, Ermentrude, while I take a look.'

She hardly felt his hands after that, and while he dealt with the lump and the faint bleeding he asked what had happened.

Mr Grant and the boy both told him at once, talking together.

'The police?'

'They said they were on their way.'

The professor said gravely, 'It is largely due to the quick thinking and courage of both of you that Ermentrude isn't more severely injured. I'll get her to hospital just as soon as the police get here.'

They came a few minutes later, took statements from Mr Grant and the boy, agreed with the professor that Ermentrude wasn't in a fit state to say anything at the moment and agreed to interview her later. 'We will lock the door and keep the key at the station.' The officer swept his gaze round the bare room. 'No one lives here?'

'Yes, me,' said Ermentrude. 'Just for a few weeks—until someone wants to buy it. Do you want me to explain?' She opened her eyes and closed them again.

'Wait until you know what you're talking about,' advised the professor bracingly. He spoke to one of the officers. 'Miss Foster is staying here for a short time; her parents have moved and she has stayed behind to settle things up.' He added, 'You will want to see her, of course. She will be staying at my house.' He gave the address, heedless of Emmy's mutterings.

'Now, if I might have a blanket in which to wrap her, I'll take her straight to St Luke's. I'm a consultant there. She needs to be X-rayed.'

Emmy heard this in a muzzy fashion. It wouldn't do at all; she must say something. She lifted her head too quickly, and then bent it over the sink just in time. The professor held her head in a matter-of-fact way while the others averted their gaze.

'The blanket?' asked the professor again, and the boy went upstairs and came back with her handbag and the quilt from Emmy's bed. The professor cleaned her up in a businesslike manner, wrapped her in the quilt and picked her up.

'If I'm not at my home I'll be at the hospital.' He thanked Mr Grant and the boy, bade the officers a civil goodnight, propped Emmy in the back of the car and, when she began to mumble a protest, told her to be quiet.

He said it in a very gentle voice, though. She closed

her eyes, lying back in the comfortable seat, and tried to forget her raging headache.

At the hospital she was whisked straight to X-Ray. She was vaguely aware of the radiographer complaining good-naturedly to the professor and of lying on a trolley for what seemed hours.

'No harm done,' said the professor quietly in her ear. 'I'm going to see to that lump, and then you can be put to bed and sleep.'

She was wheeled to Casualty then, and lay quietly while he bent over her, peering into her eyes, putting a dressing on her head. She was drowsy now, but his quiet voice mingling with Sister's brisk tone was soothing. She really didn't care what happened next.

When he lifted her into the car once more, she said, 'Not here…' But since the professor took no notice of her she closed her eyes again. She had been given a pill to swallow in Casualty; her headache was almost bearable and she felt nicely sleepy.

Beaker was waiting when the professor reached his house, carried Emmy indoors and asked, 'You got Mrs Burge to come round? I had no time to give you details. If I carry Miss Foster upstairs perhaps she will help her to bed.'

'She's upstairs waiting, sir. What a to-do. The poor young lady—knocked out, was she?'

'Yes. I'll tell you presently, Beaker. I could do with a drink, and I expect you could, too. Did Mrs Burge make any objections?'

'Not her! I fetched her like you told me to, and she'll stay as long as she's wanted.'

The professor was going upstairs with Emmy, fast asleep now, in his arms. 'Splendid.'

Mrs Burge met him on the small landing. 'In the

small guest room, sir. Just you lay her down on the bed and I'll make her comfortable.'

She was a tall, bony woman with hair screwed into an old-fashioned bun and a sharp nose. A widow, she had been coming each day to help Beaker for some time now, having let it be known from the outset that through no fault of her own she had fallen on hard times and needed to earn her living.

Beaker got on well with her, and she had developed an admiration for the professor, so that being routed out of her bed in the early hours of the morning was something she bore with equanimity. She said now, 'Just you leave the young lady to me, sir, and go and have a nap—you'll be dead on your feet and a day's work ahead of you.'

The professor said, 'Yes, Mrs Burge,' in a meek voice, merely adding that he would be up presently just to make sure that Emmy's pulse was steady and that she slept still. 'I know I leave her in good hands,' he told Mrs Burge, and she bridled with pleasure.

For all her somewhat forbidding appearance she was a kind-hearted woman. She tucked Emmy, still sleeping, into bed, dimmed the bedside light and sat down in the comfortable armchair, keeping faithful watch.

'She's not moved,' she told the professor presently. 'Sleeping like a baby.'

He bent over the bed, took Emmy's pulse and felt her head.

'I'll leave these pills for her to take, Mrs Burge. See that she has plenty to drink, and if she wants to eat, so much the better. A couple of days in bed and she'll be quite herself. There's only the mildest of concussions, and the cut will heal quickly.

'I'm going to the hospital in an hour or so and shall be there all day. Ring me if you're worried. Beaker will give you all the assistance you require, and once Ermentrude is awake there is no reason why you shouldn't leave her from time to time. I'll be back presently when I've had breakfast so that you can have yours with Beaker.'

He went away to shower and dress and eat his breakfast and then returned, and Mrs Burge went downstairs to where Beaker was waiting with eggs and bacon.

Emmy hadn't stirred; the professor sat down in a chair, watching her. She suited the room, he decided—quite a small room, but charming with its white furniture, its walls covered with a delicate paper of pale pink roses and soft green leaves. The curtains were white, and the bedspread matched the wallpaper exactly. It was a room he had planned with the help of his younger sister, whose small daughter slept in it when they visited him.

'Though once you're married, Ruerd,' she had told him laughingly, 'you'll need it for your own daughter.'

Emmy, with her hair all over the pillow, looked very young and not at all plain, he decided. When Mrs Burge came back he said a word or two to her, bent over the bed once more and stopped himself just in time from kissing Emmy.

It was late in the morning when Emmy woke, to stare up into Mrs Burge's face. She was on the point of asking 'Where am I?' and remembered that only heroines in books said that. Instead she said, 'I feel perfectly all right; I should like to get up.'

'Not just yet, love. I'm going to bring you a nice little pot of tea and something tasty to eat. You're to sit up a bit if you feel like it. I'll put another pillow behind you. There…'

'I don't remember very clearly,' began Emmy. 'I was taken to the hospital and I went to sleep.'

'Why, you're snug and safe here in Professor ter Mennolt's house, dearie, and me and Beaker are keeping an eye on you. He's gone to the hospital, but he'll be home this evening.'

Emmy sat up too suddenly and winced. 'I can't stay here. There's no one at the house—the estate agent won't know—someone might want to buy it…'

'Leave everything to the professor, ducks. You may be sure he'll have thought of what's to be done.'

Mrs Burge went away and came back presently with a tray daintily laid with fine china—a teapot, cup and saucer, milk and sugar. 'Drink this, there's a good girl,' she said. 'Beaker's getting you a nice little lunch and then you must have another nap.'

'I'm quite able to get up,' said Emmy, to Mrs Burge's departing back.

'You'll stay just where you are until I say you may get out of bed,' said the professor from the door. 'Feeling better?'

'Yes, thank you. I'm sorry I've given you all so much trouble. Couldn't I have stayed in hospital and then gone home?'

'No,' said the professor. 'You will stay here today and tomorrow, and then we will decide what is to be done. I have phoned the estate agent. He has a set of keys for your house and will deal with anyone who wishes to view it. The police will come some time this afternoon to ask you a few questions if you feel up to it.'

'You're very kind, sir, and I'm grateful. I'll be quite well by tomorrow, I can go…'

'Where?' He was leaning over the foot of the bed, watching her.

She took a sip of tea. 'I'm sure Mrs Grimes would put me up.'

'Mrs Grimes—the lady with the powerful voice? Don't talk nonsense, Ermentrude.' He glanced up as Mrs Burge came in with a tray. 'Here is your lunch; eat all of it and drink all the lemonade in that jug. I'll be back this evening.'

He went away and presently out of the house, for he had a clinic that early afternoon. He had missed lunch in order to see Ermentrude, and had only time to swallow a cup of coffee before his first patient arrived.

Emmy ate her lunch under Mrs Burge's watchful eye and, rather to her surprise, went to sleep again to wake and find another tray of tea, and Mrs Burge shaking out a gossamer-fine nightie.

'If you feel up to it, I'm to help you have a bath, love. You're to borrow one of the professor's sister's nighties. You'll feel a whole lot better.'

'Would someone be able to fetch my clothes so that I can go home tomorrow?' asked Emmy.

'Beaker will run me over this evening. You just tell me what you want and I'll pack it up for you. Professor ter Mennolt's got the keys.'

'Oh, thank you. You're very kind. Were you here when I came last night?'

'Yes—Beaker fetched me—three o'clock in the morning...'

'You must be so tired. I'm quite all right, Mrs Burge. Can't you go home and have a good sleep?'

'Bless you, ducks, I'm as right as a trivet; don't you worry your head about me. Now, how about a bath?'

Getting carefully out of bed, Emmy discovered that she still had a headache and for the moment wished very much to crawl back between the sheets. But the thought of being seen in her present neglected state got her onto her feet and into the adjoining bathroom, and once in the warm, scented water with Mrs Burge sponging her gently she began to feel better.

'I suppose I can't wash my hair?'

'Lawks, no, love. I'll give it a bit of a comb, but I daren't go messing about with it until the professor says so.'

'It's only a small cut,' said Emmy, anxious to look her best.

'And a lump the size of an egg—that'll take a day or two. A proper crack on the head and no mistake. Lucky that neighbour saw the light and the men running away. It could have been a lot worse,' said Mrs Burge with a gloomy relish.

Emmy, dried, powdered and in the kind of nightgown she had often dreamed of possessing, sat carefully in a chair while Mrs Burge made her bed and shook up her pillows. Once more settled against them, Emmy sighed with relief. It was absurd that a bang on the head should make her feel so tired. She closed her eyes and went to sleep.

Which was how the professor found her when he got home. He stood looking down at her for a long minute, and in turn was watched by Mrs Burge.

They went out of the room together. 'Go home, Mrs Burge,' he told her. 'You've been more than kind. If you could come in tomorrow, I would be most grateful. I must contrive to get Ermentrude down to her parents—they are in Dorset and know nothing of this. They are moving house, and I don't wish to make things more difficult for them than I must. Another day of quiet rest here and I think I might drive her down on the following day…'

Mrs Burge crossed her arms across her thin chest. 'Begging your pardon, sir, but I'll be back here to sleep tonight.'

He didn't smile, but said gravely, 'That would be good of you, Mrs Burge, as long as you find that convenient.'

'It's convenient.' She nodded. 'And I'll make sure the young lady's all right tomorrow.'

'I'm in your debt, Mrs Burge. Come back when you like this evening. Is there a room ready for you?'

'Yes, sir, I saw to that myself.' She hesitated. 'Miss Ermentrude did ask if someone could fetch her clothes. I said I'd go this evening…'

'Tell me when you want to go; I'll drive you over. Perhaps you had better ask her if she needs anything else. Money or papers of any sort.'

Emmy woke presently and, feeling much better, made a list of what she needed and gave it to Mrs Burge.

'I'm off home for a bit,' said that lady. 'But I'll be back this evening. Beaker will bring you up some supper presently. You just lie there like a good girl.'

So Emmy lay back and, despite a slight headache, tried to make plans. Once she had been pronounced fit, she decided, she would go back to the house. She didn't much fancy being there alone, but reassured herself with the thought that lightning never struck twice in the same place… She would go to the estate agents again, too, and there was only another week or so until Christmas now.

Her thoughts were interrupted by the professor and her supper tray.

He greeted her with an impersonal hello. 'Beaker has done his best, so be sure and eat everything.'

He put the tray down, set the bed table across her knees and plumped up her pillows. 'I think you might get up tomorrow—potter round the house, go into the garden—well wrapped-up. I'll take you home the day after.'

'You're very kind, but I must go back to the house, just in case someone wants to buy it. I mean, I can't afford to miss a chance. It'll have to be left empty when I go home at Christmas, and you know how awful houses look when they're empty. So if you don't mind…'

'I do mind, Ermentrude, and you'll do as I say. I'll phone the estate agent if it will set your mind at rest and rearrange things. Do you want me to tell your parents what has happened?'

'Oh, no—they're getting the house straight, and Father's at the school all day so it's taking a bit of time. They've enough to worry about. They don't need to know anyway.'

'Just as you wish. Does Mrs Burge know what to fetch for you?'

'Yes, thank you. I gave her a list. I've only a few clothes there; Mother took the rest with her.'

'Then I'll say goodnight, Ermentrude. Sleep well.'

She was left to eat her supper, a delicious meal Beaker had devised with a good deal of thought. It was he who came to get the tray later, bringing with him fresh lemonade and a fragile china plate with mouth-watering biscuits.

'I make them myself, miss,' he told her, beaming at her praise of the supper. 'Mrs Burge will look in on you when she gets back, with a nice drop of hot milk.'

'Thank you, Beaker, you have been so kind and I'm giving you a lot of extra work.'

'A pleasure, miss.'

'I heard Charlie barking…'

'A spirited dog, miss, and a pleasure to have in the house. Humphrey and he are quite partial to each other. When you come downstairs tomorrow he will be delighted to see you.'

Emmy, left alone, ate some of the biscuits, drank some of the lemonade and thought about the professor.

His household ran on oiled wheels, that was obvious. His Anneliese, when she married him, would have very little to do—a little tasteful flower-arranging perhaps, occasional shopping, although she thought that Beaker might not like that. And of course later there would be the children to look after.

Emmy frowned. She tried to imagine Anneliese nursing a baby, changing nappies or coping with a toddler and failed. She gave up thinking about it and thought about the professor instead, wishing he would come home again and come and see her. She liked him, she decided, even though he was difficult to get to know. Then, why should he wish her to know too much about him? She had no place in his life.

Much later she heard the front door close, and Charlie barking. He and Mrs Burge were home. She lay, watching the door. When it opened Mrs Burge came in, a suitcase in one hand, a glass of milk in the other.

'Still awake? I've brought everything you asked for, and Professor ter Mennolt went to see the estate agent at his home and fixed things up. No one's been to look at the house.' Mrs Burge's sniff implied that she wasn't surprised at that. 'We looked everywhere to make sure that things were just so. And there's some post. Would you like to read it now?'

She put the milk on the bedside table. 'Drink your milk first. It's time you were sleeping.'

Emmy asked hesitantly, 'Are you going home now, Mrs Burge?'

'No, ducks. I'll be here, just across the landing, if you want me. Now I'll just hang up your things…'

Emmy stifled disappointment. There was no reason why the professor should wish to see her. He must, in fact, be heartily sick of her by now, disrupting his life.

* * *

The professor was talking on the phone. Presently he got his coat, ushered Charlie into the back of the car and, with a word to Beaker, drove himself to St Luke's where one of his patients was giving rise to anxiety.

He got home an hour later, ate the dinner which Beaker served him with the air of someone who had long learned not to mind when his carefully prepared meals were eaten hours after they should have been, and went to his study to work at his desk with the faithful Charlie sprawled over his feet.

Waking the following morning, Emmy decided that she felt perfectly well again. She ate her breakfast in bed, since Mrs Burge told her sternly not to get up till later.

'Professor ter Mennolt went off an hour ago,' she told Emmy. 'What a life that man leads, never an hour to call his own.'

Which wasn't quite true, but Emmy knew what she meant. 'I suppose all doctors are at everyone's beck and call, but it must be a rewarding life.'

'Well, let's hope he gets his reward; he deserves it,' said Mrs Burge. 'Time that fiancée of his made up her mind to marry him.' She sniffed. 'Wants too much, if you ask me. Doesn't like this house—too small, she says…'

'Too small?' Emmy put down her cup. 'But it's a big house—I mean, big enough for a family.'

'Huh,' said Mrs Burge forcefully. 'Never mind a family, she likes to entertain—dinner parties and friends visiting. She doesn't much like Beaker, either.'

Emmy, aware that she shouldn't be gossiping, nonetheless asked, 'But why not? He's the nicest person…'

'True enough, love. Looks after the professor a treat.'

'So do you, Mrs Burge.'

'Me? I come in each day to give a hand, like. Been

doing it for years, ever since the professor bought the house. A very nice home he's made of it, too. I have heard that he's got a tip-top place in Holland, too. Well, it stands to reason, doesn't it? He's over there for the best part of the year—only comes here for a month or two, though he pops over if he's needed. Much in demand, he is.'

She picked up Emmy's tray. 'Now, you have a nice bath and get dressed and come downstairs when you're ready. I'll be around and just you call if you want me. We'd better pack your things later on; the professor's driving you home in the morning.'

So Emmy got herself out of bed, first taking a look at her lump before going to the bathroom. The swelling had almost gone and the cut was healing nicely. She stared at her reflection for several moments; she looked a fright, and she was going to wash her hair before anyone told her not to.

Bathed, and with her hair in a damp plait, she went downstairs to find Beaker hovering in the hall.

His, 'Good morning, miss,' was affable. 'There's a cup of coffee in the small sitting room; it's nice and cosy there.'

He led the way and opened a door onto a quite small room at the back of the house. It was furnished very comfortably, and there was a fire burning in the elegant fireplace. A small armchair had been drawn up to it, flanked by a table on which were newspapers and a magazine or two. Sitting in front of the fire, waving his tail, asking to be noticed, was Charlie.

Emmy, sitting down, could think of nothing more delightful than to be the owner of such a room and such a dog, with a faithful old friend like Beaker smoothing out life's wrinkles. She said on a happy sigh, 'This is such a lovely house, Beaker, and everything is so beautifully polished and cared for.'

Beaker allowed himself to smile. 'The master and I, we're happy here, or so I hope, miss.' He went, soft-footed, to the door. 'I'll leave you to drink your coffee; lunch will be at one o'clock.'

He opened the door and she could hear Mrs Burge Hoovering somewhere.

'I suppose the professor won't be home for lunch?'

'No, miss. Late afternoon. He has an evening engagement.'

She put on her coat and went into the garden with Charlie after lunch. For one belonging to a town house the garden was surprisingly large, and cleverly planned to make the most of its space. She wandered up and down while Charlie pottered, and presently when they went indoors she sought out Beaker.

'Do you suppose I might take Charlie for a walk?' she asked him.

Beaker looked disapproving. 'I don't think the professor would care for that, miss. Charlie has had a long walk, early this morning with his master. He will go out again when the professor comes home. There's a nice fire burning in the drawing room. Mrs Burge asked me to let you know that she'll be back this evening if you should need any help with your packing. I understand that you are to make an early start.'

So Emmy retreated to the drawing room and curled up by the fire with Charlie beside her and Humphrey on her lap. She leafed through the newspapers and magazines on the table beside her, not reading them, her mind busy with her future. Christmas was too close for her to look for work; she would stay at home and help to get their new house to rights. There would be curtains to sew and hang, possessions to be stowed away in cupboards.

She wondered what the house was like. Her mother had written to tell her that it was delightful, but had had no time to describe it. There had been a slight hitch, she had written; the previous occupant's furniture was for the most part still in the house owing to some delay in its transport. 'But,' her mother had written, 'we shall be quite settled in by the time you come.'

Beaker brought tea presently; tiny sandwiches, fairy cakes and a chocolate cake which he assured her he had baked especially for her. 'Most young ladies enjoy them,' he told her.

Emmy was swallowing the last morsel when Charlie bounded to his feet, barking, and a moment later the professor came into the room.

His 'Hello,' was friendly and casual. He sat down, then enquired how she felt and cut himself a slice of cake.

'I'll run you home in the morning,' he told her. 'The day after tomorrow I shall be going to Holland.'

'There's no need,' said Emmy.

'Don't be silly,' said the professor at his most bracing. 'You can't go back to an empty house, and in a very short time you would be going home anyway. There seems little chance of selling the house at the moment; I phoned the agent this morning. There's nothing of value left there, is there?'

She shook her head. 'No, only my bed and the bedclothes and a few bits of furniture.'

'There you are, then. We'll leave at eight o'clock.' He got up. 'Charlie and I are going for our walk—I shall be out tonight. Beaker's looking after you?'

'Oh, yes, thank you.'

'Mrs Burge will come again this evening. Ask for anything you want.'

His smile was remote as he went away.

She was still sitting there when he returned an hour later with Charlie, but he didn't come into the drawing room, and later still she heard him leave the house once more. Beaker, opening the door for Charlie to come in, said that Mrs Burge was in the kitchen if she needed her for anything. 'I'll be serving dinner in half an hour, Miss. May I pour you a glass of sherry?'

It might lift her unexpected gloom, thought Emmy, accepting. Why she should feel so downcast she had no idea; she should have been on the top of the world—leaving London and that pokey house and going to live miles away in Dorset. She wouldn't miss anything or anyone, she told herself, and the professor, for one, would be glad to see her go; she had caused enough disruption in his life.

Beaker had taken great pains with dinner—mushroom soup, sole *à la femme*, creamed potatoes and baby sprouts, and an apricot pavlova to follow these. He poured her a glass of wine too, murmuring that the professor had told him to do so.

She drank her coffee in Humphrey's company and then, since she was heartily sick of her own company, went in search of Mrs Burge. There was still some packing to do, and that lady came willingly enough to give her help, even though it wasn't necessary. It passed an hour or so in comfortable chat and presently Emmy said that she would go to bed.

'We're to go early in the morning, so I'll say goodbye, Mrs Burge, and thank you for being so kind and helpful.'

'Bless you, ducks, it's been a pleasure, and I'll be up

to see you off. Beaker will have breakfast on the table sharp at half past seven—I'll give you a call at seven, shall I?'

She turned on her way out. 'I must say you look a sight better than when you got here.'

Emmy, alone, went to the triple looking-glass on the dressing table and took a good look. If she was looking better now she must have looked a perfect fright before. No wonder the professor showed little interest in her company. Anyway, she reminded herself, his mind would be on Anneliese.

She woke in the morning to find her bedside lamp on and Mrs Burge standing there with a tray of tea.

'It's a nasty old day,' said Mrs Burge. 'Still dark, too. You've got half an hour. The professor's already up and out with Charlie.'

The thought of keeping him waiting spurred Emmy on to dress with speed. She was downstairs with only moments to spare as he and Charlie came into the house.

His good morning was spoken warmly. He's glad I'm going, thought Emmy as she answered cheerfully.

'There's still time to put me on a train,' she told him as they sat down to breakfast. 'It would save you a miserable drive.'

He didn't bother to answer. 'The roads will be pretty empty for another hour or so,' he observed, just as though she hadn't spoken. 'We should get to Littleton Mangate by mid-morning. Ready to leave, are you?'

Emmy went to thank Beaker and Mrs Burge, and got into her coat while Beaker fetched her case down to the car. It was bitterly cold, and she took a few quick breaths before she got into the car, glad to see Charlie already sprawling on the back seat. It was almost like having a third person in the car, even though he obviously intended to go to sleep.

It was striking eight o'clock as they drove away, starting the tedious first part of their journey through London's streets and presently the suburbs.

CHAPTER SIX

IT WAS still quite dark, and the rain was turning to sleet. The professor didn't speak and Emmy made no attempt to talk. In any case she couldn't think of anything to say. The weather, that useful topic of conversation, was hardly conducive to small talk, and he had never struck her as a man who enjoyed talking for the sake of it. She stared out of the window and watched the city streets gradually give way to rows of semi-detached houses with neat front gardens, and these in turn recede to be replaced by larger houses set in their own gardens and then, at last, open country and the motorway.

Beyond asking her if she was warm enough and comfortable, the professor remained silent. Emmy sat back in her comfortable seat and thought about her future. She had thought about it rather a lot in the last few days, largely because she didn't want to think too much about the past few weeks.

She was going to miss the professor, she admitted to herself. She wouldn't see him again after today, but she hoped that he would be happy with Anneliese. He had annoyed her on several occasions, but he was a good man and kind—the sort of kindness which was practical, and if he sometimes spoke his mind rather too frankly she supposed he was entitled to do so.

As the motorway merged into the A303 he turned the car into the service station. 'Coffee? We've made good time. You go on in; I'll take Charlie for a quick trot. I'll see you in the café.'

The place was full, which made their lack of conversation easier to bear. Emmy, painstakingly making small talk and receiving nothing but brief, polite replies, presently gave up. On a wave of ill humour she said, 'Well, if you don't want to talk, we won't.' She added hastily, going red in the face, 'I'm sorry, that was rude. I expect you have a lot to think about.'

He looked at her thoughtfully. 'Yes, Ermentrude, I have. And, strangely, in your company I do not feel compelled to keep up a flow of chat.'

'That's all right, then.' She smiled at him, for it seemed to her that he had paid her a compliment.

They drove on presently through worsening weather. All the same her heart lifted at the sight of open fields and small villages. Nearing their journey's end, the professor turned off the A303 and took a narrow cross-country road, and Emmy said, 'You know the way? You've been here before?'

'No.' He turned to smile at her. 'I looked at the map. We're almost there.'

Shortly after that they went through a village and turned off into a lane overhung with bare winter trees. Round a corner, within their view, was Emmy's new house.

The professor brought the car to a halt, and after a moment's silence Emmy said, 'Oh, this can't be it,' although she knew that it was. The lodge itself was charming, even on a winter's day, but its charm was completely obliterated by the conglomeration of things around it, leaving it half-buried. Her father's car stood at the open gate, for the garage was overflowing with furniture. There was more furniture stacked and covered by tarpaulins in heaps in front of the house, a van parked on the small lawn to one side of the lodge and a stack of pipes under a hedge.

'Oh, whatever has happened?' asked Emmy. 'Surely Father hasn't…'

The professor put a large hand on hers. 'Supposing we go and have a look?'

He got out of the car and went to open her door and then let Charlie out, and together they went up the narrow path to the house.

It wasn't locked. Emmy opened it and called, 'Mother?'

They heard Mrs Foster's surprised voice from somewhere in the house and a moment later she came into the tiny hall.

'Darling—Emmy, how lovely to see you. We didn't expect you…' She looked at the professor. 'Is everything all right?'

He shook hands. 'I think it is we who should be asking you that, Mrs Foster.'

Mrs Foster had an arm round Emmy. 'Come into the kitchen; it's the only room that's comfortable. We hoped to be settled in by the time you came, Emmy. There's been a hitch…'

She led them to the kitchen with Charlie at their heels. 'Sit down; I'll make us some coffee.'

The kitchen wasn't quite warm enough, but it was furnished with a table and chairs, and there were two easy chairs at each side of the small Aga. China and crockery, knives and forks, spoons and mugs and glasses were arranged on a built-in dresser and there was a pretty latticed window over the sink.

Mrs Foster waved a hand. 'Of course all this is temporary; in a week or two we shall be settled in.'

'Mother, what has happened?' Emmy sat down at the table. Enoch and Snoodles had jumped onto her lap while George investigated Charlie.

The professor was still standing, leaning against the wall, silent. Only when Mrs Foster handed round the coffee mugs and sat down did he take a chair.

'So unfortunate,' said Mrs Foster. 'Mr Bennett, whom your father replaced, died suddenly the very day I moved down here. His furniture was to have been taken to his sister's house where he intended to live, but, of course, she didn't want it, and anyway he had willed it to a nephew who lives somewhere in the north of England. He intends to come and decide what to do with it, but he's put it off twice already and says there's no need for it to be put in store as he'll deal with it when he comes. Only he doesn't come and here we are, half in and half out as it were.'

She drank from her mug. 'Your father is extremely happy here, and since he's away for most of the day we manage very well. School breaks up tomorrow, so he will be free after that. We didn't tell you, Emmy, because we hoped—still do hope—that Mr Bennett's nephew will do something about the furniture.'

'Whose van is that outside?' asked Emmy.

'The plumber, dear. There's something wrong with the boiler—he says he'll have it right in a day or two.' Mrs Foster looked worried. 'I'm so sorry we weren't ready for you, but we'll manage. You may have to sleep on the sofa; it's in the sitting room.' She looked doubtful. 'There's furniture all over the place, I'm afraid, but we can clear a space...'

She looked at Emmy. 'I don't suppose the house is sold, Emmy?'

'No, Mother, but there have been several people to look at it. The agent's got the keys...'

'We didn't expect you just yet.' Her mother looked enquiring. 'Has something gone wrong?'

'I'll tell you later,' said Emmy. She turned to the professor, who still hadn't uttered a word. 'It was very kind of you to bring me here,' she said. 'I hope it hasn't upset your day too much.'

'Should I be told something?' asked her mother.

'Later, Mother,' said Emmy quickly. 'I'm sure Professor ter Mennolt wants to get back to London as quickly as possible.'

The professor allowed himself a small smile. He said quietly, 'There is a great deal you should be told, Mrs Foster, and if I may I'll tell it, for I can see that Ermentrude won't say a word until I'm out of the way.'

'emmy's been ill,' said Mrs Foster in a motherly panic.

'Allow me to explain.' And, when Emmy opened her mouth to speak, he said, 'No, Ermentrude, do not interrupt me.'

He explained. His account of Emmy's misfortunes was succinct, even dry. He sounded, thought Emmy, listening to his calm voice, as if he were dictating a diagnosis, explaining something to a sister on a ward round.

When he had finished, Mrs Foster said, 'We are deeply grateful to you—my husband and I. I don't know how we can thank you enough for taking such care of Emmy.'

'A pleasure,' said the professor in a noncommittal voice which made Emmy frown. Of course it hadn't been a pleasure; she had been a nuisance. She hoped that he would go now so that she need never see him again. The thought gave her such a pang of unhappiness that she went quite pale.

He had no intention of going. He accepted Mrs

Foster's invitation to share the snack lunch she was preparing, and remarked that he would like to have a talk with Mr Foster.

'He comes home for lunch?' he enquired blandly.

'Well, no. He has it at school, but he's got a free hour at two o'clock; he told me this morning.'

'Splendid. If I may, I'll walk up to the school and have a chat.'

Emmy was on the point of asking what about when he caught her eye.

'No, Ermentrude, don't ask!' The animals had settled before the stove. The professor got up. 'I'll bring in your things, Ermentrude.'

He sounded impersonal and nonchalant, but something stopped her from asking the questions hovering on her tongue. Why should he want to talk to her father? she wondered.

They had their lunch presently—tinned soup and toasted cheese—sitting round the kitchen table, and Mrs Foster and the professor were never at a loss for conversation. Emmy thought of the silent journey they had just made and wondered what it was that kept him silent in her company. It was a relief when he got into his coat again and started on the five-minute walk to the school.

Mr Foster, if he was surprised to see the professor, didn't say so. He led the way to a small room near the classrooms, remarking that they would be undisturbed there.

'You want to see me, Professor?' He gave him a sharp glance. 'Is this to do with Emmy? She isn't ill? You say she is with her mother...'

'No, no. She has had a mild concussion and a nasty cut on the head, but, if you will allow me, I will explain...'

Which he did in the same dry manner which he had

employed at the lodge. Only this time he added rather more detail.

'I am deeply indebted to you,' said Mr Foster. 'Emmy didn't say a word—if she had done so my wife would have returned to London immediately.'

'Of course. Ermentrude was determined that you should know nothing about it. It was unfortunate that she should have been made redundant with such short notice, although I believe she wasn't unduly put out about that. I had no idea that she was alone in the house until I returned to London.'

Mr Foster gave him a thoughtful look and wondered why the professor should sound concerned, but he said nothing. 'Well, once we have got this business of the furniture and the plumbing settled, we shall be able to settle down nicely. I'm sure that Emmy will find a job, and in the meantime there's plenty for her to do at home.'

'Unfortunate that Christmas is so close,' observed the professor. 'Is it likely that you will be settled in by then?'

Mr Foster frowned. 'Unfortunately, no. I had a phone message this morning—this nephew is unable to deal with the removal of Mr Bennett's furniture until after Christmas. He suggests that it stays where it is for the moment. I suppose we shall be able to manage…'

'Well, now, as to that, may I offer a suggestion? Bearing in mind that Ermentrude is still not completely recovered, and the discomforts you are living in, would you consider…?'

Emmy and her mother, left on their own, rummaged around, finding blankets and pillows. 'There's a mattress in the little bedroom upstairs, if you could manage on that for a few nights,' suggested Mrs Foster worriedly. 'If only they would take all this furniture away…'

Emmy, making up some sort of a bed, declared that she would be quite all right. 'It won't be for long,' she said cheerfully. 'I'll be more comfortable here than I was in London. And Father's got his job—that's what matters.'

She went downstairs to feed the animals. 'The professor and Charlie are a long time,' she observed. 'I hope Charlie hasn't got lost. It's almost tea time, too, and I'm sure he wants to get back to London.'

The professor wasn't lost, nor was Charlie. Having concluded his talk with Mr Foster, the professor had whistled to his dog and set off for a walk, having agreed to return to the school when Mr Foster should be free to return home.

The unpleasant weather hadn't improved at all. Sleet and wet snow fell from time to time from a grey sky rapidly darkening, and the lanes he walked along were half-frozen mud. He was unaware of the weather, his thoughts miles away.

'I am, of course, mad,' he told Charlie. 'No man in his right senses would have conceived such a plan without due regard to the pitfalls and disadvantages. And what is Anneliese going to think?'

Upon reflection he thought that he didn't much mind what she felt. She had been sufficiently well brought up to treat his guests civilly, and if she and Ermentrude were to cross swords he felt reasonably sure that Ermentrude would give as good as she got. Besides, Anneliese wouldn't be staying at his home, although he expected to see a good deal of her.

He waited patiently while Charlie investigated a tree. Surely Anneliese would understand that he couldn't leave Ermentrude and her parents to spend Christmas in a house brim-full of someone else's furniture and inadequate plumbing, especially as he had been the means of their move there in the first place. Perhaps he had rather over-emphasised Ermentrude's need to recuperate after concussion, but it had successfully decided her father to accept his offer.

He strode back to the school to meet Mr Foster and accompany him back to the lodge.

Emmy was making tea when they got there.

'You're wet,' she said unnecessarily. 'And you'll be very late back home. I've made toast, and there's a bowl of food for Charlie when you've dried him off. There's an old towel hanging on the back of the kitchen door. Give me that coat; I'll hang it on a chair by the Aga or you'll catch your death of cold.'

The professor, meekly doing as he was told, reflected that Ermentrude sounded just like a wife. He tried to imagine Anneliese talking like that and failed, but then she would never allow herself to be in a situation such as Emmy was now. She would have demanded to be taken to the nearest hotel. He laughed at the thought, and Emmy looked round at him in surprise. The professor didn't laugh often.

He helped her father out of his wet jacket, poured the tea and called her mother, who was hanging curtains in the small bedroom.

'They'll have to do,' she said, coming into the kitchen. 'I've pinned them up for the moment, and it does make the room look cosier.'

She smiled at the professor. 'Did you have a nice walk? Do sit down. Let Charlie lie by the stove; he must be tired. It's a wretched evening for you to travel.'

Emmy handed round toast and a pot of jam. The tea, in an assortment of cups and saucers, was hot and strong. She watched the professor spread jam on his toast and take a bite, and thought of Beaker's dainty teas with the fine china and little cakes. He looked up and caught her eye and smiled.

Mr Foster drank his tea and put down his cup. 'Professor ter Mennolt has made us a most generous offer. He considers that Emmy needs rest after her accident, and that as a medical man he cannot like the idea of her remaining here while the house is in such a state of confusion. He has most kindly offered to take us over to Holland for the Christmas period to stay in his house there. He will be going the day after tomorrow—'

'You said tomorrow…' interrupted Emmy.

'I find that I am unable to get away until the following day,' said the professor smoothly. 'But I shall be delighted to have you as my guests for a few days. Hopefully by the time you return the problems in this house will be resolved.' He added blandly, 'As a doctor, I would feel it very wrong of me to allow Ermentrude to stay here until she is quite fit.'

Emmy drew a deep breath. She didn't think he meant a word of it; he might look and sound like the learned man he undoubtedly was but his suggestion was preposterous. Besides, there was nothing wrong with her. She opened her mouth to say so and closed it again, swallowing her protest. She didn't stand a chance against that weighty professional manner.

She listened to her mother receiving his offer with delighted relief.

'Surely we shall upset your plans for Christmas? Your family and guests? How will you let them know? And all the extra work…'

The professor sounded reassuring. 'I'm sure you don't need to worry, Mrs Foster. If you can face the idea of Christmas in Holland, I can assure you that you will all be most welcome. Rather short notice, I'm afraid, but if you could manage to be ready by midday on the day after tomorrow?'

Mr and Mrs Foster exchanged glances. It was an offer they could hardly refuse. On their way they would have scrambled through the festive season somehow or other, always hopeful that Mr Bennett's furniture would have been moved by the time Emmy arrived. But now that seemed unlikely, and with Christmas in such a muddle, and Emmy not quite herself…

Mrs Foster said simply, 'Thank you for a most generous offer; we accept with pleasure. Only don't let us interfere with any of your family arrangements. I mean, we are happy just to have a bed and a roof over our heads…'

The professor smiled. 'It will be a pleasure to have you—I always think the more the merrier at Christmas, don't you?'

'Your family will be there?'

'I have two sisters with children and a younger brother. I'm sure they will be delighted to meet you.'

He got up. 'You will forgive me if I leave you now?'

He shook hands with Mr and Mrs Foster, but Ermentrude he patted on the shoulder in a casual manner and told her to take care.

When he had gone, Mrs Foster said, 'What a delightful man, and how kind he is. You know, Emmy, your father and I were at our wits' end wondering what to do about Christmas, and along comes Professor ter Mennolt and settles it all for us—just like that.'

Mr Foster was watching Emmy's face. 'A good man, and very well thought of in his profession, I believe. He tells me that he is engaged to be married. I dare say we shall meet his fiancée.'

Emmy said in a bright voice, 'Oh, I have met her—she came to St Luke's one day to see him—she'd been staying over here. She's beautiful, you know. Fair and slender, and has the most gorgeous clothes.'

'Did you like her?' asked her mother.

'No,' said Emmy. 'But I expect that was because she was the kind of person I would like to be and aren't.'

'Well,' said her mother briskly, 'let's get tidied up here and then think about what clothes to take with us. I've that long black skirt and that rather nice crêpe de Chine blouse; that'll do for the evening. What about you, Emmy?'

'Well, there's the brown velvet; that'll do.' It would have to; she had no other suitable dress for the evening. She thought for a moment. 'I could go in the jacket and skirt, and wear my coat over them. A blouse or two, and a sweater...I don't suppose we'll be there for more than a few days.'

'If we sell the house, you shall have some new clothes, and now your father's got this splendid post...'

'Oh, I've plenty of clothes,' said Emmy airily. 'And they don't matter. It's marvellous that Father's here, and this is a dear little house.'

She looked round her at the muddle—chairs stacked in corners, a wardrobe in the hall, Mr Bennett's piano still in the sitting room. They looked at each other and burst out laughing. 'When you're able to settle in,' said Emmy.

The professor, with Charlie beside him, drove back to Chelsea. 'I do not know what possessed me,' he told his companion. 'Anneliese is not going to like my unexpected guests, and yet what else could I do? Would you like to spend Christmas in such cold chaos? No, of course you wouldn't. Common humanity dictated that I should do something about it... Let me think...'

By the time he had reached his home his plans were made. Over the dinner which Beaker set before him he went through them carefully, and presently went to his study and picked up the phone.

Beaker, bringing his coffee later, coughed gently. 'Mrs Burge and I, sir, we miss Miss Foster.'

The professor looked at him over his spectacles. 'So do I, Beaker. By the way, she and her parents are going to Holland with me for Christmas. Due to unavoidable circumstances, the house they have moved to is unfit to live in for the moment and they have nowhere to go.'

Beaker's face remained impassive. 'A good idea, if I may say so, sir. The young lady isn't quite herself after that nasty attack.'

'Just so, Beaker. I shan't be leaving until the day after tomorrow—pack a few things for me, will you? Enough for a week.'

Beaker gone, the professor buried his commanding nose in a weighty tome and forgot everything else. It was only as he was going to bed that he remembered that he should have phoned Anneliese. It would be better to tell her when he got to Holland, perhaps. He felt sure that she would be as warmly welcoming to his unexpected guests as his sisters had promised to be.

Emmy slept badly; a mattress on the floor, surrounded by odds and ends of furniture which creaked and sighed during the night, was hardly conducive to a restful night. Nor were her thoughts—largely of the professor—none of which were of a sensible nature.

She got up heavy-eyed and her mother said, 'The professor is quite right, Emmy, you don't look at all yourself.' She eyed her much loved daughter worriedly. 'Was it very uncomfortable on the mattress? There's no room to put up a bed, and anyway we haven't got one until we can get yours from the house in London. Your father can sleep there tonight and you can come in with me...'

'I was very comfortable,' said Emmy. 'But there was such a lot to think about that I didn't sleep very well. I expect I'm excited.'

Mrs Foster put the eggs for breakfast on to boil. 'So am I. We'll pack presently—your father's going up to the school to find out where the nearest kennels are, then he can take these three later this evening.'

'I hope they'll be all right, but it's only for a few days. Wouldn't it be marvellous if we came back and found all Mr Bennett's furniture gone and the plumbing repaired?'

'We mustn't expect too much, but it would be nice. Directly after Christmas your father will go up to London and see the estate agent and arrange for your bed to be brought down here. You need never go back there unless you want to, Emmy.' Her mother turned round to smile at her. 'Oh, Emmy, isn't it all too good to be true?'

There was a good deal to do—cases to pack, hair to wash, hands to be attended to.

'I do hope the professor won't feel ashamed of us,' said Mrs Foster.

Emmy said quite passionately, 'No, Mother, he's not like that. He's kind and, and—' She paused. 'Well, he's nice.' And, when her mother gave her a surprised look, she added, 'He's quite tiresome at times too.'

Mrs Foster wisely said nothing.

They all went to bed early in a house strangely silent now that George and Snoodles and Enoch had been taken, protesting fiercely, to the kennels near Shaftesbury. Emmy had another wakeful night, worrying about her clothes and whether the professor might be regretting his generosity—and what would Anneliese think when she knew? She dropped off finally and had a nightmare, wherein his family, grotesquely hideous, shouted abuse at her. She was only too glad when it was time to get up.

They made the house as secure as they could, piling the furniture tidily under the tarpaulins and tying them down, parking her father's car as near the house as possible and covering it with more tarpaulins. There was just time to have a cup of coffee before the professor was due to arrive.

He came punctually, relaxed and pleasant, drank the coffee he was offered, stowed the luggage in the boot and invited everyone to get into the car.

Mr Foster was told to sit in front, for, as the professor pointed out, he might need directions. 'We're going from Dover—the hovercraft. It's quick, and there is quite a long journey on the other side.'

He got in and turned to look at Mrs Foster. 'Passports?' he asked. 'Keys and so forth? So easily forgotten at the last minute, and I have rushed you.'

'I think we've got everything, Professor…'

'Would you call me Ruerd?' His glance slid over Emmy's rather pale face, but he didn't say anything to her.

It was another cold day but it wasn't raining, although the sky was dark. The professor drove steadily, going across country to pick up the motorway outside Southampton and turning inland at Chichester to pick up the A27 and then the A259. He stopped in Hawkshurst at a pub in the little town where they had soup and sandwiches.

'Are we in good time for the hovercraft,' asked Mrs Foster anxiously.

'Plenty of time,' he assured her. 'It takes longer this way, I believe, but the motorway up to London and down to Dover would have been packed with traffic.'

'You've been this way before?' asked Emmy's father.

'No, but it seemed a good route. On a fine day it must be very pleasant. I dislike motorways, but I have to use them frequently.'

They drove on presently, joining the A20 as they neared Dover. From the warmth of the car Emmy surveyed the wintry scene outside. How awful if she was to be seasick...

She forgot about it in the excitement of going on board, and, once there, since it was rather like sitting in a superior bus, she forgot about feeling sick and settled down beside her mother, sharing the tea they had been brought and eating the biscuits. Her father had gone to sleep and the professor, with a word of apology, had taken out some papers from a pocket, put on his spectacles and was absorbing their contents.

It was rough but not unbearably so. All the same it was nice to get back into the car.

'Not too tired?' asked the professor, and, once clear of the traffic around Calais, sent the car surging forward, out of France and into Belgium, where he took the road to Ghent and then on into Holland.

Emmy looked out of the window and thought the country looked rather flat and uninteresting. Instead she studied the back of the professor's head, and wished that she were sitting beside him. She caught the thought up short before it could go any further. All this excitement was going to her head, and any silly ideas must be squashed at once. Circumstances had thrown them together; circumstances would very shortly part them. That was an end of that.

She sighed, and then choked on a breath when the professor asked, 'What's the matter, Ermentrude?'

She had forgotten that he could see her in his mirror above the dashboard. 'Nothing, nothing,' she repeated. 'I'm fine. It's all very interesting.'

Which, considering it was now almost dark and the view held no interest whatsoever, was a silly answer.

It was completely dark by the time he turned in at his own gates and she saw the lights streaming from the house ahead of them. She hadn't expected anything like this. A substantial villa, perhaps, or a roomy townhouse, but not this large, square house, with its big windows and imposing front door.

As they got out of the car the door opened and Solly and Tip dashed out, barking a welcome—a welcome offered in a more sedate fashion by Cokker, who greeted the guests as though three people arriving for Christmas without more than a few hours' warning was an everyday occurrence.

The hall was warm and splendidly lighted and there was a Christmas tree in one corner, not yet decorated. Cokker took coats and scarves, and the whole party crossed the hall and went into the drawing room.

'Oh, what a beautiful room!' said Mrs Foster.

'I'm glad you like it. Shall we have a drink before you go to your rooms? Would dinner in half an hour suit you?'

'Yes, please.' Mrs Foster beamed at him. 'I don't know about anyone else, but I'm famished.' She sat down by the fire and looked around her, frankly admiring. 'Ruerd, this is so beautiful and yet you choose to live a good part of your life in England?'

'I go where my work is,' he told her, smiling. 'I'm very happy in Chelsea, but this is my home.'

He crossed to the drinks table and went to sit by Mr

Foster, talking about their journey, leaving Emmy to sit with her mother. Presently Cokker came, and with him a tall, stout woman, no longer young but very upright.

'Ah, Tiele,' said the professor. 'My housekeeper and Cokker's wife. She doesn't speak English but I'm sure you will manage very well.'

He said something to her in what Emmy supposed was Dutch.

'Tiele is from Friesland, so we speak Friese together…'

'You're not Dutch? You're Friesian?' asked Emmy.

'I had a Friesian grandmother,' he told her. 'Tiele will take you upstairs, and when you are ready will you come back here again? Don't hurry; you must be tired.'

On their way to the door Emmy stopped by him. 'Aren't you tired?' she asked him.

He smiled down at her. 'No. When I'm with people I like or doing something I enjoy I'm never tired.'

He smiled slowly and she turned away and followed her mother, father and Tiele up the wide, curving staircase. It was inevitable, I suppose, she thought, that sooner or later I should fall in love with him. Only it's a pity I couldn't have waited until we were back home and there would be no chance of seeing him again. I must, decided Emmy firmly, be very circumspect in my manner towards him.

There were a number of rooms leading from the gallery which encircled the stairs. Emmy watched her parents disappear into one at the front of the house before she was led by Tiele to a room on the opposite side. It was not a very large room, but it was furnished beautifully with a canopied bed, a William the Fourth dressing table in tulip wood, two Georgian *bergères* upholstered in the same pale pink of the curtains and bedspread, and a mahogany bedside table—an elegant Georgian trifle.

The one long window opened onto a small wrought-iron balcony; she peeped out onto the dark outside and turned back thankfully to the cheerful light of the rose-shaded lamps. There was a clothes cupboard too, built into one wall, and a small, quite perfect bathroom.

Emmy prowled around, picking things up and putting them down again. 'I wonder,' she said out loud, 'if Anneliese knows how lucky she is?'

She tidied herself then, brushed her hair, powdered her nose and went to fetch her parents.

'Darling,' said her mother worriedly. 'Should we have come? I mean, just look at everything…'

Her father said sensibly, 'This is Ruerd's home, my dear, and he has made us welcome. Never mind if it is a mansion or a cottage. I fancy that it is immaterial to him, and it should be to us.'

They went down to the drawing room and found the professor standing before his hearth, the dogs pressed up against him.

'You have all you want?' he asked Mrs Foster. 'Do say if you need anything, won't you? I rushed you here with very little time to decide what to pack.'

When Cokker came the professor said, 'I believe dinner is on the table. And if you aren't too tired later, sir, I'd like to show you some first editions I have. I recently found Robert Herrick's *Hesperides*—seventeenth century, but perhaps you would advise me as to the exact date?'

The dining room was as magnificent as the drawing room, with a pedestal table in mahogany ringed around by twelve chairs, those at the head and foot of the table being carvers upholstered in red leather. It was a large room, with plenty of space for the massive side table along one wall and the small serving table facing it.

There were a number of paintings on the walls. Emmy, anxious not to appear nosy, determined to have a good look at them when there was no one about. At the moment she was delighted to keep her attention on the delicious food she was being offered. Smoked salmon with wafer-thin brown bread and butter, roast pheasant with game chips and an assortment of vegetables, and following these a *crème brûlée*.

They had coffee in the drawing room and presently the professor took Mr Foster away to his library, first of all wishing Mrs Foster and Emmy a good night. 'Breakfast is at half past eight, but if you would like to have it in bed you have only to say so. Sleep well.' His gaze dwelt on Emmy's face for a moment and she looked away quickly.

She was going to stay awake, she thought, lying in a scented bath. There were a great many problems to mull over—and the most important one was how to forget the professor as quickly as possible. If it's only infatuation, she thought, I can get over it once I've stopped seeing him.

She got into bed and lay admiring her surroundings before putting out the bedside light, prepared to lie awake and worry. She had reckoned without the comfort of the bed and the long day behind her. With a last dreamy thought of the professor, she slept.

CHAPTER SEVEN

EMMY was wakened in the morning by a sturdy young girl in a coloured pinafore, bearing a tray of tea. She beamed at Emmy, drew the curtains back, giggled cheerfully and went away.

Emmy drank her tea and hopped out of bed intent on looking out of the window. She opened it and stepped cautiously onto the balcony. The tiles were icy and her toes curled under with the cold, but the air was fresh and smelled of the sea.

She took great gulping breaths and peered down to the garden below. It was more than a garden; it stretched away towards what looked like rough grass, and beyond that she could glimpse the sea. She took her fill of the view and then looked down again. Directly under the balcony the professor was standing, looking up at her, the dogs beside him.

He wished her good morning. 'And go and put some clothes on, Ermentrude, and come outside.' He laughed then.

She said haughtily, 'Good morning, Professor. I think not, thank you. I'm cold.'

'Well, of course you are with only a nightie on. Get dressed and come on down. You need the exercise.'

Emmy felt light-headed at the sight of him, standing there, laughing at her.

She said, 'All right, ten minutes,' and whisked herself back into her room, leaving the professor wondering why the sight of her in a sensible nightdress with her hair hanging untidily in a cloud around her shoulders, should so disturb him in a way which Anneliese, even in the most exquisite gown, never had. He reminded himself that Anneliese would be coming to dinner that evening, and regretted the impulse to invite Emmy to join him.

She came through the side door to meet him, wrapped in her coat, a scarf over her hair, sensible shoes on her feet. Tip and Solly made much of her, and she said, 'Oh, what a pity that Charlie isn't here, too.'

'I think that Beaker might not like that. Charlie is his darling, as much loved as Humphrey.'

They had begun to walk down the length of the garden, and at its end he opened a wicket gate and led the way over rough grass until they reached the edge of the dunes with the sea beyond. There was a strong wind blowing, whipping the waves high, turning the water to a tumultuous steel-grey.

The professor put an arm round Emmy's shoulders to steady her. 'Like it?'

'Oh, yes, it's heavenly! And so quiet—I mean, no people, no cars…'

'Just us,' said the professor.

It wasn't full daylight, but she could see the wide sand stretching away on either side of them, disappearing into the early-morning gloom.

'You could walk for miles,' said Emmy. 'How far?'

'All the way to den Helder in the north and to the Hoek in the south.'

'You must think of this when you are in London…'

'Yes. I suppose that one day I'll come to live here permanently.'

'I expect you will want to do that when you're married and have a family,' said Emmy, and felt the pain which the words were giving her. Would Anneliese stand here with him, watching the stormy sea and blown by the wind? And his children? She pictured a whole clutch of them and dismissed the thought. Anneliese would have one child—two, perhaps—but no more than that.

She felt tears well under her eyelids. Ruerd would be a splendid father and his home was large enough to accommodate a whole bunch of children, but that would never happen.

'You're crying,' said the professor. 'Why?'

'It's the wind; it makes my eyes water. The air is like sucking ice cubes from the fridge, isn't it?'

He smiled then. 'An apt description. Let us go back and have breakfast before we decorate the tree—a morning's work. We will come again—whatever the weather, it is always a splendid view.

Breakfast was a cheerful meal; her parents had slept well and the talk was wholly of Christmas and the forthcoming gaiety.

'My sisters will come later today, my brother tomorrow. Anneliese—my fiancée—will be coming this evening to dinner.'

'We look forward to meeting her,' said Mrs Foster, politely untruthful. Maternal instinct warned her that Anneliese wasn't going to like finding them at Ruerd's house. Although from all accounts she had nothing to fear from Emmy, thought Mrs Foster sadly. A darling girl, but with no looks. A man as handsome as Ruerd would surely choose a beautiful woman for his wife.

They decorated the tree after breakfast, hanging it with glass baubles, tinsel, little china angels and a great many fairy lights. On top, of course, there was a fairy doll—given after Christmas to the youngest of his nieces, the professor told them.

'You have several nieces?' asked Mrs Foster.

'Three so far, and four nephews. I do hope you like children…'

'Indeed I do. Ruerd, we feel terrible at not having any presents to give.'

'Please don't worry about that. They have so many gifts that they lose count as to whom they are from.'

Emmy, making paper chains for the nursery, found him beside her.

'After lunch we'll go over the house, if you would like that, but, in the meantime, will you bring those upstairs and we'll hang them before the children get here?'

The nursery was at the back of the house behind a baize door. There was a night nursery, too, and a bedroom for nanny, a small kitchenette and a splendidly equipped bathroom.

'The children sleep here, but they go where they like in the house. Children should be with their parents as much as possible, don't you agree?'

'Well, of course. Otherwise they're not a family, are they?' She stood there, handing him the chains as he fastened them in festoons between the walls. 'Did you sleep here, too?'

'Oh, yes. Until I was eight years old. On our eighth birthdays we were given our own bedrooms.'

He hung the chains, and turned to stare at her. 'You like my home, Ermentrude?'

'Yes, indeed I do. I think you must be very happy here.'

She walked to the door, uneasy under his look. 'At what time do your sisters arrive?'

His voice was reassuringly casual again. 'Very shortly after lunch. It will be chaos for the rest of the afternoon, I expect. Several friends will be coming to dinner.'

She paused as they reached the stairs. 'You have been so kind to us, Professor, but that doesn't mean you have to include us in your family gatherings.' She saw his quick frown. 'I've put that badly, but you know quite well what I mean, don't you? Mother and Father and I would be quite happy if you would like us to dine alone. I mean, you weren't expecting us…'

She had made him angry. She started down the staircase and wished that she had held her tongue, but she had had to say it. Perhaps if she hadn't fallen in love with him she wouldn't have felt the urge to make it clear to him that they were on sufferance, even if it was a kindly sufferance.

He put out a hand and stopped her, turned her round to face him, and when he spoke it was in a rigidly controlled voice which masked his anger.

'Never say such a thing to me again, Ermentrude. You and your parents are my guests, and welcome in my house. Be good enough to remember that.'

She stood quietly under his hand. 'All right, I won't,' she told him. 'Don't be so annoyed, there's no need.'

He smiled then. 'Should I beg your pardon? Did I startle you?'

'Oh, no. I think I've always known that you conceal your feelings.' She met his look and went pink. 'Now it's me who should say sorry. Goodness me, I wouldn't have dared talk to you like that at St Luke's. It must be because we're here.'

He studied her face, nodded and went on down the stairs, his hand still on her arm.

Lunch was a cheerful meal. The professor and Mr Foster seemed to have a great deal in common; neither was at a loss for a subject although they were careful to include Mrs Foster and Emmy.

Shortly afterwards the first of the guests arrived. The house seemed suddenly to be full of children, racing around, shouting and laughing, hugging the dogs, hanging onto their uncle, absorbing Emmy and her parents into their lives as though they had always been there.

There were only four of them but it seemed more—three boys and a girl, the eldest six years and the youngest two. A rather fierce Scottish nanny came with them, but she took one look at Emmy's unassuming person and allowed her to be taken over by her charges. So Emmy was coaxed to go to the nursery with the children and their mother, a tall young woman with the professor's good looks. She had shaken Emmy by the hand, and liked her.

'Joke,' she said with a smile. 'It sounds like part of an egg but it's spelt like a joke. I do hope you like children. Mine run wild at Christmas, and Ruerd spoils them. My sister Alemke will be here shortly; she's got a boy and two girls, and a baby on the way.' She grinned at Emmy. 'Are we all a bit overpowering?'

'No, no. I like children. Only, you see, the professor is so—well, remote at the hospital. It's hard to think of him with a family.'

'I know just what you mean.' Joke made a face. 'He loves children, but I don't think Anneliese, his fiancée, likes them very much. I sound critical, don't I? Well, I am. Why he has to marry someone like her I'll never know. Suitable, I suppose.'

She took Emmy's arm. 'I'm so glad you're here. Only I hope the children aren't going to plague you.'

'I shan't mind a bit. How old are your sister's children?'

'The boy is five, and the girls—twins—almost three. Let's go down and have tea.'

Her sister had arrived when they got down to the drawing room and there were more children, who, undeterred by language problems, took possession of Emmy.

Alemke was very like her sister, only younger. 'Isn't this fun?' she said in English as good as Emmy's own. 'I love a crowd. Our husbands will come later, and I suppose Aunt Beatrix will be here and Uncle Cor and Grandmother ter Mennolt. She's a bit fierce, but don't mind her. There'll be Ruerd's friends, too; it should be great fun. And Anneliese, of course.'

The sisters exchanged looks. 'We don't like her, though we try very hard to do so,' said Joke.

'She's very beautiful,' said Emmy, anxious to be fair.

'You've met her?'

'She came to St Luke's when I was working there, to see the professor.'

'Do you always call Ruerd "professor"?' asked Joke.

'Well, yes. He's—he's... Well, it's difficult to explain, but the hospital— He's a senior consultant and I was on the telephone exchange.'

Alemke took her arm. 'Come over here and sit with us while we have tea, and tell us about the hospital—wasn't there a bomb or something? Ruerd mentioned it vaguely. Anneliese was over there, wasn't she?'

Emmy accepted a delicate china cup of tea and a tiny biscuit.

'Yes, it must have been very difficult for the professor because, of course, he was busier than usual.'

Joke and Alemke exchanged a quick look. Here was

the answer to their prayers. This small girl with the plain face and the beautiful eyes was exactly what they had in mind for their brother. They had seen with satisfaction that, beyond a few civil remarks, he had avoided Emmy and she had gone out of her way to stay at the other end of the room. A good sign, but it was unfortunate that Ruerd had given his promise to Anneliese. Who would be coming that evening, no doubt looking more beautiful than ever.

The children, excited but sleepy, were led away after tea to be bathed and given supper and be put to bed, and everyone else went away to dress for the evening. Emmy had seen with pleasure that her parents were enjoying themselves and were perfectly at ease in their grand surroundings. She reminded herself that before her father had been made redundant he and her mother had had a pleasant social life. It was only when they had gone to London and he had been out of work that they had had to change their ways.

Emmy took a long time dressing. The result looked very much as usual to her anxious eyes as she studied her person in the pier-glass. The brown dress was best described as useful, its colour mouse-like, guaranteed to turn the wearer into a nonentity, its modest style such that it could be worn year after year without even being noticed.

Emmy had bought it at a sale, searching for a dress to wear to the annual hospital ball at St Luke's two years previously, knowing that it would have to last for a number of years even if its outings were scanty. It hardly added to her looks, although it couldn't disguise her pretty figure.

She went slowly down the staircase, hoping that no one would notice her.

The professor noticed—and knew then why Emmy hadn't wanted to join his other guests. He crossed the hall to meet her at the foot of the staircase, and took her hand with a smile and a nod at her person. He said in exactly the right tone of casual approval, 'Very nice, Ermentrude. Come and meet the rest of my guests.'

His brothers-in-law were there now, but he took her first to an old lady sitting by the console table.

'Aunt Beatrix, this is Ermentrude Foster who is staying here over Christmas with her parents—you have already met them.'

The old lady looked her up and down and held out a hand. 'Ah, yes. You have an unusual name. Perhaps you are an unusual girl?'

Emmy shook the old hand. 'No, no. I'm very ordinary.'

Aunt Beatrix patted the stool at her feet. 'Sit down and tell me what you do.' She shot a glance at Emmy. 'You do do something?'

'Well, yes.' Emmy told her of the job at St Luke's. 'But, now Father has a post in Dorset, I can live there and find something to do while I train.'

'What for?'

'I want to embroider—really complicated embroidery, you know? Tapestry work and smocking on babies' dresses and drawn thread work. And when I know enough I'd like to open a small shop.'

'Not get married?'

'I expect if someone asked me, and I loved him, I'd like to get married,' said Emmy.

The professor had wandered back. 'Come and meet Rik and Hugo and the others.' He put a hand on her shoulder and led her from one to the other, and then paused by Anneliese, who was superb in red chiffon, delicately made-up, her hair an artless mass of loose curls.

'Remember Ermentrude?' asked the professor cheerfully.

'Of course I do.' Anneliese studied the brown dress slowly and smiled a nasty little smile. 'What a rush for you, coming here at a moment's notice. Ruerd told me all about it, of course. You must feel very grateful to him. Such a bore for you, having no time to buy some decent clothes. Still, I suppose you're only here for a couple of days.'

'Yes, I expect we are,' said Emmy in a carefully controlled voice. Just then the professor was called away. Anneliese turned round and spoke to a tall, stout woman chatting nearby. 'Mother, come and meet this girl Ruerd is helping yet again.'

Mevrouw van Moule ignored the hand Emmy put out. She had cold eyes and a mean mouth, and Emmy thought, In twenty years' time Anneliese will look like that.

'I dare say you find all this rather awkward, do you not? You worked in a hospital, I understand.'

'Yes,' said Emmy pleasantly. 'An honest day's work, like the professor. He does an honest day's work, too.' She smiled sweetly at Anneliese. 'What kind of work do you do, Anneliese?'

'Anneliese is far too delicate and sensitive to work,' declared her mother. 'In any case she has no need to do so. She will marry Professor ter Mennolt very shortly.'

'Yes, I did know.' Emmy smiled at them both. It was a difficult thing to do; she wanted to slap them, and shake Anneliese until her teeth rattled in her head. 'So nice to see you again,' she told Anneliese, and crossed the room to join her mother and father, who were talking to an elderly couple, cousins of the professor.

The professor's two sisters, watching her from the other end of the room, saw her pink cheeks and lifted chin and wondered what Anneliese had said to her. When the professor joined them for a moment, Joke said, 'Ruerd, why did you leave Emmy with Anneliese and her mother? They've upset her. You know how nasty Anneliese can be.' She caught her brother's eye. 'All right, I shouldn't have said that. But her mother's there, too…'

She wandered away and presently fetched up beside Emmy.

'You crossed swords,' she said into Emmy's ear. 'Were they absolutely awful?'

'Yes.'

'I hope you gave them as good as you got,' said Joke.

'Well, no. I wanted to very badly, but I couldn't, could I? I'm a guest here, aren't I? And I couldn't answer back.'

'Why not?'

'Anneliese is going to marry Ruerd. He—he must love her, and it would hurt him if she were upset.'

Joke tucked her hand in her arm. 'Emmy, dear, would you mind if Ruerd was upset?'

'Yes, of course. He's—he's kind and patient and very generous, and he deserves to be happy.' Emmy looked at Joke, unaware of the feelings showing so plainly in her face.

'Yes, he does,' said Joke gravely. 'Come and meet some more of the family. We're endless, aren't we? Have you met my grandmother?'

Twenty people sat down to dinner presently. The table had been extended and more chairs arranged round it, but there was still plenty of room. Emmy, sitting between one of the brothers-in-law and a jovial man—an old friend of the family—could see her parents on the other side of the table, obviously enjoying themselves.

The professor sat at the head of the table, of course, with Anneliese beside him and his grandmother on his other hand. Emmy looked away and concentrated on something else. There was plenty to concentrate upon. The table for a start, with the lace table mats, sparkling glass and polished silver. There was an epergne at its centre, filled with holly, Christmas roses and trailing ivy, and candles in silver candelabra.

Dinner lived up to the splendour of the table: sorrel soup, mustard-grilled sole, raised game pie with braised celery, brussels sprouts with chestnuts, spinach purée and creamed potatoes, and to follow a selection of desserts.

Emmy, finding it difficult to choose between a mouth-watering trifle and a milanaise soufflé, remembered the bread and jam they had once eaten and blushed. She blushed again when the professor caught her eye and smiled. Perhaps he had remembered, too, although how he had thought of anything else but his beautiful Anneliese sitting beside him…

Emmy, savouring the trifle, saw that Anneliese was toying with a water ice. No wonder she was so slim. Not slim, thought Emmy—bony. And, however gorgeous her dress was, it didn't disguise Anneliese's lack of bosom. Listening politely to the old friend of the family talking about his garden, Emmy was thankfully aware that her own bosom left nothing to be desired. A pity about the brown dress, of course, but, since the professor had barely glanced at her, it hardly mattered—a potato sack would have done just as well.

Dinner over, the party repaired to the drawing room and Emmy went to sit by her mother.

Mrs Foster was enjoying herself. 'This is delightful, Emmy. When I think that we might still be at the lodge, surrounded by someone else's furniture… I do wish we had brought a present for Ruerd.'

'Well, there wasn't time, Mother. Perhaps we can

send him something when we get back home. Has he said how long we're staying here?'

'No, but he told your father that he has to return to England on Boxing Day, so I expect we shall go back with him then.' Mrs Foster added, 'I don't like his fiancée; she'll not make him a good wife.'

They were joined by other guests then, and the rest of the evening passed pleasantly enough. Around midnight Anneliese and her mother went home. She went from one group to the other, laughing and talking, her hand on the professor's sleeve, barely pausing to wish Emmy and her mother goodnight.

'I'll be back tomorrow,' she told them. 'Ruerd has excellent servants but they need supervision. So fortunate that Ruerd offered you a roof over your heads for Christmas. Of course, it was the least anyone could do.'

She gave them a brittle smile and left them.

'I don't like her,' said Mrs Foster softly.

'She's beautiful,' said Emmy. 'She will be a most suitable wife for Ruerd.'

Alemke joined them then and they chattered together, presently joined by several other guests, until people began to drift home. All this while the professor had contrived to be at the other end of the room, going from one group to the other, pausing briefly to say something to Mrs Foster, hoping that Emmy was enjoying herself. The perfect host.

The next day was Christmas Eve, and Anneliese arrived for lunch wrapped in cashmere and a quilted silk jacket. At least she came alone this time, playing her part as the future mistress of Ruerd's house with a charm which set Emmy's teeth on edge.

Somehow she managed to make Emmy feel that she

was receiving charity, even while she smiled and talked and ordered Cokker about as though she were already his mistress. He was called away to the phone, and she took the opportunity to alter the arrangements for lunch, reprimand Cokker for some trivial fault and point out to Emmy in a sugary voice that there would be guests for lunch and had she nothing more suitable to wear?

'No, I haven't,' said Emmy coldly. 'And if you don't wish to sit down to the table with me, please say so. I'm sure the professor won't mind if I and my mother and father have something on a tray in another room.' She added, 'I'll go and find him and tell him so…'

Anneliese said urgently, 'No, no, I didn't mean… It was only a suggestion. I'm sure you look quite nice, and everyone knows—'

'What does everyone know?' asked the professor from the door.

He looked from one to the other of them, and Emmy said in a wooden voice, 'Oh, you must ask Anneliese that,' and went past him out of the room.

The professor said quietly, 'The Fosters are my guests, Anneliese. I hope that you remember that—and that you are in my house!'

She leaned up to kiss his cheek. 'Dear Ruerd, of course I remember. But Emmy isn't happy, you know; this isn't her kind of life. She told me just now that she and her parents would be much happier having lunch by themselves. I told her that she looked quite nice—she's so sensitive about her clothes—and that everyone knew they had no time to pack sufficient clothes.'

She shrugged her shoulders. 'I've done my best, Ruerd.' She flashed him a smile. 'I'm going to talk to your sisters; I've hardly had time to speak to them.'

The professor stood for a moment after she had left

him, deep in thought. Then he wandered off, away from the drawing room where everyone was having a drink before lunch, opening and closing doors quietly until he found Emmy in the garden room, standing by the great stone sink, doing nothing.

He closed the door behind him and stood leaning against it. 'You know, Emmy, it doesn't really matter in the least what clothes you are wearing. Anneliese tells me that you feel inadequately dressed and are shy of joining my guests. I do know that clothes matter to a woman, but the woman wearing them matters much more.

'Everyone likes you, Emmy, and you know me well enough by now to know that I don't say anything I don't mean. Indeed, they like you so much that Joke wants you to stay a few weeks and help her with the children while Nanny goes on holiday. Would you consider that? I shall be in England, Rik has to go to Switzerland for ten days on business, and she would love to have your company and help.'

Emmy had had her back to him, but she turned round now. 'I wouldn't believe a word of that if it was someone else, but you wouldn't lie to me, would you?'

'No, Emmy.'

'Joke would really like me to stay and help with the children? I'd like that very much. But what about Mother and Father?'

'I'll take them back when I go in two days' time. Probably by then the problem of the furniture will have been settled.' He smiled. 'They will have everything as they want it by the time you get back.'

'I'll stay if Joke would like that,' said Emmy.

'She'll be delighted. Now come and eat your lunch—we will talk to your mother and father presently.'

She sat next to him at lunch, with Rik on her other

side and Hugo across the table, and between them they had her laughing and talking, all thoughts of her clothes forgotten. That afternoon she went for a walk with Joke and Alemke and the children, down to the village and back again, walking fast in a cold wind and under a grey sky.

'There'll be snow later,' said Joke. 'Will you come to church tomorrow, Emmy? The family goes, and anyone else who'd like to. We have midday lunch and a gigantic feast in the evening. The children stay up for it and it's bedlam.'

There was tea round the fire when they got back, with Anneliese acting as hostess, although, when Joke and Alemke joined the others, she said with a titter, 'Oh, dear, I shouldn't be doing this—Joke, do forgive me. I am so used to being here that sometimes I feel that I am already married.'

Several people gave her a surprised look, but no one said anything until Alemke started to talk about their walk.

The professor wasn't there and neither, Emmy saw, were her mother and father. She wondered if Anneliese knew that she had been asked to stay on after Christmas and decided that she didn't—for Anneliese was being gracious, talking to her in her rather loud voice, saying how glad she would be to be back in her own house, and did she know what kind of job she hoped to get?

Emmy ate Christmas cake and said placidly that she had no idea. Her heart ached with love for Ruerd but nothing of that showed in her serene face, nicely flushed by her walk.

She didn't have to suffer Anneliese's condescending conversation for long; she was called over to a group reminiscing about earlier Christmases, and presently Aunt Beatrix joined them, with Cokker close behind, bringing fresh tea. Everyone clustered around her, and Anneliese said bossily, 'I'll ring for sandwiches; Cokker should have brought them.'

Aunt Beatrix paused in her talk to say loudly, 'You'll do nothing of the kind. If I want sandwiches, Cokker will bring them. I dare say you mean well,' went on Aunt Beatrix tartly, 'but please remember that I am a member of the family and familiar with the household.' She added sharply, 'Why aren't you with Ruerd? You see little enough of each other.'

'He's doing something—he said he would have his tea in the study.' Anneliese added self-righteously, 'I never interfere with his work, *mevrouw*.'

Aunt Beatrix gave a well-bred snort. She said something in Dutch which, of course, Emmy didn't understand and which made Anneliese look uncomfortable.

Cokker returned then, set a covered dish before Aunt Beatrix, removed the lid to reveal hot buttered toast and then slid behind Emmy's chair. 'If you will come with me, miss, your mother requires you.'

Emmy got up. 'There's nothing wrong?' she asked him quietly, and he shook his head and smiled. 'You will excuse me, *mevrouw*,' said Emmy quietly. 'My mother is asking for me.'

She went unhurriedly from the room, following Cokker into the hall as Aunt Beatrix, reverting to her own tongue, said, 'There goes a girl with pretty manners. I approve of her.'

A remark tantamount, in the eyes of her family, to receiving a medal.

Cokker led the way across the hall and opened the study door, ushered Emmy into the room and closed the door gently behind her. The professor was there, sitting at his desk, and her mother and father were sitting comfortably in the two leather chairs on either side of the small fireplace, in which a brisk fire burned.

There was a tea tray beside her mother's chair and the professor, who had stood up as Emmy went in, asked, 'You have had your tea, Ermentrude? Would you like another cup, perhaps?'

Emmy sat down composedly, her insides in a turmoil. I must learn to control my feelings, she reflected, and said briskly, 'Cokker said that Mother wanted to see me.'

'Well, yes, dear—we all do. Ruerd was telling us that his sister would like you to stay for a while and help with her children. We think it's a splendid idea but, of course, you must do what you like. Though, as Ruerd says, you really need a holiday and a change of scene, and we can get the lodge put to rights before you come back home.'

Emmy could hear the relief in her mother's voice. The prospect of getting the lodge in order while cherishing her daughter—who, according to the professor, needed a quiet and comfortable life for a few weeks—was daunting. The lodge would be cold and damp, and there were tea-chests of things to be unpacked, not to mention getting meals and household chores. Having a semi-invalid around the place would be no help at all. Much as she loved her child, Mrs Foster could be forgiven for welcoming the solving of an awkward problem.

Wasn't too much concern being expressed about her health? wondered Emmy. After all, it had only been a bang on the head, and she felt perfectly all right.

'I'll be glad to stay for a little while and help Joke with the children,' she said composedly.

'Splendid,' said the professor. 'Ermentrude will be in good hands, Mrs Foster. Cokker and Tiele will look after my sister and the children and Ermentrude. Alemke will go home directly after Christmas, and so will Aunt Beatrix and the cousins. It will be nice for Cokker to have someone in the house. Joke will be here for a couple of weeks, I believe, and I'll see that Ermentrude will have a comfortable journey home.'

He's talking just as though I wasn't here, reflected Emmy. For two pins I'd say… He smiled at her then and she found herself smiling back, quite forgetting his high-handedness.

Dinner that evening was festive. Emmy wished that she had a dress to do justice to the occasion, but the brown velvet had to pass muster once again. Anneliese, in the splendour of gold tissue and chiffon, gave her a slight smile as she entered the drawing room—much more eloquent than words.

Despite that, Emmy enjoyed herself. Tonight it was mushrooms in garlic, roast pheasant and red cabbage and a mouth-watering selection of desserts. And a delicious red wine which Emmy found very uplifting to the spirits.

Anneliese's father came to drive her home later, and Emmy felt everyone relax. It was an hour or two later before the party broke up, everyone going to their beds, in a very convivial mood. She had hardly spoken to the professor, and his goodnight was friendly and casual.

'A delightful evening,' said Mrs Foster, bidding Emmy goodnight at her bedroom door. 'Ruerd is a delightful man and a splendid host. Although I cannot see how he could possibly be in love with Anneliese. A nasty, conceited woman, if you ask me.'

'She's beautiful,' said Emmy, and kissed her mother goodnight.

Christmas Day proved to be everything it should be. After breakfast everyone, children included, loaded themselves into cars and drove to the village church, where Emmy was delighted to hear carols just as she would have expected to hear in England—only they were sung in Dutch, of course. The tunes were the same; she sang the English words and the professor, standing beside her, smiled to himself.

Lunch was a buffet, with the children on their best behaviour because once lunch was over they would all go into the hall and the presents would be handed out from under the tree, now splendidly lighted. Everyone was there—Cokker and Tiele and the housemaids and the gardener—but no Anneliese.

'She'll come this evening,' whispered Joke. She added waspishly, 'When the children are all in bed and there is no danger of sticky fingers.'

Handing out the presents took a long time; there was a great deal of unwrapping of parcels and exclamations of delight at their contents, and the children went from one to the other, showing off their gifts. There was a present for Mrs Foster, too—an evening handbag of great elegance—and for Mr Foster a box of cigars. For Emmy there was a blue cashmere scarf, the colour of a pale winter sky. It was soft and fine, and she stroked it gently. Every time she wore it, she promised herself, she would remember the professor.

Tea was noisy and cheerful but, very soon afterwards, the children—now tired and cross—were swept away to their beds. Nanny came to fetch them, looking harassed, and Emmy asked Joke if she might go with her. 'Just to help a bit,' she said diffidently.

'Oh, would you like to?' Joke beamed at her. 'Alemke has a headache, but I'll be up presently to say goodnight. You'd truly like to? I mean, don't feel that you must.'

Emmy smiled. 'I'd like to.'

She slipped away and spent the next hour under Nanny's stern eye, getting damp from splashed bathwater and warm from coaxing small, wriggling bodies into nightclothes. They were all settled at last and, with a nod of thanks from Nanny, Emmy went back downstairs. Everyone was dressing for dinner, she realised as she reached the hall.

Not quite everyone; she found the professor beside her.

She turned to go back upstairs again. 'I ought to be changing,' she said quickly. 'Thank you for my scarf. I've never had anything cashmere before.'

He didn't say anything, but wrapped his great arms round her and kissed her.

She was so taken by surprise that she didn't do anything for a moment. She had no breath anyway. The kiss hadn't been a social peck; it had lingered far too long. And besides, she had the odd feeling that something was alight inside her, giving her the pleasant feeling that she could float in the air if she wished. If that was what a kiss did to one, she thought hazily, then one must avoid being kissed again.

She disentangled herself. 'You shouldn't…' she began. 'What I mean is, you mustn't kiss me. Anneliese wouldn't like it…'

He was staring down at her, an odd look on his face. 'But you did, Ermentrude?'

She nodded. 'It's not fair to her,' she said, and then, unable to help herself, asked, 'Why did you do it?'

He smiled. 'My dear Ermentrude, look up above our heads. Mistletoe—see? A mistletoe kiss, permissible even between the truest strangers. And really we aren't much more than that, are we?'

He gave her an avuncular pat on the shoulder. 'Run along and dress or you will be late for drinks.'

Emmy didn't say anything; her throat was crowded with tears and she could feel the hot colour creeping into her face. She flew up the staircase without a sound. Somewhere to hide, she thought unhappily. He was laughing at me.

But the professor wasn't laughing.

CHAPTER EIGHT

THERE was very little time left for Emmy to dress. Which was perhaps just as well. She lay too long in the bath and had to tear into her clothes, zipping up the brown dress with furious fingers, brushing her hair until her eyes watered.

She had made a fool of herself; the professor must have been amused, he must have seen how his kiss had affected her—like a silly schoolgirl, she told her reflection. If only she didn't love him she would hate him. She would be very cool for the entire evening, let him see that she considered his kiss—his mistletoe kiss, she reminded herself—was no consequence at all.

Her mother and father had already gone downstairs; she hurried after them just in time to see Anneliese making an entrance. Vivid peacock-blue taffeta this evening. In a style slightly too girlish for the wearer, decided Emmy waspishly, before going to greet Grandmother ter Mennolt—who had spent most of the day in her room but had now joined the family party, wearing purple velvet and a cashmere shawl fastened with the largest diamond brooch Emmy had ever set eyes on.

Emmy wished her good evening and would have moved away, but the old lady caught her arm. 'Stay, child. I have seen very little of you. I enjoyed a talk with your parents. They return tomorrow?'

'Yes, *mevrouw*. I'm staying for a little while to help Joke while her nanny goes on holiday.'

'You will be here for the New Year? It is an important occasion to us in Holland.'

'I don't know; I shouldn't think so. Will it be a family gathering again?'

'Yes, but just for the evening. You are enjoying yourself?'

'Yes, thank you. Very much.'

'Excellent. Now run along and join the others.' The old lady smiled. 'I must confess that I prefer the quiet of my room, but it is Christmas and one must make merry!'

Which described the evening very well—drinks before dinner sent everyone into the dining room full of *bonhomie*, to sit down to a traditional Christmas dinner—turkey, Christmas pudding, mince pies, crackers, port and walnuts…

The cousin sitting next to Emmy, whose name she had forgotten, accepted a second mince pie. 'Of course, not all Dutch families celebrate as we do here. This is typically English, is it not? But you see we have married into English families from time to time, and this is one of the delightful customs we have adopted. Will you be here for the New Year?'

'I don't know. I don't expect so. I'm only staying for a few days while Nanny has a holiday.'

'We return home tomorrow—all of us. But we shall be here again for New Year. But only for one night. We are that rare thing—a happy family. We enjoy meeting each other quite frequently. You have brothers and sisters?'

'No, there is just me. But I have always been happy at home.'

'The children like you…'

'Well, I like them.' She smiled at him and turned to the elderly man on her other side. She wasn't sure who he was, and his English was heavily accented, but he was, like everyone else—except Anneliese and her parents—friendly towards her.

After dinner everyone went back to the drawing room, to talk and gossip, going from group to group, and Emmy found herself swept up by Joke, listening to the lively chatter, enjoying herself and quite forgetting the brown dress and the way in which the professor avoided her.

It was while Joke, her arm linked in Emmy's, was talking to friends of the professor's—a youngish couple and something, she gathered, to do with one of the hospitals—that Anneliese joined them.

She tapped Emmy on the arm. 'Ruerd tells me you are to stay here for a few weeks as nanny to Joke's children. How fortunate you are, Emmy, to find work so easily after your lovely holiday.' She gave a titter. 'Let us hope that it hasn't given you ideas above your station.'

Emmy reminded herself that this was the professor's fiancée and that after this evening she need not, with any luck, ever see her again. Which was just as well, for the temptation to slap her was very strong.

She said in a gentle voice, aware that her companions were bating their breath, 'I'm sure you will agree with me that work at any level is preferable to idling away one's life, wasting money on unsuitable clothes—' she cast an eloquent eye at Anneliese's flat chest '—and wasting one's days doing nothing.'

If I sound like a prig, that's too bad, thought Emmy, and smiled her sweetest smile.

Now what would happen?

Joke said instantly, 'You're quite right, Emmy—I'm

sure you agree, Anneliese.' And she was backed up by murmurs from her companions.

Anneliese, red in the face, said sharply, 'Well, of course I do. Excuse me, I must speak to Aunt Beatrix…'

'You mean *our* aunt Beatrix,' said Joke in a voice of kindly reproval. Anneliese shot her a look of pure dislike and went away without another word.

'I simply must learn to hold my tongue,' said Joke, and giggled. 'I'm afraid I shall be a very nasty sister-in-law. Alemke is much more civil, although it plays havoc with her temper.'

She caught Emmy's sleeve. 'Come and talk to Grandmother. She will be going back to den Haag in the morning. Well, everyone will be going, won't they? Ruerd last of all, after lunch, and that leaves you and the children and me, Emmy.'

'I shall like that,' said Emmy. She was still shaking with rage. Anneliese would go to Ruerd and tell him how rude she had been, and he would never speak to her again…

She was talking to her mother when Anneliese went home with her parents. She gave them no more than a cool nod as she swept past them. The professor, as a good host should, saw them into their car and when he came back went to talk to his grandmother. It wasn't until everyone was dispersing much later to their beds that he came to wish the Fosters a good night and to hope that they had enjoyed their evening. 'I trust that you enjoyed yourself, too, Ermentrude,' he observed, looking down his splendid nose at her.

How nice if one could voice one's true thoughts and feelings, thought Emmy, assuring him in a polite voice that she had had a splendid evening.

He said, 'Good, good. I have to go to Leiden in the morning, but I shall see you before we go after lunch.'

For the last time, thought Emmy, and kissed her mother and father goodnight and went up the staircase to her bed.

Once breakfast was over in the morning people began to leave—stopping for a last-minute gossip, going back to find something they'd forgotten to pack, exchanging last-minute messages. They went at last, and within minutes the professor had got into his car and driven away too, leaving Emmy and her parents with Joke and the children.

Mrs Foster went away to finish her packing and Mr Foster retired to the library to read the *Daily Telegraph*, which Cokker had conjured up from somewhere. Since Joke wanted to talk to Tiele about the running of the house once the professor had gone, Emmy dressed the children in their outdoor things, wrapped herself in her coat, tied a scarf over her head and took them off to the village, with Solly and Tip for company.

They bought sweets in the small village shop and the dogs crunched the biscuits old Mevrouw Kamp offered them while she took a good look at Emmy, nodding and smiling while the children talked. Emmy had no doubt that it was about her, but the old lady looked friendly enough and, when she offered the children a sweetie from the jar on the counter, she offered Emmy one too. It tasted horrid, but she chewed it with apparent pleasure and wondered what it was.

'*Zoute* drop,' she was told. 'And weren't they delicious?'

For anyone partial to a sweet made of salt probably they were, thought Emmy, and swallowed the last morsel thankfully.

They lunched early as the professor wanted to leave

by one o'clock. He joined in the talk—teasing the children, making last-minute arrangements with his sister, discussing the latest news with Mr Foster. But, although he was careful to see that Emmy had all that she wanted and was included in the talk, he had little to say to her.

I shan't see him again, thought Emmy, and I can't bear it. She brightened, though, when she remembered that she would be going back to England later and there was a chance that he might take her if he was on one of his flying visits to one or other of the hospitals. The thought cheered her so much that she was able to bid him goodbye with brisk friendliness and thank him suitably for her visit. 'It was a lovely Christmas,' she told him, and offered a hand, to have it engulfed in his.

His brief, too cheerful, 'Yes, it was, wasn't it?' made it only too plain that behind his good manners he didn't care tuppence…

She bade her mother and father goodbye, pleased to see what a lot of good these few days had done them. A little luxury never harmed anyone, she reflected, and hoped that the lodge would be quickly restored to normal.

'When you get home everything will be sorted out,' her mother assured her. 'Your father and I feel so rested we can tackle anything. Take care of yourself, love, won't you? Ruerd says you could do with a few more days before you go job-hunting.'

If it hadn't been for the children the house would have seemed very quiet once its master had driven away, but the rest of the day was taken up with the pleasurable task of re-examining the presents which they had had at Christmas, and a visit to the village shop once more to buy paper and envelopes for the less pleasurable task of writing the thank-you letters.

On the following day they all got into Joke's car and drove along the coast as far as Alkmaar. The cheese museum was closed for the winter, but there was the clock, with its mechanical figures circling round it on each hour, and the lovely cathedral church, as well as the picturesque old houses and shops. They lunched in a small café, off *erwtensoep*—a pea soup so thick that a spoon could stand upright in it—and *roggebrood*. The children made Emmy repeat the names after them, rolling around with laughter at her efforts.

It was a surprisingly happy day, and Emmy was kept too busy to think about the professor. Only that night as she got into bed did she spare him a thought. He would be back in Chelsea by now, with Beaker looking after him. He would have phoned Anneliese, of course. He would miss her, thought Emmy sleepily, although how a man could miss anyone as disagreeable as she was a bit of a puzzle.

There was a phone call from her mother in the morning. They had had a splendid trip back; Ruerd had taken them right to their door, and there had been a letter waiting for them, telling them that the furniture would be removed in a day's time.

'So now we can get things straight,' said her mother happily. 'And Ruerd is so splendid—he unloaded a box of the most delicious food for us, and a bottle of champagne. One meets such a person so seldom in life, and when one does it is so often for a brief period. We shall miss him. He sent his kind regards, by the way, love.'

An empty, meaningless phrase, reflected Emmy.

She was to have the children all day as Joke was going to den Haag to the hairdresser's and to do some shopping. It was a bright, cold day, so, with everyone well wrapped-up, she led them down to the sea, tramping along the sand with Tip and Solly gavotting around them. They all threw sticks, racing up and down, shouting and laughing to each other, playing tag, daring each other to run to the water's edge and back.

Emmy shouted with them; there was no one else to hear or see them, and the air was exhilarating. They trooped back presently, tired and hungry, to eat the lunch Cokker had waiting for them and then go to the nursery, where they sat around the table playing cards—the littlest one on Emmy's lap, her head tucked into Emmy's shoulder, half asleep.

They had tea there presently and, since Joke wasn't back yet, Emmy set about getting them ready for bed. Bathed and clad in dressing gowns they were eating their suppers when their mother returned.

'emmy, you must be worn out. I never meant to be so long, but I met some friends and had lunch with them and then I had the shopping to do. Have you hated it?'

'I've enjoyed every minute,' said Emmy quite truthfully. 'I had a lovely day; I only hope the children did, too.'

'Well, tomorrow we're all going to den Haag to have lunch with my mother and father. They were away for Christmas—in Denmark with a widowed aunt. They'll be here for New Year, though. You did know that we had parents living?'

'The professor mentioned it.'

'Christmas wasn't quite the same without them, but we'll all be here in a few days.'

'You want me to come with you tomorrow?' asked Emmy. 'I'm quite happy to stay here—I mean, it's family…'

Joke smiled. 'I want you to come if you will, Emmy.' She wondered if she should tell her that her parents had been told all about her by Ruerd, and decided not to. It was his business. They had never been a family to interfere with each other's lives, although she and Alemke very much wished to dissuade him from marrying Anneliese.

There was undoubtedly something Ruerd was keeping to himself, and neither of them had seen any sign of love or even affection in his manner towards Anneliese, although he was attentive to her needs and always concerned for her comfort. Good manners wouldn't allow him to be otherwise. And he had been careful to avoid being alone with Emmy at Christmas. Always polite towards her, his friendliness also aloof. Knowing her brother, Joke knew that he wouldn't break his word to Anneliese, although she strongly suspected that he had more than a casual interest in Emmy.

They drove to den Haag in good spirits in the morning. The children spoke a little English and Emmy taught them some of the old-fashioned nursery rhymes, which they sang for most of the way. Only as they reached a long, stately avenue with large houses on each side of it did Emmy suggest that they should stop. Joke drove up the short drive of one of these houses and stopped before its ponderous door. 'Well, here we are,' she declared. 'Oma and Opa will be waiting.'

The door opened as they reached it and a stout, elderly woman welcomed them.

'This is Nynke,' said Joke, and Emmy shook hands and waited while the children hugged and kissed her. 'The housekeeper. She has been with us since I was a little girl.' It was her turn to be hugged and kissed before they all went into the hall to take off coats and scarves and gloves, and go through the arched double doors Nynke was holding open for them.

The elderly couple waiting for them at the end of the

long, narrow room made an imposing pair. The professor's parents were tall—his father with the massive frame he had passed on to his son, and his mother an imposing, rather stout figure. They both had grey hair, and his father was still a handsome man, but his mother, despite her elegant bearing, had a homely face, spared from downright plainness by a pair of very blue eyes.

No wonder he has fallen in love with Anneliese, reflected Emmy, with that lovely face and golden hair. The children swarmed over their grandparents, although they were careful to mind their manners, and presently stood quietly while Joke greeted her parents.

'And this is Emmy,' she said, and put a hand on Emmy's arm. 'I am so glad to have her with me for a few days—she's been staying with her parents over Christmas at Huis ter Mennolt. Rik's away, and it's lovely to have company.'

Emmy shook hands, warmed by friendly smiles and greetings in almost accentless English. Presently Mevrouw ter Mennolt drew her to one side and, over coffee and tiny almond biscuits, begged her to tell her something of herself.

'Ruerd mentioned that he had guests from England when he phoned us. You know him well?'

The nice, plain face smiled, the blue eyes twinkled. Emmy embarked on a brief résumé of her acquaintance with the professor, happily unaware that her companion had already had a detailed account from her son. It was what he *hadn't* said which had convinced his mother that he was more than a little interested in Emmy.

Watching Emmy's face, almost as plain as her own, she wished heartily for a miracle before Anneliese managed to get her son to the altar. Mevrouw ter Mennolt had tried hard to like her, since her son was to marry the girl, but she had had no success, and Anneliese, confident in her beauty and charm, had never made an effort to gain her future mother-in-law's affection.

Emmy would, however, do very nicely. Joke had told her that she was right for Ruerd, and she found herself agreeing. The children liked her and that, for a doting grandmother, was an important point. She hadn't forgotten Anneliese once flying into a rage during a visit because Joke's youngest had accidentally put a grubby little paw on Anneliese's white skirt. It was a pity that Ruerd hadn't been there, for her lovely face had grown ugly with temper. Besides, this quiet, rather shabbily dressed girl might be the one woman in the world who understood Ruerd, a man whose feelings ran deep and hidden from all but those who loved him.

Emmy was handed over to her host presently, and although she was at first wary of this older edition of the professor he put her at her ease in minutes, talking about gardening, dogs and cats, and presently he bade her fetch her coat.

'We have a garden here,' he told her. 'Not as splendid as that at Huis ter Mennolt, but sufficient for us and Max. Let us take the dogs for a quick run before lunch.'

They went through the house, into a conservatory, out of doors onto a terrace and down some steps to the garden below. Max, the black Labrador, Solly and Tip went with them, going off the path to search for imaginary rabbits, while Emmy and Ruerd's father walked briskly down its considerable length to the shrubbery at the end.

All the while they talked. At least, the old man talked, and a great deal of what he said concerned his son. Emmy learned more about Ruerd in fifteen minutes than she had in all the weeks she had known him. She listened avidly; soon she would never see him again, so every small scrap of information about him was precious, to be stored away, to be mulled over in a future empty of him.

Back at the house she led the children away to have their hands washed and their hair combed before lunch. They went up the stairs and into one of the bathrooms—old-fashioned like the rest of the house, but lacking nothing in comfort. She liked the house. It wasn't like Huis ter Mennolt; it had been built at a later date—mid-nineteenth century, she guessed—and the furniture was solid and beautifully cared for. Beidermeier? she thought, not knowing much about it. Its walls were hung with family portraits and she longed to study them as she urged the children downstairs once again, all talking at once and laughing at her attempts to understand them.

She was offered dry sherry in the drawing room while the children drank something pink and fizzy—a special drink they always had at their grandmother's, they told her, before they all went into the dining room for lunch.

It was a pleasant meal, with the children on their best behaviour and conversation which went well with eating the lamb chops which followed the celery soup—nothing deep which required long pauses while something was debated and explained—and nothing personal. No one, thought Emmy, had mentioned Anneliese once, which, since she was so soon to be a member of the family, seemed strange.

Christmas was discussed, and plans for the New Year.

'We shall all meet again at Huis ter Mennolt,' explained Joke. 'Just for dinner in the evening, and to wish each other a happy New Year. Ruerd will come back just for a day or two; he never misses.'

They sat around after lunch, and presently, when the children became restive, Emmy sat them round a table at the other end of the drawing room and suggested cards. 'Snap', 'beggar your neighbour' and 'beat your neighbour out of doors' she had already taught them, and they settled down to play. Presently she was making as much noise as they were.

It was a large room; the three persons at the other end of it were able to talk without hindrance, and, even if Emmy could have heard them, she couldn't have understood a word. Good manners required them to talk in English while she was with them, but now they embarked on the subject nearest to their hearts—Ruerd.

They would have been much cheered if they had known that he was in his office at St Luke's, sitting at his desk piled with patients' notes, charts and department reports, none of which he was reading. He was thinking about Emmy.

When he returned to Holland in a few days' time, he would ask Anneliese to release him from their engagement. It was a step he was reluctant to take for, although he had no feeling for her any more, he had no wish to humiliate her with her friends. But to marry her when he loved Ermentrude was out of the question. Supposing Ermentrude wouldn't have him? He smiled a little; then he would have to remain a bachelor for the rest of his days.

He would have his lovely home in Holland, his pleasant house in Chelsea, his dogs, his work...but a bleak prospect without her.

Joke, Emmy and the children drove back to Huis ter Mennolt after tea. With the coming of evening it was much colder. 'We shall probably have some snow before much longer,' said Joke. 'Do you skate, Emmy?'

'No, only roller-skating when I was a little girl. We don't get much snow at home.'

'Well, we can teach you while you are here.' Joke added quickly, 'Nanny isn't coming back for another couple of days. Her mother has the flu, and she doesn't want to give it to the children. You won't mind staying for a few days longer?'

Emmy didn't mind. She didn't mind where she was if the professor wasn't going to be there too.

'You've heard from your mother?' asked Joke.

'Yes; everything is going very well at last. The furniture will be gone today and the plumber has almost finished whatever it was he had to do. By the time the term starts they should be well settled in. I ought to have been there to help…'

'Well, Ruerd advised against it, didn't he? And I dare say your mother would have worried over you if you had worked too hard or got wet.'

'Well, yes, I suppose so.'

Emmy eased the smallest child onto her lap so that Solly could lean against her shoulder. Tip was in front with the eldest boy. It was a bit of a squash in the big car, but it was warm and comfortable, smelling of damp dog and the peppermints the children were eating.

The next morning Joke went back to den Haag. 'Cokker will look after you all,' she told Emmy. 'Take the children out if you like. They're getting excited about New Year. Everyone will be coming tomorrow in time for lunch, but Ruerd phoned to say he won't get here until the evening. I hope he'll stay for a few days this time. He'll take you back with him when he does go. If that suits you?' Joke studied Emmy's face. 'You do feel better for the change? I haven't asked you to do too much?'

'I've loved every minute,' said Emmy truthfully. 'I like the children and I love this house and the seashore, and you've all been so kind to me and Mother and Father.'

'You must come and see us again,' said Joke, and looked at Emmy to see how she felt about that.

'I expect I shall have a job, but it's kind of you to invite me.'

'Ruerd could always bring you over when he comes,' persisted Joke.

'Well, I don't suppose we shall see each other. I mean, he's in London and I'll be in Dorset.'

'Will you mind that?' said Joke.

Emmy bent over the French knitting she was fixing for one of the girls.

'Yes. The professor has helped me so often—you know, when things have happened. He—he always seemed to be there, if you see what I mean. I shall always be grateful to him.'

Joke said airily, 'Yes, coincidence is a strange thing, isn't it? Some people call it fate. Well, I'm off. Ask Cokker or Tiele for anything you want. I'll try and be back in time for tea, but if the traffic's heavy I may be a bit late.'

The day was much as other days—going down to the seashore, running races on the sand, with Emmy carrying the youngest, joining in the shouting and laughing and then going back to piping hot soup and *crokettes*, and, since it was almost New Year, *poffertjes*—tiny pancakes sprinkled with sugar.

The two smallest children were led upstairs to rest then, and the other two went to the billiard room where they were allowed to play snooker on the small table at one end of the room.

Which left Emmy with an hour or so to herself. She

went back to the drawing room and began a slow round of the portraits and then a careful study of the contents of the two great display cabinets on either side of the fireplace. She was admiring a group of figurines—Meissen, she thought—when Cokker came into the room.

'Juffrouw van Moule has called,' he told her. 'I have said that *mevrouw* is out, but she wishes to see you, miss.'

'Me? Whatever for?' asked Emmy. 'I expect I'd better see her, hadn't I, Cokker? I don't expect she'll stay, do you? But if the children want anything, could you please ask Tiele to go to them?'

'Yes, miss, and you will ring if you want me?'

'Thank you, Cokker.'

Anneliese came into the room with the self-assurance of someone who knew that she looked perfection itself. Indeed she was beautiful, wrapped in a soft blue wool coat, with a high-crowned Melusine hat perched on her fair hair. She took the coat off and tossed it onto a chair, sent gloves and handbag after it and sat down in one of the small easy chairs.

'Still here, Ermentrude.' It wasn't a question but a statement. 'Hanging on until the last minute. Not that it will do you any good. Ruerd must be heartily tired of you, but that is what happens when one does a good deed—one is condemned to repeat it unendingly. Still, you have had a splendid holiday, have you not? He intends that you should return to England directly after New Year. He will be staying on here for a time; we have the wedding arrangements to complete. You did know that we are to marry in January?'

She looked at Emmy's face. 'No, I see that you did not know. I expect he knew that I would tell you. So much easier for me to do it, is it not? It is embarrassing for him, knowing that you are in love with him, although heaven knows he has never given you the least encouragement. I suppose someone like you, living such a dull life, has to make do with daydreams.'

Anneliese smiled and sat back in her chair.

'It seems to me,' said Emmy, in a voice she willed to keep steady, 'that you are talking a great deal of nonsense. Is that why you came? And you haven't told me anything new. I know that you and the professor are to be married, and I know that I am going back to England as soon as Nanny is back, and I know that you have been very rude and rather spiteful.'

She watched with satisfaction as Anneliese flushed brightly. 'I believe in being outspoken too. We dislike each other; I have no use for girls like you. Go back to England and find some clerk or shopkeeper to marry you. It is a pity that you ever had a taste of our kind of life.' She eyed Emmy shrewdly. 'You do believe me, don't you, about our marriage?'

And when Emmy didn't answer she said, 'I'll prove it.'

She got up and went to the phone on one of the side-tables. 'Ruerd's house number,' she said over her shoulder. 'If he isn't there I will ring the hospital.' She began to dial. 'And you know what I shall say? I shall tell him that you don't believe me, that you hope in your heart that he loves you and that you will continue to pester him and try and spoil his happiness.'

'You don't need to phone,' said Emmy quietly. 'I didn't believe you, but perhaps there is truth in what you say. I shall go back to England as soon as I can and I shan't see him again.'

Anneliese came back to her chair. 'And you'll say nothing when he comes here tomorrow? A pity you have to be here, but it can't be helped. Luckily there will be a number of people here; he won't have time to talk to you.'

'He never has talked to me,' said Emmy. 'Only as a guest.' Emmy got up. 'I expect you would like to go now. I don't know why you have thought of me as a—well, a rival, I suppose. You're beautiful, and I'm sure you will make the professor a most suitable wife. I hope you will both be happy.'

The words had almost choked her, but she had said them. Anneliese looked surprised, but she got into her coat, picked up her gloves and bag and went out of the room without another word. Cokker appeared a minute later.

'I have prepared a pot of tea, miss; I am sure you would enjoy it.'

Emmy managed a smile. 'Oh, Cokker, thank you. I'd love it.'

He came with the tray and set it down beside her chair. 'The English, I understand, drink tea at any time, but especially at moments of great joy or despair.'

'Yes, Cokker, you are quite right; they do.'

She wasn't going to cry, she told herself, drinking the hot tea, forcing it down over the lump of tears in her throat.

She tried not to think about the things Anneliese had said. They had been spiteful, but they had had the ring of truth. Had she been so transparent in her feelings towards Ruerd? She had thought—and how silly and stupid she had been—that his kiss under the mistletoe had meant something. She didn't know what, but it had been like a spark between them. Perhaps Anneliese was right and she had been allowing herself to daydream.

Emmy went pale at the thought of meeting him, but she had the rest of the day and most of tomorrow in which to pull herself together, and the first chance she got she would go back to England.

* * *

The children had their tea and she began on the leisurely task of getting them to bed after a rousing game of ludo. They were in their dressing gowns and eating their suppers when Joke got back, and it wasn't until she and Emmy had dined that Emmy asked her when Nanny would be coming back.

'You are not happy. I have given you too much to do—the children all day long…'

'No, no. I love it here and I like being with the children, only I think that I should go home as soon as Nanny comes back. I don't mean to sound ungrateful—it's been like a lovely holiday—but I must start looking for a job.'

Emmy spoke briskly but her face was sad, and Joke wondered why. She had her answer as Emmy went on in a determinedly cheerful voice, 'Anneliese called this afternoon. I should have told you sooner, but there were so many other things to talk about with the children. She only stayed for a few minutes.'

'Why did she come here? What did she say?'

'Nothing, really; she just sort of popped in. She didn't leave any messages for you. Perhaps she wanted to know something to do with tomorrow. She will be coming, of course.'

'Oh, yes, she will be here. Was she civil? She doesn't like you much, does she?'

'No; I don't know why. She was quite polite.'

I could tell you why, thought Joke—you've stolen Ruerd's heart, something Anneliese knows she can never do.

She said aloud, 'Nanny phoned this evening while you were getting the children into bed. She will be back the day after tomorrow. I hate to see you go, Emmy.'

'I shan't forget any of you, or this house and the people in it,' said Emmy.

She had no time to think about her own plans. The house was in a bustle, getting ready for the guests. Tiele was in the kitchen making piles of *oliebolljes*—a kind of doughnut which everyone ate at New Year—and the maids were hurrying here and there, laying the table for a buffet lunch and getting a guest room ready in case Grandmother ter Mennolt should need to rest.

'She never misses,' said Joke. 'She and Aunt Beatrix live together at Wassenaar—that's a suburb of den Haag. They have a housekeeper and Jon, the chauffeur, who sees to the garden and stokes the boiler and so on. The aunts and uncles and cousins you met at Christmas will come—oh, and Anneliese, of course.'

Almost everyone came for lunch, although guests were still arriving during the afternoon. Anneliese had arrived for lunch, behaving, as Joke said sourly, as though she were already the mistress of the house. Her parents were with her, and a youngish man whom she introduced as an old friend who had recently returned to Holland.

'We lost touch,' she explained. 'We were quite close…' She smiled charmingly and he put an arm round her waist and smiled down at her. She had spoken in Dutch, and Alemke had whispered a translation in Emmy's ear.

'How dare she bring that man here?' she added. 'And Ruerd won't be here until quite late this evening… Oh, how I wish something would happen…'

Sometimes a wish is granted. The professor, by dint of working twice as hard as usual, was ready to leave

Chelsea by the late morning. Seen off by Beaker and Charlie, he drove to Dover, crossed over the channel and made good time to his house. It was dark when he arrived, and the windows were ablaze. He let himself in through a side door, pleased to be home, and even more pleased at the thought of seeing Emmy again. He walked along the curved passage behind the hall and then paused at a half-open door of a small sitting room, seldom used. Whoever was there sounded like Anneliese. He opened the door and went in.

CHAPTER NINE

IT WAS indeed Anneliese, in the arms of a man the professor didn't know, being kissed and kissing with unmistakable ardour.

With such ardour that they didn't see him. He stood in the doorway, watching them, until the man caught sight of him, pushed Anneliese away and then caught her hand in his.

The professor strolled into the room. 'I don't think I have had the pleasure of meeting you,' he said pleasantly. 'Anneliese, please introduce me to your friend.'

Anneliese was for once at a loss for words. The man held out a hand. 'Hubold Koppelar, an old friend of Anneliese.'

The professor ignored the hand. He looked down his splendid nose at Koppelar. 'How old?' he asked. 'Before Anneliese became engaged to me?'

Anneliese had found her tongue. 'Of course it was. Hubold went away to Canada; I thought he would never come back...'

The professor took out his spectacles, put them on and looked at her carefully. 'So you made do with me?'

Anneliese tossed her head. 'Well, what else was there to do? I want a home and money, like any other woman.'

'I am now no longer necessary to your plans for the future, though?' asked the professor gently. 'Consider yourself free, Anneliese, if that is what you want.'

Hubold drew her hand through his arm. 'She wants it, all right. Of course, we hadn't meant it to be like this—we would have let you down lightly…'

The professor's eyes were like flint, but he smiled. 'Very good of you. And now the matter is settled there is no need for us to meet again, is there? I regret that I cannot show you the door at this moment, but the New Year is an occasion in this house and I won't have it spoilt. I must ask you both to remain and behave normally until after midnight. Now, let us go together and meet my guests…'

So Emmy, about to go upstairs to get into the despised brown dress, was one of the first to see him come into the hall, with Anneliese on one side of him and the man she had brought with her on the other. It was easy to escape for everyone else surged forward to meet him.

'Ruerd, how lovely,' cried Joke. 'We didn't expect you until much later…'

'An unexpected surprise,' said the professor, and watched Emmy's small person disappear up the staircase. Nothing of his feelings showed on his face.

He made some laughing remark to Anneliese and went to talk to his grandmother and father and mother, then presently to mingle with his guests before everyone went away to change for the evening.

Emmy didn't waste much time on dressing. She took a uninterested look at her person in the looking-glass, put a few extra pins into the coil of hair in the nape of her neck and went along to the nursery to make sure that the children were ready for bed. As a great treat, they were to be roused just before midnight and brought downstairs to greet the New Year, on the understanding that they went to their beds punctually and went to sleep.

It seemed unlikely that they would, thought Emmy, tucking them in while she wondered how best to arrange her departure just as soon as possible.

To travel on New Year's Day would be impossible, but if she could see the professor in the morning and ask him to arrange for her to travel on the following day she would only need to stay one more day. And with so many people in the house it would be easy enough to keep out of the way. Anyway, he would surely be wrapped up in Anneliese. Emmy would get up early and pack, just in case there was some way of leaving sooner.

Fortune smiled on her for once. Sitting in a quiet corner of the drawing room was Oom Domus, middle-aged and a widower. He told her that he was going to the Hook of Holland to catch the ferry to England late on New Year's Day. 'It sails at midnight, as you may know. There will be almost no trains and buses or ferries tomorrow. It is very much a national holiday here.'

'Do you drive there?' asked Emmy.

'Yes; I'm going to stay with friends in Warwickshire.'

Emmy took a quick breath. 'Would you mind very much giving me a lift as far as Dover? I'm going back to England now that Nanny will be back tomorrow.'

If Oom Domus was surprised he didn't show it. 'My dear young lady, I shall be delighted. You live in Dorset, do you not? Far better if I drive you on to London and drop you off at whichever station you want.'

'You're very kind. I—I haven't seen the professor to tell him yet, but I'm sure he won't mind.'

Oom Domus had watched Ruerd not looking at Emmy, just as she was careful not to look at him. He thought it likely that both of them would mind, but he wasn't going to say so. He said easily, 'I shall leave around seven o'clock tomorrow evening, my dear. That will give you plenty of time to enjoy your day.'

As far as Emmy was concerned the day was going to be far too long. She wanted to get away as quickly as she could, away from Ruerd and his lovely home, and away from Anneliese.

Aunt Beatrix joined them then, and Emmy looked around her at the laughing and talking people near her. There was no sign of the professor for the moment, but Anneliese was there, as beautiful as ever, in yards of trailing chiffon. She was laughing a great deal, and looked flushed. Excitement at seeing Ruerd again? Or drinking too much?

Emmy took a second glass of sherry when Cokker offered it; perhaps if she drank everything she was offered during the evening it would be over more quickly. She caught sight of the professor's handsome features as he came across the room; she tossed back the sherry and beat a retreat into a group of cousins, who smilingly welcomed her and switched to English as easily as changing hats.

If the professor had noticed this, he gave no sign, merely passed the time of day with his uncle and went to talk to Joke.

'You look like a cat who's swallowed the cream,' she told him. 'What's going on behind that bland face of yours?'

When he only smiled she said, 'Nanny's back tomorrow. Have you arranged to take Emmy home?'

'No, not yet.'

'For some reason she's keen to go as soon as possible—said she has to find a job.'

'I'll talk to her when there's a quiet moment. Here's Cokker to tell us that dinner is served.'

Twenty persons sat down to the table which had been extended for the occasion, and Emmy found herself between two of the professor's friends—pleasant, middle-aged men who knew England well and kept up a lively conversation throughout the meal.

Emmy, very slightly muzzy from her tossed-back sherry, ate her mushrooms in garlic and cream, drank a glass of white wine with the lobster Thermidor and a glass of red wine with the kidneys in a calvados and cream sauce. And another glass of sweet white wine with the trifle and mince pies…

The meal was leisurely and the talk lively. The professor's father, sitting at the head of the table, listened gravely to Anneliese, who was so animated that Emmy decided that she really had drunk too much. Like me, reflected Emmy uneasily. He had Grandmother ter Mennolt on his other side, who, excepting when good manners demanded, ignored Anneliese. The professor was at the other end of the table, sitting beside his mother with Aunt Beatrix on his other side. Emmy wondered why he and Anneliese weren't sitting together. Perhaps there was a precedent about these occasions…

They had coffee at the table so that it was well after eleven o'clock before everyone went back to the drawing room. Anneliese was with Ruerd now, her friend at the other end of the room talking to Joke's husband. Emmy wondered if the professor would make some sort of announcement about his forthcoming marriage; Anneliese had told her that it was to be within the next few weeks, and presumably everyone there would be invited.

Nothing was said, and just before twelve o'clock she

slipped away to rouse the children and bring them down to the drawing room. The older ones were awake—she suspected that they hadn't been to sleep yet—but the smaller ones needed a good deal of rousing. She was joined by Joke and Alemke presently, and they led the children downstairs, where they stood, owl-eyed and excited, each with a small glass of lemonade with which to greet the New Year.

Someone had tuned into the BBC, and Cokker was going round filling glasses with champagne. The maids and the gardener had joined them by now, and there was a ripple of excitement as Big Ben struck the first stroke. There were cries of *Gelukkige Niewe Jaar!* and the children screamed with delight as the first of the fireworks outside the drawing-room windows were set off.

Everyone was darting to and fro, kissing and shaking hands and wishing each other good luck and happiness. Emmy was kissed and greeted too, standing a little to one side with the smallest child—already half-asleep again despite the fireworks—tucked against her shoulder. Even Anneliese paused by her, but not to wish her well. All she said was, 'Tomorrow you will be back in England.'

Hubold Koppelar, circling the group, paused by her, looked her over and went past her without a word. He wasn't sure who she was; one of the maids, he supposed, detailed to look after the children. Anneliese would tell him later. For the moment they were keeping prudently apart, mindful of the professor's words, uttered so quietly but not to be ignored.

Emmy had been edging round the room, avoiding the professor as he went from one group to the other, exchanging greetings, but he finally caught up with her. She held out a hand and said stiffly, looking no higher than his tie, 'A happy New Year, Professor.'

He took the hand and held it fast. 'Don't worry, Ermentrude. I'm not going to kiss you; not here and now.'

He smiled down at her and her heart turned over.

'We shall have a chance to talk tomorrow morning,' he told her. 'Or perhaps presently, when the children are back in bed.'

Emmy gazed at him, quite unable to think of anything to say, looking so sad that he started to ask her what was the matter—to be interrupted by Aunt Beatrix, asking him briskly if he would have a word with his grandmother.

He let Emmy's hand go at last. 'Later,' he said, and smiled with such tenderness that she swallowed tears.

She watched his massive back disappear amongst his guests. He was letting her down lightly, letting her see that he was going to ignore a situation embarrassing to them both. She felt hot all over at the thought.

It was a relief to escape with the children and put them back into their beds. She wouldn't be missed, and although there was a buffet supper she couldn't have swallowed a morsel. She went to her room, undressed and got into bed, lying awake until long after the house was quiet.

There was no one at breakfast when she went downstairs in the morning. Cokker brought her coffee and toast, which she didn't want. Later, she promised herself, when the professor had a few minutes to spare, she would explain about going back to England with Oom Domus. He would be pleased; it made a neat end to an awkward situation. Anneliese would have got her way, too... She hadn't seen Anneliese after those few words; she supposed that she was spending the night here and would probably stay on now the professor was home.

Emmy got up and went to look out of the window. Ruerd was coming towards the house with Tip and

Solly, coming from the direction of the shore. If she had the chance she would go once more just to watch the wintry North Sea and then walk back over the dunes along the path which would afford her a glimpse of the house beyond the garden. It was something she wanted to remember for always.

She went back upstairs before he reached the house; the children must be wakened and urged to dress and clean their teeth. Joke had said that they would be leaving that afternoon at the same time as Alemke and her husband and children.

'Everyone else will go before lunch,' she had told Emmy. 'My mother and father will stay for lunch, of course, but Grandmother and Aunt Beatrix will go at the same time as the others.'

Cousins and aunts and uncles and family and friends began to take their leave soon after breakfast, and, once they had gone, Emmy suggested that she should take the children down for a last scamper on the sands.

'Oh, would you?' asked Joke. 'Just for an hour, so they can let off steam? Nanny will be waiting for us when we get home. They're going to miss you, Emmy.'

The professor was in his study with his father. Emmy bundled the children into their coats, wrapped herself up against the winter weather outside and hurried them away before he should return. She still had to tell him that she was leaving, but perhaps a brisk run out of doors would give her the courage to do so.

At the end of an hour, she marshalled her charges into some sort of order and went back to the house, and, since their boots and shoes were covered in damp sand and frost, they went in through the side door. It wasn't until it was too late to retreat that she saw the professor standing there, holding the door open.

The children milled around him, chattering like magpies, but presently he said something to them and they trooped away, leaving Emmy without a backward glance. She did her best to slide past the professor's bulk.

'I'll just go and help the children,' she began. And then went on ashamed of her cowardice, 'I wanted to see you, Professor. I'd like to go back to England today, if you don't mind. Oom Domus said he would give me a lift this evening.' When he said nothing she added, 'I've had a lovely time here, and you've been so kind. I'm very grateful, but it's time I went back to England.'

He glanced at her and looked away. 'Stay a few more days, Ermentrude. I'll take you back when I go.'

'I'd like to go today—and it's so convenient, isn't it? I mean, Oom Domus is going over to England this evening.'

'You have no wish to stay?' he asked, in what she thought was a very casual voice. 'We must talk…'

'No—no. I'd like to go as soon as possible.'

'By all means go with Oom Domus.' He stood aside. 'Don't let me keep you; I expect that you have things to do. Lunch will be in half an hour or so.'

She slipped past him, and then stopped as he said, without turning round, 'You have avoided me, Ermentrude. You have a reason?'

'Yes, but I don't want to talk about it. It's—personal.' She paused. 'It's something I'd rather not talk about,' she repeated.

When he didn't answer, she went away. It hadn't been at all satisfactory; she had expected him to be relieved, even if he expressed polite regret at her sudden departure. He had sounded withdrawn, as though it didn't matter whether she came or went. Probably it *didn't* matter, she told herself firmly. He must surely be relieved to bring to an end what could only have been an embarrassing episode. As for the kiss, what to her had been a glorious moment in her life had surely been a mere passing incident in his.

She went to her room and sat down to think about it. She could, of course, write to him, but what would be the point? He would think that she was wishful of continuing their friendship—had it been friendship? She no longer knew—and that would be the last thing he would want with his marriage to Anneliese imminent. Best leave things as they were, she decided, and tidied her hair, looked rather despairingly at her pale face and went down to lunch.

She had been dreading that, but there was no need. The professor offered her sherry with easy friendliness and during lunch kept the conversation to light-hearted topics, never once touching on her departure. It seemed to her that he was no longer interested in it.

She made the excuse that she still had some last-minute packing to do after lunch. If she remained in the drawing room it would mean that everyone would have to speak in English, and it was quite likely they wanted to discuss family matters in their own language. It had surprised her that Anneliese hadn't come to lunch—perhaps Ruerd was going to her home later that day. Everyone would be gone by the late afternoon and he would be able to do as he pleased.

Of course, she had no packing to do. She went and sat by the window and stared out at the garden and the dunes and the sea beyond. It would be dark in a few hours, but the sun had struggled through the clouds now, and the pale sunlight warmed the bare trees and turned the dull-grey sea into silver. It wouldn't last long; there were clouds banking up on the horizon, and a bitter wind.

She was turning away from the window when she saw the professor with his dogs, striding down the garden and across the dunes. He was bare-headed, but wearing his sheepskin jacket so that he looked even larger than he was.

She watched him for a moment, and then on an impulse put on her own coat, tied a scarf over her head and went quietly downstairs and out of the side door. The wind took her breath as she started down the long garden, intent on reaching Ruerd while she still had the courage. She was going away, but she had given him no reason and he was entitled to that, and out here in the bleakness of the seashore it would be easier to tell him.

The wind was coming off the sea and she found it slow going; the dunes were narrow here, but they were slippery—full of hollows and unexpected hillocks. By the time she reached the sands the professor was standing by the water, watching the waves tumbling towards him.

The sun had gone again. She walked towards him, soundless on the sand, and when she reached him put out a hand and touched his sleeve.

He turned and looked at her then, and she saw how grim he looked and how tired. She forgot her speech for a moment.

'You ought not to be out in this weather without a hat,' she told him. And then, 'I can't go away without telling you why I'm going, Ruerd. I wasn't going to—Anneliese asked me not to say anything—but perhaps she won't mind if you explain to her… I'm going because I'm in love with you. You know that, don't you? She told me so. I'm sorry you found out; I didn't think it showed. It must have been awkward for you.'

She looked away from him. 'You do see that I had to

tell you? But now that I have you can forget all about it. You've been kind. More than kind.' She gulped. 'I'm sure you will be very happy with Anneliese...'

If she had intended to say anything more she was given no opportunity to do so. Wrapped so tightly in his arms that she could hardly breathe she heard his voice roaring above the noise of the wind and waves.

'Kind? Kind? My darling girl, I have not been kind. I have been in love with you since the moment I first saw you, spending hours thinking up ways of seeing more of you and knowing that I had given Anneliese my promise to marry her. It has been something unbearable I never wish to live through again.'

He bent his head and kissed her. It was even better than the kiss under the mistletoe, and highly satisfactory. All the same, Emmy muttered, 'Anneliese...?'

'Anneliese no longer wishes to marry me. Forget her, my darling, and listen to me. We shall marry, you and I, and live happily ever after. You do believe that?'

Emmy peeped up into his face, no longer grim and tired but full of tenderness and love. She nodded. 'Yes, Ruerd. Oh, yes. But what about Anneliese?'

He kissed her soundly. 'We will talk later; I'm going to kiss you again.'

'Very well,' said Emmy. 'I don't mind if you do.'

They stood, the pair of them, just for a while in their own world, oblivious of the wind and the waves and the dogs running to and fro.

Heaven, thought Emmy happily, isn't necessarily sunshine and blue skies—and she reached up to put her arms round her professor's neck.

At the end of the garden, Oom Domus, coming to look for her, adjusted his binoculars, took a good look and hurried back to the house. He would have a lonely trip to England, but what did that matter? He was bursting with good news.

OUTBACK ANGEL

BY
MARGARET WAY

Harlequin Mills & Boon™

Margaret Way takes great pleasure in her work and works hard at her pleasure. She enjoys tearing off to the beach with her family at weekends, loves haunting galleries and auctions and is completely given over to French champagne 'for every possible joyous occasion'. She was born and educated in the river city of Brisbane, Australia, and now lives within sight and sound of beautiful Moreton Bay.

CHAPTER ONE

THE heat and clamour of the day had been frightful, Jake reflected. Truly exhausting even for him. It had been easy enough rounding up the mob on the spinifex plains at the height of the Dry, fields of burnt gold like an endless harvest of wheat, but galloping after cattle in rough terrain was no fun. And dangerous.

Last year his Brit jackeroo, Charlie Middleton, had sustained a back injury as a result of his boundless derring-do and yen for action and had to undergo surgery, which mercifully turned out fine. Charlie, the Honourable Charles Middleton, no less, was back on the job a whole lot less inclined to go swashbuckling around the bush. He really liked Charlie and mostly looked on his enthusiasm and sense of adventure with favour, but the ever-present hazards had to be taken seriously. Driving cleanskins, the unbranded cattle, out of their hiding places was one of them. The horned beasts, dangerous on that count alone, buried themselves deep in the vast network of lignum thickets that wrapped themselves around the waterways and billabongs, finding green havens after the semidesert with its scorching red sands.

This was the final muster before Christmas. The Big One, though work procedures had been revolutionised since he was a boy. Today on the station good chopper pilots—and he was one of them—matched the skills of the pioneer stockmen when it came to moving cattle. The name of the game was efficiency and the use of helicopters had greatly increased the speed of the musters as well as cutting the workforce. But there were some places the choppers couldn't safely go, so the horses got involved, every last one of them well trained. That was his job. Overseeing their management.

A man had to be multi-skilled these days to survive on the land. He was a smart businessman, too. He had a degree in commerce behind him. A man for all seasons you might say.

And speaking of seasons, the Wet had officially begun in the tropical north of his giant state of Queensland, but not one drop of rain had fallen on his neck of the woods; the far south-west of the state, the Channel Country, riverine desert with some of the loneliest, most dramatic landscapes on the planet. Home to the nation's cattle kings. He guessed he had to be one of them now.

Jake McCord. Cattle king. Jake was grittier than Jonathon, his real name. Of course his father had come up with the alternative. He supposed it was reasonably close. Only his mother had called him Jonathon. Three years after his father's premature death—Clive McCord had been bitten in the leg by a poisonous copperhead while out on one of his solitary desert walkabouts—he still thought of himself as the heir apparent. The man in waiting. He supposed it was to his credit he had never thought of himself as being overshadowed by his father when his father had clearly enjoyed cracking the whip as a means of keeping everyone around him under control.

Especially his son. However, in his case, his father had never tasted success. Some inbred fighting spirit had allowed him to shrug and take it. He knew a lot of people in their far-flung Outback community put the discord between father and son down to Clive McCord's not unrare jealousy of his heir and his deep-seated bitterness. The fact was, both of their lives had been tragically disrupted by the death of beautiful, much loved, Roxanne, wife and mother, in a riding accident on the station when Jake was barely six. From then on his father had turned into another person, with hardly a nodding tolerance for others, not drawing closer to his bereft child, but seeming to blame him for living when his wife hadn't. There was ample proof that sort of thing sometimes happened.

The total lack of love and approval had left him damaged

he supposed. It had certainly charged him with a lot of hurt and anger and an almost chronic wariness that even extended into his love life. He supposed it was all about his mother and his idealisation of her. It had been very hard on his girlfriends because one way or another they had all fallen short. Or perhaps he believed that love was an illusion. Yet he had known love when his mother was alive. He was still capable of remembering. Her loss had been overwhelming and it had come at a bad time in a child's life.

Two years after his mother's death, Stacy had come along. Stacy, his stepmother, his father's second wife. Poor Stacy! God what a life she'd had with such a hard strange man who'd only married her because she was nothing like his late wife, but she was young, gentle and tractable and could provide from her delicate body more sons to work the giant station. All Stacy could manage was his half sister, Gillian, who had proved as easy to dominate as her mother, flinching whenever her father's hard gaze fell on her. It would have been easier for Gillian had she been a McCabe in appearance. His clan tended to be really handsome people with a surplus of self-confidence. Gillian favoured her mother. Pretty, sure, but living life under a modern-day despot who never saw her as any kind of asset had clipped Gilly's wings. Sometimes he thought it hadn't helped anyone when he'd come so repeatedly to their defence. It had only made his father look more harshly on all of them.

McCord's sudden violent death was an appalling shock when they all thought he was going to live forever, but in the end he hadn't been mourned. Stacy and Gillian had made a pretence at grief—surely it was expected—but it wasn't in Jake to play the hypocrite. All of them after the initial shock had felt a vast sense of release. For such a rich and powerful man, his father had had few genuine friends except for an old aboriginal called Jindii, an Eaglehawk man, who sometimes joined McCord on his wanderings. Jindii, a desert nomad, had passed back and forth across the station for as long as anyone could remember. In fact the old man had to be at least one hundred and looked every minute of it. Jindii still wandered the Wild Heart. So did his father for that matter. In spirit anyway. He had scattered his father's ashes in a high-noon ritual, watching them disappear in a sea of mirage to become part of the eternal shifting sands.

So now he was McCord, the master of Coori Downs. Coori was an aboriginal word meaning flowers. And vast vistas of desert flora was what the first Scottish-born McCord settler in Australia had seen when he and an explorer friend had passed through the Channel Country on their journey to the Central Queensland plains in the early 1800s. Jake had whole sections of his ancestor's diaries off pat....

"Wildflowers marching to the horizons!" His ancestor had written. "Mile after mile of them, as far as a man can see. A sight that gave me a sense of God; of great kinship with this ancient earth. Under those infinite desert gardens, surely the mightiest on earth, lay the bones of the explorers who had perished. Men like Kingsley and me. Ordinary men but adventurers, too. Men of vision. It seemed impossible such displays could exist under the blazing sun. There were countless millions of daisies with white and gold petals like paper. Pink succulents, yellow poppies, delicate, fragrant indigo, purple, brilliant red bushes that looked like they'd caught fire. And grasses of lilac, silver and pale green were waving their feathery plumes before the wind. A wonderful, wonderful sight, breath-taking in its unexpectedness. It was like entering Paradise after the savagery of the country through which we had passed, harsh and unforgiving enough to break a man's spirit. The temptation to stay in this flowering wilderness was enormous but Kingsley rightly reminded me we had to meet up with the main party at an isolated settlement eight days hence."

His intrepid ancestor had returned ten years later, to almost the exact spot, this time with his family, his wife and four sons, to lay the foundation for the McCord dynasty. It had proved a hard life with undreamed-of tribulations, but the family had survived and triumphed. The days of the pioneers had been meticulously recorded in several diaries.

It was a harsh code Jake had lived under himself. Not materially, the reputed family wealth was no fiction. His father deserved respect for the management of his heritage. Coori had prospered under his stewardship, but somehow from a twisted soul his father had set about trying to deplete his only son's resources. But in the best tradition of his forefathers, it had only made Jake tougher. Survival of the fittest was the name of the game. A man still had to contend with the rules of the jungle.

As for Stacy? She hadn't had much of a life. Married off at eighteen to a man of difficult character almost twenty years her senior. Just to add to it, Stacy had to live with the fact she was in a triangular marriage, even if her rival was a tragic ghost, the memory of his mother, Roxanne.

Her portrait had never come down. It continued to hang above the mantelpiece in the Yellow Drawing Room. A study of a beautiful young woman on the eve of her marriage to one of the most eligible young men in the country, Clive McCord of the McCord pioneering dynasty. He tried to remember his father as a young man. Certainly his early childhood memories had been filled with happy times. Enough to sustain him.

But the young Clive McCord had all but disappeared the day they brought his wife in on a stretcher, slender neck broken in a fall from her beloved Arabian mare, Habibah, though she'd been an experienced horsewoman. His father had shot Habibah where it stood, sweating and trembling. Jake remembered that bright, shining, beautiful animal crashing to the ground as vividly as though it were yesterday. He remembered his screams of protest, rushing to his father, grasping him around the legs in an effort to divert his aim. Habibah was his mother's horse. She would never have wanted it destroyed. It was an accident, but it may as well have been murder so far as his father was concerned. Despite the agony of his son, Clive McCord had pulled the trigger, his insides burning with grief and rage.

I've such a memory, he thought, feeling a moment of depression, it burdens me. He stopped on his journey from the stables to the house to eye a falcon about to drop on its prey. He clapped his hands, looking skyward at the blazing desert sunset.

"Scat!" Immediately the falcon flew off with a sharp, predatory and mournful cry that startled the family cat, Tosca, who had the same colouring as Jake. It amused him, though Stacy always said he was more like a lion. He bent to the cat, as it purred in contentment and wound itself around his leg, stroking and murmuring a few endearments that Tosca seemed to enjoy. He loved all animals though he'd had his arguments with wild camels and dingoes. He loved horses especially, it was a love born and bred in him. Horses were essential to his unique way of life. He was highly skilled at educating them and keeping them fit and sound in tough conditions. He couldn't help knowing that he was widely regarded as a superb rider and polo player, as well.

The truly frustrating thing was while he was a damned good judge of a horse's character, he hadn't had such luck with women. One in particular had hurt him, but that was in his university days. Her name was Michelle. She was a few years older, and a smooth, smooth, operator. She played games when one thing he prized in a relationship was trust. And he didn't share. He was still waiting like a fool for that thunderbolt from the heavens, the perfect woman, or perfect for him, and he was twenty-eight years old. A man of strong passions, but he made damn sure they didn't appear too near the surface. How different life would be with that one woman. He still hadn't closed his mind on the idea he would find her. Or she would find him. God knows he had little time to go courting. That was the curse of the man on the land.

He heaved a weary sigh. He found sweet and endearing his stepmother and half sister. He loved them for their gentle caring natures but even at the best of times they weren't women to lean on. They had an excellent housekeeper in Clary. Clary had her own little band of household staff, part aboriginal girls born on the station, gone away to school, but happy to come back. Still, the homestead by any standards was a mansion and Clary wasn't getting any younger. The house girls needed direction. He certainly didn't need Stacy and Gilly to help him run the station and their two out-stations hundreds of miles away in Central Queensland, but it would have been brilliant had they been more confident and competent, able to run things, order up supplies, manage the domestic staff, all the sorts of things women traditionally did on an Outback station.

Like Dinah, for instance. He could just picture Dinah Campbell running the Christmas functions Coori would be hosting this year, although he had given the job to his cousin, Isobel, who ran a very successful catering business for the well-heeled in Brisbane. Even so, Dinah had come close to telling him she would have been just as good at the job, humming softly to herself as she explored all the reception rooms of the house, making suggestions as to what needed changing, a seriously desirous expression in her eyes; laughing right under his nose about Stacy's "problems" until she saw she was making him furious.

Dinah, a genuine platinum-blonde with pale green eyes, was a good-looking, totally capable and assured young woman but her strong point wasn't tact or understanding, maybe you couldn't have one without the other, and he didn't care at all for her patronising his family. He'd known Dinah since they were children. Like him, she was Outback royalty, grand-daughter to his McCord grandfather's closest friend. He had even romanced her on and off. Dinah could be good fun, as well as being good in bed. He knew she valued their long friendship, but there was something about her he couldn't really cotton on to. Could it be her lack of feeling for others? God knows he'd had enough of that, though she was always incredibly sweet to him. He was aware Dinah and her family had high hopes that one day he would "pop the question" though he had never led Dinah to believe it was only a matter of time.

Yes, he could picture Dinah organising everything perfectly, compulsively methodical, looking glamorous while she savoured playing Coori's hostess, circling the guests using all her practised charm, and supreme self-confidence that came with having a rich man for a doting dad. So why had he rejected her? In many ways she had fit the bill. She was strong, with energy to burn. She was Outback born and had lived his way of life. Moreover he needed someone. A woman he could love and live with for the rest of his life. Where the hell was she? If she ever turned up he knew he would recognise her right off.

Some of his more delicious dreams stirred... He kept seeing a pair of dark eyes. A wonderful fall of dark curly hair, glossy as a magpie's wing. Even thinking about it drew all the blood into his loins. But he didn't know a single girl with large lustrous dark eyes and a beautiful soft body that drew a man like a magnet. At one point he thought he had actually seen her someplace. Somewhere outside his dreams. Then he decided she was simply a figment of his imagination.

Stacy was waiting for him the moment he set foot in the homestead. Even after all these years she still had the capacity to surprise him. She was sitting cross-legged on the parqueted floor, flanked by the two coal-black Labradors, Juno and Jupiter, tails thumping in an ecstasy of greeting.

"What on earth are you doing down there?" He braced himself as the dogs bounded towards him.

Stacy smiled sweetly and shrugged. "Why not? It's nice and cool. Besides I've never felt comfortable in those chairs." She nodded at two very imposing and valuable antique carved mahogany hall chairs with sphinx-like figures for arms. At forty Stacy was in great shape. She still looked like a girl, with her fair hair and skin and large cloudy blue eyes. She'd lived a lifetime of constantly trying to please, but somehow she didn't show the burden of endless stress.

Arrested development, one of the acerbic McCord aunts had observed. No one in the extended family could ever work out why the high-handed, difficult and demanding Clive had married such a consistently shy and ineffectual little thing. Stacy wasn't considered interesting or exciting at all. Why, she couldn't be more different to the beautiful, vivid Roxanne whom everyone had adored and greatly mourned.

Now Stacy stood up, swaying a little because she had pins and needles in her left foot, a neat figure in her cotton shirt and jeans, the great crystal waterfall that was the hall chandelier putting highlights into her short cap of fair hair.

"Isobel called," she announced, as though conducting a conversation with his dynamo of a cousin had left her vaguely distraught.

"Oh?" At this time of year Isobel's business was running full-tilt, but she had come to his rescue yet again. Isobel, married to a well-known Federal M.P. was particularly sensitive to his plight. Kinder than most of the McCord clan, even Isobel found Stacy's lack of social and organization skills extremely unfortunate.

"So what did she want?" he prompted as Stacy seemed to have come to the end of her speech.

"Malcolm had a sick turn in the P.M.'s office." She said it like it was the high point of Malcolm's career. "He's going into hospital in the morning so they can run a few tests."

"Oh, Lord, I'll have to call her." He ran a hand through his thick hair, dismayed on two counts. He really liked Malcolm, and this could put paid to the up-coming Coori festivities. "Maybe exhaustion," he mused, hopefully. "Malcolm works harder than most."

"I didn't know any of them really worked," said Stacy who had no insight into a busy politician's life at all. "But I'm sorry about Malcolm. He's one of the few to never be nasty to me. And they're such a compatible couple."

"I guess some marriages have to work out," he offered

distractedly, his mind ticking over. Even his rock-solid cousin would be a mess if anything was really wrong with Malcolm, God forbid. And it would put paid to Isobel's indispensable services. Maybe he would have to turn to Dinah, after all. She'd really love that.

"What if Isobel can't handle our functions?" Stacy asked thoughtfully, not considering for a minute she should have a go. "You might have to fall back on Dinah. I hope you don't have to." She cast him a quick look. "Isobel flusters me, I almost have to run to catch up with her, but Dinah makes me feel an utter fool."

"Why don't you tell her off?" he suggested briskly, no longer embarrassed by his stepmother's inadequacies. "That might give both of you a good shake-up. Eventually, Dinah might even stop."

"But she's your friend!" Stacy stared at him incredulously, as if somehow that gave Dinah free rein. "I'm not game to say a word to her," she confessed, thinking even Dinah's smile had a sneer in it. "I must be such a disappointment to you, Jake." Stacy brushed her wispy fringe from her forehead. "I was certainly cut from a different cloth than the likes of Isobel and Dinah."

Wasn't that the truth! From his childhood his role had been to be supportive of Stacy. Even now Stacy couldn't speak his mother's name, though he had often caught her staring up at Roxanne's portrait. Roxanne, who even as a young bride had handled the role of mistress of a great historic station with brilliant aplomb.

"From all McCord accounts an imbecile." From nowhere tears suddenly rolled down Stacy's cheeks, though he knew from long experience anything could trigger them.

After all these years it didn't break him up. "Cut it out now," he braced her automatically, feeling it would be wise to get Gillian started on some course or other. He didn't want his half sister feeling such confusion about herself and her life. "Organising and running functions isn't the only thing in the world." The Lord is my strength and my shield, he thought wryly. He had been relying on Isobel to get them through.

"I'm really, really sorry, Jake." Stacy's tears stopped on the instant. It was taking time for her to remember with his father gone there was nothing to fear.

"Don't worry, we'll manage," Jake reassured her.

Stacy sighed with relief. Nothing ever rattles him, she thought gratefully, looking up into her stepson's dynamic face. Even terrible things. She supposed that was keeping up the McCord tradition, when the McCord tradition had beaten her down. As often happened, she had the sense of looking at his mother. The beautiful young woman her husband had never forgotten. Jake had the same glorious tawny colouring. The thick, thick, wavy hair, amber, streaked with gold. Roxanne, in the portrait, had great coils of it. Jake's was a lion's mane. They both had amber eyes to match, which were spectacularly beautiful, full of sparkle and life. The passionate nature of mother and son showed in the vitality of their expressions, the cut of the beautifully defined sensuous mouths. Mouths you couldn't look away from. Jake was tall, as had been Roxanne. At six-three, even taller than his father, young-man lean, wide shoulders narrowing to a trim waist, long taut flanks. He was superbly fit from his hard outdoor life. Jake was a wonderful-looking young man, exotic in his tawny splendour. His mother, Roxanne, had been incandescent in her beauty. Even dead, she's more alive than I am, Stacy thought ironically. She was quite quite certain she would never have survived living with Clive McCord if it weren't for his son.

Malcolm as it turned out required surgery. An ultrasound confirmed he would have to have his gall bladder removed. It would be keyhole surgery with a minimum recovery time, but his devoted wife couldn't think of leaving him. Isobel apologised to Jake twice. Jake said not to worry. But even then, worried Isobel took charge. By midmorning of the next day she left a message that she had found someone she thought would be perfect to take over her job. A wonderful young woman she had taken under her wing, with a background in fine food. Her parents owned and ran a prize-winning restaurant. Her protégée was a food writer with the up-market magazine, *Cosima,* sometimes she guested for other highly regarded magazines. She wasn't a chef as such, but a darn good cook—she had helped Isobel with several important functions. Isobel could highly recommend her. The paragon whose name was Angelica De Campo, would ring Jake that very night. If he liked the sound of her, the deal could be stitched up. There was little time to lose.

Jake received all this information when he returned to the homestead at sundown. He started to relax as his worries began to fall off him. Isobel wouldn't recommend anyone she didn't have the utmost faith in. He was at his desk in the study looking over an industry report when Miss De Campo's call came through.

''Mr. McCord?''

Her voice was so mellifluous, so much like honey, he actually slumped back in his leather chair, feeling a delicious lick of it on his tongue. ''Miss De Campo. How good of you to call.'' He on the other hand sounded quite sardonic. Sometimes, he thought ruefully, he even sounded like his father, which really bothered him.

''Isobel will have told you about me?'' Honey Throat was asking. Hell, the effect on him was fantastic! He had to control the force of his exhalation.

''The only thing she omitted to do was send a picture. I'm sure, though, you're most attractive.'' God, he wanted her to be. That voice and good looks. A winning combination! And she could cook, and handle big functions anyplace, even the middle of the Outback. What a joy! He was stunned to think there were women like that out there. Maybe she also had huge dark eyes, and beautiful, womanly breasts. Of course, being a great cook there was more than a slight possibility she could be overweight and sensitive about it. He mustn't place too much importance on a great voice.

''You can decide when you see me,'' she laughed. ''I hope I pass. That's if you want me to take over from Isobel, Mr. McCord. You might like to ask me a few questions?''

''Indeed,'' he answered, trying and succeeding in sounding the tough businessman. ''My first. You've never handled functions of this size by yourself?''

''No, not as big, but that's fine,'' she returned with pleasing poise. ''Size is no problem. I've had a lot of experience in catering to numbers. Isobel would have told you my parents are in the hospitality business. They run an excellent restaurant. I know all their sources, the top people to contact. I've done a lot of P.R. I'm currently working on a pre-Christmas party for Billie Reynolds, the millionaire stockbroker?''

She said it like it was a question and he nearly answered, ''Bah!'' Shades of his father again. ''I do recognise the name.'' Billie Reynolds fell into the serial-womanising category. Trying to count his ex-wives would be like trying to count sheep. ''How do you think it will turn out?''

''Wonderful, even if I say so myself.'' She sounded convinced. ''Billie wouldn't have hired me if I couldn't deliver. He's a perfectionist.''

''So you're brilliant then?'' he lightly mocked, positive she was.

''I work hard at what I do,'' she told him modestly. ''I've learned a great deal watching my parents and Isobel, of course. I admire her tremendously. She's enormously successful. I was quite upset when I heard about Malcolm.''

''Then you'll know his surgeon is speaking about a quick recovery.'' She had obviously drawn herself into the family circle.

''Yes. Belle and I are constantly in touch.''

Well listen to that! Belle. ''I gather you're something of a protégée?'' Another deadpan delivery. Just like his dear dad.

What if this thing grew and grew? The thought was downright scary.

"Belle is very good at spotting talent."

Was it possible she was having a go at him? He didn't actually mind.

"I'm very flattered she recommended me," she added.

"And I have to say I'm enormously relieved." He whisked away the rest of his Scotch. "At this time of year I'm nearly running on empty. You realise how isolated the station is?" There would be plenty of opportunities for showing her around.

"Isobel has described everything," she answered, totally unfazed. "As I understand it, you'll be hosting the finals of the Marsdon Polo Cup with a luncheon followed by afternoon tea. Finishing up with a gala ball that evening. The following week, there'll be a barbecue for all the staff and their families. And the Saturday before Christmas you're hosting a large party for all your relatives and friends." She sounded like she was ticking them off; she seemed a young woman of considerable competence who could handle things on her own.

Aside from Dinah, who didn't have a voice like strawberry-flavoured brandy, he had never had such an experience.

"Do I have that right?" she asked.

"I should throw in it's my birthday, as well." That might faze her.

"Is it?"

He heard the smile in her voice, resolved to hold on to his cool. "No, but I've waited all my life to have one. A party, that is."

A pause. "That sounds a little sad. But you've got plenty of time."

"How could you know I'm twenty-eight?"

"Isobel must have mentioned it."

"Then you also know I'm a bachelor?" It was perfectly clear they were flirting. Or at least he was. It amazed him. Proof positive he needed a woman clever enough to get under his skin. ''My birthday's in August by the way. I'm the definitive Leo.''

''That's interesting. So am I. Shall I write a party down under Future Projects?''

He swung around in the swivel chair. ''Well, you'd best work for me first, don't you think?''

''Great idea! Say the word and I can start. You won't find me a disappointment.''

''How expensive are you, Miss De Campo?'' She told him. Wow! Pulling in money like that was something to brag about. On the other hand Isobel, even if she was his cousin, didn't come cheap, either.

''Everything will be the best,'' she explained. ''That means expensive, but I say pay it every time. There's no substitute for quality.''

''Sure,'' he agreed laconically. ''You must take your pay home in an armoured van.''

''No, but a security guard walks me to my car. Now, why don't we discuss what you plan over Christmas?''

Why not? Maybe by August they'd be married. He let his sense of humour take over. If this woman had beautiful dark eyes he'd fall into her arms. He needed a really great love affair to free him up. It was so long since he'd had one. Hell, he'd never had one. They spoke back and forth for another ten minutes, both adopting a no-nonsense manner as they got down to detail. He asked many more questions of her, she gave all the right answers. Isobel knew her stuff. Miss Angelica De Campo was hired.

After he put the phone down, he leaned back in his chair and closed his eyes. It struck him Miss De Campo's effect on him had been dangerously seductive. Either that or it was the effects of a glancing blow to the head in the scrub.

CHAPTER TWO

JUST over a week later Angelica stepped onto the tarmac of an Outback airport terminal into a shimmering landscape of heat. Waves of it bounded up from the ground at her. For an instant it almost took her breath away, like a sudden blast from an oven, until she decided to confront it head-on, moving her long legs purposefully, eyes straight ahead, not drawing in all the admiring glances, so she was among the first to reach the air-conditioned cool of the terminal building. There she snapped her dark mane of hair back from her heat-pricked forehead. She thought of the challenging weeks ahead of her; the amount of work she had to do even with help.

Isobel had cautioned her about the heat but she didn't quite understand until it hit her. She was thankful for her olive skin and Mediterranean heritage, otherwise she thought her skin might have melted. Not that she wasn't used to heat, living in Brisbane. But there it was the languid golden heat of the tropics, with high humidity. This heat was different. It felt more like a dry bake. Still, it couldn't diminish her excitement about the project.

She was exuberant about the whole thing. She couldn't wait to get to Coori Downs, which she'd heard was remarkable. Isobel had been meaning to show her a magazine which featured quite a spread on the historic homestead but Malcolm's hospitalisation had naturally preoccupied her mind. Pity! There was supposed to be a great shot of the current cattle baron, a man, from all accounts, to turn heads. Promising!

The scope of the functions would establish what she could do, enhancing her career, but she had to say as well as the

Outback venue, she'd been mightily attracted by the prospect of meeting Isobel's cousin, Jake. He'd sounded so sexy over the phone, the memory still made her knees go weak. His father, according to Isobel, had been a regular fire-eater, but the son sounded very easy in his power, as though it fitted him like a great pair of jeans. The nicest, most considerate thing was, he was actually flying in from his desert stronghold to pick her up. She had been expecting to catch a charter flight but it was Jake who suggested he collect her. She loved people who did favours.

In the rest room she freshened up, piling her extravagant mass of hair into a knot of sorts at the back. She had no idea how long it would stay there. Her hair had a mind of its own. For the trip she'd kept her outfit simple. A white sleeveless top in a softly clingy fabric, teamed with her favourite denim mini. It showed yards of leg but she wore it unselfconsciously.

She had learned to take comfort in her jaunty thoroughbred legs even if their length did turn her into a very tall woman. She stood six feet in high heels and she wasn't one for flatties. Her height had made her a basketball star in high school. Even so she never slumped—for that she had to thank her mother who was also tall—and she held her head high even though there were lots of guys who had to look up to her. The man to sweep her off her feet, and she just knew he was out there, would have to be a latter day John Wayne. Despite that, she'd been hotly pursued for years. What did they call her in the columns? The luscious Angelica De Campo. Not that she carried an ounce of fat but she had inherited an eye-catching bust from the Italian side of the family.

Men saw her as a challenge. She remembered one in particular. A married man, a powerful, destructive, merchant banker—she had helped out catering a party for his wife—who simply wouldn't take no for an answer. As hc saw it, he could have anyone with his fat wallet. In the end, exercising her discretion—God knows what boundaries her father would have crossed for his ''little'' girl—she told her brother,

Bruno, who was six-six. Bruno managed to convince the banker to stay away or the outlook would be lousy. She hadn't asked Bruno to explain his methods. Whatever they were, they'd worked. Probably the banker thought Bruno was a paid-up member of the Mafia. Still the experience had left a nasty taste in the mouth.

Certain men could be quite frightening when they developed a fixation on a woman. Mr. Merchant Banker had been one of them, but that was a few years back. She did occasionally agonise over it, if only because she and the banker had been caught out getting physical in a near frenzy of a wrestle, she, even at her superior height fighting hard for her honour. She wished she'd seen that guy again. The one who'd looked at her so contemptuously from his extraordinary lion's eyes. She'd soon put him straight. Only she never laid eyes on him again. Not once during the intervening years and she had to admit she'd never grown tired of looking.

Embarrassments and scandals. She was very careful these days men being what they were. It seemed they only had to look at a well-endowed woman. And she came from a decent, normal, well-adjusted family.

Jake saw her before she saw him. She was staring out the plate-glass window, watching a private jet fly in. Even if the excited female attendant hadn't pointed her out—apparently Miss De Campo had made any number of appearances on television—he'd have picked her. Despite the extreme simplicity of her dress—her skirt seemed to end at her armpits—he couldn't fail to recognise the quality people generally called style. It oozed out of her and he was only looking at her side-on. She looked incredibly sexy in that unique way European women had, she seemed innocently seductive without being sultry, with her lashings of dark, mahogany hair with a decided curl. She had to have dark Italian eyes. She couldn't have looked better had he dreamed her up. He didn't even mind her height, which would have her towering over Stacy and Gillian. She wouldn't tower over him. This was a woman he could meet face-to-face.

"Miss De Campo?"

She reacted instantaneously, as if he had pushed a button, swinging around, a lovely buoyant smile on her face, sparkle of beautiful teeth; a smile that ludicrously…froze.

They stared at one another transfixed. Horror, fascination, disbelief flitted across both their faces. To put it mildly, both were shocked into a near paralysis as they began to track one another down. That party! One of those horribly mortifying incidents that reverberate forever.

She was the last woman in the world he expected. Jake was suddenly, violently, fathoms deep into the past. He felt anger and disappointment along with the most profound scarcely rational disillusionment. After all, she hadn't arrived as his mail-order bride. But over the phone she had intrigued him to the extent he had gone about his work all week with a warm secret feeling lurking in his heart; the idea she just could be the woman to fulfil his dreams. He still believed in the idea. Now all his daydreams had been swept away. Miss Angelica De Campo had a very bad habit. She played erotic games that got out of control. Memory clicked in, all the more mysterious because such picture of her he had, had only lasted a few moments. Afterwards, defiantly he had blocked her out, but other images of her were locked in his subconscious.

This was another one of those woman who drew men like bees. Women like Michelle who these days scarcely seemed to count. Even Michelle had never looked like this! Such women often gave exquisite joy before they delivered the body blows. His big problem was Miss De Campo, like Michelle, didn't adhere to his idea of decent principles. Miss De Campo was a home wrecker. A woman who got an emotional fix out of seducing married men.

It had to be almost three years since he'd attended that party thrown by Trevor and Carly Huntley. He'd had little to do with Huntley, barely making a connection. Trevor Huntley was a wealthy merchant banker, but Carly was a relative. He was in town on business. Carly had run into him coming out of his hotel, expressed her delight and surprise at seeing him, and invited him to their party that night. He'd had nothing else to do, so he'd gone along, waiting until the party was well under way before he made an appearance.

The Huntleys lived in style in a mansion on the river. Theirs was an over-the-top splendour he didn't envy. Although he'd met Huntley several times over the years, he'd never liked him, probably due to an abiding disgust with hypocrisy. Playing the part of devoted husband in public, it was common knowledge within the McCord family Huntley gave Carly a hard time. No one knew why she stayed with him. Apparently she was pretty much still in love with him. He was certainly impressive in his way, with his big, burly, dark hair, ice-blue eyes he had looks of a fading film star…

People were milling all over the house, drinking, standing, talking, dancing and generally having a good time. A very vivacious redhead—he swore she never touched a drink—had made a beeline for Jake as soon as he'd arrived. He didn't mind that as a matter of fact—she was attractive—but as the night wore on it became apparent the redhead had the vision of the two of them finishing up the evening in bed. It wasn't going to happen. He'd never said he was available.

At one point he sought refuge in what was presumably a study because the moment he opened the door, he saw a wall of books and trophies, dozens of them. A moment later he felt his insides contract as his eyes were led to where two people were locked into passionate lovemaking on the sofa.

He could hear the man's grunts of pleasure. See the rough way his hands moved. The woman was gorgeous, like something out of the Arabian Nights. She was dark-haired, great dark doe eyes. One beautiful breast with its dusky peak was totally exposed. The glimpse was blink-of-an-eye brief, yet he felt the heat of a flush spread like fire over his skin. Huntley was fondling the other breast, working the nipple, his harsh cries abruptly cutting off.

Carly's devoted Trevor. My God! He remembered the terrible sense of déjà vu. Huntley stood up staring, trying to adjust his clothing, unable to hide his arousal.

The woman buried her face in her trembling hands. Guilt? Shame? More likely she didn't want him to know her identity. "Disturbed you, did I?" He remembered his own voice, dripping acid. "Stupid of me not to knock." Hadn't the very same thing happened with Michelle? And Michelle had later claimed she wasn't even interested in the guy.

Huntley had actually given him a smile of undisguised insolence, the lust gleaming out of his eyes. "Welcome to the real world, my boy," he'd drawled, still fumbling with his clothing. "Don't look so shocked. I'm a man who always gets what he wants." He gestured to the young woman who was now sitting up on the sofa, pulling the thin strap that held up her bodice onto her shoulder, showing him only the naked gold satin of her back. "Do you blame me?"

How could he? He imagined his own hands on her. Felt instant self-disgust. He remembered he was badly shaken, alive with contempt. Now he was face-to-face with her.

The shock was so extreme he felt almost numb. This was the woman who had caused Carly so much suffering. Carly knew her husband had been having an affair, although, oddly, it wasn't this young woman who had figured in their spectacular divorce—Carly had used the family lawyers to secure a record settlement—it was a hard-faced blonde with the body of a stripper who was now the second Mrs. Huntley.

Jaw clenched, he forced himself to speak. "So you didn't go into hiding?"

"From you?" Angelica, too, was so traumatised she hardly knew what she was saying. Neither of them had made the slightest attempt to feign ignorance of the other. Both of them were instantly seized up by that shameful incident years before. Angelica's recollection of this man, however brief, was so acute, so agonising, she had to work hard to cope. Here was the tawny lion with a mane of deeply waving gold-streaked copper hair brushed back from a broad forehead. Could she ever mistake those distinctive amber eyes, or the condemnation in them? What inner trauma prompted that response?

This was the man who billowed in and out of her dreams. A man in full possession of himself and his world.

By a strange stroke of fate, Jake McCord. Her knees bumped together. ''I wonder if I could ever convince you—'' she began, turning away from the huge window.

The full glare of the sun was hitting her like a spotlight, finding no fault in her golden-olive skin. He cut her off swiftly. ''Really, Miss De Campo, I don't want to know.'' She was still staggeringly beautiful, so lusciously ripe and alive, her skin so healthy and glowing it begged to be touched. How could a woman like that have allowed herself to be mixed up in such a murky demeaning affair? How could she have allowed herself to be mauled by a callous womaniser like Huntley?

She looked at him, upset, but very ready to defend herself. After all, she had done no wrong. She, like many another woman, had been the victim of a predatory man. ''You're very judgmental, aren't you?'' she said. ''You really know nothing about what you saw years ago. I'm amazed you even remembered.''

''You did, didn't you?'' he countered, horrified by the harshness of his own tone, which in essence was an intertwining of past and present events. ''I certainly didn't see you fending him off. God knows it couldn't have been that hard.'' His eyes swept her tall, svelte body. ''Anyway, it no longer matters. Carly is re-making her life. Huntley's welcome to the ex-hooker he married. Didn't he want you after all?'' He wondered why he asked, but was forced to confront the fact he really wanted to know. ''Or didn't you want him?''

Her hair had come out of its too casual arrangement, dark masses of it atop her slender body. She put a hand to it. ''You're taking this very hard, aren't you?''

''Hell, yes,'' he drawled. ''Carly is part of my extended

family.'' And his mood was pervaded by a sense of deep disappointment.

''Have you ever tried to check out your theory with her?'' she questioned bluntly, not knowing any other way to put it.

''That you were having an affair with her ex-husband?'' he scoffed. ''Don't be ridiculous. God forbid I should have added to her worries.''

''You really should do something about your habit of jumping to conclusions, Mr. McCord,'' she suggested, seemingly unaware she was filling the air around them with her femininity and fragrance. ''One of these days, when you're prepared to listen, I'll tell you what it was all about.''

He laughed, ashamed of the swift desire he felt for her, though he had the wit to realise it was a matter outside his control. ''But, Miss De Campo, can't you see there's no way I'll listen. I regret the fact you've had to travel all the way out here, but I need to make a decision. In view of what we both know, and find embarrassing, I have to say you're not the woman I need to run our functions. I guess you're what most men would call a femme fatale. That's great up to a point, but I'm not paying for one to come out to Coori. Who knows how many guys might be prepared to make fools of themselves over you. There will be plenty around. Two polo teams, and you don't play by the rules. The womenfolk might hate you. I don't want to bump into you half-naked on a couch again either.''

''Why would you?'' she asked silkily. ''You couldn't handle it the first time. It seems to have burnt itself into your brain.''

''I'll get over it.'' He stood in front of her, shielding her from view, his face almost stern. ''You do understand my position?''

''Frankly, no.'' She tossed her exuberant mane, putting him in mind of a high-strung filly. ''We had a deal, Mr. McCord, and I'm going to hold you to it. I've put off other functions to come out here.''

''I'm quite prepared to compensate you for your trouble.''

"I'm sorry. I'm too full of pride. Right up to here!" She stepped forward and levelled a hand just beneath his arrogant nose. "I can't let you walk away from a commitment and I won't!"

"Really?" He raised a supercilious brow, hiding his unwilling admiration for her spirit. What would she be like if she were really angry? "Do you mind if we walk outside? We appear to be attracting quite a bit of attention." People were indeed looking their way, which might have a lot to do with her glorious appearance or the hostility of the body language.

"Well you will turn this into a crisis situation."

They walked out into the spiralling heat, the aromatic smell of baked earth and baked eucalyptus leaves blowing on the wind.

"Good grief, there's a kangaroo," she said, sounding as excited as a child about to make a spectacle of herself by running after it.

"You'll see plenty of them out here," he told her dryly, lulled by the lovely crooning quality of her voice.

"So I'm staying?" She turned to him hopefully, staring into his eyes. Playing him for all he was worth.

"It's hard to know what to do with you." His answer was therefore curt. At least it kept him from falling at her feet. If a latter day Cellini needed a model for the Roman goddess Venus, she was it. "I know in my bones, you're good old-fashioned Trouble."

"Would it help if I put on my half-moon reading glasses?" she asked with a kind of tart sweetness.

"You need glasses?" He felt a little shock. He didn't think she had a single flaw.

"Going on your masculine logic they might help," she answered with some of his own dryness.

"Well I've pretty much approved the mini-skirt," he told her coolly. "You don't feel self-conscious wearing it?"

"I'm not ashamed of my legs." She looked down at their

slender length, then at him. ''Have you finished checking them out?''

Not half finished, he thought. ''You're certainly very forthright, Miss De Campo.'' He glinted, inevitably reminded of the shy reticence of his stepmother and sister.

''What's good for the goose is good for the gander,'' she pronounced philosophically. ''I insist now we hold to our agreement. From all accounts you need me.''

''What do you mean?'' For a moment hostility held sway. Had she heard some unkind comments about Stacy's lack of organisational skills?

''No need to bite my head off. I'm only saying, there's very little time to find my replacement even if I'd allow it. And I do have your initial cheque. Banked,'' she stressed.

''Is there any possibility you might accept it as compensation?'' His expression hardened while he waited for her answer.

''None whatever. I've come, Mr. McCord, and I'm going to stay,'' she announced, exuding determination. ''What's more, you'll find no fault with me. I intend to work as hard as I know how.''

''Better yet you might think of a uniform.'' He glanced meaningfully at her well-endowed body, fighting down those unwelcome flares of excitement. ''Keep it simple. Nothing revealing.''

''You're very timid around women, aren't you?'' She glanced at him sidelong. The man had sex appeal coming out of his ears. ''Possibly you've had a bad experience?''

''One, but it was a long time ago. A femme fatale like you,'' he countered suavely, not allowing her to take a rise out of him. ''You must understand your staying depends on true-blue behaviour, Miss De Campo.''

''Angelica, please,'' she begged. ''Angelica. Angie. I get both. But I'm not sure I know what true-blue behaviour is.'' She widened her beautiful eyes.

''It's not playing around,'' he explained. ''Excuse the expression.'' To his consternation he found he was unable to look away from her luscious mouth.

Surprise flickered into her eyes. ''You know you've got it all wrong.'' She gazed back with considerable appeal. ''Huntley grabbed me,'' she told him simply. ''I was such an idiot to go with him.''

''Were you attracted to him?'' It seemed both monstrous and bizarre.

''Lord, no!'' She shuddered, making the clingy little top climb higher around her golden midriff. ''Men like that I don't give the time of day.''

''Really?'' He'd heard something like this before. ''Forgive me if I have to wonder why you were allowing him to maul you?''

''He was, wasn't he?'' she agreed dismally. ''All that grappling. I still remember the tumble on the couch. It wasn't my fault, I swear. But the way you were looking at me made me feel quite worthless. Odd to be innocent but found guilty.'' She pushed back tight little damp curls, marvelling at the heat. ''He found an excuse to get me into the study. I was working with a colleague that night doing the catering.''

''Did he send you a little note?''

''He spoke to me. He was the host. He was a big burly man who'd been tossing drinks down.''

''I wouldn't call you little.'' Extravagantly beautiful, maybe.

''Mr. McCord, I've been insulted about my height all my life,'' she groaned.

''I don't believe that at all.'' She had to be fishing for compliments.

''Everyone called me Shorty at school. I know they were only joking but it hurt at the time.''

''I suppose being so beautiful you needed the odd remark.'' The heat of the day wasn't bothering him, he was used to it, but he indicated they should move further under the shade of the trees. God help him if he actually touched her. She was dynamite. ''Miss McCord, I don't feel in the least sorry for you,'' he told her briskly. ''You're gorgeous. Have no doubts. One reason why I'm extremely anxious about taking you out to Coori.''

''So when do we get started?'' she asked with a surge of hope, absent-mindedly crumbling a dry eucalyptus leaf between her fingers, so she could enjoy the sharp nostalgic scent.

''The plane is over there.'' He pointed back through the trees to the light aircraft strip. It just so happened his was the only one there.

''My goodness! Unreal!'' She gave a little gasp of admiration. ''Your own private jet.''

''It's not a jet, as you very well know. It's a Beech Baron.''

''It's beautiful,'' she said, absolutely fascinated.

''Thank you.'' A shower of dry gum leaves suddenly fell from the trees, but he resisted the powerful impulse to brush them from her hair.

She shook her head, dislodging the burnished leaves herself. ''Pardon my asking, but you don't have a lady friend to pull this off?''

''What off?'' he retaliated sharply.

''Why, your functions, of course,'' she answered mildly. ''I understand your stepmother and your sister, Gillian, are a little nervous about handling something so big?''

''Nice of Isobel to tell you.'' So they'd discussed it. Why not?

''She had to tell me,'' she answered with mild reasonableness, obviously a sunny-natured woman. ''Not every woman wants to plunge into lots of catering activities. Fortunately for you, it so happens I love it.''

''So I can point the finger at Isobel for telling you about my so-called lady friend?'' He unleashed a certain toughness.

''Don't get cross,'' she coaxed. ''You probably have no idea how ferocious you can look.''

That rocked him. ''I've hardly said a word.'' He imagined

a situation where he could simply pick her up and carry her off, caveman-style.

"You obviously don't mind getting personal?" She came a step further, strangely appealing in her tallness.

"I fail to see what's personal about that."

"Talking about the length of my skirt was. Your lady friend is a fellow rancher, I understand?"

He marvelled at her cheek, giving her a cool stare. "You're not getting paid to ask questions like that, Miss De Campo. As it happens, I'm a committed bachelor."

She didn't know if he was telling the truth or having her on. Not the time, really, to tell him he could very well be the man of her dreams. That would come later. Now she settled for, "You don't look like one." Indeed he looked like the hero of some big-budget adventure movie. The sort who kept a woman's eyes glued to the screen.

He didn't appear to be taking her seriously. In fact he moved off abruptly in the direction of his lovely plane, causing her to utilise some of what she thought of as her beanstalk height to catch up.

Equally abruptly, he turned back, smiling so tigerishly, he surprised her into slamming into him. Multiple little shocks like a charge of electricity rippled through her; a little sound suspiciously like excitement escaped her. The big cat's eyes swished over her.

"And you know them all?"

Angelica felt his condemnation like an actual burden. She didn't care how long it took, she'd convince him there'd been absolutely nothing between herself and Trevor Huntley, no matter what his eyes had deceived him into thinking. Things weren't always what they seemed yet he'd already brought in a verdict. It was awful to be accused of a crime like indecent exposure when one was perfectly innocent.

"So what about my luggage?" she prompted, although she'd just remembered it herself. Some measure of proof her customary aplomb had collapsed. ‘‘Surely you don’t intend taking off without it?’’

He laughed, a sexual sardonic sound. Something he was good at. ‘‘If all your clothes are as brief as what you’re wearing,’’ he observed, ‘‘I’m surprised you’re not carrying it over your shoulder.’’

Good-natured as she was, she couldn’t contain a flicker of temper. ‘‘Obviously you don’t realise what’s going on in women’s fashions. I expect it comes with the landscape. You’re a very long way from the big city.’’

‘‘Which doesn’t mean I don’t get there part of the time to catch up.’’ He hesitated a moment, his gleaming gaze speculative. ‘‘Any chance you’ve packed a few things a couple of inches longer?’’

She responded sweetly though sparks were crackling between them. ‘‘To bring all this off successfully, and I so want to, Mr. McCord, perhaps I could arrange a showing of my wardrobe for you. You could tell me what you like and what you don’t. The kind of thing a nice girl wears. We could talk about it.’’

His amber eyes sparkled with half malice, half amusement. ‘‘Which calls for time I don’t have. You are the same woman I spoke to on the phone?’’

‘‘You have doubts?’’ She seemed to be gravitating towards him, drawn by his powerful magnetism.

‘‘It is a concern,’’ he mocked. ‘‘You don’t seem like my initial choice.’’

‘‘I’m me, I can vouch for it.’’

The handsomely defined mouth compressed. ‘‘In that case, you’d better come along. Your luggage, unless it’s been stolen, should be beside the plane by now. I know the guy who drives the van.’’

‘‘Let’s hope he’s not a cross-dresser,’’ she joked.

‘‘I beg your pardon.’’ He paused to look down at her, eyes narrowed.

‘‘I said—’’

‘‘I know what you said.’’ Despite himself he had to laugh.

Whatever else the ravishingly wanton Miss De Campo might prove to be—and he just knew she was going to be an extravagant handful—she wouldn't be dull. That's what he had liked about her in the first place.

CHAPTER THREE

FROM the air, Coori homestead, surrounded by its satellite buildings, resembled a settlement constructed on the site of an oasis. The vast areas around it, thousands upon thousands of square miles, in comparison, was practically the far side of planet Mercury. The burning, mirage-stalked earth was coloured a brilliant red, scattered densely with golden bushes like great mounds. Angelica guessed before McCord told her it was spinifex. Spinifex and sand. Out here the two went together.

"The cattle will eat it if nothing else is available," he told her casually, secretly pleased she'd been such a good passenger. She was fearless—they'd hit a few thermals—she showed great interest in her latest adventure, and she asked intelligent questions. "But spinifex has little food value for the stock. The seeds on the other hand we use to fatten horses to prime condition."

"From here it looks rather like wheat," she observed, fascinated by the spectacle, the sheer size and emptiness of a giant primitive landscape that was crisscrossed by maze after maze of water channels—swamps, lagoons, billabongs, desert streams—that appeared to be running near dry.

He nodded. "Especially at this time of year. The interior of the bushes, strangely enough, is quite cool. For that reason the lizards make their home there, but the wax content is so high the bushes can burn fiercely. When they do, they send up great clouds of black smoke for days."

"It doesn't look like you've had any rain," she said quietly, thinking drought must be really terrible to the man on the land.

His laugh was ironic. "Not for a year. Not a drop during

winter-spring. Not a single shower, but we've seen great displays of storm-clouds like a Wagnerian set that got wheeled away. We're hoping the Wet season up north will be a good one. But not too good. We can do without the floods. Just enough to flush out every water channel. When the eastern river system comes down in flood, the waterbirds fly in in their millions. The Channel Country is a major breeding ground for nomadic waterbirds. Great colonies of Ibis nest in our lignum swamps. They do us a big favour by feasting on the destructive flocks of grasshoppers that strip the grass and herbage for the stock. Then there are all sorts of ducks in their countless thousands—herons, shags, spoonbills, waterhens, egrets.''

''So where do they come from?'' she asked, turning to admire his handsome profile. He was a marvellous-looking man.

''Good question. No one seems to know. It's one of those great mysteries of the Outback. One day there's not a sign of them, but then a sudden storm, the billabongs fill and they're there literally overnight. Most other birds take days to arrive, when they sense water. Pelicans—I love the pelicans. I used to try to find their nests as a boy—turn up in favoured years to breed in our more remote swamps. Those are just the waterbirds. What will dazzle you here is the great flights of budgerigar, a phenomenon of the Outback, like the crimson chats and the finches. The hawks and the falcons prey on them. The largest bird is the wedge-tailed eagle. You'll identity it easily in flight from the wingspan. At least seven foot. The wingtips curve up. Wedge-tails can take a fair-size kangaroo.''

''Goodness.'' She tried to visualise it. ''Swooping on a medium-size kangaroo must take some doing?''

''They don't have a problem. There are plenty of predators around.'' He shrugged. ''The huge flocks of white birds you'll see are the corellas. They cover the coolabahs so densely you can scarcely see a leaf. Or a branch. And the noise when they take off is deafening. All our beautiful parrots prefer the scrub. Not that you'll have much time for sight-seeing, Miss De Campo. You're here to work.''

''I'll get up very early,'' she murmured. ''What a truly extraordinary place you live in.'' It had to have moulded him, made him special. ''You must feel like a desert chieftain?''

He glanced at her with those amazing exotic eyes. Everything about him said, ''Don't go trying to fascinate me.'' What a challenge! He confirmed it by saying, ''Don't go getting any romantic notions. I'm a hardworking cattleman. I haven't the energy to ravish females.''

''I guess desert chieftains don't have to be mad rapists,'' she joked.

''Have you been raped?'' he asked very seriously indeed, giving her a direct stare. Huntley, brute that he was, was probably capable of it. That, he couldn't bear.

''No such terrible thing has happened to me, the Lord be praised.'' She shuddered. ''No woman knows for certain if she's going to be in the wrong place at the wrong time. It's woman's universal fear. I have a guardian angel I pray to to look after me. A father who adores me. A brother who thinks a lot of me. He's built like a commando and he has a black belt.''

''Whereas all you've got is a cupboard full of basketball trophies.''

''I'm sorry I told you that,'' she said.

''You also told me you were frequently asked, 'How's the weather up there?'''

''My favourite was how did I cope with altitude sickness. People are cruel. The plainer they are, the crueller they get.''

''Whereas you're a most beautiful woman.''

''Am I?'' she asked with a small degree of surprise. She'd had plenty of compliments in her time but she hadn't been expecting too many from him. Not after that flinty-eyed reception.

''Miss De Campo, I have no intention of going soft on you,'' he assured her, as though he found her mind easy to read. ''I hope you believe it, though I'm sure your successes have been legion. I'll be watching your every move. You may have won the battle but not the war."

"Why should there be war between us? A war would get us nowhere. I'm looking for your co-operation."

"And you'll get it providing you don't take it into your head to send the senses of the male population reeling."

"As though I'd be capable of such a thing," she answered breezily. "Are we coming in to land?"

"We are," he confirmed crisply, thinking he was coming off second best with this woman. "So you can tighten your seat belt."

"Aye, aye, Captain!" She laughed as excitement set in. "Or is it 'Roger?' I have to catch up on the terminology. Anyway, I can't wait." She looked down, trying to gather in her kaleidoscope of thoughts and impressions. "Obviously it's all paid off, being a desert chieftain," she enthused. "The homestead looks huge!" And the setting was fantastic! "Who would ever have thought of building a mansion in the middle of the Never-Never?"

"We are a way out of town," he agreed dryly. "Do you think you can possibly sit quietly?"

"Just watch me." She gave him a cheerful smile, proceeding to sit as solidly as an Easter Island statue. Honey caught more flies than vinegar. Hadn't her mother told her?

They were greeted by a station hand the moment they arrived. When the young man was introduced to Angelica he muttered a, "Pleased to meet you," without lifting his head. Indeed he seemed dead-set on digging the toe of his riding boot into the baked earth.

"Shy," Angelica commented kindly when she and McCord had disposed themselves in the waiting Jeep.

"Why not?" McCord gave her a sidelong glance. "Noah was brought up in the bush. He's never seen a woman like you in his life."

"Aw shucks!" she pretended to simper. "You'll be telling me you had me pegged for a high-class callgirl in two ticks."

"You have to admit we started badly."

''You being so judgmental. The fact of the matter is you owe me an apology.'' She lifted her chin as she spoke. It had a shallow dimple he really loved. Not that he was about to tell her that.

''I'll apologise if I have to when I know the true story,'' he assured her. ''Huntley had several girlfriends and a mistress at the time. Carly knew for a fact at least one was a very glamorous brunette. That doesn't exactly clear you.''

''It doesn't condemn me, either,'' she said tartly. ''I don't want to insult you but you sound a real prude.''

''Your opinion, Miss De Campo, doesn't concern me at all. I know what I saw in that study. People were milling about. You could have screamed. You could have appealed to me for help. Had you needed it. I would have enjoyed knocking dear Trevor flat.''

''I regret to say I was too ashamed and mortified,'' Angelica confessed, appalled to hear her excuse sound so weak. ''Seconds elapsed from the moment he got me into that study to when he all but threw me on the sofa.''

He made no attempt to hide a snort of derision. ''You're not exactly a featherweight. Come to think of it, my recollection of you is a lot of woman.''

''A lot?'' she burst out wrathfully. ''Don't be ridiculous. I was a comfortable size twelve.''

''Are you sure?'' He did his best to look sceptical. ''Not that I know much about women's dress sizes, but being in the cattle business I'm a good judge of weight. I'd say you were a good stone heavier then.''

''Well, perhaps,'' she conceded, pulling a face. How did he know so much when he'd only see her for such a short time? ''These days I go to the gym. And I watch my diet. I've actually worked out quite a care program. Especially now I'm on the TV. I know I'm a big girl.''

''Big is beautiful,'' he returned, a sardonic gleam in his amber gold-speckled eyes. ''There's hardly a thing to choose between you and a supermodel.''

When they stepped into the splendid entrance hall of Coori

homestead a cute young woman around five-two, with fair hair and sky-blue eyes, dressed in cotton jeans and a T-shirt, rushed down the central staircase to greet them. ''Oh, you're here! That's lovely!'' she cried enthusiastically, directly addressing Angelica and waggling her fingers at her half brother as though he'd pulled off a great coup. ''Isobel didn't exaggerate. You're beautiful!''

It sure beat her half brother's reception, Angelica thought, immediately warming to Gillian. This girl fitted Isobel's description. Gillian was just possibly half a foot, maybe more, shorter, but what the heck! Angelica was comforted by such a welcome. ''How nice of you to say so.'' She held out her hand, returning the beaming smile.

McCord's young half sister was a mixture of shyness and appealing vulnerability. She bore no resemblance whatsoever to her half brother. ''You're Gillian, of course.''

''Gilly, please.'' Gillian took the hand extended to her, staring up at Angelica with the kind of heroine worship one usually saw reserved for school captain. ''Mum will be here in a moment,'' she explained. ''This is the second time she's changed her dress. Isobel told us you've got great style.''

''You should have seen some of my fashion disasters,'' Angelica confided, refusing to look in McCord's direction, in case he was still critically examining her denim mini.

''I'm sure you'd look wonderful in anything,'' Gillian said so sincerely Angelica wanted to hug her.

''Listen, why don't we let Miss De Campo settle in,'' McCord suggested, his tone an unexpected combination of gentleness and wry impatience.

Gillian blushed. ''Sorry, Jake.''

''No worries, Gilly.'' He lightly touched her shoulder. ''Has anything happened while I've been gone? Any messages?''

''Oh.'' Gilly made an apologetic little sound. ''I nearly forgot. The vet can make it this afternoon, after all. He'll be here around three-thirty. He's cadged a ride with Brodie.

Brodie brings the mail and supplies,'' she explained to Angelica in an aside.

''A bit of good news. Anything else?'' McCord prompted patiently. Angelica got the feeling he did that often.

''Dinah rang.'' Gillian started to gnaw at one of her fingernails. ''She's flying over Friday afternoon. She thought she might stay the weekend. Invited herself really.'' She slumped as though the high-handed Dinah was already there. ''She says she can't wait to meet Angelica.''

''And Dinah is?'' Angelica neatly questioned, more than halfway to knowing she was one of McCord's girlfriends. No revelation a man like that would have a huge following and she couldn't now overlook herself.

''Friend of the family,'' he clipped off, obviously not wanting to be pushed into any discussion. ''Now I've a few things to do before I show you around, Angelica.'' He gave her a smile of such lazy sensuality Angelica almost swooned. ''Meanwhile, Gilly can help you settle in. Your luggage will be at your door. The day will be over before I get out there but I'm leaving you in good hands.''

''Thanks, Jake!'' Gillian smiled happily.

''See you in about an hour.'' He gave Angelica another one of those looks that sizzled.

She had a mad desire to call after him, ''Have fun now,'' but wisely thought better of it. McCord was obviously a man to be reckoned with. He probably spent all his days giving orders and being obeyed. It was too bad about this Dinah. Then again, she reminded herself, he wasn't engaged. Not surprising when he had described himself as a committed bachelor, but she had the feeling that was a big hint for her. Not exactly a propitious beginning for both of them, but she refused to allow it to dampen her buoyant spirits. She had only set foot on Coori and already she was in love with its wild beauty, its history and romance. All right! The master of Coori wasn't too bad, either.

The mistress of that great station—one of the shyest people Angel had met, even more startling considering the power and influence of the family—gazed at Angelica a minute or two, then gave her an unreserved welcome that was as warm and informal as that of her daughter's.

"Oh, I'm so glad it's you," she confided sometime later, as they relaxed over iced tea. "Isobel is a dear woman—she's been very kind to me—but she's so confident in every way she makes me feel a desperate failure. You and I are going to get on well."

That shook Angelica a little. She took the frosted mint-scented glass from her mouth. "You think I'm going to make lots of mistakes?"

"Oh, no, dear, I'm sure you won't." Stacy was astonished at Angelica's quite logical interpretation. "You have that unmistakable touch of class, and laughter in your eyes. An ease of manner I find very soothing. I know you won't make me feel nervous. Beautiful women have made me nervous all my life."

"Maybe you haven't noticed I'm oversize." Angelica smiled.

"That's the surprising thing," Stacy said artlessly. "It looks just right on you. I, on the other hand, have always struggled to attain any sort of stature." She looked vaguely around the lovely sitting room furnished with a mixture of contemporary and antique pieces. "I was never right as mistress of Coori station, for instance. I'm sure you've already heard that from Isobel. Why Clive picked on humble little me remains a puzzle in the McCord family. He should have kept looking. Jake is very tolerant of my lack of organisational skills. He's been my champion since he was a little boy. Not that it did him any good. Clive couldn't tolerate the way Jake stood up to him. I think he found it threatening, even allowing for the hard man that he was. Jake can be tough when he has to be, but he has heart. My late husband was a heartless perfectionist."

Angelica had heard that, as well, but still felt shocked. "That must have been hard to live up to?"

"Oh, it runs in the family," Stacy sighed. "Thank the Lord, Jake is different. His father was from the school of biting sarcasm. It was easy to make him explode. No matter how much I tried to please him, I couldn't. The irony is, it was my only ambition."

Angelica shook her head in sympathy, nevertheless surprised by Stacy's disclosures so early in their acquaintance. She tinked the rim of her crystal glass against her white teeth. What a life it must have been, to be constantly belittled. She believed her own mother, wife, earthmother, restauranteur, superstar, would have put Clive McCord right. Men seemed to pick their mark. On the face of it Stacy McCord seemed like a natural-born victim. There wasn't going to be any small talk, either. Stacy had major traumas to unload with seemingly not a minute to lose.

"Of course in my youthful ignorance I thought loving him was enough," Stacy continued in that soft reminiscent voice. It wasn't often she found herself with a captive audience, consequently she found it difficult not to keep going. "Clive was everything I dreamed about. I thought I was in for a life of married bliss, a home of my own where I could be in charge for a change. And my parents were over the moon with such a splendid match. The McCords are an old pioneering family."

"And rich?" That upped anyone's eligibility, Angel thought.

"There's always something about money," Stacy agreed. "It made my mother so happy. She was proud of me for once. But the money didn't mean anything to me. I loved him. He was such a striking-looking man and I was little more than a silly schoolgirl. I didn't have a glimmer of an idea he'd bought me like he'd buy a pedigreed little heifer. I was young and pretty, if you can believe it. I was soft, and by the way I mean soft in the head, as well. I had no instinct for trouble. I didn't even notice Clive wasn't a bit of fun."

By this time Angelica herself didn't know whether to laugh or cry. "I doubt many people have it all together at eighteen,'' she consoled. I mean, did she? The answer was a resounding no. ''It takes time to understand human emotions and passions. If we ever do. Anyway there's nothing like getting married to bring out the best and worst in people.''

Stacy, to her credit, gave vent to a surprisingly hearty laugh. ''Why is it I think I've known you forever?''

''It happens like that.'' Angelica smiled.

''But I am talking too much.'' Stacy suddenly flushed, blotching her apple-blossom skin.

''I really appreciate the fact you trust me,'' Angelica told her with sincerity. The fact of the matter was she often received unsolicited confidences the moment people laid eyes on her. She supposed she must look kind, or they thought they'd never see her again. She'd even received off-the-cuff marriage proposals.

''I used to think if the portrait of Roxanne came down, Clive would start to forget.'' Stacy pushed at her wispy fringe, a mannerism Angelica had remarked. ''But he never did. He was absolutely faithful to her to the end. I suspect when he was dying alone out there in the desert he cried out her name. Maybe they're together again at last.''

''Maybe they are,'' Angelica said, with a kind of fascinated sadness. If she were a romance writer instead of a caterer she could have turned the whole thing into a blockbuster. ''I believe in an afterlife, but you have to let go, Stacy.''

Stacy nodded. Nodded again with great vehemence. ''Oh, it's so good to talk. Very few would be interested.''

''You're still young.'' Angelica intuited Stacy had been thinking along these lines. ''There's no reason why you can't re-marry. Happily this time. Life goes by so fast you have to grab it on the wing.''

''Oh, God!'' Stacy exclaimed almost despairingly. ''That's all very well for you. You're young and so vibrant. I don't believe I ever was. I was Little Miss Helpless. Only child syndrome. Older parents. Anyway, who'd have me?''

''A lot,'' Angelica answered dryly.

''Aha, the money.'' Stacy saw the irony.

''Don't put yourself down. You're a pretty woman.''

''Am I?'' Stacy sounded pleased and even took a very human little peek into a well-positioned gilded mirror. ''But how could I meet anyone out here?''

''Dive right in,'' Angelica advised. ''We have all these wonderful Christmas functions coming up. I absolutely love Christmas. We must have a great big tree. I know you've got one.''

''No we haven't got one,'' Stacy announced surprisingly. ''Clive only died three years ago. He didn't want any Christmas trees.''

''Why didn't you get one yourself? Even afterwards?'' Angelica was so amazed, her voice cracked.

''I think I expected Clive might come back to haunt me. Anyway if I put up a big Christmas tree you can count on its falling over.''

''It won't fall over on me,'' Angelica said. ''Have we agreed on a Christmas tree? I know exactly where it should go. The bigger the better.''

''We've no pines here, dear, only desert oaks.'' Stacy smiled.

''We'll find something,'' Angelica said. ''But getting back to our functions, you know who's coming. Surely there's an eligible man or two? There must be, I can see you smiling.''

''Really just a friend.'' Stacy's voice softened. A dead give-away. ''He's a lovely man, but I can't think he'd be all that interested in me. There are others.''

''Look on the positive side,'' Angelica advised. ''You can have what you want if you go after it. I've found it really doesn't pay to be tentative and hold back. Why don't we try to sort things out this week? I'm going to have to press you into service, if that's okay? No need to worry. You're going to enjoy it. Have fun. Offering hospitality to friends should be fun. You don't have to perform miracles. Gillian has to do her bit, too. Is there a guy in her life?''

Stacy glanced over her shoulder as though Gillian was

about to return. ''Gilly's got a crush on one of our jackeroos,'' she confided.

Angelica's jaw dropped. She thought jackeroos were supposed to keep their distance. ''Really?''

''He's a fine young man, but he's English.''

Angelica, disconcerted, just stopped herself from snorting. ''Is that a problem?'' She stared at Stacy, wondering if Stacy had been hoping for a local.

''It is in this way...'' Stacy started to clarify. ''Charlie could go back home at any time. He's here for the adventure. He read all about the Outback as a boy and fancied himself living the frontier life. They must have made it sound very glamorous. Anyway he loves it but his family will want him back home. Who could blame them? He's the Honourable Charles Middleton by the way.''

Angelica was fascinated. ''That sounds safe enough. You mean Gillian has a member of the English aristocracy in her pocket?''

''Well, it hasn't gone far, but they seem very fond of each other. Charlie is such a nice young man. Jake likes him, too, which makes things so much easier. That's where she's nipped out to.''

''To see Charlie?'' Angelica asked, further intrigued.

''They don't go a day without seeing each other.'' Stacy brushed at her fringe, torn between feeling happy for her daughter and worry. ''I pray and pray she won't get hurt. I mean, she's a real softie like me.''

''And the Honourable Charlie isn't your normal, average guy.'' Angelica nodded in understanding. ''This must be an entirely new way of life for him?''

''You'd think he was born to it.'' Stacy smiled fondly. ''Though he's had his learning curve. He finished up in hospital last year with a back injury. We were all so worried, but he made an excellent recovery. Jake keeps in contact with his family and of course Charlie does, too, but his father likes Jake to tell him how his son is getting along. I suppose you could call him much more than the normal jackeroo. He often comes up to the house for dinner. He hero worships Jake. He thinks he's marvellous even when Jake has had to tear strips off him for being too reckless. But those were the early days.''

''I'm looking forward to meeting Charlie.'' Angelica had to laugh.

Please don't take him off Gilly, Stacy thought. Most men wouldn't be able to tear their eyes away from Angelica. But she seemed such a nice girl. Generous and kind.

They were still chatting when Jake returned. He heard their laughter as he made his way to his stepmother's sitting room. Miss De Campo certainly knew how to charm people, he thought. Every time Dinah came over there was no hint of laughter from Stacy or Gilly.

Both women looked up as he entered the cool, charming room. ''How's it going?''

''We haven't stopped talking from the moment we sat down,'' Stacy told him, pink-cheeked and happy. ''In fact I haven't enjoyed myself so much in ages.''

''That's good.'' Miss De Campo was either very kind or very clever. Maybe both. He glanced at her. She had changed her eye-catching mini for an equally hot little number; a cool white cotton knit top over pink cotton jeans that sat as sweetly on her hips as the oval-dipping top clung to her breasts. She had a major talent for wearing clothes. It was no problem to imagine her naked, either. ''If we're going to look around, we'd better get started,'' he said, sounding crisp.

''Fine!'' Instantly, Angelica jumped to her feet. ''I can't wait to see around. My bedroom is simply beautiful. Very grand.''

''I decided on it, dear.'' Stacy looked pleased.

''A four-poster is a real treat for me.'' Angelica said. ''I'm really going to enjoy myself going to bed.''

You'd make me pretty damned happy, as well, Jake thought, not insured against dangerous thoughts.

They made a tour of the house, moving from room to room

of the mansion. They started with the reception rooms but Jake took little time in the beautiful Yellow Drawing Room that housed the portrait of his mother, and Angelica sensed some inner emotional struggle. They spent more time over the very fine library with its collection of rare books, and now they stood inside Clive McCord's memento- and trophy-filled study, a room Jake told her he didn't use.

Eyes dark and brilliant, Angelica looked up at the portrait of Clive McCord that dominated the generously sized room. "I must be a fanciful person but I feel the people who lived in this house all around us," she said quietly. "There's been happiness here, hope, love and sorrow."

"Certainly my father waged his own personal war against fate," Jake said without bitterness, looking into his father's painted piercingly blue eyes. He looked wonderfully handsome, arrogant, with the promise of a glorious life ahead of him. This had been painted as a companion piece to the portrait of his mother in the Yellow Drawing Room.

"It was wrong of him to make his family suffer," Angelica said gently, "but the joy must have gone out of him the day your mother was killed." She turned to look into Jake's handsome face. It wore a sombre expression, as though he remembered constant duels in this very room.

"I hate to admit it." He shrugged. "I'm a grown man, but he hurt us all. He never treated me like a son. More like a usurper whose only aim was to steal his throne from him. Contradictory really because my father always said life was meaningless."

"I expect he meant without your mother. It was very hard on Stacy."

"She told you?" And if she did, who did Stacy really have to talk to?

"Why not? Stacy accepts me as the person I am."

"Whereas I've dipped into your past?" he murmured, thinking how that had complicated things.

"Is it you don't trust me or you don't trust anyone?" she asked directly.

Something flashed in his eyes. ''Maybe I'm more like my father than I care to acknowledge.''

''Is that a fear?'' Both her voice and her expression was very soft, near tender.

It affected him so much he wanted to grab her. Pull her into his arms. Rain kisses down on the luscious mouth. Instead he said coolly, ''Is this a psychoanalysis session?''

''I think life would be unendurable if we couldn't talk to someone,'' she countered, realising there was a lot of stress in him.

''I don't know you...'' He only had to lower his head.

''Strangely, I don't feel like that.'' The atmosphere was so intimate she found herself near whispering. ''I think you fall into the category of people I've known in another life.''

''How fanciful...Angel.'' Now why had he called her that?

On his lips it sounded heavenly. ''Millions of people believe in reincarnation,'' she said, her blood racing. ''I still say I met you somewhere along the way.''

''And did you love me or hate me?'' he asked, some note in his voice sending shock waves along her nerves.

''I don't know,'' she admitted, her voice so breathy it touched his cheek. ''But I know you. I can't explain it.'' She looked back at the portrait of Clive McCord. ''That's a very powerful painting. Clearly you don't have your father's colouring, but you do have a look of him.''

''So tell me, is it the arrogance?''

''You might have a touch of it but I should think it was the arrogance of achievement. I think you're going to be a winner in life's battles, Jake McCord.''

He tried to clear the huskiness from his throat. ''Who taught you how to heal?'' he asked.

She looked at him in surprise. ''I'm not aware I have that talent.''

His amber gaze was brilliant and unblinking. ''I swear you've been using it on me since the moment you stepped off the plane.''

‘‘Maybe I’m looking for the man behind the tough façade.’’ A beautiful smile moved over her face. ‘‘My poppa is a little bit like you. Very much the dominant male in the old tradition but he has a sweet centre. My mother soon found it.’’

He was close enough to touch her. To run his fingers down her cheek, brush back the glossy dark tumble of hair. He did none of those things. Instead he asked, ‘‘Are you saying you could find mine? Always supposing I have one.’’

‘‘You must!’’ She shrugged an elegant satiny shoulder. ‘‘Stacy and Gilly love you.’’

‘‘So basically I’m a good guy,’’ he said with wry humour.

‘‘That’s about the size of it.’’ She glanced up at him, looked away quickly before he saw invitation in her eyes. For reasons she couldn’t entirely fathom she found this complex man utterly irresistible. This man who for his own reasons had decided to condemn her. But such was the power of attraction, irrational in its way. She made a silent vow to find the real man beneath. Jake McCord was one enigma she intended to solve.

CHAPTER FOUR

ONCE in a blue moon did you see showcase country kitchens like this, Angelica thought, pausing in the open doorway to admire the extraordinarily inviting king-size room. It was a delightful mix of old and new with homestead charm allied to the finest modern appliances money could buy. Such a highly functional kitchen with plenty of work spaces would make her job so much easier. In fact it would have fitted seamlessly into her parents' flagship Italian restaurant.

Her trained eye moved with approval over marble bench tops, lots of gleaming timber—cupboards, a polished hardwood floor—a timber hanging rail displaying copper utensils above a huge central work station. Along the back wall, a restaurant-size stainless-steel oven, stainless-steel refrigerators with matching freezers side by side. There was even a small informal dining area, circular table and four cottage chairs by the window where deflected sunlight streamed in. On the centre of the table stood a bright ceramic bowl full of lemons. A must in any cook's kitchen.

The housekeeper—for a godsend, they had met and taken to one another on sight—preferred to be known only as "Clary." The name suited her, Angel thought, uncertain whether Clary by chance stood for Clara, Clarice or even Clarabelle. No one had enlightened her if they even knew.

Clary would have been well into her sixties conforming to the traditional idea of "cook," stout of figure with an air of great energy, shrewd, genial eyes and a fine head of thick pepper-and-salt curls. Given the size of the homestead and the family and the stacks of visitors to the station to feed Angel could well see she would always be on the go. In a year or two, maybe less, Clary would surely want to retire and have some time to herself. Apparently she had been running the household since it was discovered the second Mrs. McCord had little aptitude for the job. Coming up twenty years? In that time Clary had created her own super-functional, super-efficient kitchen environment over which she reigned supreme.

As Angelica stood admiring a world-renowned double cooker, Clary emerged from an adjacent doorway to the rear. "Hello there, Clary," Angelica called, her admiring voice not lost on the housekeeper. "I hope I'm not disturbing you. I was just looking at your marvellous kitchen."

"You can disturb me all you like, love," Clary said comfortably, waving a hand to welcome Angelica in. "I take that as a real compliment coming from you. I see copies of *Cosima,* you know. I really like the way you write. It's infectious. And I like your recipes with all the little surprises. You make food preparation fun."

"Which, of course, it is if you love food and all the wonderful produce of the earth. I must say you've a splendid working environment here," Angelica commented, running a hand over a bench top. "Great for serious cooking. It will make the job of catering so much easier."

"That it will," Clary agreed, picking up a dish cloth to wipe away a non-existent spot. "Would you like to look at the pantry, love. It's well stocked but you'll be wanting lots more. You do need a hand?"

"You bet I do, Clary. I'm counting on it."

"I'm in." Clary injected pleasure and enthusiasm into it. "Isobel appreciates my help, too. We want to do Coori proud. You won't get Stacy, God love her, on the team though," she added wryly. "She's not domesticated, I'm afraid, but Isobel would have told you that. In the early days I used to try to show her something but she always disappeared. It used to make the master simmer, I can tell you, but it seemed to make no impression on Stacy. She didn't always pick up on his moods. You know and I know that to feed people successfully, come up with menus, et cetera, you have to love food. Like it at least. Stacy and young Gilly only eat to survive. They have little interest in what I put before them.''

Angelica, an inspired cook, who thought every woman should know her way around a kitchen, was seized by empathy. ''Gosh, that can't make you happy?''

''Especially when you're asked for toast and a boiled egg. I've been here a long time.'' Clary shrugged. ''The master, Mr. Clive, demanded the best. He grew up with his own father and mother priding themselves on keeping a good table. If one tiny thing was omitted, it was a crime as far as he was concerned. Lord could he be fierce! I dunno that I've met a worse man to this day. When I first came here I was tempted to kill him with one of my favourite kitchen knives.''

''You never considered doing a runner instead?'' Angelica laughed.

''No, love. I was down on me luck. I stuck it out. He wasn't miserable with money. I was well paid and I came to love Jake. I had no kids and loving him was the easiest thing imaginable. He was a great little guy, so brave and spirited with his father I used to get anxious for him, but he just kept getting better and better. Now he's the boss, the Lord be praised. To work for him is a pleasure. Jake truly appreciates a good meal. Sometimes I can't fill him. He works too hard. That's what worries me. He runs Coori and the out-stations and that's not his only role. He does the lot around here. When his father was alive Jake had to work until he dropped. But he hung in because Coori is his heritage.''

''A marvellous heritage,'' Angelica said fervently, pleasantly stunned the household with the exception of McCord were only too ready to confide in her.

''The best!'' Clary agreed. ''This is the pantry, love,'' she announced, waving her hand around a mini-supermarket. ''Everyday household. There are store rooms, refrigerator rooms elsewhere in the compound. We supply our own beef, lamb, pork, poultry, game. I make a beautiful red Thai kangaroo curry with coconut rice. I pride myself on keeping up with the latest trends as well as the old favourites. Of course kangaroo isn't everyone's cup of tea. A bit gamey for some, but I do some lovely cured char-grilled topside steaks, as well.''

''They'll probably go well with the barbecue,'' Angelica said. ''I have to admit I'm a bit emotional about Skippy, kangaroos being the national emblem and all. At the same time I realise we have a superb renewable resource. We'd be foolish to forget that.''

''God knows there are enough of them,'' Clary remarked. ''The annual cull is carried out under the supervision of National Parks and Wildlife. Some years when water is plentiful they're a real menace.''

''So I understand. Sometime tomorrow, Clary, when you have a minute, I'd like to sit down with you and plan out what we're going to do. We're not getting into complex food, or anything that is time-consuming. It's all about taste and using the freshest, best possible ingredients as well as providing warm hospitality. Polo day's first up. Lunch, afternoon tea. Neither will present a problem. It'll take more time working out supper for the ball.''

''Staff barbecue, no worries, either,'' Clary said. ''We're all used to them. I get lots of help from the station wives and the older kids home from boarding school. Everyone pitches in. They love it.''

''Great! Then there's the Christmas party. We'll go to town on that. And I'm so looking forward to decorating the house. Such a marvellous house! So very grand. I can feel the history. Stacy tells me you haven't had a Christmas tree since she's been here.''

Clary looked at her with a sad expression. ''The first Mrs. McCord, Jake's mother was killed just before Christmas. You didn't know that, love?''

''No.'' Angelica shook her dark head, instantly upset she might have put her foot in it.

''The master never came to terms with that.''

''I would think not. No birthday parties, either?''

"Gracious, did Jake tell you that?" Clary looked at her with admiration.

"Only in passing, as a joke."

"It was no joke," Clary said. "I know it sounds disloyal, but the master was no bundle of laughs."

"Well, Jake is McCord now. The Christmas tree will be a start. I'll be speaking to him tonight about it. We need a ceiling on the budget."

"It won't be tight, love," Clary assured her as Angelica began to walk up and down the aisles that divided the huge pantry with Clary trailing her.

"Clary this is fantastic!"

"We're so isolated, love, we can't have provisions flown in all the time. I need to make the ordering cost-effective. I handle all that side of it and I have my small staff. My girls are all part aboriginal. They're more like domestic apprentices. Leah, in particular, is very good. I rely on her a lot and don't have to keep checking all the time. She has a little daughter, Kylee. Kylee's nearly four. She's as cute as they come. Leah was treated badly by the white man who fathered her child. As soon as she fell pregnant he abandoned her. She had no money and nowhere to go. The child was born on one of the McCord out-stations. Jake gave her a job."

"That was good of him."

"He's a very responsible man. Practically a saint," Clary said earnestly. "He also put out the word. The father had to move on. He couldn't land another stockman's job in this part of the world again."

"How old is Leah?" Angelica asked, looking through a variety of staple tinned products.

"Early twenties, I reckon. She doesn't really know. She's had a hard life has our little Leah. She was removed from abusive parents."

"The abuse continued," Angelica said briefly, and shook her head.

"There's a pattern," Clary agreed sadly. "Clever little thing, too. I'd like you to meet her."

''I'll look forward to it.'' Angelica said, her voice resonating warmly. ''Little Kylee, too. What's Christmas without children? She's going to love the Christmas tree. Now what's on the menu for tonight?''

''You mean, dinner?'' For a minute Clary looked the happiest woman in the world.

''I do, too.'' Angelica gave her a smile that made Clary smile, too.

''You're going to put me on my mettle, aren't you?''

''I fancy you'll like that, Clary,'' Angelica teased.

The rest of the day melted into a flurry of activity for Angelica. With Clary well and truly onside, the task ahead of her seemed less formidable. Jake had set aside a station vehicle, a four-wheel drive, for her and she simply took off, driving around the compound and the plains beyond, grateful for the cream akubra Gillian had lent her and her own excellent sunglasses to ward off the worst of the shimmering heat.

Following Stacy's somewhat hazy instructions she found the polo fields, and gave a lot of thought to where she would set up the marquees. It had emerged in the course of conversation Jake was a marvellous player, physically and mentally tough, with wonderful co-ordination and balance. He was also captain of one of the teams contesting the Marsdon Polo Cup. She had looked the event up. She'd also read up about the game of polo knowing it was *the* game out here. Apparently the rules were quite complex so she was far from perfect on them. She'd just have to score a few points as a spectator, looking as glamorous as she possibly could. She had a great outfit anyway. She was looking forward to seeing Jake all dressed up in his polo gear, the numbered shirt, the white breeches, long boots and helmet. No wonder some women developed a mad passion for polo players.

When she saw the Great Hall she stood for a long time, arms folded, visualising what she wanted to do with the decoration. She stared up at the ceiling. Wouldn't it be great painted, perhaps a beautiful deep blue? Maybe studded with the moon and stars? Or better yet in keeping with the polo theme, floating umbrellas amid the clouds, like the ones spectators gathered under at a swank Sydney polo club she had been taken to as a visitor. She wondered what McCord would say to that idea. When she'd spoken to him on the phone that first night he'd managed to convey to her she could have her heart's desire. That was before they had meet face to face and the whole embarrassing Huntley affair with its long lingering sense of shame had rocked her respectable status and established suspicious beginnings.

Late afternoon saw her standing on the broad verandah of the upper storey, watching heat lightning flash up against an incredible sunset of blazing reds, pinks and golds. It speared forks of purple, livid green, indigo and yellow into the billowing clouds. Now nothing moved. Fifteen minutes before, the sky was a moving spectacle of birds of all colours, brilliant parrots, wave upon wave of emerald bolts of silk, the budgerigar, pink and grey galahs, the pure white sulphur-yellow-crested cockatoos, all trying to get home before the storm. A storm that never eventuated though she couldn't imagine it wasn't coming.

She was so absorbed in looking at the blazing, bruised, sky she didn't notice Jake McCord moving down the verandah towards her until he was almost upon her.

"Nothing will come of it, if that's what you're wondering," he said, tilting the akubra he wore at a rakish swagger. So catlike was his tread, she actually jumped, one hand to her heart.

"You startled me," she said unsteadily. And that wasn't the main problem. He deeply stirred and disturbed her. Once more she hoped he couldn't see her reactions to him in her face and misinterpret them as some sort of a come-on.

"I'm sorry. Shall I go back and start again?" The golden-amber eyes danced over her, causing her overstimulated heart to beat out a tattoo.

"You're here now." She made quite an effort to firm up her tone. God, he was a marvellous-looking man. She was coming to think of her attraction like a no-holds-barred thing, even as she knew it wasn't all chemical. At least having to look up at him was entirely satisfactory. Nine times out of ten she had to look down to make eye contact.

"So what have you been up to?" He came nonchalantly alongside, resting his lean, bronze arms on the white wrought-iron railing. An inch more and their fingers would touch. She could feel the blood in her veins turn to a thick golden syrup.

"I've been driving all around," she said, pleased she sounded almost normal. "I took in the polo fields. Worked out where I want to set up the tables and chairs for the spectators and the marquees. I have a favour to ask if you can manage it?"

"As long as it revolves around work." He glanced at her with mockery, thinking they were the right size for each other. Come live with me and be my love, his heart cried. Then he could go crazy with jealousy for the rest of his days.

She tilted her dimpled chin, dark eyes challenging. "What else, pray? I was thinking the ceiling of the Great Hall could do with a paint. Maybe cobalt-blue. I'd like to put a mural of sorts up there for the Polo Ball. I know just the guy who could do it."

"Another one of your admirers?" He couldn't help the taunt.

"As a matter of fact, yes. We're both creative."

"I bet! Then the answer's no." He was quite blunt.

"He's gay."

He pretended to find that bizarre when he felt a sense of relief. "Never! What did you have in mind?"

"I was thinking of stars."

He laughed shortly, wondering what it would be like making love beneath the stars.

"But then umbrellas came to mind."

"Where the hell did that come from?" His eyes were pure gold in the sun. His hair gleamed gold again against the black of his slouched hat.

''As in spectator brollies,'' she explained. ''Floating silver cups and maybe a mallet or two.''

''In which case wouldn't you colour the field green?'' He glanced at her. ''Polo is played on grass.''

''Then you like the idea?'' she said happily.

So happily he wanted to kiss her deeply. He wasn't used to happy women. Or women so charming they'd have you eating out of their hands. Despite that, he said, ''Give me a minute. You've just thrown it at me.''

''I think it would work well,'' she urged. ''We'll carry out the polo theme. Maybe frame the dance floor like a pitch. Goal at either end.''

''Why not an indoor match?''

''I thought indoor polo was gaining in popularity?''

''Not around here it isn't. We've got plenty of land. Plenty of sunshine. I was only being facetious.''

''I realise that,'' she answered kindly. ''I also want a beautiful big Christmas tree for the entrance hall. I want it to loft to the ceiling. All the lovely glittering baubles we can find. Like treasure chests spilling out Christmas angels. I want it to look—oh, magic!'' She threw up her arms, irresistibly drawing his eyes to her full, beautiful breasts. Maybe that was the intention, he thought cynically. How formidable were females. And this was a volatile, passionate woman. Alas to a fault.

''And lots of beautifully wrapped presents piled beneath the tree.'' On her face was the excitement and wonder of a child. ''I haven't as yet seen the guest list for the Christmas party but I imagine there will be children coming with their parents?''

''Quite a few, as it happens,'' he said, certain she was a woman who loved children. A woman children would love. Earthmother was written all over her. ''You'll have to order up the tree, Angel,'' he said, using his new nickname for her. ''We don't have any pines or spruce around here. A live tree would be too aromatic in the house.''

''Leave it to me.''

''I fully intend to. That's what you're here for.'' What would she do if he pulled her to him? The sudden urge was so drastic he had to refocus on that painful scene with Carly's rat of a husband. Even as he did he was forced to concede it was an out-and-out defence strategy. What the hell!

Angelica felt his abrupt change of mood. ''Don't look like you want to throw me out,'' she said.

''Is that how it seems to you?'' The flicker of desire in his amber eyes was so quick she doubted she saw it all.

''Either that or you want to eat me.''

He laughed, a wonderfully attractive sound and a total departure from the edge of severity. ''Undeniably you'd taste delicious. Are we going to get a forerunner of what you might be wearing at dinner?''

''Gracious, no. You have to wait for that.'' Her abundant hair was caught up at the back against the heat, but long curls spilled down onto the sides of her face and her nape. ''I love it here,'' she said, holding his extraordinary eyes for just a moment. This man was dynamite. For the first time in her life she really didn't trust herself. She had read about men who took a woman's breath away but up until now she hadn't actually met one.

''You can't escape the heat.'' In a gesture quite beyond him to prevent, he reached out to push one glossy strand behind her ear.

''It does take a little getting used to.'' Excitement blossomed frantically. ''It's a different heat altogether to what I'm used to.'' Heat, heat! What was he staring at? Could he see she was on fire?

''Ah, well, I'd better go take my shower,'' he said, as though tearing himself away. ''Then I want a long cold beer.''

''I can imagine.'' Her lips curved. ''Actually a cold beer sounds good to me.'' She could see them clinking glasses.

He laughed, pushing his akubra down over his eyes as the last rays of the sun blitzed the verandah with gold. ''Then get Clary to organise something on the downstairs verandah.''

Angelica shook her head. ''I won't bother Clary at all,'' she said. ''She's cooking up something special for tonight. I can handle drinks and a few nibbles without stopping our appetite.''

''Then go to it, Angel,'' he advised. He started to move off, already half drunk on her. What was her perfume? Alluring femininity. She was a seriously beautiful woman and he had seen her half naked. Probably seducing men was the usual scenario for a siren like that. ''Just give me half an hour,'' he called back, sounding surprisingly light-hearted.

''Not a minute longer,'' she answered.

Captivating as she undoubtedly was, he didn't trust her. Not one little inch. That could well be his problem, not hers. All he really knew was it was astonishingly good to have her under his roof.

CHAPTER FIVE

THE house looked splendid by night, giving Angelica a very good idea of what could be achieved for the Christmas party. The chandeliers were absolutely wonderful, antique but converted to electricity. Who had the job of cleaning them? she wondered with some awe. Clary and her girls? Or maybe Clary didn't trust the girls with the easily broken crystal. Whoever it was, Angelica didn't envy them the job. There were so many pieces to each it would take ages. But it was worth it. They cast their brilliance over the main entrance hall and the Yellow Drawing Room which, Stacy informed her, was rarely used except for special occasions, and the formal dining room which Angelica and Clary had decided they'd use that night even before knowing Gillian had invited the Honourable Charles Middleton to join them. Gillian had checked with Jake. It was all right. Did Angelica mind? Of course she didn't.

She was interested to meet the young aristocrat turned jackeroo, to discover, like Stacy, if his feelings for Gillian were encouraging or a result of fevered wishful thinking on Gillian's part. From what she'd seen of Gillian, admittedly very little, Angelica wasn't certain Gillian could handle serious hurt. From all accounts, this was Gillian's first taste of life after years of controlling by an authoritarian father. She was free and, according to her mother, in love. But Charlie came from another, much wider world.

She dressed for dinner in a style that really worked for her with her Latin looks. It could be described as Flamenco or gypsy. With her red, ankle-length flounced cotton voile skirt, she teamed a matching red top, V-necked and sleeveless, which was lovely and cool. A fancy gold belt to show off her narrow waist, long dangly earrings for a bit of chic, half a dozen bangles and a pair of her beloved very expensive high-heeled Italian gold sandals, which meant she was all of six feet. But what the heck! She'd accepted her height now. Even the wisecracks didn't jar so much.

When she went downstairs she checked in with Clary first. ''How's it going? The kitchen smells wonderful.''

''Everything organised,'' Clary reported, looking up from her preparations, highly pleased. ''I'm loving this. It's quite a thrill cooking for someone who really understands food. Just don't slam me if something doesn't quite turn out.''

''As if I'd do that,'' Angelica tutted. ''This is going to be very successful, Clary, you'll see. Nothing too adventurous considering Stacy's and Gilly's delicate palates. We'll work up to that. Artichoke hearts with foie gras for starters, racks of lamb with a green herb crust, Moroccan orange tart. What more could they want? By the way, where's your help?''

''She'll be here in a moment.'' Clary adjusted her snowy apron around her ample waist. ''She had to settle the little one, I expect.''

''So it's Leah? Good, I can get to meet her.''

She didn't have to wait long. A very slender young woman of exotic appearance with elegant, birdlike limbs, dressed in a stylish outfit with a fascinating ethnic print, came silently through the back door. Her dark skin had a high gloss. She had big, soft, gentle eyes. When she caught sight of Angelica she stood perfectly still for a moment, but Clary called to her in an encouraging voice. ''Come on in, Leah. Meet Miss De Campo. I told you all about her.''

Leah walked slowly across the room as though she had a heavy jar on her head, her dark eyes on Angelica standing so dramatically in her red dress that threw off vibrant light. ''Hello, Leah.'' Angelica put out her hand, smiling at the woman. The slender hand was like a living bird's, trembling faintly. She put Angelica in mind of a small vulnerable creature of the wild ready to take off at the slightest breath of alarm. ''I'm so pleased to meet you. I love the outfit you're wearing. I'd like to wear something like that myself.''

''Then I'll make something for you,'' the young woman announced softly, apparently having made up her mind Angelica was a friend. ''It's hand-painted to my own design.''

''It's beautiful.'' Angelica, very fashion conscious, took a closer look. ''You must be a very good dress-maker, as well,'' she concluded, impressed.

''Learned it off the nuns she did,'' Clary supplied. ''Mission school. Natural talent. 'Course the nuns couldn't teach her how to do all her lovely prints. That's her world. The dreaming. Painting and drawing is your heritage, isn't it, Leah?''

''Yes,'' Leah agreed simply.

''We'll have to talk more about this, Leah,'' Angelica said with some enthusiasm, but aware there was work to be done. ''I'd love to see more of what you do. You wear your own designs beautifully. You could have been a model walking across the room. I expect you know, quite a few indigenous designers are making it in the fashion world. There's a showing heading to Italy right now. I'm of Italian descent.''

''You're beautiful!'' Leah pronounced, pressing a finger to a spot between her brows as though therein lay a third eye. There were no waves of anger or venom around this woman as tall as a queen. Leah with her sad background was very careful about people. ''I could make something to please you,'' she said, studying Angelica's body intently. ''I know your size.''

''Just like that?'' Angelica laughed.

''Just like that.'' Leah nodded, looking up to meet Angelica's smiling eyes. ''You could wear my clothes. Not everyone can.''

''See, you're one of the lucky ones, Angelica,'' Clary said. ''Now come on, Leah, no more chatting, we've got work to do.''

"It's just like the convent." Leah flashed Angelica a white grin, bright little sparks of mischief in her melancholy eyes.

When Angelica walked into the splendid drawing room with gilt stucco work on the ceiling and around a pair of very beautiful gilt mirrors almost the size of the wall, she found Jake staring up at the portrait of his mother. For a moment she hesitated to approach him, sensitive to the feelings that surrounded Roxanne. What was he thinking of? Loss? How beautiful she was? How much he resembled her? How very different his life would have been had she lived? It must have taken a lot of inner strength to have survived his harsh upbringing with his spirit intact.

She was just about to retreat when he turned abruptly, his brilliant amber eyes moving over her from head to toe. "What took you so long?"

She answered with comic gravity. "You'll have to learn patience, Mr. McCord. Actually I wanted to have a word with Clary."

"Ah, yes!" He turned to face her squarely, his mother's painted image for a backdrop.

What a piece of work is man, Angelica thought, lost in admiration. He looked stunning in a collarless cream linen shirt and deeper-toned trousers, the light colour playing up his dark golden skin and bronzed hair.

"Clary's as taken with you as my stepmother and sister," he told her as though she may have developed a practised charm instead of inheriting it in the cradle.

"So tell me, are you feeling better about me?" she asked, with a little challenging smile.

"The points are going up," he assured her. "I know I love that dress."

"Why thank you." She dropped a perfectly balanced little curtsy.

"Are you going to dance for us later?" he asked suavely, his eyes alive with mockery.

"You mean, flamenco?"

"You are sporting that personality surely?"

"Gypsy's in," she told him airily. "It works for me. Actually I'm more interested in one of your employees."

"Oh, hell no!" He turned about.

"Why do you say that?" she asked in astonishment.

"I guess I'll just have to wait for you to tell me."

"Listen, it's Leah," she said. "Leah helps Clary in the kitchen."

"Why thank you for that helpful piece of information, Miss De Campo. I do know Leah."

"Okay, okay, you don't give me much of a chance. Leah is very gifted. She was wearing an outfit that I'd fancy wearing myself."

"See if she'll sell it to you," he suggested sardonically.

"You don't understand." She clicked her teeth in exasperation. "She designed and made it herself. She's good. I know about these things."

"I'm prepared to believe that. I've never seen anyone with so much oomph."

"Can I help it?" she countered. "The thing is, I'd really like to do something for her."

"I'm not going to stop you," he answered mildly. "Leah needs help. She's lived a hard life."

"And you rescued her?" She loved him for being kind.

"My God, years too late!" He sounded angry the young aboriginal woman had had to suffer so much pain and distress. "You'll know from Clary she has a child."

"Kylee. At least she has someone to love," Angelica said thankfully, moving to where he stood, again experiencing a sensuous arousal that was becoming familiar. "Your mother was a glorious-looking woman," she ventured gently, looking up at the painted golden eyes as she had not been invited to before.

"Spoken by a woman who could pass for Venus?"

"You think so?" A little pulse was beating up a storm in her throat.

''Oh, for God's sake, you know you're beautiful,'' he said almost roughly.

''Why do you make that sound like it's just another thing you hate about me?'' Provoked, her reaction was nearly as fierce as his. He was such an unpredictable man.

''I'm just worried you're going to use it on me.''

''On you?'' she asked with scorn. ''I'd have my work cut out.''

''That wouldn't stop you trying.''

''In another minute I'm going to slap you,'' she warned, a non-violent woman aroused.

''What did I tell you? You're a real powerhouse,'' he scoffed, unperturbed.

''You're not exactly...normal, either.'' Not with all those hard, glittery edges.

''And what is your definition of normal, my Angel?'' he asked, looking so deeply into her eyes her mind spun. ''A man who falls instantly under your spell?''

She tried to hold his amber gaze as long as she could without actually drowning. ''You're the most arrogant man I know,'' she muttered.

''You've already figured that out.'' His expression softened miraculously, became almost indulgent. ''Why any minute now we'll have a full-blown argument. Our first. I'm sorry. My mother did teach me manners. You're not exactly a guest, but you're under my roof.''

''And I have my reputation to think about.'' She turned her attention back to the portrait, staring up at the lovely, luminous face. ''You remember her well?''

''I remember some things very clearly. My father was different then. It was the suffering that made him bitter.''

''It must help you to understand that,'' she said. ''It would have been terrible for him to lose the young wife he adored. And in such a way.''

''One of the worst things in life,'' he answered sombrely.

''And for you to lose your mother,'' she added, thinking how it must have been for a small thoughtful child.

"I survived," he told her in a closed-off voice. "Nothing like a touch of the whip to keep you on course."

"It couldn't have been so easy for Stacy and Gillian, either." She was acutely aware of the tension in him. "Women can sometimes seem so much more vulnerable to the lack of love."

"You appear to know a whole lot about my family."

She coloured at his tone. "People have a tendency to confide in me."

"You think I might fit into that category?"

"How could you when you don't even have a basic trust?"

"True." The golden-amber eyes traced a course over her face, throat, to the swell of her breasts. "How did you finally get rid of Trevor?" he asked very softly. Too softly.

She shivered. "I sent my brother Bruno along to explain the situation. I think I told you, Bruno is six-six."

"Yes. That's over my head." He gave an appreciative laugh. "What does Bruno do?"

"He's spectacularly talented like me. He's a sports commentator. He's on TV. He's great-looking."

"I can well believe that. Italians are a very handsome people and you show your heritage."

"A heritage I'm very proud of. When we were kids people used to think we were twins. Anyway, Bruno put the fear of God into Trevor."

"So how did you get involved in the first place?" he asked so abruptly he might have wished to trip her up.

"I told you, but you don't want to believe it."

He shrugged a wide shoulder. "Oh, I want to believe it, Angel, but I really require a little more than your maidenly protestations."

"Your cynicism knows no bounds. Why exactly? Why are you so wary of women or is it just me? Why are you being judge, jury and executioner?"

"In all likelihood I want you to be as good as you're beautiful," he surprised himself by admitting out loud. "To answer your question, I don't exactly know why I'm so hard on you. And it is you. I've never been like this before. Maybe it was the way I was raised." He looked back up at the portrait of his mother. "I never got the chance to know my mother well. All I've had is a portrait of a beautiful woman, forever young, and a few precious memories. I've idealised her so I guess I see a woman who moves me in those terms. Can you understand any of that?"

The seriousness, even the strange appeal in his expression, made her tremble. "Yes I can. You've put your mother up on a pedestal and you expect the woman you want to occupy that lofty position, as well. That presents a dilemma when life is full of pitfalls."

"So you're saying even a woman of honourable intentions can be led astray?" He hated the suavity in his own voice, the cutting edge, when God knows he wasn't what he really intended.

"You can't eradicate Huntley from your mind, can you?" she said, almost sorrowfully. "Probably in the wake of such a dysfunctional childhood and adolescence you back away from powerful attachments. Any excuse might do. The very fact you're not married—"

He held up a lean hand. "Stop trying to push the buttons. You're not here to tell me how to live my life."

"I'm trying to help you." She laid a hesitant hand on his arm. "Moreover I'm trying to help myself. We should be able to talk it over. I don't want one unsavoury incident to spoil any friendship that might be possible between us. But you give me the impression you think I'm the sort of woman who might hurt you."

"Cut me to ribbons?" Unexpectedly, as though she were a princess, he lifted her hand, barely brushing a kiss on her silky skin. Then his velvety eyelids came down heavily over his big cat's eyes. "We've talked enough about me, Angel. You can try to redeem me if you like."

At his touch excitement raged through her. "It's a challenge!" she admitted huskily, seeing the dare in his shimmering glance. A glorious challenge! But was she ready to take it on?

Very slowly, he put a finger to the shallow dimple in her chin. ''And you've a high rate of success.''

''What do you want to hear?'' She stared back at him, willing her heart to settle. ''I've had plenty?''

I don't want another man touching you, he thought, his expression turning stormy. She was so beautiful, that abundant hair flowing around her face and over her shoulders. Her eyes were as dark as night but when she laughed they were filled with little flickering stars. He wanted to kiss her deeply, lavishly, with all the passion that beat in his blood.

''I never believed in a witch until I met you,'' he said, thinking what it would be like to keep her forever.

''Yet you still call me Angel? I have to tell you no one else has called me that.'' It seemed important to bring the fact to his attention. ''You need to think about that, Jake McCord. Because I can't be both.''

The Honourable Charles Middleton turned out to be a very charming young man, carefully dressed for the occasion in a long-sleeved blue shirt with a blue-and-navy-striped tie and jeans that sat neatly on his lanky six-foot frame. He had floppy blond sun-streaked hair, and his fine English skin was perfectly tanned. His eyes in contrast were a heavenly blue. He stared at Angelica, an incredulous expression in those eyes, as if she were a sight he hadn't been prepared for. ''Delighted to meet you, Miss De Campo,'' he said enthusiastically, as if he wouldn't have missed meeting her for the world.

That earned him a hurt look from Gillian, only as he wasn't looking in her direction he missed it.

Jake didn't. Not that he was terribly surprised. Angel was enough to distract any man.

They found their way into the dining room, Charlie exclaiming how delightful it was to be dining there. Usually the family used the smaller informal dining room overlooking the large swimming pool Jake had decided to put in. Angelica had seen it that very afternoon, amazed by the great profusion of blossoming bougainvillea spilling over the roof of the stone pool house.

''This room has such perfect proportions,'' Charlie said, lifting his blond head. ''It reminds me a little of the dining room at home. I expect it's the decorated ceiling and the panels on the walls.''

''Now then, Charlie, you know the dining room at home is at least twice as big,'' Jake said dryly.

''Well it was the banquet hall at one time.'' Charlie gave him a quick, boyish grin. ''There's an immense fireplace in the drawing room. My sister and I used to think it looked like a tomb.''

''You must miss home, Charles?'' Angel asked. Although his name had been cut to Charlie, he was actually much more a Charles in her opinion.

''Oh I do, but I love it here. As someone from a small country, it fascinates me. Australia is so vast. One can travel for days and still be in the same state.''

Gillian held out her hand. ''You must sit beside me, Charlie.''

''Yes of course,'' Charles agreed at once, smiling almost conspiratorially at Angelica.

Dinner went wonderfully well. Charles was an easy conversationalist. He had read widely, travelled widely and was very intelligent. He didn't seem to be attaching the same significance to their friendship as Gilly was, Angelica thought with a little lurch of dismay. The station was so isolated Gilly had little chance of meeting and mixing with eligible young men. Small wonder she had fallen so hard for the handsome Charles.

Leah brought in the entrees, serving quietly and efficiently, giving Angelica a little over-the-shoulder smile as she left to return to the kitchen.

''Does she really have to wear a dress like that?'' asked Gillian.

"I love it." Angelica looked up, surprised. "Don't you?"

"I think a uniform would be more suitable. Father would have insisted she wear one."

"Don't let his snobbery wear off on you, Gilly." Jake spoke quietly, aware his half sister had picked up some of their father's more sorry traits.

"Actually she's a very interesting and charming woman." Without realising, Charles added fuel to the fire. "She paints, as well, adding to her gifts. I've bought a few of her paintings. She sells them for a song. I'm very drawn to them. She uses such vivid, stylised patterns, which obviously mean something."

"They go far beyond decoration," Jake added. "The designs are important. They represent, symbolically, the great ancestral and mythical beings. What I noticed of the design of the dress she has on was magic in nature."

"Really?" Angelica was fascinated, turning her dark head to look straight into his amber eyes. She wanted him to continue but she was aware of Gillian's discomfort.

Gillian cut in, looking stunned. "You've bought paintings off Leah?" She rounded on Charles as though the news had shattered her.

"Gilly, I've often told you how talented Leah is," Jake said quickly, trying to head her off. "You can't have been listening."

"Probably you should look at Leah's paintings yourself, Gilly." Charles tapped Gillian's wrist in a series of rapid, gentle movements. "She'll show you if you ask nicely."

"I don't intend to ask at all." Gillian all but turned up her pert nose.

"Your loss." Charles laughed it off. "I bet she'd show them to you, Angelica." He looked at Angelica across the gleaming table, a bright light in his blue eyes.

"I'd really enjoy that. She's already promised me she'd make me a dress." Angelica looked to Gillian to smile, but there was no smile back. Oh dear, she thinks I'm trying to steal her boyfriend. How unfortunate. Gilly didn't realise there was a man in her life already. A man who made Charles look like a charming boy.

"You wouldn't wear it, would you, dear?" Stacy turned a surprised face.

"Of course I would." The "course" soared in surprise. She really didn't understand Stacy's and Gillian's patronising attitude, which seemed odd to her.

"You've got taste," the egalitarian Charles said, as though that settled it. "You'll look marvellous in it. You have the style to carry off the look. And the dramatic colouring." He put down his knife and fork to steeple his fingers, sitting back in his chair to consider her like a sculpture.

"For what it's worth," Jake said dryly. "I agree. So now we all have something to look forward to. Angelica in her new dress. Probably the symbols will have something to do with woman-magic."

"Oh, I love that!" Charles exclaimed delightedly.

Clary ushered in the main course, which went down very well. "This is absolutely delicious!" Charles gasped, rolling the word on his tongue. "I understand you and Clary put your heads together on the menu, Angelica?"

"Well..." Angelica caught Gillian's sulk and nearly moaned. "Clary did the actual cooking."

"I know you're marvellous, too." Charles seemed quite unaware his little pleasantries were being interpreted by Gillian and her protective mother as unacceptable gush. "I must try to get copies of *Cosima* magazine. I'd love to read your features."

"You're not in need of a husband, are you, Angelica?" Jake quipped lightly at Charlie's expense.

"What, you of all people proposing?" In turn she mocked him, tilting her chin with its provocative dimple.

"Charlie's the one who's getting carried away."

Stacy and Gillian looked at him blankly. "You're joking, aren't you, dear?" Stacy questioned finally.

"Of course I am," he gently teased, thinking Gilly might have to be brought down to earth a bit. Even so, it wasn't the moment to point out Angelica had scored big with the Honourable Charles. Even the way she said his name was having an effect on the effervescent Charlie, much like a glass of champagne.

By the time they finished dessert, the air was literally electric. The heaviness of the impending storm continued while all rain held off. Violent thunder rocked back and forth. Once the great chandeliers dimmed as lightning zigzagged across the sky with a blinding white metallic flash that lit up the long windows.

Angelica jumped in her seat, setting her dangly earrings in motion. "Gosh, this weather is making me very nervous."

To her surprised delight Jake stretched out a reassuring hand to her, touching her bare skin. "Don't let it frighten you." Heat and power flowed from him to her. She thought he could cure her if she were ill.

Afterwards Gillian, a certain determined look in her eye, bore Charles off to hear CDs that had just arrived.

"I'm so sleepy after that wonderful meal I'll probably listen with only half an ear," said Charles.

Not the most lover-like of statements, Jake thought, figuring he would have to review his assessment of the relationship based a lot on hearsay from Gilly that could be little more than feverish wishful thinking.

Stacy might have been reviewing matters, as well. She excused herself, obviously in a bit of a tizzy, saying she had a few little jobs to do without volunteering exactly what they were.

"What do you say we go for a walk?" A bit rattled himself, Jake sought Angelica's satiny bare arm.

"You're asking me to brave the storm?" She stared up at him thinking she would probably go with him to rob a bank.

"It's not a storm. It's a circus out there." Inside, as well, he thought.

"I've been waiting all my life to be hit by lightning," she informed him laconically.

He looked down at her vivid face. Red was her colour.

The colour of passion. Some mouths although not overfull were wonderfully voluptuous. He had a sudden desire to put his hands around her lovely, long throat, thumbs tilting up her chin… "Come on," he said abruptly. "We'll stay on the verandah. But I want a breath of fresh air."

Outside in the night she inhaled the ozone. Great eucalypts reared to either side of the house, branches swishing with the urgency of the wind.

"How would you describe Charlie?" he asked, coming to stand beside her. The long skirt of her dress rippled and twisted around her long legs. Her hair blew free, streaming out behind her. Her profile looked carved.

"Let me see." She turned towards him then laughed when her hair suddenly streamed around her face. "I like him. There's a certain sweetness about him. And he's really classy. Am I getting warm?"

"I'm looking for an answer. To put it bluntly, he was very taken with you."

"Is that an additional sin?" She was stung to defend herself, wondering if it was always going to be like this. "I thought he was just being pleasant."

"Pleasant and very responsive," he said dryly. "What I'm trying to get at is—and after this evening I'm confused—is he romantically interested in Gilly?"

Angel feared he wasn't. Well, not all that much. "Maybe I'm as confused as you are," she evaded.

"I don't think so. You know men."

"Please don't use Trevor Huntley again as an illustration."

"Forget him." Being so near to her was like sinking his head into a bowl of gorgeous red roses coming into full bloom. Somehow, God help him, she ignited the poet in him. Nevertheless he clipped off, "I have a family to protect."

"Gilly has to learn her own lessons," she bravely offered.

"So what are you saying? You don't think Charlie is in love with her?"

"I'm sure he enjoys her company," she said diplomatically. "We all want a bit of excitement in our lives. Gilly is a pretty girl. She could be even prettier with a little help. I'd love to take her shopping. I know exactly how she can bring out her best points.''

He groaned, stepping back. ''Oh, great! Are you sure you shouldn't get into the beauty business?''

''Looking good is my business,'' she said tartly. ''As for Charles...''

''Isn't that darling...Charles.'' He made an excellent job of mimicking her honeyed tones. So good she didn't take offence.

''I must say that's terribly good. Some people say there's a layer of Italian in my accent. You got it just right. Anyway, he is a Charles, isn't he? Not a Charlie. Apart from the fact he's an Honourable—whatever that means—he's simply not the kind of young man one calls Charlie.''

He gave a scoffing laugh. ''Tell that to the boys down at the stockmen's quarters. At least it's better than Charlie the Pom. That's all he got when he arrived.''

''Goodness, what are you people?'' she asked sternly.

Surprisingly he smiled lazily. ''Just having a bit of fun. Charlie stuck it out like the good sport he is. Now they all laugh together.''

''Sadly for Gilly, I think Charles will go home,'' she predicted, staring out into the wild night like she was seeing into the future. ''Probably when he's satisfied his sense of adventure.''

''I told you that,'' he reminded her sarcastically. ''He can't have fallen in love with Gilly if he was so easily taken with you.''

''Ah, then, but I'm a real stunner even if you're indifferent.'' She turned the sarcasm back on him. ''Seriously, and I could be wrong, I think Gilly is in love with love. She can't manage to meet many young men when she lives way out here at the back of beyond. She must be longing for affection.''

''She gets affection.'' His amber eyes turned electric.

She'd have to take a touch more care. ''No need to snap my head off,'' she protested.

''Pardon me. I've spent more time apologising to you than anyone I can think of.''

''I don't think you've spent much time apologising to anyone.'' Having spoken her piece, she bit her lip.

''Shouldn't you mention my arrogance again?''

''Wouldn't it be a good idea if we tried to be friends?''

''I thought we were really good friends already,'' he said, subjecting her to another flashing look.

''Nope.'' She shook her wind-tossed dark curls. ''We're not. We might have been only for a single incident three years ago.''

''You mean, Carly's husband trying to make violent love to you.'' He gave a hoot of derision.

''I was raised in a good Christian environment. You just can't admit it's possible to be tricked.'' Even as she spoke, her anger turned to simple shock. She looked up at the sky, one hand rising to her cheek. ''Isn't that a drop of rain?''

He slumped back against a white vine-wreathed pillar. ''My poor girl, we haven't had rain for a year.''

''I'm not stupid, you know. That's a spit of rain. There there's another one.'' She felt a great wave of something like joy. ''Feel!'' She moved over to him, holding up her face for his touch.

''You've been crying,'' he gently mocked, just barely suppressing his desire to put his hand around her narrow waist and draw her into his arms. What skin she had! God, it was like satin. She was intoxicating. So intoxicating he allowed his hand to drift over her cheek, the tips of his fingers full of sensation. ''Is this another one of your little tricks?'' he asked, coming dangerously close to breaking loose.

''Damn it, Jake.'' His touch made her turbulent, shattering what poise she had left. ''There it is again. Has it got to pelt down before you take any notice?''

He dropped his hand abruptly, refocussing, his nostrils assailed by a new element in the air. Thunder cracked again, splitting open the whole world. A great silver blade of lightning buried itself in the red earth. He was used to this climatic phenomena. He had lived with it all his life. Mostly it was spectacular pyrotechnics resulting in not a single drop of rain. Only this time it was different.

"Fantastic!" Angelica leaned over the balustrade, inhaling deeply the uniquely fresh, subtle perfume of rain. The drops came heavier onto her face, onto the top of the tongue she put out to catch them. She closed her eyes in a kind of rapture. This was what this vast parched Inland craved. Water.

Soon it wasn't enough to stand on the verandah. She had to seize the moment. She stopped only seconds to remove her beautiful expensive sandals then she ran down the low flight of stone steps, calling to Jake over her shoulder, "This is what you want, isn't it?"

Rainwater was streaming over her hair, her forehead and cheeks, down her throat, between her breasts, down over her long cotton voile skirt to her bare feet. Rain, rain, rain! After the heat it was bliss!

But Jake continued to stand on the verandah, leaning hard against the white pillar, hypnotised by the sight of her. She was doing some kind of little rain dance, rivulets of water glittering all over her, causing her red dress to closely mould her body. It almost tore the heart from him. He could feel his sensual response to her in every nerve, every muscle, every fibre. Despite his odd ambivalence, he wanted to go to her, crush her to him, mindless of the inevitable complications. He wanted to hold up her face to him, kiss that luscious, alluring mouth. He wanted to hear her moan his name. Not Jake. Jonathon. He wanted to hear his name again after all these years. Unparalleled in his experience, he wanted this woman. He wanted to kiss every inch of her naked, delectable, pliant flesh.

Getting soaking wet didn't concern her in the least. Her graceful movements, incredibly erotic to his eyes, began to change. Incredible! She had moved into a different kind of dance, a gypsy flamenco with its unique heart-stirring steps.

''Just for you,'' she called, lifting her long beautiful arms above her head while she stamped her bare feet on the glistening earth. She was the very image of a beautiful, seductive gypsy woman, confident in her powerful allure, indeed glorying in it, while he stood before her spellbound.

Then like a miracle, as if she read his every desire, she cried out to him breathlessly, ''Jonathon, what are you doing up there? Come to me. It's so wonderful!''

He needed no further invitation, his passions inflamed. His strong tanned hands clenched and unclenched. How had she known to call him Jonathon? Was it possible this woman dabbled in magic? He believed now that certain women down the ages were capable of witchcraft.

He came to her as sleekly, as powerfully, as a big cat. It even had a hint of violence in it, as though he were responding to something primitive in him. He was vaguely aware the rain was coming down heavier now. But his need to take hold of this woman was so overwhelming it became his sole interest. When he reached her, hauling her to him, his hands on her shoulders, they both gasped with the shock and excitement of it, stumbling backwards until they were totally obscured by the great golden canes, tremulously singing some kind of wind song.

Their fronds parted to contain and cocoon them as he folded her tight into his body, silencing her little jagged gasps as he took her lush mouth.

It was an explosion of desire such as he had never known. An assuagement of some deep permanent hunger. His hands were bold. They went where they wanted. To her beautiful breasts, almost too womanly, too voluptuous, for a man to bear, the nipples tight as berries, inviting the further stimulation of his fingers. He wanted her, nothing more, nothing less. He was holding her to him, his left hand locked strongly to her back. Her long dress was so wet, so slick against her body, he could have peeled it from her.

Either the kiss had gone on and on or he was kissing her again while she arched against him, mouth open, body yielding as though his sudden onslaught had gained him total dominion. When he finally came halfway to his senses, he jerked back his head, letting his hands fall to her golden hips. They were surrounded by a wilderness of wet greenery and silver rain and the heady fragrance released from the beds of white lilies that grew beneath the trees. Little tremors were flickering through his arms. He craved this woman. This purely dangerous woman who could inspire so much rapture. The rain was still falling. Real rain pouring out of the sky. He had never known anything like it The wild improbability of it all! For a woman never lost for a word, she was very quiet, weakened perhaps by the powerful momentum of his desire, as stormy and tumultuous as the elements.

''Are you all right? Tell me,'' he muttered, his voice deepened by emotion, his arm still tight around her.

But Angelica was reeling from the power of the feeling he'd unleashed. Strangely, when she no longer was, she felt like a virgin only just awakened to the full blinding rush of physical passion.

''Angel, why you?'' he asked in a dark, near melancholy voice.

That released her. Slowed the wild beating of her heart.

''Because I'm here?'' She threw up her expressive head to challenge him. A tall woman with her own tensile strength.

''You are.'' A flame jumped back and forth between them that could not be extinguished by rain, caution, or lack of trust. ''And it's magic!'' He pressed a finger into the hollow of her rain-slicked neck. The pulse was hammering. He left his finger there hoping that through her pulse he could hold on to her heart.

All hostility seemed to drain away. ''The rain tastes sweet,'' she whispered. ''Isn't that strange?''

''Nothing's strange with you.'' He spread his long tanned fingers over her throat, dipping his head so he could run his tongue over her wet cheek, gathering up the delicious moisture. His vibrant voice was almost dreamy. ''I want to make love to you, you know that?''

Yes, oh yes! She thought blindly. Tonight. For the longest, longest time. Until dawn. Everything about him called to her like a voice she was programmed to obey. Now his mouth brushed against her sensitive neck, moving back and forth.

Excitement flowed into her so she was near oblivious to the streaming rain and the pungent steam that rose from the hot earth and the tiled walkways. Tendrils of wet curls fell on her brow and her cheeks like ribbons of silk. The paradox of it all! She felt marvellously safe within his arms, and yet endangered, knowing full well this man could reach in and steal her heart.

''Jonathon, it's so sudden,'' she murmured, as his mouth sought hers again. ''Sexual attraction can't be all there is.'' Even as she protested, that same attraction was pushing her to the edge.

''Why Jonathon?'' he demanded urgently. ''Whatever prompted you to call me that? And why now? Are you mocking me?''

She was shocked he might think so. ''But your name is Jonathon. Isobel told me it was your father who renamed you Jake.''

''And you suddenly remembered?''

''Stop it.'' She lifted a hand to his mouth as if to silence him. ''If you don't want me to call you Jonathon, I won't.''

She sounded so upset he found himself full of remorse, cradling her. ''Hushhhhhhh... I do like it,'' he told her tenderly. ''You have a gift.'' It was so wonderful he couldn't properly interpret it. He could only recognise there was far more to what had passed between them than a man's driving passion and need for release. He wanted to mate with this woman. He wanted to take her to bed. At that moment he couldn't care less about old indiscretions.

Except that wasn't entirely true. He wanted her to be utterly faithful. To him. He wasn't fully aware of the extent of his needs. He only knew she was very, very special. And there was something else he was forced to consider. Once he let her into his heart she could very easily go away. He knew all about loss.

Sweet God, he had to be out of his mind. He stepped back so quickly Angelica staggered and had to clutch at his soaked shirt. "We have to get you out of this wet gear," he muttered, trying to dispel the tremendous build-up of intimacy between them with a certain curtness of tone. The skin of her face, throat and arms was shimmering with the lustre of a golden South Sea pearl. It seemed a whole lifetime had passed while they were cocooned together amid the storm-tossed palms. Time out of mind.

On the path she began to shiver and he pulled her drenched figure to him, angling his head and body so he was protecting her from the silver, slanting rain. "Are you cold?"

"A little bit." She knew it was a reaction to the loss of his body heat.

"We'll go in by the rear staircase. I'm astounded no one has come out to greet our small miracle. Maybe they're on the verandah."

The rain that had so passionately cracked down turned off like a tap. By the time they stumbled into the rear hall with the wind hammering at their backs it seemed to be all over. They could hear the sound of laughter coming from somewhere upstairs then rapturous clapping.

"That's them!" Jake said, looking down at the puddles of water at their feet. "Stay here for a moment. I'll grab a few towels. Better yet we'll try the first-aid room." He ushered her down the polished cedar-wood hallway to a doorway on the right. He lifted his hand and the light snapped on, revealing a large, white-tiled room with a high bed like those one saw in a doctor's room, and rows of glass-fronted white cabinets holding an array of medical things.

"You really should get that dress off," he said, his gaze going over her. In the glare from the fluorescent lights she still managed to look stunning, soaked to the skin, even though she'd gone from seductive gypsy to drenched woman, her gleaming hair separating into long ebony curls.

''The towel will have to do,'' she said, shaking her hair back and scattering spray. ''I'm not really cold. It's a reaction.''

''It wasn't what you were expecting,'' he said, a little raggedly, walking away to a cupboard and taking out a pair of large white towels. ''Here, catch.''

Instantly she held up her hands like the athlete she'd been. ''Got it.''

He laughed as some of the tension was cut, using a towel on himself. ''Another one for your hair.'' This time he located a hand towel, but instead of tossing it to her as before he came to stand behind her, gathering up her long hair to dry it.

''No need!'' She was quivering and breathless standing so close, aware how terribly exciting he was to her.

''But I want to.'' His voice was exquisitely gentle, doubly sensual because of it. ''Go ahead, wrap yourself in that towel.''

She obeyed, slinging the towel around her hips, sarong-style. ''What would you say is your real problem with me?'' she asked, wishing and wishing they hadn't started off so badly.

''You make me confused,'' he said with a fine edge of despair, bending his head and kissing her shoulder, then moving the neck of her dress to kiss the other. ''Why aren't you married, beautiful Angelica? A woman like you with this mane of black silk. It's superb.''

''Why aren't you?'' she countered, thinking she had never known such a wide range of sensations.

''I've never met a woman who possessed magic.''

''And I've never met the right man. Not one who could offer me more than passing pleasure.''

''You mean no dangerous rapture?'' He turned her to face the wall mirror, the difference in their colouring startling.

''Isn't that what we all want, after all?'' she asked wistfully.

''And seldom get. Even then there's a price.''

His eyes were glittering like wonderful topaz, the kind of stones princes of old used to keep for themselves. Neither of them moved. Neither of them seemingly capable of fighting out of their emotional bounds.

A laughing English voice suddenly echoed through the hallway, releasing them instantly. "I say, you two. Where are you?"

"Here, Charlie," Jake called. "The first-aid room."

"Good grief! Everything okay?" Charlie appeared in the open doorway, his look of concern turning into one of enjoyment. "You've been out in the pouring rain. Isn't that exactly what I wanted. I was mad to tear down the stairs only Gilly didn't want to get wet. Some Aussie she is when she shudders at life in the great outdoors."

"Hi, Charlie," Jake said.

"Not intruding, am I?" Now Charlie sounded a little awkward.

"Believe me, you are. Angelica and I were considering whether we should top off the evening by making violent love," Jake told him dryly.

"What!" Charlie near choked, wedging himself against the door in shock, even if Jake had used a light satiric tone. "I suppose it is almost the night for it."

"He's joking, Charles." Angelica calmed him. "Far more important to get dry. But that was a marvellous downpour. Hasn't it cooled the air!"

"And so unexpected." Charlie was fascinated by Angel's appearance, more gypsy-ish than ever and marvellously sexy. He had never seen a woman look like that in the rain before. "We've had storm-clouds darkening the sky night after night." He looked to Jake. "Heavens knows what happened tonight. A meteorologist could explain it. Usually it all goes away. Now this!"

"A miracle! Here's to our Christmas Angel," Jake said suavely, with an elegant bow in Angelica's direction. "Angelica De Campo. A woman like no other."

"I'll second that!" Charlie's voice was saturated with boyish enthusiasm.

One stormy night on Coori station and her whole life had changed course.

CHAPTER SIX

SHE was awake at first light, fascinated by the sounds of the birds. Never in her life had she heard such a glorious din. Indeed the birdsong was so loud, so sweetly piercing, she found it impossible to stay in bed. She had been given what was virtually a suite, a huge bedroom, dominated by a marvellous four-poster with carved columns—Stacy had told her Jake's great-grandfather had brought it back from India along with many other pieces of furniture and artifacts in the house. The bed was hung with ivory voile to keep out insects.

There was an adjoining bathroom that was very Victorian in its splendour—a lion-clawed bath, rich dark timberwork, rose-trellised leadlight window. On the other side of the bedroom there was a pretty sitting room-study. Now she threw back the sheer hangings, which gave her such a sense of fantasy, and swung her feet to the carpeted floor. The light was increasing. Golden rays were cutting through the pearl-grey and lemon. She had slept soundly as though those long minutes of aching passion had weakened her to the point that all she could do was sleep to regain her strength.

He hadn't come to her room. She didn't know what she would have done if he had. Exactly the same thing as had happened when they were lost in the storm? She was convinced the storm had been the propellant. It had the quality of magic about it. It had stirred her to dance in front of him, in a way that must have seemed related to a dance of seduction. Whatever it was, it had electrified him, making him for a short time lose control. But there had been other emotions merged with his desire. She had felt them. Apprehension? Remembered pain? The terrible pain when his mother had been ripped out of his life? A subconscious desire never to go through that pain again? Or the thought of one humiliating moment out of time he couldn't let go of. She even had to consider that other woman who had hurt him years ago and forever made him wary. Jake was, after all, a man of deep feelings.

Sighing quietly, Angel walked out onto the wide balcony. She hadn't bothered to put on her robe. It was dawn. Who would be around? The front of the house overlooked a great expanse of lawn, trees and circular gardens, all fed by bore water. The homestead by everyday standards was enormous. She thought it would take her weeks to get around it. Built of rosy bricks, it presented the formality and symmetry of a Georgian building set down in the vast, timeless grandeur of the Outback. It was two-storied with deep verandahs supported by soaring white columns all vine-wreathed with a beautiful mauve flower. The rooms were set out in line across the facade, with main reception rooms downstairs, bedrooms up, all rooms fitted with white-painted French doors and frosty-white decorative ironwork to enclose the surrounding verandahs. It was a splendid house that must have conjured up nostalgic memories of the homeland and the old life that was missed, all the more extraordinary because of its wild, remote setting.

It had seemed to her as she'd been shown through the house that while the furnishings, Persian rugs and paintings were magnificent, some refurbishing was in order. Money to bring in expert interior designers didn't appear to be the problem. Obviously Stacy had decided to leave well enough alone. Maybe she needed some encouragement. Jake—why had she been inspired to call him Jonathon last night? Was some spirit voice prompting her? She really didn't know—couldn't be expected to take on domestic matters when he had a huge enterprise to run. Had she been one of the McCord women she wouldn't have hesitated to have a go. New curtains for the Yellow Drawing Room would make a difference. The ones that were, though they must have been splendid when they first went up, had been allowed to fade, their golden radiance dimmed.

She realised with some amusement she was the sort of woman who was always looking to improve her surroundings. If she hadn't gotten into the food business, she would liked to have been an interior designer. That was her artistic streak. Her mother always said she had one. At least dinner last night had been a minor triumph. The master of the house, hungry after a long day's work, and his surprisingly privileged jackeroo had little difficulty polishing it off, their appreciation evident. Even Stacy and Gilly, usually light eaters, had found everything satisfying.

As she approached the wrought-iron balustrade, her satin nightdress falling opalescent around her, the horizon was suddenly gilded by a great ball of fire. Kookaburras broke into their demented cackling, a sound, nevertheless that touched her heart. She drew in a deep breath of air washed clean by that marvellous downpour of rain then lifted her arms above her, stretching…stretching…rising up onto her toes. She had just about redesigned her body over the last two years going to the gym. Now she couldn't help knowing she had a great body, but it hadn't come easily. Let's face it, she had to stick with the program and watch her diet when she was surrounded by abundant, delicious food. Of course she and Bruno broke out from time to time especially when they went over to their parents' for Sunday brunch.

A man's voice called to her. "If you bent over right now I bet you could touch your toes."

Her flush was merciless, staining her cheeks. Immediately she arched back, dropping her arms, hoping he couldn't see through her nightdress. To counter that, she stepped away from the balustrade, lest she be caught in the sun's early rays.

"What are you doing up here invading my privacy?" It came out halfway between a reprimand and an expression of pleasure.

He smiled lazily, already fully dressed in his working gear, which suited him marvellously. Bush shirt, jaunty bright blue bandana carelessly knotted around his throat, fitted jeans, high boots. The only thing missing was the cool black akubra. ‘‘I have a right, don’t you think?’’ he countered mildly. ‘‘I do own the place.’’

‘‘I wasn’t expecting you right outside my bedroom door.’’ She was suddenly as nervous as a kitten. Should she rush inside and collect her matching satin robe?

‘‘I figured it was all right, now it’s morning.’’ He answered with a touch of sarcasm.

‘‘You didn’t really think we were going to sleep together?’’ She held his gleaming gaze in case it fell to the telltale quick rise and fall of her breasts.

‘‘Then you’d better not lead me into temptation,’’ he warned. ‘‘What was that exciting little dance you did last night?’’

‘‘And didn’t you love it!’’ she softly mocked, lifting her chin and spreading her hands in an exaggerated flamenco pose. ‘‘It started out as an ode to the rain god. I presume there is one around here?’’

‘‘Very much so,’’ he confirmed, looking so sexy she thought his whole aura would engulf her. ‘‘Apparently your dance was so good he thought he’d reward you. Only one downpour, but you’ll be surprised what a difference it’ll make.’’

‘‘So I’ll have to do more dancing,’’ she said, aware of the sudden acceleration of her pulses.

‘‘I don’t know if my heart can take it.’’

‘‘Mine, either. Listen, do you mind if I get my robe?’’

He continued to walk towards her taking in that beautiful body encased in satin. ‘‘When you look absolutely luscious as you are.’’ His amber eyes were so brilliant they momentarily blinded her to her surroundings.

‘‘I’ll be back in a moment,’’ she promised.

‘‘Hurry. Because I want to have breakfast with you. Tell me, do you ride?’’

She paused in the act of shouldering into her peach satin robe. ‘‘As in trains, buses?’’

''As on horses.''

She stepped back onto the verandah, tying the braided, silken cord. ''Could I fake it?''

''No. Absolutely no. So you don't ride?''

''Why so scathing?'' she said defensively. ''I thought I was here to handle the Christmas functions. Which reminds me, I'm going to order the biggest tree I can get. It has to be synthetic. Spruce or something. As long as it's big. Is that okay? I'll arrange to have it flown in.''

''From the sound of your voice I'm meant to acquiesce.''

She curled her lovely mouth into a smile. ''Does that mean yes?''

He nodded his head, a mass of deep sun-streaked amber waves, grown a little long on the nape. ''When my mother was alive we had a tree. After she was killed everything stopped. All the fun. All the laughter. The only laughs I got were at boarding school and later at university.''

''Well, don't feel down. We're going to have a wonderful Christmas tree this year. I know the exact place for it.''

''So you've said. Where?''

''As it turns out we have to shift something,'' she said.

''What?'' He turned directly to face her, his expression rather tense.

''The library table,'' she said. ''Don't worry, it's going back.''

''Why not put it to one side of the entrance hall?''

''No, no, you have to indulge me in this,'' she said. ''Dead centre is perfect. That's the most commanding position and we can all see it in the round. Besides, the entrance hall is huge. Guests will be able to move around the tree easily providing they don't go mad and crowd it.''

''My mother used to have it there,'' he said, his gaze moving away from her to the horizon.

''Then that's lovely, isn't it?'' Angel said gently, thinking the spirit of Roxanne could be helping her.

Jake moved towards her with his silent, big-cat tread. ''Why is it I want to kiss you every time I lay eyes on you?''

"Could it be because you're falling in love with me?" she asked, full of hope, while wonderful sensations began their glide all over her skin.

"Haven't you got enough men in love with you?" He wanted to touch her urgently.

"They're in love with my cooking."

"Though very good I'm sure it's the least of your charms." He surrendered to that driving impulse. He dipped his head, very gently, but so tantalisingly covering the full sensuous curves of her mouth with his own. "Could you really love me, mixed-up mortal man?"

How could she answer when her knees were buckling?

It was ages before either of them could come up for air. Both of them were in very deep.

"I could pick you up and carry you back into the bedroom," he told her huskily, the very thought making his head swim. "You're not a virgin."

"For heaven's sake, I'm twenty-five. How many lovers have you had?" She turned it back on him.

"Collectively?" He nipped her lips gently with his beautiful white teeth.

"The family friend Dinah Campbell, I'm sure. You're a bit casual about her. Isn't she flying in Friday?"

"Hell, is she?" He released her abruptly.

"Surely you knew?" she asked in amazement. "Didn't Gilly tell you? Don't you want her to come?"

"Questions, questions," he moaned. "Dinah's coming over for one thing, I'm sure."

"She's lonely when she's not in your bed?"

His shoulders moved impatiently. "Would you believe she's never been in my bed?"

"Noooo."

"It might be every girl's dream, but not in my bedroom," he scoffed. "When I have had an affair, it's been elsewhere. No, Angelica, Dinah is coming over to check you out. She wanted to handle all the functions, you know."

"I guessed as much." Angelica arched her beautifully marked black brows. "Is she up to the job?"

"Probably," he mused, stroking his clean-cut chin.

"Then why bother with me?" She put him on the spot.

"Isobel recommended you and you charmed me when you rang."

"Of course you had no idea who I was then."

"No, I found out too late." He dredged that up, not even knowing why.

It had quite an effect on Angelica. She turned on her heel. "What a rotten thing to say. You really are a bastard."

He laughed, despite himself. "So I am. I'm sorry."

"No you're not sorry," she said sternly. "You'll say something like that again, because you're so judgmental."

"And there's the rub. I'm not usually," he said, following her into the bedroom. "It has something to do with you, my angel."

"Amoral old me." She sailed into the dressing room and began pulling out clothes. "You've got to put a stop to this, Jonathon."

He had almost made it to the door, thinking he had better leave, now he snaked out a long arm, grasping her around the waist. "Show me how."

"You want me to get in touch with your cousin first. I was the victim then. I don't want to be now."

"Sure," he sighed. "But why did Carly believe you had an affair with her husband?" Through the thrum of conflict, he was aware of the tremendous intimacy that was building up between them. He could feel her trembling. He could feel her magical body through the shining satin. She was taking him places where he had never been before. Inciting emotions that made him say contrary things to her.

Her voice was torn. "This is unbearable." She made a half-hearted movement to get away from him. "Your cousin couldn't have named me at all. Why don't you speak to her, you're such a doubting Thomas? Then, maybe, we can start all over again." She stared briefly into his eyes. Found them strangely troubled. "You'd better go now." Before this tiny scuffle tipped into something else.

"I don't think I can move from this spot."

She turned her head away, feeling close to tears. "What do you want of me, Jonathon? We scarcely know one another yet here we are—"

"Desperate to fall back on that bed," he completed her thought, his voice quiet and contemplative. "It can't be all that unusual to want a woman on sight."

"You must go," she said. "Really."

He grasped a handful of her hair and tilted up her head. "Why don't I just lock the door?"

She shook her head. "Because you think I'm a bad girl."

"No. Maybe I'm afraid of you. Of what you could do to me." He began shaking out her sleep-tousled hair. It was like skeins of heavy silk.

"Talk to me, Jonathon." She found herself winding her arms around him, almost protectively. "How could you be afraid of me? Why?"

"God knows! Feelings," he said, resting his chin on her head. "So much so soon it's like an avalanche. I didn't even know you, yet I hated seeing Huntley's hand on you. Hated him. My reaction was so excessive I veered away from remembering. Yet you stayed with me only to be brought forth in my dreams."

"As I remembered you," she confided, looking back over the intervening three years.

There was such a sweetness, an understanding to her tone he found himself continuing the moments of self exploration. "It's that loathing of Huntley, my disgust at his callous hand that makes me say harsh things," he said, shadows gathering on his golden-bronze face. "My father had the cruellest tongue and a way of glaring. I guess I worry there's more than a bit of him in me after all."

"You're not cruel, Jonathon," she said, shaking her head, imagining him as a defenceless child taking that kind of treatment from a formidable father.

''God, I hope not!'' His voice carried the sounds of his deepest concerns. ''You have that healing touch. It's true, isn't it, Angel?'' He looked down, his gaze irresistibly zooming in on her mouth, a natural tender red like crushed strawberries. He couldn't look at it without putting his own mouth to it, covering the plush, receptive surface.

A moment of sliding back into a dream world, then he put her away from him. ''You're right, I shouldn't be here. I should be doing my job. I have a station to run. But first, I want you to have breakfast with me.''

''I'll get breakfast for you, you mean,'' she told him eagerly, swinging about to spy out her clothes. ''I promise you you'll lick the plate clean.''

He laughed and walked to the door, moved by her soft, lovely mood. ''In return I'll find the time to teach you to ride,'' he promised, and sketched a brief salute. ''Ten minutes. No more.''

She waved him away, suddenly incredibly happy. ''I'm aiming for five.''

The rest of the day passed very swiftly. There was much to be done. In Clary she had a fine, capable, enthusiastic lieutenant ready to do everything to make these Christmas celebrations work. Even Stacy and Gillian got into the spirit of it. It was clear they found her quite unthreatening, indeed they all did quite a lot of laughing as Angelica took them through her plans for the various functions one by one. ''I think I might like Leah in on this,'' Angelica announced at one point. ''If you all agree she's gifted—and she certainly is if you consider the sheer professionalism of that dress—she'll be able to help out with the decoration.''

''But Mum and I want to decorate the tree, Angelica.'' Gilly looked dismayed. ''We'd love to get involved.''

''But of course. It's your home, Gilly. I'm only here as co-ordinator and supervisor. I'm talking about the Great Hall for Leah.''

''Oh, that's all right then.'' Gilly looked relieved. ''As

long as we don't have dear Dinah getting into the act. Mum and I aren't keen on Dinah." Her pretty mouth thinned.

"We should be able to avoid that," Angelica said hopefully. "I've spoken to Jake about the tree. We're going to shift the library table so it can soar dead centre."

"Shift the library table!" Stacy echoed, as though that was absolutely the worst thing that could happen. "But the library table has always been there, dear."

"Then it's time we shifted it. For the occasion anyway," Angelica coaxed. "Trust me, Stacy. It will look wonderful there."

"Yes, Mum, let Angelica handle it." Gilly joined forces. She let her blue eyes rest on Angel's tall, striking figure. Everything about her was perfect, she thought. Even her height, though she wouldn't want to be so tall herself. Angelica was wearing a simple pink top, but in a very nice sort of slinky fabric, teamed with a full pink skirt printed with huge cyclamen peonies. Not a dress-up outfit but it looked great. "I bet you brought some beautiful dresses with you," Gillian said wistfully. "If you had a moment I'd love you to take a look at what I'll be wearing. Compared to you it's all out of date. Mum and I haven't bought a thing since the last time we went shopping in Sydney. That was eighteen months ago." She groaned and let her head fall forward on the table.

"Your clothes are lovely, Gilly darling," Stacy remonstrated as if Gillian didn't fully appreciate how fortunate she was.

"No they're not, Mum. You're way behind the times." Gillian tugged rebelliously at her shirt.

"I'm sure Angelica can give you some guidance, pet." Clary patted Gillian's arm. "Why when you're all dolled up you look lovely. You too, ma'am." She nodded at Stacy. "If I was you two, I'd really go to town for the parties. Give everyone a surprise."

"But you're coming, too, Clary," Angel said. She didn't want Clary left out.

''I'm tempted to.'' Clary's cheeks went hot and ruddy with surprise.

''But of course you must!'' Stacy's face lit up as though she'd only that minute thought of it. ''You've been an absolute rock.''

''That I have!'' Clary nodded her agreement, not one to hide her light behind a bushel.

''Well, that's settled.'' Angelica looked around with satisfaction. ''We might arrange a private dressing-up, but it has to be soon just in case we decide on something completely different.''

''How? Isn't it all too late?'' Gillian looked like she mistrusted her hearing.

''Never too late,'' Angel assured her blithely. ''I have friends all over, including designers and boutique owners. Clever people who know how to dress their clients. All you need is the money.''

''We have it if we need it,'' Stacy offered, pretty much like a schoolgirl. ''Jake handles all the money. We can get it from him.''

To Angelica, the modern working woman, that was quite bizarre. It seemed Victorian in fact. She turned to Clary for a little relief. ''So you'll speak to Leah when she comes in?'' Clary rolled up her sleeves.

''Better yet I'll get her up to the house and you can speak to her.''

''Lovely.''

Angelica was in Jake's study, sending off a batch of e-mails to various distributors when Leah, wearing another one of her enchanting hand-painted dresses, tapped gently on the door.

''You wanted to see me, Miss?''

Angelica clicked the e-mail away and looked up to smile. ''Yes, Leah. Come in and take a seat. Mr. McCord has very kindly allowed me to use his study.'' She broke off as she realised Leah wasn't alone. Almost hidden behind her mother's skirt was one of the most adorable little girls Angelica had ever seen. She had a wonderfully engaging face and the huge melting black eyes of her mother, but her skin was a shade or two lighter and she had a head full of stunning toffee-coloured curls.

"You must be Kylee," Angelica said, delighted by the child. "How are you?"

The little girl grinned shyly but didn't speak, bunching her mother's skirt with her hand.

Leah gave her a little prod as though the child's silence might give offence. "Say hello to Miss."

Angelica heard the anxiety, felt a pang of pity. "That's all right, Leah," she said easily, thinking life for Leah must have been a grim business.

"She's shy."

"Hello, Miss," the child, knowing she was being talked about, piped up. Her bright expression turned earnest.

"It's lovely to meet you, Kylee. Come take a seat beside Mummy. We need to talk about all the Christmas parties we're going to have."

"With presents?" The very idea gave Kylee a huge buzz. She made a sudden rush for a chair and in the process took a tumble on the slightly raised edge of the Persian rug.

"Silly girl!" Anxiously Leah scooped her daughter up and deposited her rather hard into the leather chair. "I'm sorry, Miss," she apologised as though Angel was about to remonstrate. "I shouldn't have brought her."

"Whyever not? I love children. I'm a proud aunt already. My brother, Bruno, has a little boy just turned two. I'm godmother to two others. The children of girlfriends. Relax, Leah, everything is fine. What I want is to enlist your help with the decoration of the Great Hall. It will be in use for the Polo Ball. You're a creative person. You might be able to come up with some ideas? I believe in consulting clever people."

"Me, Miss?" Leah looked astounded.

"Yes, you, Leah." Angelica laughed. "Is that totally unexpected? Please call me Angelica, or Angie, if you like.'' She looked steadily into the young woman's eyes.

''Better not, Miss,'' Leah said simply. ''No one has ever asked me to do anything before.''

''Well this is your big chance.'' Angelica leaned forward encouragingly.

''Are children coming?'' Kylee chirruped.

''I told you you must be quiet, Kylee,'' her mother warned in a quick aside.

''All you children are coming to the staff barbecue,'' Angelica told the child kindly, trying to see beyond Leah's uptight manner to what experiences lay behind it. ''And there will be presents.''

Immediately Kylee started to bounce up and down in her chair when oddly her mother seemed distressed.

''Why, Leah, whatever's wrong?'' Angelica asked in quick concern.

''No one likes me. Or her.'' Leah dashed a hand across her cheek.

''That can't be right.'' Angelica curled her fingers tightly around her pen, almost as if she were going into battle.

''That's the way it is, Miss.'' Leah's long curly black lashes languished on her cheeks. ''I want everyone to like me but they don't. The station ladies, they don't like me. They don't want Kylee to play with their kids.''

''Have you any idea why?'' Angelica was amazed.

''Oh, different things,'' Leah said vaguely. ''I can't talk to people like I want. I can't say, hello Mick, hello Vince. I tell you, them women are funny. They think I want to take their man away. 'Course I don't. I learned men are cruel. Me own man left me. Took off whoosh, just like that the minute he knew I was pregnant. Reckoned it wasn't his. Reckoned it could have been anybody's. It was his all right. He knew.''

''Life has been hard for you, Leah,'' Angelica said, seeing that Leah needed lots of loving care let alone repair. ''Where did you get that scar?'' It was the first time Angelica had seen it. Leah wore her shoulder-length dark hair side parted and falling forward onto her cheeks. Now as she spoke she pushed the heavier side behind her ear, revealing a long welt of a scar running from temple to ear.

''The old man.'' Leah winced, putting her fingers to it. ''Ran at me with a bottle,'' she said with droll disdain. ''Drunk. Saturday night. Wasn't good to me. Reckon I'd be dead only Mr. McCord found out about me and Kylee and offered me a job at the homestead helpin' out. I'll never be able to thank him, but I try. I like it here at the house. Clary is kind to me. And my little one.'' She pointed a finger at Kylee who tried to grab it.

''But of course.'' Looking at Leah with her delicate exotic looks, a by-product of her mixed blood, Angelica could well see why some of the station wives might be wary of the effect of those looks on their menfolk. At the same time she felt Leah in her vulnerability of body and mind was seeing antipathy where there was none. She thought she might call a meeting of the station wives, citing plans for the staff barbecue as the reason. It would present an opportunity to find out why Leah should consider herself and her child outsiders. There were always two sides to a story.

Almost without thinking Angel hunted up a small notepad and a pencil and held it out across the table. ''Would you like to draw like Mummy, Kylee?'' she suggested to keep the child entertained.

Without a second's hesitation Kylee scrambled out of the chair and dashed around the desk. ''Is this mine?'' She grabbed the pad and pencil.

''If you want it to be.'' Angelica didn't think the station would miss a small notepad and pencil.

Kylee jumped back and laughed merrily. ''I like you, Miss. You're nice. Other ladies tell me to be still when I can't be still.''

''What other ladies?'' Angelica looked to Leah.

''The Missus and Miss Gillian don't like Kylee running around the house.'' Leah squeezed her elegant fingers together. "She gets away from me sometimes when I work. She's a real little monkey."

Moments later four-and-a-half-year-old Kylee jumped up and presented Angel with her finished oeuvre.

"Goodness me!" Angel held the drawing in her hands, amazed at how easily and swiftly the child had done it. It wasn't the typical simple four-year-old drawing. It was of a tree. A quite extraordinary tree with thick gnarled branches and prop roots rising out of swift impressions of rocks and tufts of grass. "Kylee, this is very good," she said, much surprised. "I like it very, very much. Aren't you a clever girl." Clearly, Kylee, like her mother, had a gift.

"She knows her alphabet. She can count. She can spell lots of words," Leah said proudly. "Better than me. The nuns could teach me how to sew but they couldn't teach me anything else. I never saw much of the classroom. I had to help a lot with me foster mum."

"Were you happy there?" Angel had grave misgivings about the foster mum.

"I hated her," Leah said. "And him. Especially him."

Angelica very nearly moaned, thanking God for her parents and her happy childhood. "Well you've produced a very talented little girl." She tried to console. "This drawing I'm sure is far beyond her age ability. It looks like a real tree."

"It is." Leah gave Angel a kind of challenging look as though a white woman, however nice, couldn't possibly know. "This tree has great power. Kylee and me often go there to talk to it. It's one of the old spirits."

"It actually looks like one," Angelica said. "I'm going to keep this, Kylee," she told the child gently, "and I'm going to find you some drawing books and coloured pens and pencils. Would you like that?"

"To take home?" Kylee asked, her eyes huge.

"Where is home?" Angelica turned in the swivel chair to ask Leah.

Leah gave a radiant smile. "Mr. McCord give us a nice

bungalow. Best place I ever lived in in me life. I can show you if you like.''

''Yes I do like, Leah.'' Angelica leaned back in the deep comfortable desk chair. ''I just can't quite figure out how I'm going to do it, but I'd like to help you. We can arrange a time for me to see your dress designs and your paintings. Charles Middleton told me he's bought a few off you and they're very good. I'm sure Charles would know.''

''And who might Charles Middleton be?'' Leah giggled.

''Why, Charlie, the jackeroo.''

''Oh, Charlie!'' Leah rolled her eyes. ''He's nice. He's funny. He's never been mean to me.''

''I should think not,'' Angelica said. ''Charlie is a gentleman. You'll have to tell me who is mean to you, Leah. We'll take it up with Mr. McCord. For now I want to tell you my idea for a theme for the Polo Ball. I was going to get someone in, though I fancy I've left it a bit late, but maybe you could handle what I have in mind. With your aboriginal blood you'd have great affinity with the land, this extraordinary channel country. I'm thinking of a mural. A kind of dream landscape. Dreamtime, if you like. Sun, rocks, billabongs, waterlilies, all those marvellous birds, the vivid coloration that comes as such a shock. On the ceiling, and perhaps a little down the walls, depending on how you feel and how it turns out.''

Leah almost jumped out of her chair. ''On the ceiling? You mean, like Michelangelo?'' she asked with a great flare of interest. ''The Sistine Chapel in Rome?''

''You know all about it?'' Okay, Angelica thought, I'm surprised.

Leah smiled, looking happy and in the process quite beautiful. ''I love looking at books about painting and artists. Only books I like. That would be a wonderful idea, but I'd have to do it all the time so I couldn't work here. I'd have to have ladders and trestles and everything.'' She threw out her arms as if to say this venture was on the level of building a city bridge.

''We'd better get cracking then,'' Angelica said. ''I want other things to figure in that landscape, Leah. It's a polo theme. Would it be pushing it to ask if you can draw animals.''

'''Course I can draw animals,'' Leah lightly scoffed. ''What kind of animals? It's not gunna be kangaroos?''

''Horses.'' Angel sat back. ''Polo ponies, to be specific, though they only call them ponies.''

''Even Kylee can draw a horse.''

''I can't,'' Angel freely admitted. ''Can't ride one, either.''

''No big deal, Miss.'' Leah smiled.

''So, a landscape, horses, floating umbrellas. The kind of striped umbrellas you see at polo matches.''

''Never been to one,'' Leah said laconically.

''Never mind. I'll get you a brolly to copy. Sporting cups. There are dozens of them just behind you. Somehow Mr. McCord managed to acquire them. You can't back out now, Leah.''

''I don't want to back out. That's great!'' said Leah, nearly leaping out of her skin with excitement.

''Brilliant!'' Angelica added for good measure, pleased at Leah's reaction. ''My own idea of the ceiling in the hall is a featureless plain. You can shape it any way you like but let it reflect the station.''

''I reckon we might get many flowers after the storm. I reckon last night was magic. It shoulda come to nothin'. I'd nearly forgotten what the rain tastes like, all clean and wet. Anyway I can draw flowers easy, the blue, blue sky, big rain bubbles like balloons. Maybe a couple of little kids sittin' under a tree. Doesn't have to be real?''

''Put your own stamp on it, Leah,'' Angelica said.

By six o'clock the following morning Angelica was down at the stables for her first riding lesson. If it was any help, she thought she was fairly brave, but she knew horses were temperamental as well as majestic creatures. If it came to a battle between her and any horse the horse would easily win. She guessed the secret had to be gentleness and sensitivity. She hoped she might be good at that.

When she arrived, right on time, Jake was already waiting for her. ''Sleep in?'' The amber eyes swept over her, taking in her appearance. She wore a short-sleeved blue cotton shirt tucked into tight-fitting designer jeans and a fancy silver and turquoise belt. On her head she wore a navy and white baseball cap turned the wrong way, and her thick hair was tied back in a plait.

She glanced at her watch. ''Right on time, McCord.''

''You're very cheeky, aren't you, for someone just about to have her first riding lesson?''

''I trust you with my life.'' She smiled, wondering how it was possible she had developed an enormous attachment to him virtually overnight. Maybe it was all the time she had dreamed of him. The years she had waited to see his unforgettable face in a crowd. An unforgettable face.

''I love the way you say that,'' he said, making a move toward her that caused a mad rush of pleasure. But then an aboriginal boy around sixteen emerged from one of the buildings in the huge stable complex, leading a bright chestnut horse.

''Here I am, boss.'' The boy laughed as though he and the horse had to be flagged down.

''Thanks, Benny.'' Jake, too, laughed as though at some private joke, then turned to give Angelica a faintly mocking look. ''Say hello to your mount for the day. Her name's Ariel. And this grinning character is Benny. I only keep him on because he's very good with the horses.''

''And I'm great muckin' out.'' Benny squinted up at Jake through the golden sunlight.

''Hello, Benny.'' Angelica smiled.

''Pleased to meet yuh, ma'am.'' Benny bobbed his curly dark head. ''Yuh doin' pretty good to get the boss to teach yuh,'' he offered cheekily.

''The question is why?'' Angelica asked.

"I'm curious to know if you're going to be your usual confident self or you're going to get jittery."

Benny smothered a laugh. "Thank you, Benny," Jake said.

"I'll be back when you need me. Good luck, ma'am."

There was so much devilment in those black eyes Angel began to examine the mare more thoroughly, wondering if its real name mightn't be Psycho. "This couldn't possibly be a set-up?" she asked thoughtlessly.

He glanced at her, narrow-eyed, as well he might. "I wouldn't dream of doing anything foolish, let alone potentially dangerous."

"God no! I'm so sorry. I spoke without thinking. Just tell me what I'm supposed to do."

"You might look and listen." He eased off. "As you can imagine the ideal is to be put on a horse before you can even walk."

"Which, of course, happened to you."

He turned to gaze at her, looking every inch the imperious male, determined not to surrender to her charm. "I don't know that I've actually met a woman who so enjoyed taking the mickey out of me."

She shrugged, trying not to laugh. "I'm not going to apologise. Especially when you can be very, very lordly. Anyway, you know what I mean."

"Yes, I do know what you mean, Miss De Campo, but then, you're outrageous."

"So you keep saying, but it feels good with you. For the rest of the lesson I promise to be on my best behaviour."

"Thank you for that. I'd hate to see you when you're behaving badly."

"Surely you don't want this to lead to an argument?" she coaxed, aware even at this hour of the morning the chemical attraction between them was highly explosive.

"The truth is I want to kiss you madly," he said with a touch of self-derision, "but we'll run overtime. Are you going to pay attention?"

She groaned with wry humour. ''That's what I want to do because when you get to know me better you'll find I'm a very sweet woman.''

He laughed shortly. ''I'd prefer if you were—''

''What?'' She threw up her dimpled chin. ''Go on, Jonathon. I challenge you to tell me what you want me to be?''

''Try being this!'' With one arm he reached for her, pulling her to him.

His skin was gold, his eyes were gold and his gaze intense. Heart pounding, she waited for his kiss, the world around them reduced to the power of two. His handsome face taut with emotional pressure, he lowered his head, kissing her so passionately, so possessively, her whole body gave one long rapturous convulsive shudder.

''Jonathon,'' she murmured when the world slowly stopped spinning, ''don't do this to me if you don't mean it.''

''Mean it?'' He steadied his voice with an effort. ''You want it. I want it. It's almost as though we have no say in the matter. At least it keeps you quiet for a time.'' He allowed himself the luxury of holding her beautiful body close.

He stopped her with one brief hard kiss, and then he looked around as though he'd just remembered where they were. The mare stood quietly, well schooled around humans. ''My mother taught me to ride,'' he volunteered.

''You don't hate horses because of what happened to her?'' Angelica asked very gently.

''That happened to my father. Not to me. For me riding and horsemanship has been one of life's greatest pleasures. My mother was a wonderful rider. Before she married—for years when she was a girl—she won many competitions for show jumping. That's why it was such a terrible irony she was killed in a riding accident.''

''Were you there?''

He stared off across the cobbled courtyard. ''I was there afterwards when they brought her in.''

''I'm sorry.'' Sympathy gripped her. ''This must still upset you.''

''God, yes!'' He sighed deeply. ''I'll never forget it to my dying day. Her horse was a glorious animal. Habibah. My father shot it right in front of me. My mother would never have wanted that. It was a terrible accident. It could happen to any one of us.''

''He was out of his mind with grief.'' Her beautiful eyes reflected his grief.

''Yes, but I always thought it was cruel and it made him cruel. It was as if another being took him over. There was no life for Stacy. Little enough for Gillian. It's obvious I look like my mother, but that was no comfort to him.''

''But your father didn't crush you or your spirit.''

He shook his head, his expression grim. ''No matter how hard he tried. Why are we discussing this, Angelica?'' He stared into her eyes. ''We shouldn't be when I'm supposed to be giving you your first riding lesson. It's all about being calm around horses. Not tense.''

''I'm a fatalist,'' Angelica said. ''I believe what's to be will be.''

He took hold of her shoulders firmly. ''Then it appears to be destiny we were fated to meet again. You're a woman who can cause extreme emotions. The agony and the ecstasy.''

''I'm afraid that's what love is,'' she pointed out quietly.

''Who's talking love?'' he questioned, looking deeply into her eyes.

''A man can't grieve over what he doesn't love.''

''No.''

''Are you afraid loving might test you too much?''

''Surely it invites terrible vulnerability? A loss of autonomy. Losing the woman one loves can shatter a man's life forever. I'm not afraid of making a commitment, Angelica. I am afraid of falling in love with the wrong woman. A career-oriented woman, maybe, who'll go off and leave me. I'm pretty much stuck here. Coori is my life.''

"Hey, tell me something I don't know," she tried to tease, though her heart contracted.

"Do you want to hear now or save it for after the lesson?" he asked laconically. "Poor old Ariel is being very patient."

"Of course she is!" Chastened, Angelica reached out an impulsive hand to stroke the mare's neck just as he'd been doing for much of the time they'd been talking, but the horse tossed its head and took a few steps back. "Already I've done something wrong," she said in dismay.

"Don't worry." His voice couldn't have been more gentle. "You moved a bit too quickly, that's all. Put your hand out and let her get your scent."

This time Angelica took her time and was rewarded when the mare lowered her muzzle into her palm, tickling it with its whiskers and snuffling contentedly. "Isn't she pretty?"

"Aren't you pretty," he said dryly. "You remind me of a high-stepping filly, as Ariel was not all that long ago. I take it you've never sat on a horse?"

She shook her head. "Never. I didn't even have a rocking horse when I was a child. Probably even as a four-year-old my legs would have touched the ground."

"Well they won't now. There's an art to all this, Angel. If you really want to ride and enjoy it you'll have to make an intelligent attempt to master the correct techniques. I'm going to tell you all about what we call the aids, the means of communicating with the horse. Legs, seat, hands, voice. It's all about learning to feel what the horse is doing beneath you and influencing those movements. You'll appreciate it's the legs that create the power—I assume you've been to the races?"

"Not only that, I've won Fashions on the Field twice. Though I was runner up first time."

"What else? You regularly back outsiders that come in at a hundred to one?"

"I'd love to tell you that. The fact is I always lose. So the legs move the horse. The rider's hands guide it hopefully in the right direction?"

"Is there anything I can tell you?"

"Yes. Are you going to allow me to get into the saddle?"

"If you think you can keep your balance. You have to sit securely and centrally."

"I can do that," she stated confidently. "This is going to be exciting."

"Not on poor old Ariel it isn't. She's a quiet, sweet-tempered, well-schooled horse. You're such a tearaway I'd hate to put you on anything else. Your voice will be a big asset. It's a voice even a horse would stop and listen to. Your voice tells the horse whether you're pleased with it or not. An extrovert person such as yourself—"

"Thank you—"

"—can coax a little more out of a quiet horse. I wouldn't put an excitable person, for instance, on an equally excitable horse."

Challenge glowed in her dark eyes. "You're saying I'm excitable?"

"You are when you and I get together."

She couldn't dispute that. "It sounds fine—doesn't it?—fatal attraction, but it's scary."

"Especially when my dreams throw up all sorts of scenarios," he admitted, releasing his breath slowly.

"You dream about me?" She was thrilled and astonished.

It would be so simple to deny it, but he didn't. It was a step forward for him. "When a man slaves all day, his dreams tend to take off. I've dreamt about you, Angel. I've even gone so far as to—"

"Don't tell me." She flushed.

He stood there in the streaming sunlight looking very handsome, male and mocking. "All right, I'll let you find out. Now do you want to mount this horse or don't you?"

She gave her long thick plait an absent flick. "Of course I do. You're the one doing the flirting."

"Flirting?" He raised a bronze brow.

"Haven't you heard the word before? I'm not complaining, mind you. I like it."

''Then you think you know what you're doing?''

''Not really,'' she confessed, ''but I'm no wimp.''

''Hell no! You're full of spirit. If I gave you a leg up do you think you could swing the other over Ariel's back? Alternatively we could mount from the fence.''

''Listen, I'm an athlete. One fit, long-legged lady.'' She was ready to rise to the challenge.

Moments later she was sitting triumphantly in the saddle, back straight, shoulders square, no suspicion of a slump.

''That was damned good!'' he exclaimed in admiration, looking up at her with approval. She was seated comfortably and balanced. It seemed she was a natural.

''Why sound so surprised?'' She looked down into his remarkable eyes.

His gaze narrowed and darkened. ''I know so little about you, but that, I guess, is all part of the excitement. Teaching you, Angel, is going to be a breeze.''

Which was exactly how it turned out.

CHAPTER SEVEN

DUSK was drawing near. Jake halted in the shade of one of the coolabahs lining a shallow gully to sweep off his akubra. God, that felt good! The cooling breeze ruffled through his sweat-soaked head, bringing some relief. He couldn't wait to have a long relaxing shower and wash his red-sand-grimed hair. It had been another day of stifling heat yet the sloping grasslands had sprouted tiny purple flowers that rode the tips of the soft cane grass in wave after wave. That was the result of one good downpour courtesy Angel's exotic rain dance. The inflammatory flamenco encore had been entirely for him and that had brought equally tumultuous results!

The air around him was deliciously scented with wild passion fruit flower. He breathed in deeply, worshipful of this great ancient land. Though the heavy purple passion fruit looked inviting and tasted good, aboriginals on the station refused to touch it. The fruit belonged to one of their spirit beings who didn't take kindly to having it stolen. Though such an idea half amused him, he rarely ate the fruit himself even when his throat was parched.

It was another remarkable sunset. Fiery-red clouds billowing on the horizon reminded him of atomic mushrooms. Now the sky was turning the colour of smoke shot through with lavender. Galahs above him chewed away contentedly on blossom and leaves, making quite a racket. His black gelding suddenly chose that moment to loudly neigh and the birds took off in a flock of pearl-grey and deep pink, shrieking in protest as they sped further down the quiet lagoon.

Everywhere in this land he loved was colour and movement. Life and death. Coori was a haven for wildlife. Even as he gazed up at the darkening vault of the sky a falcon with its claws spread casually selected a bird from the flock. It curved away with its prey to its nest in the low eroded hills. Falcons never missed. Their speed of attack was amazing. He replaced his wide-brimmed hat and rode on, aware these days there was an urgency in getting home, a feeling of pleasure and heart-lifting excitement.

It was all due to the woman he now thought of as Angel, which just showed how much she was getting to him. She certainly had power. It was extraordinary how having her in the house had made everyone, not just him, come alive. He'd almost forgotten what happiness was like; all but forgotten how beautiful life could be. Sometimes it seemed it was all backbreaking work. Even when he was near exhausted there was the business side of the operation that demanded a lot of his time.

So that was his life. A lot of work. Little time for play and even less time to find himself a wife. This was the common plight of the man on the land, especially when the situation was exacerbated by the remoteness of a cattle station. His womenfolk, Stacy and Gillian, were fragile, he knew. That was the result of the hard loveless years under his father when life had almost been reduced to a daily battle. He would be very very different with his own children. That he vowed, even as he feared some terrible tragedy could unleash a latent ruthlessness in him. He was his father's son after all. He could hear his father's voice in his own tones. It was true, as Angel had intuited, he feared his own genes.

At twenty-eight he now felt a profound need for a family of his own. He supposed he might be in search of his lost childhood through the eyes of a little son. To have a child, he needed a woman. The right woman. A woman who was capable of being the stabilising centre of family life. In so many, many ways Angel was that woman. She had strength, she had humour and a sunny, positive nature. Combined with all the rest, God knows, all he could think of these days was getting her into his bed, though he knew it wasn't going to happen without the all important development of trust.

He wanted her and from her passionate responses he couldn't fail to know she wanted him, but they both knew he had called into question her dignity. Everything really depended on him. He'd known so much uncertainty in his life, his wariness, especially with profound attachments, wasn't going to disappear overnight. Most likely he was wrong about what he thought he had seen at Carly's party. Wasn't he the man endlessly pursuing perfection? In thrall to the unattainable? From a lonely small child the portrait of his mother had kept her alive for him. She remained perfect, a princess. In reality she was a stumbling block when he sought the one special woman to measure up.

Then his eyes fell on Angel, resulting in his having to turn a spotlight on himself and his own emotional difficulties.

At least she was working wonders for Stacy and Gillian. Both were opening out like daisies after a shower of rain. It was Angel who filled the house with laughter and sunshine. She took such joy in everything it had rubbed off on his family. Even Clary, who had given him the impression she was tired of it all and wanted to retire, had found a new lease on life. She'd told him she was having a ball being Angel's "right hand."

Angel had even looked further, giving support and attention to that much abused young woman Leah. She had all kinds of ideas for Leah and her child. He knew Leah was gifted. He had seen her paintings, but he hadn't known little Kylee had inherited her mother's talent. In his broad experience aboriginal people were natural artists anyway. They'd been decorating caves since time immemorial.

When he entered the house he was confronted by a great beautiful Christmas tree—God, it had to be at least fifteen feet—soaring into the double space of the entrance hall. Its green upper branches were decorated with glittering baubles: frosty white bells, red, green, gold and silver balls, little ornaments galore. Angel was up a ladder dressed in a red T-shirt and tight jeans, an outfit that made the most of her beautiful breasts, long legs and tall willowy figure. She was busy tying a silver-winged cupid to one of the pendulous branches. A shorter ladder was set up on the other side.

"Hi!" she called brightly, giving him a lovely welcoming smile. "It arrived."

"I can see that. You haven't wasted any time. Be careful up there."

"Want to join me?" It was without provocation, more like one big kid to another.

"I'd love to, but I have to take a shower first. I'm as grimy as they come."

"You look great!" He did. All the time. He was a fabulous-looking man who somehow managed to look incredibly glamorous in cowboy gear. It was a kind of beauty that belonged only to a man, Angelica thought, staring down. Heroic. Sometimes she thought it was a beauty impossible to equal. Amber curls clung to his head and his nape. His golden-bronze skin was sheened by sweat. The rest of him took a lot of beating. He was six-three of dynamic male and superbly fit.

"Damn it all, Angel, be careful," he called at a rush, as the ladder, not all that stable, rocked slightly. No doubt due to her prolonged staring at him.

"Well, if you will distract me."

"Why start at the top?" he asked, experiencing a nostalgia that was a combination of the remembered joy and grief he kept in his heart.

"I'm very methodical," she explained. "I start at the top and work down. Gilly is going to help me. She's gone off for another box of baubles. Aren't they gorgeous?"

"I bet they cost an arm and a leg?" He gave a mock shudder, moving closer to finger a green branch.

"Of course they did, but they're positively essential."

"I agree."

He directed a smile at her that was so much like a kiss Angelica had to lean against the ladder for support.

"What's this supposed to be?" he asked, still fingering the

synthetic branch. "I'm not big on trees from the Northern Hemisphere, but I take it it's a spruce?"

"Good guess. It's supposed to be a balsam fir. I think the difference is the cones on the fir point upwards like the candles on a Christmas tree. On the spruce and other conifers they hang down."

"We learn something every day." He was about to move off when Leah, holding tightly to the hand of her little girl, arrived from the direction of the kitchen. She came to a halt when she saw Jake, giving him a sunny smile. "Evenin', Mr. McCord."

"Hello, there, Leah," he responded in an easy friendly fashion. "And how are you, Miss Kylee?" he asked, lowering his golden gaze to the child.

"I'm good," Kylee announced with a beaming smile, then immediately blotted her copy book by breaking free of her mother's restraint. She launched herself at Angelica sitting up on the ladder. "Hi, Miss?" she called happily, looking for all the world like she was about to climb up and join Angelica. Instead, before anyone could divine her intention, in the unpredictable way of children, she gave the ladder a surprisingly good shake.

Her mother shrieked, watching in horror as Angelica leaned forward in an effort to clutch the ladder's sides. It only took half a second more before her right foot became dislodged, sliding perilously out of the rung.

Please God, let me bounce, Angelica prayed on the way down. This was no time for injury, big or small.

Jake moved with alacrity, positioning himself to get his arms under her, staggering for a moment, as he struggled to hold on to her before the power in his legs steadied him and allowed him to maintain his balance.

"Gracious!" Angelica, no featherweight, wrapped her arms gratefully around his neck. "Aren't you strong?"

"I'd turn into Hercules for you." He levered her higher, feeling the familiar stirring of desire. She could always work that particular miracle.

"I don't think Hercules could do better." She arched back languorously, hair tumbling, both of them shocked out of the pleasure of the moment by the sound of Leah scolding little Kylee.

"What did you think you were doing, naughty girl?" she questioned, a reflection of the countless times she'd been asked that herself. But Kylee, used to the nervy, anxious side of her mother, scurried like a little mouse over to Jake, wrapping her arms around his long legs. "You naughty girl!" Leah fretted, making for Kylee, looking very much like she was going to smack her.

Angelica slid instantly to the ground, alerted to trouble, while Jake held up his hand.

"Stop, Leah. She's only four."

"Nearly five," Leah corrected, trying to pull out of her uptight state. "Why do I have a daughter like her? She's always getting into trouble."

"She's just a child," Jake reminded her. "You mustn't hit her, Leah. I won't allow it."

An odd kind of anger was rising from him, causing Angelica to run a soothing hand up and down his arm.

"There's no harm done," she said quickly, understanding Leah's vulnerable history. "It's anxiety that's making you cross, isn't it, Leah? You're always worried some bad thing will happen to you and Kylee?"

"I've had more'un my share of bad things," Leah responded bleakly, her expression momentarily full of the violence she'd experienced.

"That's all over now, Leah," Jake said, his tone softening.

"I hope so, Mr. McCord."

"You have my word."

He stood there every inch master of Coori station, Angelica thought. And a man of his word.

"While you're on Coori nothing bad will ever happen to you or Kylee, but you must promise me to be gentle with her. You experienced terrible things. All the more reason you can't let anything bad into Kylee's life."

Leah shook her head. ''She's all I got. I love her.''

''Of course you do,'' Jake said, knowing that was perfectly true; indeed Leah was trying very hard to make something of herself.

Still Angelica could feel he was disturbed. Very likely for reasons of his own.

''Did you want to see me, Leah?'' she asked by way of diversion, feeling Kylee's sweet little hand slip into hers.

''Yes, Miss.'' Leah was glad of the change of subject. ''It's about the Hall. I worked out lots of things I'm gunna do. I sketched it out on paper.''

''Oh that's splendid!'' Angel turned to Jake. ''We have our ideas for the Great Hall. Leah as the artist in residence is going to do it.'' Or I hope she is. A sudden wave of doubt rose to her throat. His handsome face could look so formidable sometimes.

''Really? I assume you were going to consult me?''

''Of course.'' She stared at him, surprised but then not. She could see the way his lean body was braced. ''I was waiting until we had something properly worked out.''

''I can't tell you how relieved I am to know that,'' he said crisply. ''Remember what I told you, Leah.''

''Yes, sir,'' Leah answered.

''Okay, then. I'm off to take that shower. Be seeing you, Kylee.'' His expression smoothed out into his wonderful smile.

''See yuh. Mr. Jake,'' Kylee chirruped. ''I jus' wanted Miss to come down,'' she explained. ''Didn't want to make her fall.''

''Of course you didn't.'' Angelica squeezed the child's hand. ''You can stay and help with the decorations, if you like?'' She looked to Jake to see if that was okay with him, but he was moving away.

''Jus' push her out, Miss, when you're ready,'' Leah said. ''I gotta go. I got lots to think of if I'm gunna do the Hall.''

''Let's see what you have in mind, Leah.'' Jake paused

long enough to say. ''You said you had some sketches on paper?''

''Yes, sir. I'll bring 'em.''

''Fine. I'm looking forward to seeing them. Who, by the way, is doing the flower arranging?'' He glanced back at Angelica, his amber eyes sardonic.

Before she could formulate a fitting answer, he disappeared, all powerful lean elegance.

''Now you be a good girl, Kylee.'' Leah moved to cuddle her child who threw loving arms around her mother's neck.

It offered Angelica an opportunity to hurry after Jake, catching him at the end of the passageway.

''What did you get so angry about?'' She swooped to clutch his arm.

''My dear Angelica, I'm not angry.'' He appeared to tower over her when he wasn't.

''Cross, then,'' she amended. ''I hate to mention this when you're being so lordly, but you did give me carte blanche.''

''Did I?'' He pinned her with a stare.

''Oh, Jonathon, don't be like this.'' She put out an appealing hand. ''Did my falling off the ladder shake you up?''

''You'll do anything to get attention,'' he drawled, unwilling in that moment to admit just how much.

''Are you worried Leah might mistreat Kylee?'' She looked at him with understanding and concern.

''I can't totally discount it,'' he mused. ''Violence breeds violence. I've seen it over and over again. I won't have anything happen to that child.'' A certain grimness settled on his striking features.

''I understand your fears, Jonathon.'' Angelica became aware she always used his name in their more emotional moments. ''But I think in Leah's case, you could be overreacting.''

''How much experience can you draw on?'' he challenged. ''Aren't you the young woman who had the ultimate happy childhood?''

''That doesn't mean I haven't seen a lot of unhappiness. I

have a close friend who found herself in a violent marriage. I could scarcely credit it even when I knew it was true. He's a doctor, believe it or not, from a highly respected family. He took an oath to keep people well. Kylee is a happy, bouncy, little girl. Leah is doing a good job of mothering. It's her ingrained anxieties that make her responses a little harsh. She's more bark than bite.''

''I recognise that, Angel,'' he said more reasonably, ''just as I recognise the years of pent-up anger in her. I saw enough anger in my time. Anyway what's this about the Hall?'' He shook his mood off.

''The Hall?''

''You're not losing your memory?''

''Excuse me, I was waiting until you were ready to listen. When you—''

''Cooled off?'' he supplied wryly.

''Exactly.'' Unable to stop herself she leaned forward and kissed his cheek, her soft lips deliciously rasped by his faint beard. ''You're a good man, Jonathon McCord,'' she said, ''if a tad complicated.''

''And you want a good man?''

''You could very well be my last chance,'' she said teasingly.

''Then I now pronounce you my wife.'' He set his two hands to cup her face before dropping a kiss on her mouth.

''Is that a first, or do you do it all the time?'' she asked when she was able.

''All right, the wedding's off.''

''I thought it might be.''

''Get ready to show me all this stuff with Leah,'' he called as he strode away.

''Would Sir like to see it before or after dinner?'' she called with mock servility.

''Just so I see it,'' he said.

When she returned to the hall she found Gillian in the act of sending Leah and Kylee away. Leah looked upset and

Kylee's entrancing little face was all crinkled up as if she was about to burst into tears. Angelica caught her breath in dismay wondering why Gillian, who had so much, couldn't be kinder and act less the daughter of the manor.

''Oh, Gilly, I did ask Kylee to stay,'' she said in a coaxing voice. ''Christmas is all about children, don't you think?''

Gillian stared back at her, going a little red. ''I thought it would be nice just us two,'' she protested, a young woman starved of her father's affection and excessively attached to the people she liked as a result. She liked Angel. And she liked Charlie. ''Surely Kylee should have her tea and go to bed.'' Kylee who was far from lacking in intelligence, began to sob while her mother's black eyes flashed indignantly.

''A little longer won't matter and she's here now,'' Angelica pointed out as cheerfully as she could. ''I did promise her.''

''Very well,'' Gillian replied, with that odd tightening of the lips Angelica had noted before. Probably she had copied it from her father. It didn't look natural to her.

''I don't imagine she's seen so many pretty things in her whole life.'' Angelica smiled reassuringly at Kylee who had miraculously turned off her sobs to roll her huge liquid eyes.

''Neither have I,'' Gillian answered so shortly Leah backed away.

''I'll go home now, Miss.'' She addressed Angel. ''I wanna go.''

Kylee who appeared to have a decided mind of her own and, as Angelica had so recently pointed out to Jake, was not in the least cowed, pulled free of her mother. ''Wanna stay.''

''As you wish, Leah.'' Angelica caught the little girl firmly by the hand. ''Kylee can wait with us for a while. Okay, Gilly?'' She turned to face the younger woman.

''She's welcome,'' Gillian managed to her credit, although she was still flushed.

''Don't forget Mr. McCord wants to see what we've planned, Leah,'' Angelica reminded the young aboriginal woman. ''If you wouldn't mind coming back in an hour?''

''What have you planned?'' Gillian asked, in a high, surprised voice, spinning around to stare at Leah.

''You'll see.'' Angelica promised. ''It's a design for a mural. It's to go on the ceiling of the Great Hall. That's if it all comes together.''

''And Leah is going to do it?'' Gillian's pretty blue eyes registered amazement.

''Yes she is,'' Angelica confirmed, while Leah stared fixedly at the parqueted floor. ''Leah is very artistic.''

''I'm goin', Miss,'' Leah said, acutely aware of Gillian's surprise and apparent resentment. She turned, looking so vulnerable Angel felt her heart ache with pity.

''Why is she so upset?'' Gillian asked, startled by Leah's flight.

''You were a little short with her, Gilly. I'll make sure she's all right.'' Angelica dashed after the tiny Leah, easily overtaking her before she reached the kitchen.

''Please Leah,'' she begged. ''Gillian doesn't mean anything. She's not an unkind person. It's just that she thinks she has to act in a certain way.''

Leah blinked and swallowed. ''She's not going to make a friend of an aboriginal woman, you mean. It's better to keep out of the way.''

''That's giving in, Leah. I know you're a fighter. You're going to become the person you were meant to be.''

Leah's delicate head shot up. ''Why am I hurtin'?'' she asked with simple dignity. ''Why am I always hurtin'?''

''Because you've been severely wounded,'' Angelica said. ''You never feel certain how you're going to be treated. There are lots of good people in this world who are going to help you. Try not to look for threat where there isn't. Gilly doesn't dislike or look down on you. She recognises in her heart there's a lot to you. She just finds it easier to treat you like a servant. It's the way she was reared.''

''But I am a servant,'' Leah pointed out very simply.

''You have talents to lift you into a different league. Talents you're already calling on. Everyone needs a helping hand. I've had many people kind enough to help me, now I'm going to find a way to help you."

"You'll go away."

That silenced Angelica, plunging a knife into her heart. Go away? Never see Jonathon again? It was not to be borne. "Well I'm here now," she said firmly. "It may be that you'll do very much better for yourself in the city where there's more scope for your special gifts. You do have them."

"Yes." Leah lifted her head proudly.

"So prove it," Angelica said warmly, taking Leah's fine-boned hand. "You've had to be very tough to survive lots of bad situations. I've been hired to run these functions. I have to prove myself. So do you."

Somehow that had the right effect. Leah grinned broadly. "Be back in an hour, Miss," she said.

Thirty minutes later Jake rounded the corridor into the entrance hall feeling much more relaxed and refreshed. "Hey, you've been working hard!" he called out in admiration, looking up at the Christmas tree.

The tree looked majestic dressed in lustrous bells and balls and sparkling ornaments with jewel-like glints of ruby and emerald, gold and silver.

"It's like a fairy tale, isn't it, Jake?" Gillian turned a happy, smiling face to her half brother. "Oh, I'm so looking forward to everything. It's so exciting and we're going to have tons of presents massed around the tree. Angelica has wonderful ideas for those carved nymphs on the stairs. We're going to dress up the stairway with velvet swags and painted pine cones and things."

"That sounds great, Gilly," he told her gently, his gaze moving to beautiful sensual Angelica who was holding in her hands the Christmas angel dressed in a gossamer-like white-and-gold gown with golden wings and a golden halo on her amber curls.

"We're not finished yet." She smiled her pleasure. "We've got to have fairy lights. All white, I think. Some frosty snow in the desert. But we've elected you to place our angel on top. I thought the amber curls were a nice touch.''

''You selected it with me in mind?'' He stared at her with mocking golden eyes.

''I think she's exactly right in this house,'' Angelica pronounced.

''Okay now.'' He started towards her, hoping she'd planned on lots of mistletoe when a little voice carolled, ''Wait for me!''

''Good heavens, Kylee, where did you come from?'' Jake laughed, much taken with this child as she scurried out of the shadowed passageway, gulping down cake.

''Been to the kitchen,'' she told him joyfully. ''Clary gave me tea. Are yuh gunna put the Christmas angel up, Mr. Jake?''

''On second thought, you can help me.''

''Can I?'' Kylee squealed, her huge eyes flashing sparkling lights.

''I should be able to lift you without killing myself. Now Miss Angelica was a different story.''

''I thought you were interested in Herculean tests,'' Angelica reminded him, watching him lift the child like a bundle of feathers and carry her up the ladder.

Near the top, bracing himself securely, Jake reached out his long arm while Kylee placed hers over his as he set the angel into position. ''There, done!'' he cried triumphantly.

''Done!'' Kylee threw back her toffee-coloured head and laughed then she leaned forward and gave Jake a smacking kiss on the cheek, her free hand stroking his face.

Angelica, watching this touching scene from beneath, found herself caught up by longing for a happy married life. A husband who was both lover and best friend. She also wanted children. She was twenty-five, nearing twenty-six. She couldn't help thinking she was moving further away from the optimum time to have children. And she wanted four. It was the dilemma facing many career women like her. Put off having children into the late thirties never mind the forties and risk not being able to conceive at all. The medical profession had aired their warnings.

Gillian grabbed her hand. "Would you believe that little kid kissing Jake?"

"I think it's lovely, don't you?" Angel's dark eyes were on man and child as they slowly descended the ladder.

"Yes, she's a cute little thing." Gillian gave a warm smile. "Wherever did she get those orange curls?"

"I guess we'll never know. Could be genetic, but surely there are aboriginal tribes in the Centre with blond and bronze hair?"

"Yes there are," Gillian recalled. "Leah is very attractive, isn't she, in her way?"

"Very," Angelica agreed. "It would be wonderful if she could find herself a good man this time. She and Kylee deserve a better life."

"She should thank Jake for rescuing her," Gillian said. "Not everyone cares, you know."

"Well I do," said Angelica with emphasis.

CHAPTER EIGHT

FROM the moment Dinah Campbell arrived Angelica could see why Stacy and Gillian found her an intimidating guest in their home. The forceful Dinah acted as if she were the owner of Coori with the McCord women brief tenants. Dinah Campbell wasn't one of the world's underdogs. She was supremely self-confident, and always looked everyone straight in the eye. Physically very attractive, she had genuine platinum-blond hair, which she wore in a short, sexy tousled crop, apple-green eyes, good lightly tanned skin, trim athletic body, and to cap it off she was a cool dresser. All in all she made a very eye-catching package.

But her manner! Miss Campbell appeared to attach much importance to herself as the only child of a landowning family with money to burn. Dinah herself already possessed more money than she actually needed from her maternal grandfather with the full expectation of in time gathering in the lot. The trouble was, wealth didn't always vouchsafe niceness of manners, Angelica thought, watching Dinah airkiss first her hostess then Gilly, making it seem they were honoured to have her pop in, before turning what used to be called a gimlet eye on Angel.

"So you're the caterer?" she asked for openers, managing to make it sound vaguely insulting.

"I see myself more as a Celebrity Organiser." Angelica smiled, determined not to take offence. "Angelica De Campo. How are you, Miss Campbell?"

"Oh fine, fine." Though Dinah's accent was well-educated, her voice timbre was not all that easy on the ear. "Good heavens, you must be all of six feet?" She directed her gaze to some point above Angelica's dark head as though clouds were billowing there.

Used as they were to Dinah's abrasive style, Stacy and Gillian looked at one another shell-shocked, but Angelica laughed it off.

"Yes," she said calmly. "All it takes is two inches of heel."

"I imagine it's a sore point?" Dinah's green eyes were so drilling she could have been trying to punch holes in Angelica's glowing, olive-skinned flesh.

"Not at all. I figure it means I can eat more," Angelica said tongue-in-cheek. They were all still standing on the verandah where they had grouped to greet the Outback aristocrat but now Angelica decided the only course open to her was to excuse herself.

"Lovely to meet you, Miss Campbell." She smiled, already on the move. Everyone told little white lies as a social lubricant. "I must see how Leah's getting on."

She couldn't have picked a better cue. "Leah? Really?" Dinah's artfully darkened eyebrows shot up to her shaggy fringe. "Isn't she the aboriginal girl with the child? Why would you have to see her?" It was clearly a demand that needed answering but even Angelica was at a loss as to a civil response. She looked to Stacy as mistress of Coori to say something, to put Miss Campbell in her place would be good—but Stacy's mouth opened and closed soundlessly. Plainly in Dinah's company she lost all confidence when confidence wasn't her thing.

Dinah was still waiting for an explanation, wearing a slightly frowning expression. After all, she had asked a question.

Well that's it, Angelica thought. Obviously she believes everything that happens on Coori is her business and her long friendship with Jake is going to end in only one way. With a spectacular Outback wedding. The joining of two dynasties. McCord-Campbell. Such-was-life Angelica had to ask herself if it mightn't be true, and she herself fitted into the Passing

Sexy Fling category. ''Leah is being a great help to me,'' she offered finally, continuing to sound pleasant and calm.

''Please come back for lunch,'' Stacy called after her, looking nerve-racked.

''Will do.'' Angelica took off down the front steps before she threw caution to the winds, giving Stacy and Gillian a cheerful little wave. Both of them for their own good had to find their tongues.

Dinah meanwhile went to the balustrade, peering after Angelica's rapidly receding figure. She was intent on finding out which way Miss De Campo was heading. It appeared she was making for the Great Hall, which really begged another question.

''Well!'' she said co-conspiratorially, turning back to the McCord women with raised brows. ''She's a surprise.''

''Who?'' Stacy enquired, just to hold up the inevitable.

''Why, Miss De Campo. Who else?'' Dinah shrugged.

''In what way?'' This was awful. This was excruciating, Stacy thought. Couldn't Angelica have stayed? Stacy regarded Angelica as very brave.

''She's a little bit too sure of herself,'' Dinah said. ''When one thinks about it, she's only here to do a job. She even swaggers.''

''Crap!'' Gillian, having picked up that crude expression from Charlie, decided to use it.

''Well I never!'' Dinah looked at Gillian, near aghast. ''That's very rude isn't it, Gilly?''

''I thought you were the one being rude.'' Gillian darted a desperate look towards her mother. ''Angelica is a lovely person. She's very kind.'' And more than a match for you.

''Well she would be, wouldn't she?'' Dinah lightly jeered. ''As I said, she's here to do a job. A job, incidentally, I could have done with pleasure.''

''But Jake couldn't have had enough confidence in you,'' Gillian said, going red. ''I don't want to be unpleasant, Dinah, you're our guest. But I hope you're not going to start on Angelica because she's so beautiful.''

Dinah pondered that almost derisively. ''Beautiful?'' Maybe to Gillian's standards was implied. ''She's very striking sure, but, Gilly, and I'm sure this is your true opinion, she's way too tall. In fact she'd be very hard-pressed to find a man who didn't have to look up at her.''

''Jake doesn't,'' Stacy offered with satisfaction, then immediately looked away to get back her strength.

But Dinah viewed Stacy's small neatly dressed figure as though Stacy had been attempting a little joke. ''Jake doesn't have to look up to any woman,'' she offered complacently, ''but knowing Jake as well as I do, I've only one thing to say. She's definitely not his cup of tea. And that bust! It's really too voluptuous.''

''Well no one is ever going to say that about me as long as I live,'' Gillian, who was flat-chested, complained. ''Busts are definitely big time.''

Angelica found Leah and Kylee in the Great Hall. Kylee, seated at a little child-size desk, was happily trying to copy what her mother was doing while Leah was up on a trestle working on one side of her mural.

They both cried, ''Hi!'' as soon as Angelica walked in, their faces near identical in the contentment of expression. Leah had already solved the big problem of covering the background by having one of the maintenance men on the station allotted to her by Jake spray paint the ceiling and the back feature wall a beautiful dense blue like the skies over Coori.

By the time Angelica walked in Leah had completed a whole section with balloons rising into the sky like a spring of giant fresh-water bubbles. The day before she had painted in Angel's surrealistic idea of floating umbrellas and several large silver trophy cups copied from those in Jake's study. There was considerably more to be done but she had made a great start. The four-foot section of the rear wall was to become a billabong featuring the magnificent species of waterlilies unique to the Channel Country and Coori station.

This was Leah's wish as the waterlily flower was the totemic ancestor of her coastal tribe. Connecting billabong to sky from the drawing board design would be a range of amethyst hills.

"That's coming along beautifully, Leah," Angelica called, thrilled by Leah's progress. It confirmed Leah's talent and Angelica's faith in her. She had since seen a large portfolio of Leah's work full of wonderful imagery and the fantasy of aboriginal mythology as well as Coori landscapes filtered through aboriginal eyes. It was a style, entirely natural, that combined elements of both worlds. Aboriginal culture and that of the white man's.

To Angelica's thinking in terms of commercial success, it seemed to give Leah's work an edge. Whoever had given Leah lessons—a nun at the mission—knew what she was about.

"I'm happy, Miss," Leah said, a sense of workmanship and pride her normal demeanour these days.

"So you should be," Angelica said admiringly. "You're going to make a name for yourself with this."

"Mr. McCord likes it." Leah grinned. "He said he can't wait for me to start paintin' the horses. He loves horses."

"So do I," said Angelica, who continued diligently with her early morning and late-afternoon lessons, enjoying herself immensely while she was at it. She had a marvellously helpful teacher, a complete professional, who freely admitted she had a good natural seat and good hands. This made his job that much easier.

Leah's design featured three polo ponies and riders during play. The front rider was to be clearly recognisable as Jake wearing his Number 3 jersey, the position for a team's most experienced player and usually the captain. This was Leah's idea.

Angelica stayed on for a while, making sure to praise little Kylee for her efforts, delighted the child had inherited her mother's talent. Rather than return to the lounge and Dinah Campbell she thought she'd go in search of Jake. She knew from their morning conversation he was schooling the best of the latest pool of brumbies. She had never heard him use the term "breaking in." It would be interesting to see him and Dinah together. That wouldn't happen until a pre-dinner drink unless Dinah took it into her head to find Jake, as well. It couldn't have been more obvious she had little in common with Stacy and Gillian while Stacy and Gillian appeared to find Dinah exhausting.

What of Jake? Angelica steeled herself for the answer. She took the Pajero in the direction of the Four Mile where she knew there were holding yards following the chain of billabongs. Coori station seemed to go on forever. She had only seen its boundaries from the air. A lake-size expanse of lagoon looked wonderfully inviting shimmering through the trees. It appeared deep enough but the water must have contracted because it was surrounded by a wide sandy beach. Reed beds abounded and the ubiquitous waterlily. In this particular lagoon it was the lavender-blue of the lotus lily sacred to the ancient Egyptians. For as long as she could remember there had always been talk of an ancient Egyptian presence in Australia especially in the tropical north. The beautiful lotus lily was native to both countries.

Slowing her vehicle, she first heard then saw a small waterfall cascading down the worn-smooth rock face at the back of the lagoon. And this was drought, except for that one miraculous downpour. She wondered what the waterfall would be like in times of flood or the wet years when probably it would be huge. A tree stretched its long branches over the lagoon and she thought it would be a marvellous place for the children on the station to hang a rope to jump from. Just as she thought it she saw an old rope dangling from one of the branches and laughed aloud thinking someone had already had the bright idea.

When she arrived at the Four Mile she found Jake working his magic on a wild stallion. She parked in the shade and walked quietly across the lightly grassed space, her face alight with interest. Three stockmen had taken up learning positions on the opposite side of the railed enclosure and she waved to them, watching them doff their dusty wide-brimmed hats before she found herself a nice comfortable spot around the fence.

Jake glanced at her briefly, but he didn't speak, clearly focused on the job. She, however, felt a sense of longing that was like an actual weight. She was, she realised, in so deep she craved the sight of him. The brumby looked a fine specimen, not poor at all for its life lived in the semi-arid desert fringe. She knew brumbies could become useful and tractable working horses. She wasn't sure what stage Jake was at, or indeed what the stages were, but the horse wasn't bucking or pawing the ground. It looked entirely controllable, probably due to Jake's unique skill.

Eventually as she watched with great interest, the horse was saddled and Jake mounted quietly, gently urging the animal forward. She supposed a considerable amount of work had gone into the lead-up processes for the horse to accept the saddle then the rider. Maybe the final schooling? The horse moved off at a steady controlled pace.

Moments later Jake dismounted, handing over the reins to one of the stockmen and calling a few instructions. Apparently it was someone else's turn to try their hand. In another enclosure a distance away she could see a number of horses milling, their hooves raising a bright rust-red cloud of dust. Jake had already told her large numbers of brumbies roamed the vast Outback stations.

He loped towards her, his lean powerful frame so extraordinarily graceful in its movements she felt a great thrust of sexual excitement, which extended from her heart through her groin to her legs. He was magnificent. She couldn't help but imagine what it would be like to lie beside him in a big soft beautiful bed!

"This is a pleasant surprise," he drawled, thinking if they were on their own he couldn't be responsible for what happened.

"I'm only sorry I didn't come sooner." Her smile was a

ray of sunshine in her vivid face. ''I take it that horse has been through any number of stages to allow you to ride it like that?''

He pushed his akubra lazily further down over his eyes. ''Ma'am, you take it right. Schooling horses is a job I really enjoy. I find it pleasurable and a challenge. We don't need as many station horses as we used to. Helicopters and motor bikes have taken over the musters, but I like to put the best of the brumbies to use. The rest can run free. It's time-consuming, this so-called business of breaking horses in. Coori adopted the British method of breaking horses in from the earliest days. The big difference was that over there horses were used to humans from the beginning and so were more tractable and well-behaved. Our brumbies roamed a vast wilderness and never saw a single human soul. Consequently they're damned wild. And fierce.''

''So a gentleman in Britain could walk right up to an unschooled horse and pat its nose while an Outback man had a far more dangerous time of it.''

''You bet!'' He yanked at the red bandana around his strong bronzed throat. ''If they ever managed to catch the strongest and fleetest. A wild horse's response to a direct approach would be to bolt like merry hell. In my grandfather's day when he was still a young man his best friend, a fine horseman, was killed on the station. He made the fatal mistake of walking away from a brumby that was being broken in. The horse lashed out with its hinds legs, smashing his arm, shoulder and finally near caved in the side of his head.''

''How terrible!'' Angelica said weakly.

''Horses are unpredictable creatures.'' He shrugged. ''They can bite, rear or strike savagely with their front and rear feet. That's why good horsemen take pride in their ability to ride any horse with safety and facility.''

''Have you been thrown?'' She looked back at him with the greatest sense of pleasure.

He sent her an amused glance. ''I've taken my share of

falls, but strangely I've never broken anything. There's an expertise in taking a fall as well. As for you, you're making an improvement every day."

She executed a little bow. "Thank you. I have a top-rate teacher. You're surprisingly patient."

One bronzed brow shot up. "What do you mean, surprisingly?" he scoffed.

"You're a man who doesn't suffer fools gladly."

His golden gaze narrowed over her. "I can't believe you're calling yourself a fool."

"You know what I mean. Anyway I'm very grateful to you. When I go home I'm going to keep up my riding."

In an exquisitely gentle gesture that surprised the both of them he reached out to tilt up her chin, her skin petals to his touch. "And what if you can't bear to leave me?"

"I have to return." It came out in a sigh. God, how she wanted to stay.

"So we're just having an affair?" He looked deeply into her dark eyes, as he fought against the overwhelming urge to gather her into his arms.

"Are we? There's been no sex." A bittersweet little smile touched her lips.

"I thought that was your idea." His tone was half mocking, half quizzical, but he was watching her very intently.

"I want you to treat me differently to every other woman you've ever known in your life," she burst out so emotively she had to turn her head away to regain her composure. "And speaking of girlfriends..." After a moment she swung back, her voice even again. "Dinah Campbell has arrived. I've never known a woman who piloted her own plane."

"Dinah's had a licence since she was eighteen," he said, jamming his hands into his jeans' pockets just in case he reached for her again. Damn, he could scarcely keep his hands off her. "The Piper was her father's twenty-first birthday present to her."

"Which makes it remarkably easy to pop in and out," she pointed out dryly.

"Light aircraft is a way of life out here, Angelica. Not a luxury, a necessity."

"You don't have to say a word more. I just find it fascinating."

"And how did you find Dinah?"

She automatically braced. "Like an aristocrat out of those old British movies, ordering the servants about."

"In other words, a bit of a snob?"

"Exactly. I will say she's very attractive. You've told me she's very competent, as well—no doubt as a bed mate—what interests me is, apart from the fact you probably played naked as little children, what attracted you to her?"

"Jealous?" His hands came free to trap her. He caught a long coil of hair and wound it around his wrist.

"Not yet. Mind you I could be." She tugged back a little, but he didn't let go. "So, what went wrong?"

"You mean, between Dinah and me?" He flicked his wrist over, drawing her closer.

"Stop stalling, McCord. I'll get around to questioning you about your other affairs later. For now, just the imperious Dinah."

"I don't like the way she treats people, either, which echoes your concerns."

"Outback aristocrat and all that?"

"Dinah would be a snob anywhere," he said wryly, and let the length of her curly hair go, watching it bounce back. "Outback people are generally very down to earth."

"Perhaps I'll find she's down to earth when I get to know her better. I certainly wouldn't like to jeopardise your relationship with her."

"We're friends. I don't want to make love to her. Is that plain enough?"

"But you do know what she's like in bed? Average. Good. Sensational?"

He shifted to lean back against the fence, elegant even in a slouch. "Mind your own business, Angel Face."

Her brow lifted. "Understand it is my business. We're

already involved. To some degree anyway. I'll try again. What about marriage to Dinah? Have you ever thought about it? It would be a union of two Outback dynasties, after all."

"Except I want you."

"Why? Do you think you could tell me?" Now she stared near pleadingly into his golden mesmeric eyes.

Why didn't he? He had a deep underlying wish to do so but always there was the emotional hurdle. "Well, you're not exactly ugly," he evaded, taking the easy way out. "Not stupid, either. You're amazingly sexy. I can't get you out of my head."

"Or into your bed," she pointed out quietly.

"Isn't this some kind of foreplay?" There was challenge in his tone. Didn't she make the world come alive for him?

"It worked for Anne Boleyn." She smiled.

"Ah, but wasn't she the one who lost her head?"

"Admittedly she had her problems." She glanced at her watch. "Well, stimulating as this conversation is, I must tear myself away. I promised Stacy I'd return for lunch."

"Then I'll walk you to the car," he said in a gallant manner. "Have you everything settled for the weekend?"

"Everything but the weather. There's nothing for you to worry about. We're all going to have a marvellous day. I can't wait to see you play polo. I expect you're absolutely super?"

"I can't lie." His answer was droll. He opened the door for her. "Have you ever been in a steady relationship, Angel?"

She was sensitive to the gravity behind their habitual banter. "What's steady?" she asked. "More than a week?"

"When are you going to be serious? Or is it too much to expect?"

"You should t-talk!" She almost stuttered at his arrogance. "The two of us need to work on some issues."

His smile was beautiful, maddening unsettling. "Okay."

"Look, I'm normal." She drew a breath. "I'm twenty-five

until my next birthday. I've had a couple of fairly steady relationships.''

''Do you want to get married?''

''Of course I do.'' She stared at him, baffled.

''What, years from now? You, the career girl with your beautiful face in magazines and on TV? Hell, they could even want you for the movies. When exactly do you plan to marry? The near future? Or is it career first?''

''Oh go to hell!'' She'd give her career away for him anyday. Taut as a wire, she rushed past him to get into the vehicle, only their bodies were so irresistibly bent to each other, her breasts crushed against his chest. She swung into the driver's seat, hot-cheeked, aroused nipples straining against her T-shirt. ''I hope to marry just as soon as I can,'' she said, working herself into a minifury, ''but you can bet your life it won't be to anyone as insufferable as you!''

Her remark led to one blazing, retaliatory kiss through the window. It was passion perfectly balanced with punishment.

''Know what, Angel?'' His golden eyes mocked. ''You might find it hard to get insufferable old me out of your system.''

The hell was she'd come to that conclusion herself. Angelica drove off in a flurry of red dust, anger and a crazy rapture roaring through her head.

Damn that man, McCord!

CHAPTER NINE

BY THE Friday before the polo final and the gala ball, Dinah Campbell was still with them. In fact, as Stacy put it, she'd as good as moved in. She had brought all necessary luggage with her—including her evening dress and possibly a tiara. As she pointed out in the time-honoured tradition of Coori she had come for a prolonged stay. Coori boasted many bedrooms from the old days when relatives and friends who made the long journey stayed for some time, so there was no difficulty accommodating her. She was, however, visibly put out when she discovered that Angelica occupied the very best guest suite, the one she considered her suite. Obviously she truly believed, if no one else did, that she was going to marry Jake.

"She's not happy!" Gillian conveyed to Angelica, then relaxed into a fit of the giggles. "What about you move out?"

"But, Gilly, I think she expects me to."

"She's a stuck-up cow!" Gilly returned irreverently.

What was heart-warming was to see Gillian in particular come out of her shell so far as her interaction with Dinah was concerned. Even Stacy, who wasn't given to tart remarks, had come out with a surprising few after being on the receiving end of Dinah's curiously loaded comments. It was almost a form of heckling, Angel thought, fired up by protectiveness. Basically Dinah was a bitch. That was until Jake walked into the house. Then a great transformation took place. Dinah turned herself into the woman every man wants. She set out to charm him. She became all warmth and caring, eager to share station concerns, indicating she was the ideal choice for a wife.

At the dinner table, always beautifully turned out, she rose effortlessly to sparkling conversation, prompting him to tell stories of the many, many days, months, years they had spent together, all the while hanging on his every word.

Then, when Jake was out of the house she reverted to strutting her stuff, expelling oddly cutting little comments and upsetting Clary with questions as how the house was run, as if it were only a matter of time before Clary would be dumped and she would reign as mistress of a grand station. Sometimes Angelica had to place herself bodily between Clary and Dinah in case Clary, who had a fiery Irish temper, had armed herself with a sheaf of kitchen knives.

As for Angelica herself! She had to contend with endless interruptions and interventions as Dinah, to Angelica's intense irritation, gave herself the role of supervisor and interrogator. "Two heads are better than one!" she would say with a grating false laugh, coming to stare over Angelica's shoulder at some plan Angelica and Clary had stitched up until Angelica put her palms down firmly over the paper.

"Of course I could have done this and saved Jake a lot of money, but he was a little bit worried I might tire myself out. You're such a big strong woman." At this point she stared fixedly at Angelica's bosom as though it were massive.

Dinah, in fact, became so annoying Angelica and Jake had a brief exchange of words before he left the homestead on the Friday morning. "Look, she's your ex-girlfriend and she's really bugging me," Angelica cried, catching him as he ran down the front steps. "I have so much to do and she's a nuisance."

Jake, who was actually fed up with Dinah himself and worried about one of his prize beasts, rounded on the indignant Angelica. "Kill her," he said, golden eyes flashing.

"You're saying you're agreeable?"

"I'm saying I'm too damned busy to listen to this, Angel," he answered brusquely. "You're a smart girl. There's nothing wrong with your tongue, either. Tell her off."

"Oh, right! The only person off the hook is you," she said

tartly. "God, what a difference when you hove into sight. Okay I'll handle it," she called loudly as he gave her a back-handed wave and moved off with great purpose and energy. "Next time you can get somebody else in."

It all came to a head around noon, as the sky turned blue-black. Great thunder-heads streaming tails behind them like comets were building up in the sky. Angelica, hot and bothered, returned to the house from her inspection of the marquees already set up around the polo ground worried sick rain would ruin everything. They had all worked so hard, including the station hands Jake put at her disposal. Their number included Charlie who had kept them all laughing and Gillian especially happy.

Now this! Even if it didn't rain they could experience a wild windstorm or a dust storm that could bring the marquees down, tip over all the tables and chairs and rip the bunting to shreds. She didn't like Jake out in this, either, although she knew perfectly well he had lived with these extraordinary climatic conditions all his life.

She had only set foot in the entrance hall when a distant crack of thunder rolled around the hill country and little Kylee descended on her with a yelp. "It's all right, sweetheart." Angelica bent to the child, hugging her, thinking she was frightened of the thunder when Dinah suddenly appeared looking positively dragon-like.

"That child again!" she fumed. "I told her not to run around the house—so many valuable things…the Chinese porcelains alone—but she doesn't take the slightest notice. She behaves very badly. There's no way I would allow her or any other willful child in the house. She simply doesn't know what it is to be careful. Small wonder!"

"Do you mind, Dinah?" Angelica interrupted the tirade. "She's frightened of the thunder."

Kylee looked up at Angelica, small face wearing a frown. "No, I'm not, Miss. I'm frightened of her. But you're here now."

"Oh, yes, Mary Poppins!" Dinah took a crack at Angelica.

"Surely you realise there's really something very negligent about all this," she pointed out, not unreasonably had she used a different tone. But there she stood, the next mistress of Coori, guarding her future possessions. That was how she saw it in her own mind at least. "And if you don't mind my saying so—" as though anyone could stop her "—you shouldn't have put this tree here," she told Angelica as if she had no sense at all. "It's the wrong place entirely. It obstructs the traffic. One would have thought you'd know better."

"'Cause we like it," Kylee suddenly yelled in a voice extraordinarily shrill for one so tiny. "You can't touch it, lady. I'll tell Mr. Jake on yuh."

"Is that child actually speaking to me?" Dinah hissed her disbelief.

"It would appear so." Angel refrained from laughing because Kylee had been rude.

"Apologise to Miss Campbell, Kylee."

"No I ain't," said Kylee with almost adult disgust.

This time Angelica was forced to smother a laugh. "Well, no one can say I didn't try. Perhaps you can leave Kylee alone, Dinah," she suggested. "I'll keep an eye on her." She used Dinah's name when Dinah made a point of never using hers.

"Surely it's her mother's job?" Dinah's rasping tones were threaded with disapproval. "Whatever is she doing in the Great Hall? It must be clean by now?"

"She's paintin'," Kylee spoke up, pressing her heated face against Angelica's hand. "Don't want you there!"

Angelica bent down to the child, who apparently, for all Jake's concerns, feared no one. "You're being very rude, you know, Kylee," she chided softly.

"Sorry, Miss."

"Am I missing something here?" Dinah looked as though Kylee's words had set off an alarm.

"Just keep out of the Great Hall, Dinah, if you don't mind," Angelica asked. Leah was putting the finishing touches to her mural, which was so exactly what Angelica wanted and she didn't want Leah upset in any way.

"Since when have you been giving orders?" Dinah looked at Angelica with a twisted smile. "I'm a close friend of the family. Who exactly are you, when it's all said and done."

"She's Miss," Kylee yelled, clutching at Angelica like two sisters sticking together. "Go away, lady."

"This has gone quite far enough," Dinah cried promptly. "That child is truly out of hand."

Her expression was so outraged Angelica found herself losing her cool.

"God, Dinah, when was the last time you were nice to her? It might come as a surprise but it's not your job to chastise Kylee."

"Indeed it is, thank you very much. It'll be the day when some little aboriginal mite dares shout at me. It's not done."

"Say sorry, Kylee," Angelica prompted once more, "it is rude to shout at people." Kylee really hadn't been too respectful.

"I'm hot," Kylee said instead. "Can I go for a swim?"

"Watch out, she'll probably want to go in the homestead pool," Dinah said in her most sarcastic tone.

"That's an idea." Angelica swung the child up into her arms. "You're not the only one, Kylee, who feels like cooling off."

By four o'clock Angelica was convinced they were in for torrential rain. She'd already had the men move all the tables and chairs they'd so carefully set up into the shelter of the two large marquees. Everyone had agreed there seemed to be a wetness in the air, which meant a chance of rain. Stormclouds now covered the great vault of the sky entirely.

She and Clary were left standing on the verandah staring up at the heavens that periodically flashed bursts of light like someone was running from one heavenly room to the other, throwing switches. "This is going to ruin everything," Angelica groaned, easing her T-shirt from her damp midriff.

"Try not to worry, love." Clary, equally worried, did her best to comfort her. "It might come to nothing. I've seen it happen too many times before."

"But what if the wind gets up?" Angelica said.

"The marquees will be all right, love. It's not as though we're expecting a cyclone."

"What about a dust storm?" Angelica fretted. She had never seen one but she had seen pictures of Outback dust storms and they were horrendous!

"Look, love, whatever happens, happens." Clary, who had seen it all, flood drought, dust storms, the lot, spoke philosophically.

"I know. It's just that we've all worked so hard, Clary. Stacy and Gilly have really pulled their weight, too."

"They've done well," Clary agreed, surprised and pleased at the way they'd all worked together. "You've made it so much fun for them. They haven't had a lot of fun."

"Not with a family friend like Dinah Campbell around." Angelica leaned closer to Clary to whisper, "Where is she now, for goodness' sake?"

"Gone after Mr. Jake, my darling," Clary told her dryly. "That's what she does. Go after Mr. Jake."

"Do you reckon she might get him?" Angelica asked. God, what a dismal thought.

"Reckon you might if you want the job," Clary shocked her by saying. "It isn't exactly what you're used to out here. You're on your way to being a celebrity all right."

"Don't you think I'd fit in?" Angelica, who had no desire to be a celebrity, turned to Clary with a very serious expression on her face.

Clary threw back her head and laughed. "Listen, love, you fitted in from day one. You've been good for us all. Like a cure. I see the way Mr. Jake lights up when you're coming. I hear the way he calls you Angel."

"That doesn't mean he won't forget me when I'm gone."

"It could be up to you, love," Clary mused. "You're the

one with the city career. Mr. Jake can't leave here. This is his heritage. He'll never abandon it."

"I couldn't think of him elsewhere," Angelica answered simply. "He's not only the most committed, he has to be the best-looking cattleman on earth."

"You're not kiddin'!" Clary laughed with almost motherly pride. "Now I've got things to do. You can't keep fretting about this storm. It's either going to come to nothing or all hell will break loose."

"So why doesn't Jake come home?" Angelica asked anxiously as another drum roll of thunder echoed around the hills.

"He's been used to this his whole life. Don't you go worryin' about him. He can look after himself."

But Angelica felt as edgy as a cat on a hot tin roof. She couldn't follow Clary inside. Instead she ran down the steps intent on making one more circuit of the polo grounds....

When Jake did return to the homestead fifteen minutes later, he went in search of Angelica, knowing she would be concerned about the storm and its possible effect on all her hard work and planning. Even nearing sundown it was still scorchingly hot but there was a wet smell in the air. Personally having studied the sky he didn't think it would amount to much, but to a city person, like Angelica, it could be very frightening. These storm fronts, messengers of the monsoon season made everyone cranky. It was a case of all the drama without the relief of a drop of rain.

Tomorrow they would all gather for the final of the polo cup. It would be played in fierce heat but it had all been done before. People were used to it. He was prepared to take a very large bet it would be played under peacock-blue cloudless skies. He found Stacy and Gillian in the plant-filled conservatory at the rear of the house. Both of them turned smiling faces to him.

"Hi! Where's everyone?"

"If you mean Angelica, and I think you do, she's with

Clary.'' Stacy smiled. ''If you mean Dinah, she's in her room. She said the heat was giving her a headache. She tries to spend as little time with us as she can.''

''The next time she wants to come, put her off,'' Jake suggested.

''She's just so hard to put off.'' Stacy sighed.

''Maybe not if you try. I think I'll find Angel. She must be worried this storm will build into heavy rain.''

''Yes. She's so much at home here you forget she's a city girl,'' Stacy said. ''That was awfully nice of her getting the right evening dresses flown in to us. She must have described us exactly to her friend. Colouring, sizes, everything. They fit perfectly.''

''And it gives us a great chance to shine!'' Gillian showed her delight. ''Maybe Charlie will really fall in love with me. Up to date he hasn't.''

''You've got Charlie on the brain,'' her mother complained. ''Admittedly he is a fine young man, but Ty Caswell thinks the world of you.''

''I already know that, Mum.''

''Personally I think Ty suits you better,'' offered Jake. The very last thing he wanted was for Gillian to know heartbreak when Charlie went home. And that's what he was going to do when his big adventure was over.

Angel wasn't with Clary. She wasn't anywhere in the house. She wasn't in the Great Hall, either. He stopped long enough to admire Leah's mural, amazed at how good it was and the speed with which she had done it. Angel, being an angel, had given him her considered opinion, amounting to a little lecture, that Leah should be given a helping hand to relocate in Sydney where there would be more scope for her talents. Importantly, too, there were service and support groups within the aboriginal community in the city. Good aboriginal art was much sought after, both at home and abroad. Leah was good. And she had her dress-designing skills with ambitions thrown in. He sort of liked the idea of sponsoring her and little Kylee. God knows, after what Leah had suffered she deserved a helping hand.

A quick check confirmed the four-wheel drive had gone. Probably she had gone out to the polo grounds again, unable to settle. She could even want to camp out there tonight. He tried not to think of them both in one sleeping bag together. He was sick with wanting her. Sick of all his primitive urges. They were forever lapping at his senses. Willpower wouldn't work. He had fallen madly in love with Angelica De Campo. And faster than he thought possible. How was that for a swift slide into spellbound? Yet would a woman like that bury her beauty and talents in the remoteness of an Outback station? Maybe she was totally unattainable as an Outback wife. But not as a woman. He knew what he could do to her once he got her in his arms. Create a world within a world for them...

He was halfway to the grounds riding one of the station motor bikes when he spotted the Pajero coming over the crest of a ridge. It was travelling wickedly fast and he began to curse with anxiety. He couldn't bear to see her crash.

Slow down, girl. What's the race?

Another minute more and he knew. Smoke.

"God!" In among the spiralling column of dirty grey smoke he saw a shooting flame then a great shower of sparks. He realised instantly what had happened. A tree had ignited. He had lived through years when the station was dotted with spot fires. The wind was coming from the direction of the blaze. He caught a blast of heat and aromatic burning gum oil in his face. The danger zone was about a kilometre from the polo grounds. It was uncanny the way fire ran in lines and trees lined the ridge. With the wind behind the bushfire it could just miss the polo grounds. Unless the wind shifted. He opened up the throttle, slamming down hard as he tore up and over the rising ground until he met up with Angelica.

She brought the four-wheel drive to a shuddering halt, jumping out, calling to him as she ran. "Jonathon, thank God, you're here. Lightning hit a tree. It absolutely exploded.

The whole thing ignited right in front of my eyes. It was so scary. I was parked under it only a few moments before.''

He raced to her, grabbed her arms, held her fast. ''Are you okay?'' He searched her face, seeing anxiety but not a flicker of panic in her great dark eyes.

''I'm fine.'' She was now. She felt the force of his strength and inner energy. ''I don't know about your vehicle. A chunk of burning wood hit the roof hard but it must have fallen away.''

''I'm not worried about the damned vehicle,'' he said tautly. ''I was worried about you. All I want you to do now is get the men. It won't take them long to spot the flames. We want the water truck, backpacks, hessian bags, buckets, anything. They know the drill. We can't let this spread and there's no time.''

''I'll get them,'' she said, already on the run. ''What are you going to do?''

''I'm going to take a closer look.''

''Be careful!'' she yelled, her voice competing against the thunder. Even as she spoke another tree ignited, the canopy of branches throwing up great multi-coloured sparks like a fireworks display. If it weren't so frightening it would have been beautiful.

''Go on, Angel. Move it,'' he ordered, pretty shortly.

She didn't waste another second. She leapt into the vehicle and took off, reaching the compound in record time. The men were already alerted, swiftly going about their business. Everything they could use had been assembled.

''You don't have to come, Angelica.'' She and Charlie had become quite friendly, now he made a beeline for her, an odd excitement on his young handsome face. ''It could be bad up there. Really bad if the fire takes hold.''

''I'm coming all the same,'' she said. ''I want to be there. I want to help.''

''Then you'd better take this.'' He shoved a scarf into her hand. ''Put it over your face once we're up there. You won't want to breathe in the smoke.''

"Thanks, Charlie. Take care." Her voice resonated with concern. She watched him swing onto the side of the water truck equipped with barrels of water and a big yellow fire hose. Travelling towards their destination they all saw the fires take hold. Burn-offs had already taken place over most of the vast station during the Dry but the line of trees on the ridge had been left as a windbreak. Now the canopies were on fire, looking for all the world like a line of streetlights at night.

When they arrived at the fire front the men threw themselves into action, but Jake, once he caught sight of Angelica, strode towards her, his dynamic face grim. "This is no place for you." Already the wind was blasting embers across the dusty clearing. "Go back to the house."

"I can help," she protested, drawing on her own inner strength. "I'm another pair of hands. I won't get too close to it."

He held her a hair's-breadth away, staring down into her eyes. "Don't think for a minute it can't get close to you," he warned, lean body taut, nerves tense.

"Why don't you let me take one of those backpacks?" she shouted over the frightening crackle of the flames and the continuous roar of thunder. "I'm strong. Please, Jonathon, let me stay. I don't want you to be alone."

"You're not counting the men?" Abruptly he gave a crooked smile, a flash of white teeth in a smoke-grimed face. "Okay. Grab one. You know how to pump the water? But the moment I tell you to go, you'll go, understand?"

"I promise." She was inordinately pleased he trusted her to do something. She jumped to pick up a backpack while Jake strode away to the water truck.

Charlie surged forward to help her put the backpack on. "I wouldn't miss this," he told her, bending close so she could hear him.

"You must be mad." She recognised his excitement.

He lifted his blond head to scan the lurid sky. "My problem is, I have to have excitement. Will you just look at that spectacle!'' Billowing black clouds, shot through with silver and livid green, made a fantastic backdrop for the searing orange-gold flames.

''After all the work we put in there, I'd say it was heading towards the polo grounds.''

''Then we shouldn't be standing here talking,'' she clipped off.

''Okay, ma'am.'' Charlie saluted her with his devil-may-care grin. ''I like your spirit!''

It would have been a miracle if the skies had opened and sent down torrential rain. Only miracles didn't happen on demand. For three hours the fires continued to rage, jumping from tree to tree, the branches falling in fiery clumps causing ripples of tiny flames to skitter across the dry grass and smouldering leaves. All of them worked with their clothes, wet and steamy, clinging to them, for they had all doused themselves with the hoses. Once a small branch like a flaming torch fell not a metre from Angelica and she bit back a scream. That was close! She could have taken it on the head or the shoulder and been badly burned. She felt a wave of relief.

Jake's glistening blackened face appeared close to her. ''That's it, Angel. Go,'' he ordered harshly. ''For God's sake, that branch nearly hit you.'' He made a grab for her hand. ''Come on.'' Her hand was so oily, so grimy, it slithered out of his.

''We're getting there, aren't we?'' She took a long, dry, painful swallow. It seemed to her they were, though the very air was burning.

''I don't want you here. You've done well. I'm proud of you, but you can't stay. Get going.''

''All right.'' She turned away obediently, as she saw him agitated and angry. Now she was feeling dizzy, dying for one gulp of water.

''Please be careful,'' she begged, her heart in her eyes.

"I'll wait for you." She realised she was so exhausted she was on the verge of tears.

"I'll be okay," he shouted, turning to put out a spot fire on the ground with a few powerful sweeps of a hessian bag. "I'm not telling you one more time, Angel. Go."

She did just that, finding her way back to her vehicle. Her body felt like it was made of lead. Her mind was full of anxiety and an unfamiliar sensation she knew was pure panic. She was bound to Jake McCord in the most powerful way. She loved him. His life meant everything.

Angelica climbed wearily into the driver's seat and began to pray.

"Whatever possessed you to go up there?"

She'd only just arrived back at the homestead when Dinah thrust her face through the open window. Obviously she felt no need to ask Angelica how she was or if the fire was coming under control. The big thing was to tear down the front stairs the moment she spotted the four-wheel drive coming in so she could be first to ask the questions. "Don't you know anything about danger?" she scolded. "I bet Jake didn't thank you for getting yourself involved."

"Got a message for you," Angelica said laconically, opening out the door so smartly Dinah was forced to jump back. "He did." She resisted the urge to give Dinah a good shove.

"I don't believe that for a minute," Dinah gasped, staggering back. "I'm sure he told you to go away."

Angelica nodded wearily. "He did in the end, but I know I was of help."

"You could have placed the men in danger." Dinah continued the attack, uncaring of Angel's visible exhaustion. "They don't need a woman to get in the middle of things. The risks are too great. The men are trained."

"Go away, Dinah," Angelica said very quietly. Too quietly. Before the remnants of her self-control floated off into the night.

"If you actually cared," Dinah told her piously, sounding

like a woman with a great capacity for emotional involvement, ''Stacy and Gillian were very worried about you.''

''I take it you weren't.''

Silence. Then... ''I knew Jake would send you on your way.'' Dinah was not a pretty sight in her jealousy and anger.

''Then he took his time about it. I'd say I've been up there two hours and more.'' Angelica normally so light-footed, dragged her steps as she started towards the house.

''Either you'd do anything to get Jake's attention or you're insane.'' Dinah came after her, her mind suddenly filled with doomed dreams.

''Anything else you'd like to add?'' Angelica turned so abruptly Dinah almost slammed into her.

''Yes.'' Dinah's green eyes were twin daggers as she threw down the challenge. Now was a good time. Everything being as rotten as it was. ''Just make sure you don't try to come between Jake and me.''

Angelica surveyed Dinah from her superior height. ''If you disappeared off the face of the earth I bet you he wouldn't notice.''

Dinah lost it. ''I don't give a stuff what you think,'' she said furiously. ''You'll be gone the day after the Christmas party. We'll never see you again.''

''When I've already got Jake to sign me up for his birthday party?''

''Wha-a-t?'' Dinah visibly recoiled.

''You heard. Jake is starting to get a real appreciation for my talents.''

''All the sex appeal?'' Dinah sneered, almost demented with jealousy. ''Slut. I bet there are a lot of wild stories about you.''

''You wish. Then you could take them all to Jake. Personally I have no idea what slut means. But if you asked me what a super-bitch was I could tell you.''

Up on the verandah Stacy and Gillian peered into the night anxiously. It had been a long worrying time and Dinah hadn't made things better with her incessant criticisms of Angelica.

"Oh, we're so glad you're back, Angelica, dear." Stacy flew down the steps the instant Angelica came into sight. "How's it going up there?" She lifted her eyes to the illuminated ridge. "It doesn't seem anywhere near as threatening, thank God."

"I'd say they were getting over the top of things at last," Angelica told her as they stood at the bottom of the steps. "Lighting hit a tree. That's what started it off."

"Angie, Angie, are you all right?" Now Gillian appeared, running down the short flight of steps to join them. "Why, you poor thing, you look exhausted. We would have been out of our minds with worry only we knew Jake was with you. You're very brave to have stayed. Fire is terrifying." She stared up into Angelica's face, thinking her a heroine.

"I'm as tough as old leather boots," Angelica laughed, when she felt more like slipping to her knees.

"Or too stupid to know better," Dinah suggested harshly, pleased Miss De Campo looked decidedly unsexy for once.

"Dinah, please don't! Now's not the time," Stacy begged, utterly dismayed by Dinah's attitude. Gillian, however, was wrought up enough to reach out and give Dinah a good push.

"You just won't shut up, will you, Dinah?" she said. "Leave Angie alone. Who do you think you are anyway? You treat Mum and I like dirt in our own home. You think Jake's in love with you and he's not. For God's sake, get a grip."

Dinah, fell back, utterly shocked, groping for words. "I can't believe you did that, Gilly," she said, feeling her shoulder like Gillian had broken the bone.

"No, you thought I was too much of a wimp," Gillian said. "Father practically made sure I was, though he was hospitable enough to you. Both of you rotten snobs. Leave Angie alone. She's our friend. Can't you see she's reeling on her feet?"

"Maybe it will teach her a lesson," Dinah cried the harder, thoroughly startled by Gillian's growth in self-confidence. She flinched in faked pain. "I'll be telling Jake just how rude you've been to me, Gilly.'' she threatened. ''I don't know why you should attack your poor father, either. He was quite charming to me.''

''Oh, sure!'' Gillian snorted. ''Father just exuded charm. You could have told him all about my rudeness for all I care, because boy, it was worth it. Your rudeness on the other hand has gone on long enough.''

''Gilly, darling, Dinah is our guest,'' Stacy wailed, wondering where it was all going to end.

''She invited herself.''

''So is Jake complaining?'' Dinah asked. ''I think you're getting very much above yourself, Gilly.''

Gillian threw back her head and laughed. ''That's priceless coming from you. Anyway it's Angie who needs our attention.''

''Yes, dear. Come inside,'' Stacy pleaded, all but wringing her hands. ''You'll feel much better after a long shower.'' She looked back towards the ridge where billows of smoke still filled the dark night. ''I think the fire has gone as far as it's going to,'' she said with great hope. ''There's never a dull moment around here. We've got our big day tomorrow.''

''Put it off,'' said Dinah with considerable disdain. The very last thing she wanted was for Angelica's efforts to amount to a great success.

''Put it off?'' Both McCord women looked at her in disbelief. ''That's impossible. It looks like Jake and the men have the fire under control,'' Stacy pointed out. ''We have to go ahead. People will expect it. I'm sure Jake will want us to.''

''Besides, we've all worked ourselves silly,'' Angelica said, having taken up a position against the stone pillar for support.

''So, dear,'' said Stacy most affectionately, ''when are you going to take your shower?''

''Just as soon as I can get myself around the back,'' Angelica replied. ''I can't go through the front door like this.'' She glanced down at her ruined shirt and jeans.

"Not when you're positively dripping dirty water," said Dinah with a kind of relish. "I think I'll be the one to greet Jake when he returns."

It was nearing midnight before Jake and his team felt confident to return to the home compound. They had watched and waited for any sign of a flare-up. Then around eleven they had a patch of rain. It was nothing approaching the substantial downpour they wanted, just an erratic scatter of heavy drops. Still, it was enough to dampen the ground and allow the temperature to drop.

The lights were on at the homestead. He expected Stacy and Gilly would be waiting. They had never been active women like Angel who wanted to pitch in there and help. His father would have forbidden them anyway. Both of them were frightened of the spot fires that broke out somewhere on the station every summer. Even then, Coori was prepared. Not only prepared but blessed. It had its interlocking system of creeks, bores, billabongs, lagoons, swamps. Wypanga Creek was one of the reasons they hadn't had a roaring bushfire on their hands tonight.

Angel had certainly pulled her weight, sharing the burden with the men. He blamed himself though for not sending her home earlier. Had that flaming branch hit her she could have been badly burnt. He found the thought devastating, like a punch in the gut but she had simply shrugged it off. Still he had allowed her to get herself exhausted. Oh hell! He swore he would make it up to her.

They had their big day tomorrow and the ball at night. He knew he would be reinvigorated after a few hours' sleep. His life was a hard one, physically demanding. Angel for all her fitness and positive attitudes was a woman. No woman had the same capacity for hard physical toil as a man. She had worked her beautiful butt off tonight. He would never forget it. He would never forget the way she had looked at him, her heart in her eyes. He knew she would be waiting for him as she had promised.

For long minutes he forgot Dinah was in the house. Dinah who was supposed to be in love with him. It seemed extraordinary now he had ever considered Dinah as a wife. Even in passing. They had shared a friendship for most of their lives. His father had wanted the marriage. His father had actually approved of Dinah when he had been a man who'd approved of very few. Maybe that was one of the reasons he couldn't really cotton to Dinah. She had what was for him a terrible flaw. She lacked heart.

He had to have a serious talk with Dinah. Level with her, though he had tried often enough in the past. It only held her back to persist with this bred-in idea marriage was the only answer for people like them.

He trudged up the front steps to the verandah intending to sit a few moments with the women before taking himself off to the shower block at the rear of the house. He was far too begrimed for anything else. At his halting footsteps, Stacy, followed by Gillian then Dinah, rushed out to greet him.

Stacy had tears in her eyes. "Jake, darling. What can I say?"

She made to hug him but he drew back laughing, holding up his hands. "For God's sake, Stacy, I'm filthy!"

"Would I care?"

"Let's leave the hugs until morning." He grinned. "I must look like the survivor of a war."

To Dinah, who despite her best efforts came in third in their race to the door, he looked marvellous. A living sculpture of a wild man, his glorious hair near crow-black with stray locks of gold, his skin so darkened his eyes glittered like topaz gems. Why couldn't he see they were meant for each other? That Angelica woman was the danger. But she had taken herself off to bed, thank God, leaving her, Dinah, to support him. She could easily get rid of Stacy and Gillian. She'd done it any number of times over the years.

Only it didn't work out that way. They talked for a little while. Clary emerged in her nightclothes to check everything was all right, when suddenly Jake stood up, his manner signalling conversation was at an end for the night.

''We've got a big day tomorrow,'' he said, already moving down the front steps. ''I want it to be special. I want you girls to look your best. Which means you need your beauty sleep. I'm sorry Angel went off to bed. I wanted to thank her for everything she did.''

He tried to keep his deep disappointment out of his voice. She had promised him she'd wait, but he didn't blame her in the least for finding her bed. She had a demanding day coming up. It wasn't fair to her after such a traumatic night. But still he grieved.

As the others retired, Dinah rushed forward to slide her arms around him with a rush of blood to the face. ''Why don't you come to my room afterwards?'' She pitched her voice low. ''Let me comfort you. I so want to.''

He forced a smile. ''I think a good scrub is what I need, Dinah. Thanks for caring.''

Dinah only nodded. ''I'll leave my door unlocked,'' she whispered, not a whit concerned by the fact her expensive white linen shirt was now badly soiled from contact with his body.

It took him less than a minute to let himself in the rear of the house, then walk down the passageway to what the family called the ''wet'' room. Stacy and Gillian rarely if ever used it but the men of the house always had after a hard day in the saddle. The room contained several shower cubicles along one wall. Washbasins to the other side topped by mirrors to shave. There were cupboards that ran down the centre of the room to divide one area from the other. A long bench to sit on. It had a lot in common with a men's locker room.

Once inside, he switched on the light, before locking the door. He wouldn't put it past Dinah to chase him up. He wished for the ten thousandth time she'd find someone else. Her preoccupation with becoming mistress of Coori amounted to an obsession. He started shucking off his clothes as he rounded the line of cabinets to find towels. Tired and filthy as he was, a profound longing to see Angel swept over him.

He said her name. His special name for her. He didn't know if he said it aloud. A few seconds more and he staggered to a halt, his surprise giving way to a great surge of joy. For a moment he couldn't even believe his eyes.

There she was fast asleep on the floor. A small light above her illuminated her sleeping face. She was nearly as begrimed as he was, her beautiful skin covered in black streaks like a soldier's camouflage. Her shoulders were mashed up against a locker.

''Angel!'' He squatted down. ''Angel, my darling, what are you doing asleep on the floor?'' He groaned with the intense feeling he couldn't hold back. ''Sweetheart, wake up,'' he said softly, allowing his fingers to curl around her dimpled chin.

She didn't move.

He slid his arms around her, intending to pull her up, but her eyelashes flickered, then her head pitched forward a little towards his chest.

''Jonathon!'' She peered up at him, slightly frowning as though she doubted he was really there. But she could see his remarkable eyes shining out of his blackened face. She reached out and placed the tips of her fingers against his cheek. Checking if he was real flesh. ''You're back!'' Her voice betrayed her wonder.

''It's all over. The fire's out. It's past midnight. What happened to you?''

She gave a shaky laugh, dumbstruck she hadn't made it up off the floor. ''Would you believe I was going to take a shower. I was much too wet and dirty to go into the house. Here seemed the right place. I walked along to get a towel, but I must have felt dizzy for a moment. I plonked down here to recover, but I guess sleep overcame me. I don't seem to have moved.''

''Well you have to move now,'' he said. ''Let me help you. You need a shower, then bed.'' Gently, very gently, he wrapped his arms around her, pulling her to her feet. Even in his condition he felt driving desire and protectiveness at opposite poles. She smelt of fire, as he knew he did, but it might have been the ultimate fragrance. Her long hair was covered in a fine red dust.

"I think I've forgotten how to walk." She gave a little laugh that came out like a sob.

"I'll carry you." All he knew was, he wanted her in his arms.

"I know you're very strong but you must be dead on your feet, as well."

He wasn't. Not now. His blood was running like a molten river of lava.

"Have we got any shampoo?" she asked as he deposited her outside the first cubicle.

"We've got everything," he said with certainty. Clary made sure of it.

"You need to clean up as much as I do," she called after him with concern.

"So you take that shower recess and I'll take the one at the end. Does that fit in with your idea of the proprieties?"

"Proprieties depend on the situation at the time," she said wryly, possessed by the image of him. Even after battling a fire, soot-blackened, he was startlingly virile and handsome.

Her long hair that when the wind caught it reminded him of a raven's wing was filmed with grime. He touched her, putting the plastic bottle of shampoo into her hand. All tiredness had sloughed away from him like the skin of a desert snake. Nevertheless he got himself mobile. "You can get undressed. I promise I won't look."

"What's so terrible about a naked woman?" Exhilaration made her laugh.

"A beautiful, seductive, naked woman," he amended dryly. "You have too much power. The aborigines call it woman-magic. I discovered that when I first kissed you. What do you imagine would happen if I suddenly turned around?"

"You won't."

He heard the smile in her voice. "Why not?"

"Because you gave your word. Anyway, I'm ready."

"Good. I'll leave a couple of towels and a robe on the bench."

She turned on the taps, standing under the good strong spray that felt like a waterfall. She held up her face as exhaustion slid away with the soot. "Oh, this is heaven!" she cried, intensely aware he was only a short distance away, but not fazed by anything. For that moment—for long minutes until she was squeaky-clean—that was enough. She knew she wasn't in control of herself. She didn't care. Her heart's flutter was so pronounced she could feel it beating under her palm.

She soaped every inch of her body while she imagined soaping him. She could even feel the bronze-velvet texture of his skin. The scent of shampoo and boronia-perfumed soap surrounded her like a cloud. It was a marvellous feeling to get clean.

Finally when her ablutions were over, she slid open the door, hearing Jake humming quietly to himself as he continued to shower. He had a tuneful baritone. An old love song. She knew every word...

A profound daring swept over her. She slipped into the man's white towelling robe that was too big for her, padding softly in the direction of his shower cubicle. "Jonathon, how are you?" she called.

There was a short silence then she heard his voice. "To tell you the truth I'm longing for you to join me, though we both know what that would result in."

The vibrant tones were edged with self mockery.

"I'm already here." She placed her hand on the chrome knob, impelled to open the steam-clouded door.

The male perfection of his body stopped her in her tracks. He was an athlete, with the stature of a warrior. He was bronze all over, with no line of white anywhere. She knew the men on the station didn't give a damn about skinny-dipping after working in the intense heat. The hair at his groin was the same bright amber as the thick waves of his head. Rivulets of water ran down his noble body, a body classical in its construction. He glistened like a man freshly scrubbed.

"God, Angel!" Her impulsive action had knocked the breath from him.

"Stop me if you want to," she said, finding it impossible to move or look away.

"You know things will get out of hand?" He gave her fair warning, making no attempt to turn away from her ravished eyes.

"In that event I'm coming in." Very slowly she slid the robe down her body, allowing it to drop to the tiled floor.

Her eyes were enormous, deep and liquid, black as night. Her hair ran down her back like a bolt of satin. He stood beneath the running water transfixed by her as she had been transfixed by him. Undressed she seemed even more slender than she was in her clothes. Her shoulders were beautiful, sloping away from her long graceful neck. Her waist beneath her exquisite full breasts designed to be fondled, caressed by a man's hand, seemed tiny by comparison. He felt sure he could span it. Her stomach was taut, her hips gently rounded. A tiny patch of black silk veiled her secret core. Her legs were as perfect as any woman's could be. She was the reincarnation of a goddess.

The sense of inevitability was dazzling. He felt a rush of primitive passion he could not fight off. Face drawn, he took hold of her almost fiercely, pulling her with great urgency into the cubicle. There he backed her up against the glass wall, one arm locked tightly around her waist. He used his knee to separate her beautiful legs. The shock of having her naked, trembling flesh against him was so great it might have been mistaken for inner conflict. He could feel the muscles of his face and his body tautening as it came into intimate contact with hers. He could feel his manhood instantly react, swelling with power and desire. She had made it clear she wanted him. Now he would never let her get away.

They were both bathed in steam. Heat rushing inside and

out. His heart pounding, he cupped her moisture-slicked breasts, bent his head to her nipples, flushed with colour. He felt her shudder with rapture as his tongue flicked back and forth, before his mouth came down suckling passionately but with an underlying tenderness he scarcely knew was his gift.

"Jonathon," she cried out, gasping.

"I'm powerless to stop." Now he ground her hips against his as she came up on her toes to accommodate him.

"I don't want you to stop." Her body clung like some wondrous, sinuous vine. "I long for you."

He lost himself then. Lost everything but her. Exultantly he possessed her wet mouth; twining his tongue around hers, thrilled by a depth of passion that matched his own. He let his hands move down over her body, groaning with pleasure at the brush of his hands against her olive, scented flesh. She made him so happy. It was perfect. It was torture. He was deliberately holding back in the tumultuous pursuit of sensation. He wanted to pleasure her as she was delighting him. He wanted to prolong this experience like no other, conscious a tide of excitement was welling higher and higher.

Now suddenly with closed eyes, he placed a finger at the entrance to her vagina. Nothing more. Yet it unleashed a great torrent of emotion. Her moans changed in tone, coming in melting gasps, like she was losing her breath. He wanted to fill her with his driving male lust and his longing, with his love. He wanted to mate with her. He was saturated with excitement. Outside of himself.

"Angel!" He gazed down into her face. Passion had redefined her superb bone structure, the skin so taut she looked chiselled. She was magic! He had no intention of ever letting her get away.

CHAPTER TEN

AT DAWN they melded into each other again. They had spent the night together in Jake's huge king-size bed, making love so glorious the memory of it would never be erased. Later, they were stunned by the revelation they slept wrapped in each other's arms. Not two separate people but close enough for one. Now they re-sought that passionate connection while beyond the verandah, the great symphony of birds brought music to their sexual rapture.

When finally Jake rose to his feet, she put out her arms to entice him back to her side. "Don't go." She wore nothing but the sheet that barely covered her breasts. He could see the deep cleft between them like a smudge of lavender on her olive-ivory skin.

"It's getting late." If he re-entered that bed, he felt he would never get up again.

"Yes. Yes, I know." She sighed voluptuously. "Just sit down for a moment more." She waited then nestled her head beneath his arm to kiss his ribs. "You are the most wonderful lover."

"Good enough to make you stay with me?" He stared down at her. For all their passionate lovemaking, hitherto unimagined or even dreamed of, neither had uttered those momentous words, "I love you."

"It's marvellous here." She continued to kiss his flesh. "I want it always to be like this. You and me. Come back to bed." She moved over enticingly.

He smiled, amber eyes brilliant. There wasn't a trace of tiredness in him for all the experiences of the day before and the fact they'd had little repose. "Don't tempt me," he said very dryly.

''A little longer. I've never known anyone like you.'' She knelt to cover his shoulders in kisses, her breasts curving in satin globes against his back. ''One more time,'' she sighed.

''You're insatiable!'' My God, and he wasn't? ''Don't we have a full day?''

She kissed beneath his ear. ''I thought time had stood still.''

''Angel…'' He was weakening, desire rippling into his body on a king tide.

''Tonight then?'' she whispered.

''Yes.'' He pulled her down so her beautiful glossy hair spilled all over her face. ''Tomorrow, as well. And the next day. And the next day…'' His voice was hypnotic. ''I can't get enough of you.''

''Kiss me,'' she begged, aware of the fluttering that had started up in the pit of her stomach and moved to between her legs.

''I shouldn't,'' he murmured, moving the silky cascade of hair from her face. Nevertheless he risked it.

And was completely lost.

For Angelica the day moved on a high. Nothing went wrong. Nothing could go wrong such was the happiness and optimism of her emotional level. She was in love with the most wonderful man. She believed he loved her, both of them overwhelmed by an experience so divine it was like the gates of heaven had been opened to them, leaving them voiceless with reverence. Even the mercury favoured them, dropping a few degrees though it soared again during the afternoon's play.

The main match, the Marsdon Cup final, was played under brilliantly hot cloudless skies. This didn't appear to deter either players or spectators though the liquid refreshments disappeared at express rate.

The women, looking cool and glamorous, sat on rattan chairs beneath peppermint-striped and fringed umbrellas, slowly sipping long frosted drinks, locked into general conversation and gossip interspersed with cries of bravo and much clapping. The men who weren't playing confined themselves to closely following the match and rehashing their days of glory in the saddle. Polo was the game.

Jake's team, coming in as the underdogs because they had lost one of their best players, was pulling together strongly. On a hunch Jake had substituted Charlie as the Number 1 front player. Charlie, it had to be admitted, had a bit of a wild streak he hadn't yet tamed, but he was a crack horseman and suited to the job of keeping well up the pitch, taking forward passes and shooting for goal.

Both of them, Angelica considered, along with the rest of the female spectators, looked outrageously sexy, the only two golden boys among the dark-haired competitors.

"Charlie's not in love with me, is he?" sighed Gillian, who was looking very chic thanks to a smart new outfit and a little help from Angelica with her hair and make-up. "Why did I ever think he was?"

"Maybe you were in love with love?" Angelica turned lazily to smile at her.

"He's handsome, though, isn't he?"

"He sure is." Angel gave a nod of assent. "He'll be handsomer in a few years."

"You're the one he fancies," Gillian said, surprising her. "He fancied you right off."

"Oh nonsense!" Angel straightened in her rattan chair. "Charlie and I are friendly, that's all. He's very good company, also he was a big help to us." Besides, I'm madly, deeply, wildly in love with your half brother, she omitted to add.

Gillian shrugged that off. "No. I'm not glamorous enough, or exciting enough for Charlie. I'm the girl next door. You're more his style. The truth is I'm far more suited to Ty Caswell. Jake's right."

"To really find out, Gilly, you should do what Charlie's doing. Spread your wings," Angel suggested.

"How exactly?" Gillian eyed her.

"Why not take a job in the city for a while?"

"They'd sack me," Gillian said.

"Why not undertake a course of study? There must be something you'd like to do?"

"I'm not terribly bright, you know," Gillian asserted wryly. "Father was always going on about what a fool I was. He told me I took after Mum. Seems odd, doesn't it, when Jake excelled at everything, academically and on the sports field. All the McCords are clever, influential people. Anyway I don't have to work. Father left me a lot of money. He did it because he had a low opinion of me no doubt."

"It sounds more like he robbed you and your mother of all confidence," Angel said gently. "We'll talk about this some more. Your mother told me she'd like the two of you to visit the cities more. Oh, look, Jake's turned the play back to attack."

"That's why he's the captain," Gillian said smugly. "He's the strongest and best player and he's trained his ponies to be very agile and responsive. They're fast and quick-thinking, too. We should win. That will put Ty's nose out of joint. His team thought they would take it."

Jake's team did win by the narrowest of margins, making for a thrilling, cliffhanger finish. The cup was presented by the wife of one of the biggest property owners in the country—a philanthropist polo devotee—and soon after the grounds cleared as everyone took advantage of the cooling down of late afternoon. The women were all in favour of resting before the expected high jinks of the ball. These functions were known to go right through the night as Outback people extracted every ounce of enjoyment from these legendary weekends.

Coori homestead was crowded with the guests quarters and staff quarters so full that the neighbouring stations helped out with the accommodation. The homestead was looking magnificent and very festive. The splendid tree was such a talking point. They had all worked hard to make sure everything gleamed, sparkled, shone. The flowers, lavish and beautifully arrange had been flown in, as had seasoned professionals in the hospitality business, with capabilities well known to Angelica. The catering, later described in a glossy magazine as sumptuous, was well in hand.

The Great Hall looked marvellous thanks to Leah's loving, whimsical, imaginative efforts, but no way could Angelica get Leah to agree to joining in the social events.

"Better I don't," she told Angelica, not really disappointed. "I've had a great time. Though I couldn't have done it without you, Miss."

"Just you wait until others can see what you can do, Leah," Angelica promised. Prophetically as it turned out.

Being in charge of the festivities Angelica had little time to sit around, though several times she tried it. Her job was to circulate and see Coori's guests were being well looked after. With everyone so complimentary, smiles, nods, waves all 'round, Dinah Campbell emerged the odd woman out.

Dinah let loose her poisonous envy and jealousy the moment she could. It had begun at her first sight of Angelica standing on the homestead verandah, looking like some film star in her prime. But since she had caught sight of Angelica emerging from Jake's room at dawn, wearing only a man's navy silk robe, her outrage had reached massive proportions. Who was this woman to push the man she loved from her life? Dinah burned with anger and humiliation at the utter unfairness of it. She had survived Jake's other affairs. If she put her mind to it she could survive this one equally well.

At her first opportunity—it wasn't easy because Miss De Campo was being made welcome everywhere—Dinah yielded completely to the jealous ferment that was in her.

"Aren't you a piece of work?" She forcibly steered Angel away from the crowd with a tight grip on her arm.

"You're too kind." Angelica smiled sweetly as people appeared to be watching their every move. "But please do get your hand off my arm. I have a brother with a black belt. He's shown me a few moves."

"God knows you're big enough," Dinah sneered. "Why you wear high heels I'll never know."

They were a distance off, standing beneath the shade of a coolibah, before Dinah released Angelica's arm. "I take it you have a problem?" Angelica eyed the other woman closely, a trifle unnerved by the odd expression in Dinah's eyes, which had turned a livid green.

"I do," Dinah confirmed.

Angelica looked back at the milling crowd. The match was over. Tea, coffee and drinks were still being served in the big marquee. It had been an afternoon of triumph for Coori station. Now this! She wondered whether Dinah was capable of making a scene. She decided she probably was. For all her disdain and general air of superiority Dinah was short on grace. "I only hope you're going to tell me because I have many things left to do." The best part making herself beautiful for Jake.

Dinah looked at her with great contempt. "Like sleeping with Jake? That's right. Don't look away. I saw you sneaking away from his room first thing this morning."

Angelica sighed. "I just knew I couldn't get a clean getaway. Not with you in the house. No wonder you look so jealous." Though she spoke mildly, she was angered by the thought Dinah had been spying on them. "So tell me, what were you doing up at dawn? And at Jake's end of the house? Or don't you need an excuse?"

"Not me!" Dinah glared at her. "You think I haven't been there before?" She flashed Angelica a pitying look. "How could you be such a fool? I've been Jake's girl ever since I can remember. Don't think he's seriously interested in you. What he sees is earthiness. And availability. You exude vulgar sex. You're the one who's been making all the play. Men are permanently unfaithful. Even Jake."

Angelica merely stared at her. "Are you saying this happens in your happy family? I'm sorry. My parents have had a wonderful thirty-year marriage loving only each other. As for Jake, I'd be shocked to know he was promiscuous."

"You know absolutely nothing about Jake," Dinah hissed. "Ever since you arrived you've been working hard to drive him to the limit flaunting that long black hair and your bosom. You've bewitched him if you ask me."

"What would you have me do?" Angelica mocked, secure in the knowledge she had a beautiful body. "Bind my chest down?"

"You might be more modest. You're the kind of woman tailor-made for an affair. Not walking up the aisle. Jake has these affairs from time to time. But he always comes back to me."

"I don't believe that. I can't," Angelica answered quietly, feeling the happiness of the day slipping away.

"No, because you don't want to," Dinah said. "He's dropped all the others. Not me. I'm prepared to hang in there for as long as it takes. As for you! You shared an experience. Fighting the fire together. Jake gave in to lust. That's all it was. You were just an extra service."

"The Bimbo and the Cattle Baron," Angelica mocked. "Forbidden fruit."

"Whatever he does, Jake knows he can come back to me."

"Do you realise you could be wasting your life?" Angelica asked almost kindly.

"I know what I'm about." Dinah's green eyes blazed. "Your little flutter will add up to a great big nothing, you'll see. Try to remember, in a few days' time you go home. And I'll be absolutely ecstatic to see you go."

"Hang on a moment. I believe the family are hoping to see you go first?"

"If you're talking about Stacy and Gillian, they'd better get used to seeing me around. Jake has asked my entire family to the Christmas party, didn't you know?"

"So you figure you can hang around until then?"

"Why not?" Dinah shrugged.

"At least you're thick-skinned," Angelica said. "I wouldn't be too certain if the real lady of the house doesn't politely suggest you buzz off. I think she's had enough of you, but she dislikes unpleasantness."

"You mean she's a real wimp. Everyone thinks so."

"You'd better not let Jake hear you say that."

"As if I would. I'm not a fool, you know."

"That's a matter of opinion," Angelica snapped. "I know exactly what I think of you. Now you must excuse me. It's a shame to waste such a lovely afternoon talking bunkum to you. 'Bye now."

Dinah's response was to turn on her heel, lips drawn back in a single word. "Bitch!"

It came out quite loudly. Several people turned to stare at her. Some had had a taste of Dinah Campbell's sharp tongue in the past and it still rankled. Good to see the uppity Miss Campbell blow her cool.

By ten o'clock the ball was in full swing. The award-winning band, flown in by charter, played joyously. Everyone was exhilarated and on great form, the women dressed in many bright hues resembled a field of multi-coloured sparkling flowers, smiling radiantly at their men. Leah's billowy cloud ceiling was a great success, the talk of the evening in fact. Guests when they first entered the Great Hall stood in rapt silence to consider it, heads upturned, their expressions filled with pleasure, interest and a measure of surprise. The improvised waterlily lagoon beneath a canopy of trees was rhapsodical, very much suggesting Coori's landscape, inspiring the wealthy philanthropist to remark he could find work for such a talented young lady.

Iridescent dragonflies dipped over the silvered green waters, the magnificent waterlilies painted in their range of colours—pink, white, red, blue, cream—holding their lovely heads above the floating emerald pads. Others admired the floating umbrellas and sporting cups, the way Leah had captured the action of the three polo players, the Number 3 player clearly identifiable as Jake. The whole effect was captivating with considerable technical fluency.

"Gosh, you can even hear the thundering hooves," said Charlie, resplendent in black tie. "Jake looks like a god, doesn't he?" he laughed. He turned to look at Angelica, thinking her a perfect vision. "You look absolutely gorgeous. Tall, slender, beautiful!" He tore his eyes away exclaiming, "That dress! I love it. Did I tell you?"

"At least twice." Angelica smiled, laying a hand on his jacketed arm. "But I don't mind hearing it again."

"This is grand." Charlie was determined to make a night of it. "What I'd really like is to dance. Game?"

"I'd love it!" Angelica answered promptly.

Charlie led her out onto the floor chortling. He'd dreamed of having a flutter with a magnificent female. Maybe he might finally get lucky. His two-year stint on a great Australian cattle station had been an adventure. He didn't believe he would ever forget it. But he accepted he would be going home. One day, like Jake, whom he admired enormously, he would have to take his father's place. But for now? Angelica was smiling at him and her big beautiful dark eyes looked so inviting. She was without question the most beautiful woman in the room. And the most exciting. His sense of adventure was at work again!

Standing in the middle of a crowd of friends, Jake saw them take the floor. They looked spectacular. Charlie, off duty, dressed in a dinner jacket, was every inch the Honourable Charles Middleton. And he had such a great zest for life. Not that it hadn't gotten him into his fair share of trouble. No one could miss the fact either that Charlie found Angel a real knockout. His expression, which he didn't bother to hide, was a dead give-away. Much as he liked Charlie, Jake was startled to discover he didn't like the way Charlie had Angel locked in his arms. Charlie, frankly, looked in seventh heaven. Angel looked what? Indulgent? The two of them got on well. Ah well, enjoy yourself for the time being, Charlie, Jake thought silently. That woman is mine.

It was hard to listen to what the senator was saying when

he couldn't take his eyes off them. Angel was wearing the most beautiful dress he'd ever seen and there were some stunning dresses out there on the dance floor. The young women in particular, just loved these social occasions as it gave them the opportunity to dress up. Everyone made sure they looked their very best, going all out on the gowns. Gillian in a deep pink strapless organza dress with a skirt that looked like petals had never looked prettier. Stacy, too, had done him proud in sequined blue that showed off her youthful petite figure. But Angel. Wow!

How to describe that dress? It was very, very sexy and very imaginative. Not like the usual evening dress at all but a creation in gold, silver and sage green with ribbons and all kinds of fancy beadwork and sequins. A man could never describe it. The slip bodice was low-cut, revealing the swell of her beautiful breasts, the skirt had a deep flounce that showed a lot of leg. She looked like a film star. God, yes! Charlie thought so, too. He'd go and cut in just as soon as the senator stopped talking.

Charlie was a fast worker. Challenge dictated his every move. Not that Charlie knew anything about his involvement with Angel. Neither of them had put their feelings on display. Rather the reverse. Charlie was light-footed, light-hearted. Angel appeared to be floating… Hell, Charlie was tap dancing!

"…so in the end it was my lucky night!" the senator concluded, while they all laughed heartily.

Dinah, in emerald-green silk satin, her platinum hair artfully tousled, laughed, too, though her gaze had long since shifted away from the senator to follow Jake's. That woman with too much of her body on display was dancing with Charles Middleton! Surely that wasn't cracking Jake up? She was hardly the solid, faithful type.

And didn't Charles look polished. Unrecognisable, really, from the station jackeroo. Not that he'd ever been treated like one. As far as she knew Gilly had had a crush on Charles. That was a cause for amusement. Not that one could blame the poor little thing, though she did look remarkably glamorous tonight. Stacy did, too.

It was getting tiresome, Miss De Campo's interference. Apparently she had helped them achieve what they had never achieved before. An appearance in line with the McCord family status. Stacy had sprung another surprise getting it together with Leif Standford, the financier, who owned a string of winning race horses. Leif, a widower, would eventually remarry, but Dinah would never have thought ineffectual little Stacy would take his eye. Yet they'd been glued to one another's side all night. Extraordinary!

To top it off, Charles, it now appeared, was very interested in the dark-eyed, dark-haired Miss De Campo's anatomy, if nothing else. Unless she was very much mistaken, Jake didn't like it at all. His golden eyes might look lazy beneath his marked, bronze brows, he had a smile on his beautiful mouth, but she knew Jake. He was watching Charles and the Mediterranean sex goddess like the proverbial hawk. Surely this was a god-sent opportunity to do a little mischief? Jake really should see that woman for what she was. Specifically, a tart. There must be some way to work it, to push Charles and Miss De Campo together.

This was a party, after all, and there was plenty of alcohol. The last time she'd seen Charles at one of these do's he'd been quite frenetic. What she had in mind was a dawn orgy. Her Jake wouldn't be happy about that. Well now it was payback time! Revenge was her middle name.

Charles handed Angelica over without demur. "That was great, Angelica!" he said, laughing into her beautiful, black-lashed eyes. "Now the boss is here, I'll have to hand you over."

"Goodbye, Charlie," Jake drawled. "Stay away."

"I'll be back!" Charlie grinned boldly.

"I feel I can't let you out of my sight," Jake muttered, gathering her hungrily close. It was an action that plunged them into passionate intimacy.

"Sounds fine to me," Angelica answered huskily. She'd

been having fun with the debonair Charlie, but she'd been longing for the moment when Jake would cross the room and take her into his arms. He wore a white dinner jacket and the effect against his tawny colouring and golden-bronze skin was startlingly attractive. He was a powerfully sexual man yet he seemed quite unaware of it and his extraordinary looks.

"Watch Charlie," he said, with an unconscious little edge.

She drew back a little to stare into his amber eyes. "Don't you trust me?"

"I don't trust Charlie," he told her dryly. "When Charlie gets a mad idea into his head he takes off. He's extremely impulsive."

"Why he's a few years younger than I am," she pointed out in amazement. Indeed she thought of Charlie as still a boy.

"Sure," he softly jeered, "and I'm thinking he's getting carried away."

"Good thinking on your part." She had to laugh, aware of Charlie's youthful interest. "I can handle Charles."

"I'm glad to hear it."

"He's only having fun. You don't think you're a little bit jealous?" Looking into his eyes gave her enormous pleasure.

"I can promise I will be. I don't want anyone to put their arms around you but me." The whole truth and nothing but the truth.

"I love that." She sighed and flushed like a rose. It was such rapture to be in his arms. Every cell in her body reacted.

"I adore that dress. It's beautiful. The only thing I'd like more is to peel it off you."

The sensuality in his voice made her tremble. "I'm going to let you." She raised her huge dark eyes to him.

They were made desperately lovely because of some shadow she wore on the lids, a mysterious green like her dress. Had he really made endless love to her? Made her come over and over or had he only dreamt it? He would have died for a kiss at that moment, his desire for her so powerful he was almost afraid of it. He hadn't thought himself such a vulnerable man. But he was where she was concerned. Without even trying she attracted every male within range. It was a power she had and that power, he knew, wouldn't cease. She'd probably have it when she was an old lady. The man who married her would have to be prepared for fighting off all comers even if she was a woman of unquestioned loyalty. He was in love with her. Within days in fact of asking her to marry him. If she said yes, could there be a better Christmas?

"What would I do if you went away?" he mused aloud.

"I'm not leaving." She intended it to sound like a little joke, instead her voice betrayed her. It was intense and emotional. Why? She loved him.

"I just cannot believe this has all happened so quickly," he said, smoothing his cheek against her glossy hair.

"But what a miracle!" she breathed.

Across the Great Hall Dinah watched them with a cold weight on her heart. She had never seen Jake like this before. Not with anyone. He'd gone overboard for this woman, who had to be really clever. Well, she could be clever, too. Certain things she knew Jake hated. Unfaithfulness was one of them. She remembered his outburst when their friends, the Hammonds, broke up. They'd all suspected Lucienne had been having an affair. Jake hadn't liked that one little bit. Jake liked to think marriage was forever.

It was easy for Dinah to get Charles to dance with her. Better yet, she thought he was a little drunk, though his movements were controlled enough. "I saw you dancing with Miss De Campo," she said archly, cocking her platinum head to one side. "Now there's a swinger. A real party-party girl, if you know what I mean?"

"I adore her," said Charles, thinking he had never succeeded in liking Jake's ex-girlfriend, Dinah Campbell. So what if she was good-looking and her family was supposed to be loaded? There was a hardness behind the expensive wrapping and those pretty, cool green eyes. Frankly he didn't think she was good enough for Jake.

"And she likes you," Dinah continued, playing him as though he were a simple child. "She finds you thoroughly attractive, sophisticated and worldly. Not difficult to see why. You look marvellous in black tie, and of course you are the Honourable Charles Middleton. It shows."

If only she weren't such an embarrassing snob!

"You've made quite an impression on her."

For a moment Charles was quite overcome. That beautiful woman attracted to him? That was a huge coup. It stunned him. "How do you know?" he demanded, maddened he hadn't had a clue.

"Why she told me, obviously," Dinah trilled. "I'm sure she'd be yours if you want."

Charles wanted badly. Man was born to sow his wild oats! Supper came and went though it was more like a banquet. The buffet tables were laden with the most delectable food including ham, turkey, chicken, beef, served in hot or cold dishes. Magnificent seafood had been flown in from tropical North Queensland—lobster, crab, the Gulf's famous prawns, oysters nestling in ice; pasta dishes, all kinds of salads. There was a separate buffet table for the splendid desserts. Waiters circled constantly, refilling champagne flutes. It couldn't have been more splendid or more festive. Christmas was definitely in the air.

It was around two in the morning when that daredevil Charles suggested a treasure hunt. Treasure hunts went off very well at home and they did offer distinct romantic possibilities. It was a huge inducement to know Angelica was attracted to him. After all, he had plenty to offer. The younger guests received the suggestion with much clapping and cheering.

The boundaries were set and included the avenues of walkways connecting the Great Hall with the homestead as well as the Great Hall and its immediate grounds. The homestead itself was off limits. The treasure was to be planted by Jake, as master of Coori station and their host.

Once Jake moved off—he was given ten minutes to find a suitable hiding place—Charlie seized Angelica's hand. "You're with me," he said, flushed with triumph. "Jake can't be in the game. He knows where the treasure's hidden."

His mood was infectious. Though Charlie was almost an adolescent, he was good fun. Out under the stars they heard peals of giggles; girl's voices, light, sweet and young. The black-velvet sky was ribboned by the Milky Way, a glorious diamond haze containing billions of stars.

It was utterly beautiful! Angelica looked up, marking the stars that made up the constellation of the Southern Cross. It hung over the homestead's great roof, easy to pick out in the pure desert air. The star furthest to the south was a star of the first magnitude. East and north, the second magnitude. To the west, a star of the third magnitude. In ancient times it was visible in Babylonia and Greece.

"You're not supposed to be star-gazing," Charlie whispered in her ear, his excitement gathering by the moment. "We're looking for treasure. Or we're supposed to be." He wondered wildly if he should kiss her now. But just as he thought it, he had to think again. Another couple followed them up.

"You behave yourself, Charlie," said the guy, one of the members of the opposing polo team.

"Isn't that what I always do," Charlie quipped, leading Angelica across the springy grass to one of the vine-covered bowers, its flowers glowing radiantly.

"I'm not sure Jake would plant it here." She smiled, not much caring. The breeze was glorious, carrying the marvellous perfume of the purple boronia that grew wild. It was a fantastic night. She was so happy! Her thoughts were entirely of Jake. Not of Charlie, greatly misled.

For a while Charlie made a pretence of looking for the treasure, shaking out plants and looking around and beneath all the stone garden benches. They were moving further away from the lights that blazed around the Great Hall. The home gardens had been lit for the occasion, a veritable fairyland, but there were delicious pockets of dark.

Finally Charlie couldn't stand it. He stood stock-still, staring down into Angelica's pearlescent face. It took a special kind of man to lead a celibate life. It was not a life for him!

"What then?" she whispered, wondering why he had stopped.

"Oh, Angelica, why didn't you tell me you were attracted to me?" he asked tenderly.

That brought Angelica back to earth with a crash. "Charlie," she exhaled in shock, "I'm not attracted to you."

But heat was flowing into Charlie at the rate of knots. He put his hands on her shoulders, revelling in the feel of her bones and her satiny, perfumed skin. "You don't mean that." Not since Dinah's revelation.

"I absolutely do." She tried to sound stern and failed. "If you don't stop being silly, I'm going back."

But Charlie, intoxicated on all fronts, was under a pounding, painful desire. God knows, he didn't get to meet too many beautiful women miles way out in the bush. "You can't!" he protested in a spectacularly loud voice.

"Shh, be quiet!" Embarrassed, Angel looked back over her shoulder.

"No. Angelica, there's a good side to this," he informed her.

"Really, what?"

"I can afford to come to Sydney to see you. I could spend some time in the New Year with you."

"Oh, Charlie, no more!" Angel pleaded, unwilling to hurt his feelings. "You're being ridiculous. I've never given you the slightest encouragement. Not now. Not ever. I think you've had a bit too much to drink. We really ought to go back."

"Not until I've kissed you," Charlie said masterfully. It had always worked with Gilly. With a smooth slide of muscle he hauled her up against him, kissing her frantically though she tried to jerk her head back.

"You're beautiful, so beautiful!" His young voice literally shook with excitement. "You wanted that, didn't you?"

What she really wanted to do was sock him, her long hair thrashing from side to side as she attempted to wrestle him off. "Charlie, stop this," she gritted. "Someone will come along."

"Let them. Oh, hell, Angelica, did you have to kick me?" Charlie broke off to press his hand against his shin. "The truth is I'm mad about you. I just realised it. Dinah Campbell tipped me off."

"Dinah Campbell?" Angelica felt a red tide of anger as Charlie straightened, locking a finger around her wrist.

"Yes, Dinah," he confided. "I don't like her much but she did me a favour." Charlie, with a huge capacity for pleasure, reached for her again, holding her face still in his hands while he planted an emotion-charged kiss on her mouth. "I'll do the right thing by you," he muttered when he was able to talk at all.

"Hey, don't worry!" Angelica kicked him again and Charlie gave a moan of pain, perceiving through an alcohol-induced fog, Dinah, sinister sort of girl that she was, might have led him astray. Angelica didn't appear to be keen on him after all. "Don't be like this," he coaxed. "Really, Dinah's the one who should be shot. The bitch! I'm so sorry. I was out of line. Let's kiss and make up." He risked placing an arm around her, bending his blond head. He wanted to steal a kiss one last time!

Simultaneously Jake found them, silhouetted against nearby lights. Which was exactly what Dinah had planned on. To all appearances they were locked in each other's arms, enjoying a smouldering kiss. Angel's long hair was cascading down her back. One shoulder was entirely bare, as the thin strap of her gown slid down her arm, revealing more of her breast. Her skin glowed in the semi-dark.

He went to earth with his deepest emotions. He realised

he'd always lived that way. He wondered briefly if she were a nymphomaniac, and quickly rejected it disgustedly as part of the jealousy process. More likely men couldn't keep their hands off her. Either way it would be hell to be married to her.

Blessed with excellent night vision he stared for a long while hoping with all his heart Angel when released would reach back and slap Charlie's handsome face. She didn't. Instead they spoke quietly for a moment, dark and fair heads together as though planning another assignation. Then Angel turned away no doubt to return to the Hall. And she was going alone. Charlie, just like in a movie, skulked off in the opposite direction.

Head down, moving so innocently in her exquisite seductive gown, she almost walked into him. "Jake!" She clutched her throat. She seemed guilty, as though caught in the act.

"Have you ever tried getting treatment?" he asked acidly, knowing full well pain was making him lash out even as it heightened his desire.

She placed a gentle, restraining hand on his arm. "Charlie is drunk," she explained, much as she might say little Kylee was being naughty. "You know what he's like. He lost it for a while."

"You mean another one went off the deep end?" It sounded brutal. He didn't want that, but he was injured.

"Men being what they are," she said with hurt sarcasm. "Look, I like Charlie. He's just a boy."

"Some boy!" he responded tight-lipped, wanting to crush her mouth under his. The problem was he was too proud. And so afraid of loving. He abandoned himself to jealous rage, doubly angry because he had never really experienced the emotion before. In fact he was in awe of it. He had never depended on anyone outside his beloved mother for emotional support, until he met this woman. "So far as I could see he had his tongue down your throat," he bit off. Even as he said it he felt wretched.

"How would you know? Have you got X-ray vision?"

she challenged him, her own temper rising though she scented his hard desire.

"You're damned right I have. What did you go with him for anyway?"

"You want to forbid me to walk with anyone else?" She leaned towards him as though he, not Charlie, would be the recipient of a good back-hander.

"I think I told you to watch out for Charlie," he said harshly.

"That's me, a siren, luring men onto the rocks. Can't you trust me for five minutes, Jonathon?"

He took a deep breath, feeling it shake in his throat. "God knows I want to." Why couldn't he say, "I love you"? Or was he going to be trapped forever? "I thought we had something valuable," he said. "Something important. Something that would lead us to make vows. But for God's sake, do you have to lead every man in sight into temptation?" He knew he should stop but he couldn't, enwrapped in a lifetime of bitter disappointments.

Her beautiful face registered anger and pain. "Of course I do!" She gave another angry laugh. "It's never the man's fault, is it? I'd have a lifetime of getting the blame from you if we were married."

"Oh, so you thought I was going to ask you to marry me?" he asked with a touch of his father's cruelty. It sounded like an obscenity in his own ears.

"Weren't you?" she seethed. "Or was I just another one of your affairs? Dinah told me you had them from time to time. She also told poor alcohol-impaired Charlie that I had the hots for him. Or words to that effect."

"Dinah did?" He felt sick. Like he'd done some irreparable damage by rushing into judgment when she could simply be telling the truth.

"That's right. Are you surprised? Dinah, your friend," she said fiercely. "She wanted to discredit me. And she knows all about you. More than I do, at any rate. She knows what a puritan you are. The worse kind of man. Like your father."

A stricken silence. ''I didn't mean that.'' Her voice shook. ''You make me so angry, but I didn't mean it.''

''Maybe you're right,'' he said, his grave face poised above her. ''There are certain things I want from the woman I'd ask to be my wife. I thought I'd met her. I don't count Charlie. I understand what stage Charlie's at. But I meant nothing to you. You could have stopped him. Charlie might be a bit drunk but he's not the kind to force a woman.''

''Really? I thought you were all that kind,'' she returned cuttingly, pain clawing at her. ''The world could drown in a woman's tears. You're a long way from being my ideal man, Jonathon McCord. In fact, I don't want you to ever speak to me again. Except on business.'' With that, she gathered her long skirt with one hand and started to stalk off, turning abruptly to warn, ''And if you say one more nasty word about me, I'm going to sue you for defamation of character. I'll tell Bruno, as well, though he mightn't have as easy a time knocking you flat like he did Trevor. I don't give men a great big come-on, as you desperately want to believe. I don't think you'll ever get over losing your mother. Loving comes with punishment in your book. In a good marriage—and I know because my parents have one—there's trust on both sides. It's time you learned something about it. Good night!''

He went after her, stung insufferably by her little speech. ''Don't you dare go to bed.'' When he desperately wanted her there. ''You're working, remember?'' Hell, how stupid, but there didn't seem to be a way around this pain.

''I think I'll hand over to Stacy if you don't mind.''

The fact her cheek glistened with a tear came as a near physical blow to his heart. ''God, Angel, I'm sorry.'' His anger totally collapsed, revealing his very real love for her. ''I'm sure you're right in everything you say. It's me, not you. I had a terrible childhood and it's made me hard. Wanting you is something over which I have no control, when control has always been my thing.''

''I don't think you could ever change.'' She bit her lip, dreadfully upset.

''I love you.'' The words burst forth, though they seemed to give her no satisfaction. ''I hoped you loved me. I thought what we had was perfect.''

''Nothing's perfect, Jonathon.'' She sighed shakily and turned away.

CHAPTER ELEVEN

BY MID-AFTERNOON of the following day the guests with the exception of Dinah Campbell and Leif Standford had returned home. He'd realised for some time his stepmother had a soft spot for Leif and that was one of the reasons he'd been invited to the match. Now it seemed Leif returned Stacy's affections. He hoped the friendship would progress. God knows, Stacy had had little marital happiness. Leif was a good man.

As for Dinah, he planned a quiet talk with her, stung with distaste for what she had attempted to do. Charlie could get himself into enough trouble without anyone's help. Not that he was worried about Charlie. Charlie would always fall on his feet. He was more worried about himself.

It seemed a dreadful thing now he had expected the worst of Angel, then throw it at her. He had never been like this before. He had never been head over heels in love before. He had never had so many struggles going on in his head and body. He'd seen her only once that day, so vividly darkly beautiful she made the breath catch in his throat. She showed no signs of the upset of the night before, or the fact she'd probably only had an hour or two's sleep. She'd said a polite, "Good morning," and gone on her way. It shook him up a little but there were too many distractions. Guests had to be ferried to the airstrip, fare-welled. Everyone agreed it was the best day ever. Or at least until next year, though Angel's efforts would be very hard indeed to top. Not in his experience anyway.

"If I were you, son," the senator told him confidentially, grasping him by the shoulder, "I'd marry that girl. She's everything you're going to need in a wife. We have high hopes for you politically."

It wasn't the first time he'd heard it and his general thoughts had been at some stage he might be able to do some good for the man on the land. But Angel? He could never allow her to end the relationship if he had to go down on his bended knee and beg forgiveness.

He caught up with Dinah as she was walking back to the homestead after a stroll in the home gardens. He was determined to have it out. She gave him a bright smile and a wide-eyed-innocent look.

"Thank goodness they've all gone," she said, as if they were in perfect agreement, "though we did have a marvellous night."

"You certainly did trying to spread mischief." He came out with it, directly watching her smile disappear.

"She told you," she said flatly, colour staining her cheeks.

"Yes, she did. Seeing her in his arms made me crazy just like you intended. Charlie knows nothing about Angel and me."

"And what about Angelica and you?" Dinah spat.

"I love her," he said simply. "I loved her the moment I set eyes on her."

"You lusted after her, don't you think?" she retorted with great bitterness.

"That, too. A man lusts after his woman. But I want her heart and her mind. I want all of her."

"God knows there's enough," she said roughly, tormenting herself with what might have been.

Jake looked away from her and her naked jealousy, unhappy it had come this far. "I've never wanted to hurt you, Dinah. I made you no promises. What we had wasn't near enough for commitment. You'll find someone else if you can fight out of your obsession with being mistress of Coori. You want the house as much as me. Don't you think I've seen you looking at it?"

"Because I could do so much with it," she said strongly.

"I'm right for you, Jake. Can't you see that? I've loved you all my life. She'll give you hell."

He laughed sharply. "Even if she did it would be worth it, but Angelica is a good woman. I'm the one with the demon. You met him. He was my dad."

"Your father approved of me," she reminded him. "He wanted us to get married."

He nodded, his deep-seated anger and resentment of his late father finally spent. "That's so, Dinah, but Dad's gone for good. You mightn't think it now, but we'd have been miserable together."

"Not true, Jake," she protested, touching her fingers to her eyelids to suppress the pain that was starting up, "I love you."

"If you do, it hasn't made either of us happy," Jake murmured quietly. "I'm sorry, Dinah. My advice to you is to go home. I don't want you to stay on for the Christmas party. I figure we can have the house to ourselves for a change. I've seen you patronising my stepmother and my sister. I've never liked it. They don't like it, either."

"But I will see you at Christmas?" she pleaded, seemingly unable to accept rejection.

"It might be better if you don't," he answered. "I'm going to ask Angel to marry me. I want her to forgive me for being such a fool."

Finally the magnitude of her mistake got through to her. Face flaming, Dinah turned away, making for the house to pack her luggage. "You are a fool," she burst out explosively over her shoulder. "And I hate you both. She's going to lead you a merry dance. She'll drive you up the wall."

"I'll get used to it. Believe me!" He heard himself laughing. It felt wonderful. Liberating. Now he had to make his peace with Angel. He'd better make it good.

Dinah, storming into the house, was confronted by the sight of the woman she now hated with a passion. She was stacking even more presents under the towering Christmas tree, her face full of a nauseating maternal tenderness. Quite the Madonna. Dinah, an arch conservative, still thought the Christmas tree would have looked better put to one side, not dominating the entrance hall with its gaudiness and overkill. Just like Miss De Campo herself. With her, apparently the object of her affection, was the aboriginal child Kylee, with the big black eyes, the tousled ginger curls and the woefully cheeky tongue. She was gleefully sitting among the pile of expensively wrapped boxes pulling at a spectacular red-and-gold decoration atop one box.

"Leave that alone," Dinah called out sharply, wishing Jake had never laid eyes on this woman. She could have hung in there and become mistress of this house. She could have put everyone and everything straight. She could have been such an asset to Jake. She had the right sort of backbone.

They both turned to stare at her. Woman and child. "Go away, lady," the child piped up.

Angelica shook her head quickly. "No, Kylee. Be a good girl now."

"As if she'd know how! And you encourage her." Dinah dissolved into a sick rage. "You don't know anything about the way we do things around here. That child has no place in the house. She should be with her mother. She's the house girl, isn't she? A domestic."

"Well, yes, that's the way you see things, Dinah," Angelica said. "I don't. By the way, your plan nearly succeeded last night."

Dinah's eyes appraised her with hatred. "I know. I've been speaking to Jake. He's disgusted with you."

"Disgusted with himself more like it!" Jake appeared in the open doorway, staring across at Angelica for a long moment, his repentant heart in his amber eyes. "It's time you left Coori, Dinah," he advised, almost kindly. "I'm in love with Angelica. She's the only woman for me."

"You'll be sorry, Jake," Dinah warned, a crazy energy building up in her. Finally she cracked, hopelessness and humiliation taking its toll. She looked around wildly for something to throw. Something to break. Her hand closed on one of a pair of bronze winged figures. She threw it wildly, not at Jake, but at Angelica, who had wrecked all their lives.

With excellent reflexes, Angelica bent sideways sheltering Kylee with her body. The statue crashed into the Christmas tree, dislodging several ornaments and breaking a porcelain cupid.

"See what you done!" Kylee cried, already scrambling to her feet. "You're a nasty lady!" she squealed, bursting into tears.

Angelica levered herself up, watching Dinah fly up the stairs. "Go after her, Jonathon. She can't fly anywhere in that condition."

"Are you giving me orders?" He spun to face her, heartened beyond words she had called him Jonathon.

"Yes I am. You said you love me, goddamn it!"

"You drive me crazy nearly as much," he retorted, revelling in her response.

"Luv, luv!" Excitedly, Kylee started to dance, waving her little arms and twisting her knees like the natural dancer she was. "All we need is luv!" she shouted.

"Kylee's got the right idea." Jake strode to Angelica, pulling her to her feet. "I love you. Love you. Love you," he breathed. "You're my every want. My every need. I want you to marry me," he whispered in her ear. "I know this isn't the right moment. I'm going to ask you again later."

"What makes you think I'm going to say yes?" She stretched out a gentle hand to touch his face.

"We'll see." He looked down at her so thrillingly it evoked mental pictures of the two of them in his great bed, locked in each other's arms.

"Am I going to get a present for Christmas, Mr. Jake?" Kylee stopped gyrating long enough to ask.

"Sure you are, sweetheart." He reached out to muss her curls. "I'm going to send you a Christmas present every year. Wherever you are." A promise he was destined to keep.

"Oh, great!" Kylee was overwhelmed with joy, showing it in her smiling little face. "I love Christmas. I love the little

Christ child. I love Mary and Joseph and the manger. I love Mummy and you and Miss. And oh yes, Clary. She's always got something nice for me.''

''And I'll have something nice for you,'' Jake murmured for Angelica alone. ''Only you. Only you.''

To Kylee's absolute delight Mr. Jake kissed Miss. It was a lovely long kiss that went on and on. Both of them had their eyes closed.

Exactly a year later they had their first baby. They called her Noelle. She was utterly adored. She had her father's amber locks and right from the beginning her mother's melting dark eyes.

As for Jonathon and Angelica?

Each new day filled them with fresh wonder. Coori station was once more a happy place.

All it took was an angel.

THE CHRISTMAS MARRIAGE MISSION

BY

HELEN BROOKS

Harlequin Mills & Boon™

Helen Brooks lives in Northamptonshire and is married with three children. As she is a committed Christian, busy housewife and mother, her spare time is at a premium, but her hobbies include reading, swimming, gardening and walking her two energetic, inquisitive and very endearing young dogs. Her long-cherished aspiration to write became a reality when she put pen to paper on reaching the age of forty, and sent the result off to Harlequin Mills & Boon™.

CHAPTER ONE

THE offices were lush, very lush—all muted tones of ochre and buttery yellows on pale maple flooring, and, although Kay could sense a discreet urgency behind the glass doors she was passing on her way to the big chief's domain, the overall air of tranquillity was not disturbed. The glass lift that had transported her from the thickly carpeted reception to the fifth floor had been the last word in elegance too.

She knocked on the door with the nameplate reading 'Miss Jenna Wright, Mr Grey's secretary', and waited until the woman inside raised her head from the word processor in front of her before opening it. Nevertheless, the beautiful cold face in front of Kay did not return her smile, and such was the expression in the carefully made up green eyes that Kay found herself speaking coolly as she said, 'I've a package for Mr Grey. I understand it is urgent.'

Still the woman did not smile or speak, merely holding out her hand for the large manila envelope with an imperiousness that was insulting all by itself.

Mr Grey's secretary obviously thought it beneath her to speak to a humble delivery agent, Kay thought wryly, aware that the woman's gaze had taken in every crease and mark on her biking jacket and leathers. She walked across to the large desk and placed the envelope in the red-taloned hand waiting for it, and it was only then the thin, scarlet-painted mouth opened briefly to say, 'Wait outside until Mr Grey has looked at it.'

Charming. Kay turned abruptly, aware her cheeks were flushing, and left the office without another word. She stood quietly for a second in the corridor outside, willing the colour in her cheeks to subside before she was forced to speak to the other woman again, and then walked over to where an area was set aside for visitors. Seating herself on one of the big plump sofas, she reached for a glossy magazine. When Mr Grey's secretary wanted her—and she had already been told by the firm who had hired her to take the documents to Grey Cargo International there would be a reply—she could jolly well come and find her!

In spite of her irritation, as the minutes ticked by Kay found herself engrossed in the story of a massively fat woman who had decided to have her stomach stapled. The article chronicled the highs and lows of the woman's two-year fight to become the size twelve she'd been before her husband had left her after their two children had died in an accident. Kay was so taken up with the battle that she found herself grinning like a Cheshire cat when the 'after' picture showed a slim, confident, smiling woman on the arm of a new man, and she was just muttering what she would have liked to have done to the first husband who had deserted his wife when she'd needed him the most—thereby contributing to the eating disorder she'd developed—when she became aware she wasn't alone.

She raised defensive brown eyes, expecting to see the perfectly coiffured figure of the secretary in front of her, and then froze for a second as an amused smoky voice said, 'Interesting?'

The man was tall, six feet two at least, and aggressively handsome in a hard, cold way, his silver-blue eyes and black hair holding no signs of softness or warmth, and his lean, powerful body intimidating.

'I...I'm sorry?' It was all she could manage through the wave of shock that had her rooted to the seat.

'The magazine.' He gestured at it almost impatiently. 'Is it the latest fashion, or a new hairdo which is so riveting?'

The condescension was so overtly patronising that it worked like an injection of adrenalin. Kay jumped to her feet, pushing back her mass of thick curly red-brown hair, which always exploded into riotous disarray every time she took off her crash helmet—and which she had long since given up trying to control—and took a deep breath. 'Neither,' she said icily. 'Just an article which reaffirms what swines men are, actually, although perhaps that's not very fair on pigs.'

He blinked. 'Right.' There was a brief pause and she noted with some satisfaction that both the amusement and condescension had vanished when he said coldly, 'You are the courier, I take it?'

Well, it was better than delivery girl, which she was sure was how the secretary would have referred to her. Kay nodded. 'Yes, I am,' she said coolly, her heart beginning to thump harder as it dawned on her this must be Mitchell Grey himself.

He said nothing for a moment, but then he didn't have to—the arctic eyes said it all. Kay was well aware that at a slender five feet five she wasn't the average courier, but, as her firm dealt only with the delivery of documents, letters and small packages, brawn didn't come into it. Her ancient but trustworthy 100 cc motorbike could nip through the traffic jams that sometimes snarled up Romford town centre, which was all she asked of it.

'How long have you worked for Sherwood Delivery?' The words themselves were innocuous enough; his tone suggested the firm must have been crazy to take her on.

It was therefore with a great deal of inward pleasure, none of which was betrayed in her cool voice and blank face, that Kay said, 'Ever since I formed the company three years ago.'

He didn't blink this time, which said a lot for his self-control, Kay had to admit, but she just *knew* she had surprised him again, even though his face was deadpan. He continued to watch her steadily, the silver-hued eyes narrowing, before he walked across to where she was now standing.

Kay was immediately aware of feeling dwarfed, which in the circumstances was not pleasant, but she instinctively raised her small chin as she waited for his response.

'Sit down, Miss...?'

'Sherwood. *Mrs* Sherwood.' And game, set and match to me, I think, Kay thought delightedly. It might teach him not to make so many high-handed assumptions in the future at least?

She saw him glance at her ringless hands as she took the seat she had just vacated, but as she watched him seat himself opposite the sofa she made no attempt to explain further. It was none of his business.

'Three years.' He sat back, one ankle resting on the other knee in a very masculine pose. 'Why haven't I heard of your company before this?'

Keep calm and don't gabble, Kay warned herself silently. He was no doubt well aware of the faintly menacing air he gave off and probably well versed in the art of subtle—and not so subtle—intimidation. But he didn't frighten her, not for a minute!

'Probably because we are still very small,' she said evenly. 'We deal with files, documents, letters, photographs—that kind of thing.' She knew it had been an urgent document she had delivered to him today from a firm of solicitors in the town, a document that needed a signature, but that was all she had been told.

'Your husband is a partner in the company?' he enquired softly.

'No.' It had been all the explanation she'd been going to give but, when the silence stretched and lengthened unbearably, she found herself saying stiffly, 'I'm divorced. I founded the company after we'd parted; he was never involved with it.' She glanced at the envelope in his hand, her voice dismissive when she said, 'If the document is ready, I'll take it now, shall I? I understand it's urgent.'

He didn't reply to this. What he did say—the cool, smoky voice deep and low—was, 'I would like to be able to understand how you got started, Mrs Sherwood. Small business ventures are fascinating, don't you think? What prompted you to choose such an...unusual career move?'

Career move? Kay stared at him, her big brown eyes betraying none of the whirling confusion in her head. Not so much a career move as survival.

For a moment she was tempted to spring up, grab the letter and make a dash for it, but common sense prevailed. She didn't like his cold contemplation one bit, and sitting here in these lavish, grand offices in her old scuffed leathers opposite a man who looked as if he was clothed by Armani at the very least, was not her idea of fun. But insignificant as he made her feel, she wasn't going to give him the satisfaction of thinking he had unnerved her.

She resisted the impulse to fiddle with her hair, deeply regretting that she hadn't taken the time to pull it back into a pony-tail as she normally did when she removed her helmet, and marshalled her racing thoughts. The bare outline, that was all he needed to hear. Nothing personal.

And then he completely threw her off balance just as

she was about to begin when he said, 'How old are you, anyway, if it isn't a rude question?'

It was. *Very* rude, in Kay's opinion. Resentment darkened the brown of her eyes to ebony, but she managed to keep her voice under control when she said crisply, 'I am twenty-six,' her tone adding silently, Not that it's any of your business.

The carved lips twitched a little. 'You don't look a day over eighteen.'

If she had a pound for every time she'd been told how young she looked she would never need to work again, Kay thought irritably. And she hated having it drummed home. Unfortunately her elfin features combined with a liberal dusting of freckles across her nose contributed to the overall image of a teenager, and when she tried to remedy the situation she always ended up looking like a little girl playing at dressing up.

She reminded herself that the customer was always right—although in her experience they rarely were—and took a deep breath. 'You asked how I got started,' she reminded him evenly. 'It was almost by chance, actually. I was asked to pop a letter in to someone as a favour one day; the sender knew I lived in the same street and the letter was urgent.'

He interrupted her, asking smoothly, 'Who was the sender?'

'My boss.' It was meant to be succinct.

'And you were working for...?' He had ignored her tone.

'A small accountant's.' And she'd hated every minute, loathed it, but it had been a job and she had needed one desperately. Having left university with a degree in Business Studies, she'd felt she ought to put it to use but from the first day had felt like a square peg in a round hole.

'Anyway,' she continued, trying to ignore the intent gaze, 'I started to think a bit. I knew there was always the Post Office and the railway, to say nothing of special services and so on, but when I made a few enquiries I found that lots of companies sent urgent messages—files, documents and so on—by taxi or by means of a large company car. Sometimes a Rover car or something equivalent with a chauffeur would travel twenty miles for one letter. I'm cheaper and faster.'

''I'm sure you are, Mrs Sherwood.' It was very dry.

Kay continued to look somewhere over his left shoulder as she went on, 'I drafted and designed a leaflet and a local printer ran it for me—'

'What did it say?'

She did look at him then—she hated being interrupted and twice in as many minutes had 'the customer is always right' scenario flying out of the window. He was gazing at her quizzically, his big body lazy and relaxed and his arms draped either side of the back of the sofa, and the sharp words she had been about to voice died in her throat as sheer sexual magnetism hit her like a bolt of lightning.

There was a small—and for Kay—fraught silence before she managed to pull herself together and say quickly, 'Something along the lines that we could give fast, direct, door-to-door service for delivery of documents and letters etc. anywhere in the Romford area. Same-day service guaranteed and to phone for immediate attention.'

'We?'

'My brother was out of work at the time and he was available to man the phone and see if my idea worked. It did, so within two months I'd given my notice and joined him. We started off with just the motorbike—' she indicated her leathers '—but now we have two vans and one of my brother's friends works for us. We have our own office in town since last year and so much work we're thinking of taking on someone else.'

He sat up straight, the movement causing a response in Kay she could well have done without. 'Impressive.' He nodded slowly. 'Have you a business card?'

'Sure.' She had flushed scarlet but she couldn't help it—the red hair went hand in hand with a porcelain skin that was prone to blushing. She fumbled in her leathers and brought out one of their neat little cards, handing it to him as they both rose to their feet.

'I mustn't keep you any longer.' He passed her the manila envelope, suddenly dismissive.

He was towering over her again and as he reached out and shook her hand, enclosing her small paw in his long, lean fingers, it took all of Kay's control not to snatch her hand away as she felt the contact of his flesh. Which was crazy, ridiculous, she told herself desperately, as were the ripples in her blood as the faint but delicious smell of him teased her nostrils for a second or two.

'Goodbye, Mrs Sherwood.' Mitchell Grey was fully aware that the small, slender girl in front of him had appeared to tell him plenty but in fact had said nothing—about herself, that was. With her mop of shoulder-length curls and Pollyanna freckles that stood out on her creamy skin like sprinkled spice, she was definitely not his type. No way. His women were elegant, exquisitely dressed and cosmopolitan, and more importantly they knew the score. A good time and plenty of fun and laughs on both sides while it lasted. And he always made sure it didn't last *too* long, he thought grimly, watching her until she disappeared from view into the waiting lift.

So what had made him want to know more about—he consulted the card in his hand—Kay Sherwood? he asked himself silently, vaguely irritated with himself.

A scrubbed and sweet-sixteen type if ever he saw one. Although she wasn't sixteen, was she. And she was a married woman—or had been married, someone who had started a fledgling business in the present uneasy climate and succeeded at it too.

His frown deepened. Most people who started up in business on their own gained their first business experiences in another job. Then they adapted a special skill or special knowledge to a new idea, or branched out on their own thinking they could do better than the company they worked for. The young woman who had just walked out of the office—Mitchell refused to dwell on the memory of the rounded bottom under the leathers swaying provocatively as she'd disappeared—had plunged in without all that, which showed she had plenty of guts and determination. So what was her story?

And then he mentally shrugged all thoughts of Kay Sherwood away. He was already late for a business appointment in the heart of London and his chauffeur had been waiting for fifteen minutes. What was he standing here for? The hard, astute business brain kicked in and he strode over to the lift, now utterly focused on the coming meeting, which he knew would be a difficult one. As the doors opened he slipped the business card in the top pocket of his jacket, but not before a small separate section of his mind had filed away the name and telephone number for future reference.

'So what was so bad about him asking you a few questions about the business, Kay?' Kay's mother's brown eyes were puzzled, understandably so, Kay had to admit. When she actually repeated what Mitchell Grey had said word for word it didn't convey anything of the man's arrogance or the atmosphere that had been present between them.

'He was—well...just altogether irritating,' she finished lamely.

Leonora stared at her daughter for a moment more before saying diplomatically, 'Well, forget about him now, okay? It's doubtful if your paths will ever cross again and you've enough on your plate to concern yourself with as it is. You haven't forgotten it's the school's autumn fête this evening?'

'The twins wouldn't let me.' Kay smiled wryly and her mother smiled back.

'They're two live wires,' Leonora Brown admitted ruefully. 'But you were like that at their age, into everything and the whole world one gigantic adventure.'

Kay nodded, still smiling, but inwardly she was thinking, I was like that right up to the time I met Perry and then it was like I changed overnight. Why couldn't I see what he was doing to me?

She dropped her eyes from her mother's face, taking a sip of her coffee. They said love was blind, but in her case it had been a question of deaf, dumb *and* blind.

As her mother continued to chat on, the while chopping and slicing vegetables for the chicken casserole they were having for dinner, Kay gave every appearance of listening but her mind had taken a trip into the past.

She had gone out with Perry for a year before they had got married on her twenty-first birthday, the same month they had both finished at university, but within a couple of months of the wedding she had been forced to admit to herself she had made a terrible mistake. The cocoon of university life, and especially the last frantic year when she had worked as she'd never worked before, had masked so much that had been wrong in their relationship.

Perry had been young, good-looking and very charismatic, drawing people to him like moths to a flame with the power of his electric personality, but he had also been a cold-blooded, manipulative control freak—at least with her. She had been so crazy about him, and so busy—it having been her final year—that she hadn't even noticed that they'd done everything *his* way. But a few weeks into the marriage, due to a chance meeting with an old school-friend, she had been jolted free of the soporific bubble he'd carefully manufactured round her.

What had she been doing with herself? her old friend had asked in all innocence. Had she been ill? She looked terrible. Was she working too hard?

The conversation had been awkward on both sides and Kay hadn't prolonged the encounter, but when she had got home to the one-bedroomed flat in Belgravia she and Perry had been renting she had taken a long, hard look at herself in the bathroom mirror. Her hair had been strained into a tight knot at the back of her head—Perry hated it loose—and she'd been wearing no make-up—Perry disliked any artifice—but it hadn't been that so much as the drawn look to her mouth and the expression in her eyes that had brought her up short.

She looked dowdy and plain, she'd realised suddenly, glancing down at the dress she'd been wearing—one of many things Perry had insisted on buying her. She was killing herself trying to please Perry in every tiny thing rather than having to endure his cutting comments and icy silences when she said or did something he didn't agree with.

She'd stood there, in stunned shock, for some minutes. How long had this been going on? she'd asked herself numbly as reality had hit. They were happy, weren't they? She was so lucky to have him—wasn't she? He treated her so well, was so kind to her...

And the answer sounded in her head—everything was

wonderful when she was doing exactly as *he* wanted; he was the best husband in the world then. He told her how to dress, how to wear her hair; he was the one who decided when they went out and when they stayed in, even what programmes they watched on TV. Their friends were *his* friends; they ate the kind of food *he* liked and drank the wine he chose.

She had rubbed a shaky hand over her face, her mind racing. It hadn't been like that in the beginning, had it? Not for the first month or two. But then an insidious change had taken place and the most absurd thing, the preposterous, stupid and *unbelievable* thing, was that she hadn't seen it till now. She just hadn't realised it had been happening. Because he was such fun and so irresistible and mesmerising when he was being nice, it hadn't dawned on her that she was subconsciously subjugating her own persona all the time. It was as if she had turned into someone else, someone...alien. Even the fact that he had persuaded her not to look for a job immediately, but spend some time getting the flat round and creating a home for them now took on a new significance.

'I want to be able to picture you here when I'm away,' he had said beguilingly when she'd made noises about using her degree. 'Know you'll be here when I get home. We don't need your salary, darling, not at the moment, and, with me working for Dad, money will never be tight.'

She had stared at herself for some time that day. And then she'd run a hot bath, washed her hair and creamed herself all over with a frighteningly expensive body lotion that had been a Christmas present from her parents. After getting dressed in a pair of tight black jeans and little top she'd found pushed in the back of her wardrobe—remnants from pre-Perry days—she had carefully made up her face and teased her hair into soft waves about her face.

It had taken ages—her hair always wanted to go its own way and curl outrageously—but eventually she'd begun to recognise the girl in the mirror.

She had gone out and bought two steaks for dinner rather than labour over the chicken dhansak Perry had ordered, and she'd collected a paper detailing job vacancies at the same time.

When Perry had got home that evening he had found a dining table romantically set for two with candles and wine, a smiling, perfumed and groomed wife, and six envelopes containing job applications ready for posting. Even now she didn't like to think of the things he had said and how cruel he'd been, but it had been the beginning of the end.

By the time she had realised she was pregnant a little while later—she had been taking the pill but had been ill with a stomach upset at one point, not that that had stopped Perry from all but forcing himself on her one night—the discovery that Perry had begun an affair with one of the secretaries in his father's catering firm had finished the marriage completely. It had been a time of heartache and desperation and misery, but through it all she'd discovered she was stronger than she had suspected.

She had stayed on at the flat after she'd thrown Perry out, working right up to three weeks before the twins' birth and returning shortly after once she had found a good nursery. She had hated leaving them, but Perry's maintenance payments had not been forthcoming and as he had upped and left the area shortly after the birth she'd had little choice, other than moving back in with her parents. And somehow, and she couldn't have explained to a living soul why, that would have seemed like the final defeat, much as she loved her mother and father.

Then had come her father's massive heart attack, followed by the news his dabbling in the stock market had left his widow almost penniless. At the same time her married brother had lost his job just before his wife had been due to give birth to their second child.

Kay raised her head now, coming back to the present as she heard the front door slam. This meant their neighbour had dropped the twins off after school; several of them had got an efficient rota system established.

'Mummy!' As the kitchen door burst open and two little flame-haired figures catapulted into the room Kay prepared herself for the onslaught of small arms and legs with a feeling of deep thankfulness. Her girls were her life, her breath, her reason for living. They had brought her through the worst period of her life, her nurture of their tiny bodies in her womb meaning she hadn't been able to let herself sink into the abyss of despair she'd felt at the time of her marriage breakup, and their birth filling her with wonder and joy that these two tiny, perfect little babies were really hers. All hers.

'Mummy, I got a gold star today for sitting as still as a mouse during storytime.'

'And Miss Henson's put my picture on the wall. It's you, Mummy, and Grandma.'

'A picture's not as good as a gold star, is it, Mummy?'

'It is. It is as good. Better! Isn't it, Mummy?'

Both Georgia and Emily had clambered onto her lap, their arms wrapped round her neck as they struggled for prime position, all but choking her in the process.

She was saved by the ringing of the proverbial bell.

'It's for you.' Her mother had answered the telephone, which had begun to ring just as the twins had entered the room, and as Kay disentangled herself, kissing both small faces and telling them they were very clever girls, the older woman hissed quietly, 'It's him, Kay. That Mr Grey you told me about.'

'What?' Her mother had her hand over the mouthpiece, which was just as well considering how high-pitched Kay's voice had suddenly become.

Leonora now flapped her hand frantically as she pressed the receiver against her chest, mouthing, 'Quiet, he'll hear you.'

Kay looked down at the telephone as though it would scald her, making no effort to take it as she whispered back, 'How do you know it's him?'

'He said, of course, unless you know more than one Mitchell Grey?'

How on earth had he got this number? The card had given the office number but that was all. Kay took the phone, holding it gingerly as she said, 'Hallo? This is Kay Sherwood.'

'Good evening, Mrs Sherwood.' The deep voice held the texture of seductively soft velvet over finely honed steel. 'I hope you don't mind my calling you at home; I did try the number you gave me but a Mr Brown—your brother, I understand?—told me I was more likely to catch you at home at this time of the day.'

Cheers, thanks, Peter. Kay tried to inject a note of enthusiasm into her voice when she said, 'Not at all, Mr Grey. How can I help you?'

There was the briefest of pauses before the compelling voice spoke again. 'I wondered if you are free tomorrow evening?'

It would be true to say Kay had never been so surprised in her life. She knew her mouth had dropped open, and something in her face even stopped the squabbling of the twins because they, like her mother, were now staring at her curiously.

Kay's brain was racing, her thoughts tumbling over each other. He couldn't mean he was suggesting a date? He couldn't, could he? No, he must mean some sort of job. An evening delivery maybe? That must be it.

And then she was disabused of this idea when he added, 'I've tickets for the theatre, and I thought perhaps a spot of dinner first?'

Say something, Kay told herself. Anything. Except yes. She moistened her lips. 'I'm sorry, Mr Grey, but I'm busy tomorrow night,' she lied politely.

'Next week some time?'

She stared frantically at the three very interested faces at the kitchen table, and when no help was forthcoming said carefully, 'I'm sorry but this is really a very busy time for us at the moment and it's all hands to the plough.'

'You don't take time out to eat?' he asked smoothly, continuing before she had a chance to reply, 'How about lunch instead, then? And before you tell me how sorry you are again, perhaps I ought to mention that I was hoping to discuss a business proposition I had in mind.'

So it hadn't been a date! Kay was so relieved she spoke without thinking, not realising how her voice had changed. 'A business proposition? Oh, of course, Mr Grey,' she said eagerly. 'Shall we say Monday?'

'Let's.' It was dry in the extreme. 'I'll call at your office at one o'clock. Goodbye, Mrs Sherwood.'

And he had put down the phone before it dawned on her that one didn't normally suggest theatre and dinner to discuss a business proposal.

CHAPTER TWO

If Kay picked up the telephone once on Monday morning to cancel her lunch with Mitchell Grey, she picked it up a hundred times. She'd thought of little else during the weekend, going over their conversation in her mind until her brain was buzzing and her nerves were frazzled.

One moment she was telling herself that it was the height of arrogance to think that a man like him—clearly very wealthy, successful and drop-dead gorgeous—would ask her for a date, and that the proposed meeting must—*must*—be a business one. Then the memory of his voice when he had suggested the theatre and dinner would reverberate in her head, firing the panic button.

She had telephoned Peter as soon as she had put down the phone from Mitchell Grey on Friday afternoon, but her brother hadn't been particularly helpful.

'Why did I give him your home number?' Peter said breezily when she challenged him. 'Well, why not? It's not a secret, is it? You're not ex-directory or anything like that.'

Kay bit down on her lip and prayed for patience. She loved Peter dearly, and his wife and two boys meant a great deal to her, but just at that moment in time she could have hit him hard without a shred of remorse.

After a few more minutes of questioning, Peter grew impatient. 'What do you mean, how did he sound?' he asked her irritably. 'What sort of dumb question is that? I *told* you—he phoned up and wanted to speak to you, said he'd talked to you earlier in the day and there was something more he wanted to discuss. When I said you weren't around he asked if you'd got a number where he could contact you, and so I said yes. Not the deepest or most meaningful conversation in the world admittedly, but there it is.'

Kay mentally cancelled the new sound system she'd been planning to buy him for Christmas and substituted a pair of socks instead. 'I don't want to see him,' she said tightly.

'Don't, then.' Peter spoke with true brotherly compassion.

'It's not as easy as that. What if he *does* want to discuss something that would do the firm some good? What then?'

'Kay, correct me if I'm wrong but we're talking lunch here, aren't we? The guy isn't suggesting you go up and see his etchings or nip off to Bournemouth for a dirty weekend. What's your problem?'

She slammed the phone down then, telling the twins their uncle was the most irritating man in the world before they all got ready to leave for the autumn fête whereby her mind was taken off Mitchell Grey for a little while.

Peter's last words came back to her now as she glanced nervously at her wrist-watch. Ten minutes and counting. She shut her eyes tightly for a second before she opened them again, speaking out loud into the small office they rented on the ground floor of a converted house. 'So, what *is* your problem?'

She didn't know, she admitted miserably, which wasn't like her. She was a practical person at heart, not given to flights of fancy or goose-pimply feelings, but there was something about Mitchell Grey...

It didn't help that both Peter and Tom were out on deliveries either, which meant she was waiting all alone without any conversation to take her mind off the forthcoming encounter. Peter might be the most exasperating soul on earth at times, and Tom could be nearly as bad, but at least there was never a dull moment when the two of them were around. Of course she could have wandered in to either the watch repairer's or the accountant's—the two other offices on the ground floor of the premises—and passed the time of day for a while, but with no one else to man the phone it would have been an indulgence.

She glanced down at her lightly structured jacket and short skirt in shot blue silk, which had cost her an arm and a leg in the summer, and which had been bought for the wedding of her cousin, and again blessed the fact that the October day was mild and sunny. She hadn't spent much on decent clothes lately—the twins always seemed to outgrow their shoes before she could blink and there always were a hundred and one things to buy before she indulged herself—but then she didn't really need anything. Her leathers were her working clothes, and the nearest she ever got to going out was taking the twins to the park or swimming at the local pool.

Had she scrubbed up sufficiently well to hold her own on a lunch appointment with Mitchell Grey? For the umpteenth time since she'd arrived at the office that morning she opened the bottom drawer of her desk and fished out the small hand mirror she kept there.

Wide brown eyes set under brows that were fine and straight stared back anxiously, a couple of coats of mascara the only make-up she was wearing. She patted one or two errant curls back into the high loose pony-tail on top of her head, the style deceptively casual considering it had taken an hour to complete first thing that morning.

'You have beautiful hair.'

Her head shot up at the same time as she hastily threw

the mirror back into the drawer, slamming it shut and breaking a nail in the process.

Mitchell Grey was standing just inside the open office door, and in the same moment that Kay registered the hard, handsome face, full of sharply defined angles and planes made all the more threatening by the jet-black hair, she mentally cursed the fact that, after her being on watch the whole morning, he had to sneak up on her at the very moment she was at a disadvantage.

Her voice reflected some of what she was feeling when she said, 'Mr Grey. I didn't hear you come in.'

He raised his eyebrows, his voice lazy and faintly amused. 'I apologise.'

'No, I didn't mean—' She stopped abruptly. She *had* meant, actually, she told herself ungrammatically, and she was blowed if she was going to say otherwise, business proposition or no business proposition. She compressed her soft mouth, and then saw his lips twitch with a dart of fury. He thought this was funny, did he? He thought *she* was funny?

She rose to her feet as gracefully as her old saggy chair would allow, tweaking her skirt into place when she saw the silver eyes rest briefly on the inordinate amount of leg the action had revealed. 'You found us all right, then?' She moved across to him with her hand outstretched, determined to seize hold of the situation.

He nodded, his voice now holding the sort of gentleness that suggested he was humouring her when he said, 'My chauffeur was born and bred in these parts; I don't think there's an alley or back way he isn't familiar with.'

His chauffeur. Oh, wow. But of course a man like Mitchell Grey would have a chauffeur, she told herself helplessly. He probably hadn't meant it that way but it was a subtle reminder that he was the one holding all the aces and that she couldn't afford to be touchy around him—not until she knew whether it was going to cost them hard cash, at least.

'You said something about a business proposition?' she asked him now as their hands connected.

'Let's get on our way first.'

He didn't have to ask twice. The feel of his warm, hard flesh had unnerved her every bit as much as it had before, and more so considering they were alone here. Besides which, she hadn't really appreciated just how tatty their premises were until he had walked in—designer perfection personified, she thought nastily, wishing she could honestly tell herself there were something of the dandy about him but knowing it wouldn't be true. He was all male. Intimidatingly so.

She found herself fumbling with the key as she locked the door to the office, vitally aware of the tall figure waiting for her by the front door of the building, and once they emerged into the busy street and he took her elbow it was all she could do not to pull away. 'The car's over here.' He guided her across the pavement full of lunchtime shoppers towards a long, sleek Bentley parked on double yellow lines, a uniformed chauffeur sitting impassively in the front seat.

Once in the leather-clad interior Kay had a brief tussle with her skirt before sitting as primly as it would allow. Why hadn't she noticed how short it was at Caroline's wedding? she asked herself as a mortifyingly large expanse of nylon-clad flesh made itself known. Probably because Mitchell Grey wasn't at the nuptials was the answer to that, she admitted irritably.

'Relax, Kay.'

The shock of hearing her name spoken by the richly dark voice brought her head swinging round to meet his gaze, and she saw the silver-blue eyes were narrowed thoughtfully on her face.

'I beg your pardon?' She tried for icy hauteur but the effect was ruined by her breathlessness. He was close, very close in the confines of the car, and like once before the subtle sexy aftershave he wore had her pulse rate flying.

'You're tense, keyed up,' he said soothingly, 'and there is no need to be, really. Look, would it help if I came clean and admitted right now that there is no business proposition? That this is intended to be just a nice meal in comfortable surroundings where we can chat and get to know each other a little?'

Would it help? Would it—? 'Stop the car!'

'I'm sorry?'

Even if it had been possible for so ruthless and attractive a man to look innocent, his mild response to her yelp of outrage wouldn't have deceived her. She glared at him, her face flushed and her mouth set, and it was incredibly galling to see he wasn't in the least ashamed of himself.

'I said, stop the car,' Kay ground out through clenched teeth.

'All in good time.' And he had the effrontery to try a smile that she supposed he imagined made him irresistible. 'I want to explain first. You had clearly made up your mind that you didn't want to see me again—'

'How right you are,' she snarled softly.

'And so all this deception is entirely your fault,' he continued silkily.

'*My* fault?'

'Of course.' He had settled back in the seat as he'd spoken and he was so obviously enjoying her discomfiture that Kay would have slapped him if she'd dared. But she didn't. Much as she hated to admit it to herself.

'Now look, Mr Grey, I don't know what sort of game you think you are playing but you've picked the wrong girl,' she said with acid sharpness. 'I don't like the caveman approach, if that's what you're thinking, and frankly I find your attitude offensive. I want out of this car and right now.' She fumbled with the handle but wasn't surprised to find the door was locked.

'Aren't you overreacting a little?' he asked mildly. 'All I want to do is to take you to lunch.'

This couldn't be happening. She couldn't really be locked in a car with a virtual stranger being taken to goodness knew where. She took the last thought a step further when she said, 'My mother knows I have a luncheon engagement with you today, Mr Grey, as well as my brother.'

'I should hope so. It would be very unwise not to inform at least one person of your whereabouts in this day and age in which we live,' he said smoothly.

The dark head had turned to look out of the window a few moments before but now he turned back to face her, one dark eyebrow quirked mockingly as he added, 'We're here. Now try to act your age and pretend you are a cool and contained businesswoman being brought out to lunch by a male colleague, okay? That will save us both any embarrassment.'

Embarrassment? She couldn't imagine Mitchell Grey ever suffering that emotion in the whole of his life. There was arrogance, and then there was this man, and she didn't even have a word to describe him. Not one she could repeat in civilised company, anyway. If anyone needed taking down a peg or two it was him.

She glanced out of the window of the car as it drew to a stop outside a restaurant she had heard about but never entered—mainly because the cost of a meal there would necessitate taking out a second mortgage—and it was in that moment the idea occurred to her. She glanced at the big dark figure next to her and found his gaze was on her face, a disturbing gleam at the back of his eyes. What was he thinking? What did he expect her to do right at this moment? She rather suspected he was prepared for the fact that she might turn tail and march off, and she really wouldn't put it past him to manhandle her into the building, awkward though it would be for both of them.

He was a control freak if ever she'd met one—and she had, first hand, she thought tightly as Perry's face flashed across the screen of her mind for a second. But she wasn't going to put up with this, not for a moment. Her starry-eyed devotion to Perry had nearly ruined her life and the days had long since gone when she would allow a man to dictate to her.

It had been an uphill struggle for months when, after her father had died and her mother had needed her, she had come back to Romford, leaving her London flat and taking out a mortgage on the tiny house they now all lived in. Her salary had not allowed her to take on more than a small, two-bedroomed place, and even then Ivy Cottage had been dilapidated and in need of renovation. But the 1920's former ale house had had an endearing air about it, the two bedrooms overlooking what once had been a pretty garden filled with topiary, flower borders, a rockery and even an original brick well, but on their first visit to view had resembled a miniature jungle.

Her father's bad investments had meant her mother had brought nothing to the kitty, but gradually, with lots of help from Peter and his friends, they had repaired and painted and made good, transforming shabby into chic. Now the panelled front door of Ivy Cottage opened into a beamed sitting room with an open fireplace, which was cosy and charming, the kitchen-diner adequate for their needs, although Kay had to admit there wasn't room to swing a cat when Peter and his family came round for a meal. But with the twins in one bedroom and Kay and her mother sharing the other, they were happy, and the garden had proved to be a little oasis all year round. Most of all, though, the move back to Romford had saved her mother from slipping into the nervous breakdown the doctor had said was imminent. Leonora had had to take on the care of the twins during the day while Kay worked—nursery fees now being out of the question—and being wanted and useful again, as well as having her daughter and grandchildren with her permanently, had been the stimulant the older woman had needed.

It had been a fight to survive for a while after Perry had gone, but she had not only survived but managed to provide a secure home for the girls and her mother as well as establishing what was now a thriving little business, Kay thought as she climbed out of the car, ignoring Mitchell Grey's outstretched hand. There was no way she was being walked over by this arrogant brute of a man, and he was going to learn that the hard way very soon. She was self-governing now, independent.

She walked ahead of him into the restaurant, a strange prickly sensation running up and down her spine as they paused just within the doors and he took her elbow, speaking to the head waiter who had flown to their side. 'Ah, Angelo. You have my table ready?'

'Of course, Mr Grey.'

The man didn't actually bow them to the small discreet table set at an angle where they could see but not be on view, but the obsequiousness was enough to set Kay's teeth further on edge. If people were like this with Mitchell Grey no wonder the man's ego was inflated to jumbo size!

'Would you like a cocktail while you look at the menu?' The wine waiter had appeared at their side the moment they'd been seated. 'I can recommend the Smouldering Liaison,' Mitchell Grey said, blandly enough but Kay had noticed the lingering amusement curling his mouth.

'Cocktails in the lunch hour?' She raised what she hoped were coldly disapproving eyebrows.

'I'm not driving.' He settled back in his seat, pulling his tie loose and undoing the first couple of buttons of his shirt as he spoke. 'Are you?'

Kay cleared her dry throat. His powerful masculinity was all the more flagrant for its casual unconsciousness and she didn't like the way her body had reacted to what was a perfectly normal action on his part. 'No,' she admitted coolly. Peter and Tom were handling the driving for today, and although Peter had picked her up in one of the vans that morning she had planned to take a taxi for the short ride home, knowing her brother would be late back. 'But I like to be alert in the afternoon.'

'I'm sure you do.'

Four small words, but he managed to make them sound insulting, Kay thought angrily. She bit back on the hot words burning her tongue, glancing at the cocktail menu again. Perhaps she *would* have a drink at that, she decided. She needed a spot of Dutch courage if she was going to carry out her idea to put Mitchell Grey in his place.

''I'll have a Sweet Revenge, please,' she said primly, choosing the cocktail purely for its name rather than the mix of coconut rum, gin, tequila and banana essence it contained.

He whistled slowly through his teeth. 'Are you sure? It has a kick like a mule.'

'Revenge always has.' She smiled sweetly. She wanted him to remember what she'd chosen for a long, long time.

He shrugged broad shoulders. 'A Sweet Revenge for the lady,' he said lazily to the waiter, 'and I'll have a Wolf in Sheep's Clothing.'

Except in this case it was definitely a wolf in wolf's clothing, Kay thought, staring at the hard, rugged profile in the moment before he turned his head and looked at her again. And she certainly wasn't Little Red Riding Hood.

'How long are you going to be annoyed with me?' he asked her softly after a couple of seconds had ticked by.

She forced herself not to lower her gaze although the ice-blue eyes with their silver hue were piercing. 'You think I should be grateful you tricked me into having lunch with you?'

'Not exactly.' His eyes glinted at her and she knew he wasn't taking any of this seriously. It was more galling than words could express. 'But surely there are worse crimes than taking a beautiful woman out to eat?'

'You insinuated you had work for my firm.' If he thought he could sweet talk her he had another think coming. Beautiful woman indeed! Kay refused to acknowledge her accelerating pulse.

'But you'd already told me you had more work than you knew what to do with so I didn't think you'd mind too much.' He smiled. Kay did not. 'Added to which I had tried the honest approach first only to be shot down in flames. You left me with no other option,' he cajoled silkily.

This was a ridiculous conversation. She stared coldly at him, willing her fluttering heart to behave. His smoky warm voice and the sexy curve to his mouth were part of a blatant seduction programme, that was as clear as the nose on his face. Probably he'd tried this approach before and it had worked like a dream; she didn't think he got turned down too often. In fact it was very probable he had never got turned down before. It just showed you were never too old for a new experience, she told herself with secret relish.

The waiter arrived with their cocktails before she had a chance to say anything, the head waiter popping up like a genie out of a bottle a moment later with two elaborate and heavily embossed menus. 'The lobster and scallops with caviare garnish is highly recommended today, Mr Grey,' he murmured smoothly. 'Or perhaps the black leg chicken with wild mushrooms and asparagus? I'll leave you to contemplate for a few moments.'

'Thank you, Angelo. And could we have a bottle of that rather pleasant Moët et Chandon I had last time, the rosé? You do like rosé champagne?' he added, turning to Kay as he spoke the last words.

'I drink little else,' she replied with a brittle smile. If he thought he could buy her with a bottle of good champagne he was even more arrogant than she'd supposed.

The head waiter bustled off, after a somewhat nervous glance in Kay's direction, and she hastily took a sip of her creamy yellow cocktail. It was okay until it hit the back of her throat, and then the delicious taste was superseded by eye-watering heat. He hadn't exaggerated the kick of the mule bit, Kay was forced to acknowledge, and then—aware of a quietly amused gaze trained on her face—she forced herself to take another sip. It wasn't so bad now she was prepared for it, and she didn't glance directly across the table until the moisture in her eyes had subsided and she was fully in control of herself.

'Delicious,' she said serenely.

'I'm glad you like it,' he returned gravely.

Sarcastic swine. Kay made a great play of studying the menu. She felt hot and flustered and she was determined not to let it show. She was going to be dignified and icy to the end or die in the attempt.

The head waiter did his rabbit-out-of-a-hat trick in the next instant, seemingly materialising out of thin air and taking their order with profuse delight. As he glided away Kay glanced round the softly lighted, elegant surroundings, the low hum of gentle conversation and the general air of affluence suiting the bon viveur diners perfectly.

It would be better if she ate her first course before putting her plan into action; it would lull him into a false sense of security and have more effect in the long run. So... Conversation. She had to at least appear to have accepted the status quo.

'Mr Grey—'

'Mitchell, please,' he reproved her gently.

Kay nodded stiffly. 'Mitchell,' she continued evenly, 'I really don't see why it was so important I accepted a dinner invitation with you. I should imagine there are any number of women who would be only too pleased to accompany you.'

He settled himself further into his chair, finishing his cocktail and placing the empty glass on the table before he said, 'Possibly.' And if he were truthful he would have added that he didn't understand fully why he had pursued what was obviously a non-starter either. He prided himself on being a very rational and judicious man; irrationalism was not an option. So what was it about this slender woman with her mop of hair and freckles that had got under his skin? Much as he hated to admit it, he hadn't been able to get her out of his mind for more than a few minutes at a time since he'd set eyes on her.

Kay stared at him. Possibly—was that all he was going to say on the matter? He met her gaze, his eyes crystal-sharp and unblinking, his sensual mouth curved cynically.

'But you didn't feel inclined to take advantage of their services?' she asked with deliberate innuendo.

He smiled lazily. 'Are you casting aspersions on my ability to acquire a woman, Kay? I can assure you I have never needed to pay for one.'

'I didn't think for a minute you had.' And she hadn't—it had just been rather a cheap jibe to annoy him, she admitted silently, not liking herself. She wouldn't have dreamt of behaving like this normally; it was all his fault!

'Good.' He looked at her quietly for a moment. 'Tell me a little about yourself.'

'I thought I already had.' She forced a quick smile. 'It's your turn, surely? How would your CV read?'

'Well, let's see.' The wine waiter appeared with the champagne in an ice bucket. Mitchell waited until all the formalities of tasting and such were out of the way and they were alone again before he continued, 'Name, Mitchell Charles Grey. Age, thirty-five. Marital status, single, Mother, Irish, Father, English, both died in a car crash when I was fifteen. I started my own company at the age of twenty by investing all my inheritance in it along with a whopping great bank loan, and by the age of thirty had branched out to include premises in Southampton, Portsmouth and Plymouth. Anything else you'd like to know?'

Masses, and she didn't like that, Kay acknowledged, a sudden tightness in her chest. She didn't want to be interested in this man, not in any way. 'You're very successful,' she prevaricated carefully.

He nodded. False modesty was obviously not one of his failings.

'And happy?' she added evenly.

'Happy?' He didn't answer immediately, his eyes narrowing. 'Happiness is such a fragile emotion, don't you think? And not one I believe in, to be honest.'

'No?' She couldn't help it, she had to know more. 'So what *do* you believe in?'

'Hard work, determination, wealth, success. The first two giving rise to the latter when combined with that magical element called luck.'

'Right.' She finished her cocktail and hoped the waiter would bring the watercress soufflé and wholemead bread she'd ordered for her starter very soon. She was feeling distinctly light-headed. She looked at her glass of sparkling champagne and knew she didn't dare try even a sip until she'd eaten something. 'So you're a self-made man who enjoys his autonomy. Would that be a fair summing up?' she asked calmly.

'I dare say.' His brow crinkled into a quizzical ruffle. 'How about you? Are you a self-made woman who enjoys *her* autonomy?'

Self-made woman was on the grand side for her little tuppenny enterprise compared with Grey Cargo International, but Kay didn't feel inclined to point that out right now. She nodded. 'Yes.'

'And is there a current boyfriend lurking in the background somewhere?' he asked casually.

That would be the day. She'd had one or two dates in the last three years but only when she'd made it absolutely clear it was on a friends-only basis. Apart from the fact that she had no intention of introducing the odd 'uncle' to the twins, she simply didn't want to ever get heavily involved with a man again, or at least not for the foreseeable future. Maybe when the twins were grown up and off her hands she might consider a relationship if the right man came along, but he would have to understand that the whole marriage thing, even a for-ever type commitment, was out of the question. She had gone there and done that, she had the mental and emotional scars to prove it. She would never give anyone power over her like that again.

Kay took a deep breath. 'A boyfriend?' she said evenly. 'No. I haven't got the time or the inclination for romantic attachments of any kind.'

He shifted in his chair, leaning towards her as he said, 'That's a little harsh, isn't it? Was your marriage really that bad?'

She had absolutely no intention of discussing her marriage or anything else of a personal nature with this man. She looked into the hard, handsome face, folding her hands in her lap to emphasise she was perfectly relaxed and in control. 'It's over,' she said coolly, 'and I never look back or discuss the past.'

'In other words I can mind my own business?' He folded his arms over his chest, contemplating her with the penetrating, astute gaze she found so disturbing. 'What about a family in the future, children? Aren't you a bit young to close the door on that?'

She didn't answer this directly. What she did say was, 'What about you? Is that what you want—hearth, home and family?' her tone disbelieving.

He gave her a hard look before a grudging smile touched the carved lips. *'Touché,'* he murmured softly. 'No, as you've so rightly discerned, that is not what I want. I don't see myself as a family man. Children deserve absolute commitment, both from parents to the child and from parent to parent, and the possibility of wanting to stay faithful to the same woman for the rest of one's life seems ludicrous to me. And if one party does stray it can make family life hell on earth.'

His face had remained the same as he'd spoken but there had been something, just the faintest note in his voice, that made Kay say, 'Is that what happened to you as a child?' before she could stop herself.

For a moment she thought he wasn't going to answer her, and then he said, his voice very even, 'This is getting a little deep for a lunchtime chat, isn't it?' There followed the briefest of pauses before he added, 'Yes, that is what happened to me,' and, looking beyond her, 'Ah, here comes the food. I trust you will find it enjoyable. I find the chef here one of the best I've come across.'

Kay felt thoroughly put in her place. Why, oh, why had she asked him that? She hadn't meant to. Here was she determined not to reveal a thing about herself and she had gone and asked him something so personal that even a close friend would have hesitated to intrude. She began to eat the soufflé without tasting it, her cheeks burning.

'It's all right, Kay.'

The quiet voice brought her eyes up from the soufflé dish and she found he was looking at her, unsmiling but with a curious expression on his face. With anyone else but Mitchell Grey she would have thought it was gentleness.

'If I hadn't wanted to answer I wouldn't have done. Okay?'

He'd known she felt bad. She could feel her cheeks glowing still more as she nodded before saying, 'I had no right to ask such a personal question; we're strangers, after all.'

'I would like to think that isn't quite true.'

She lowered her gaze and began to eat again, her taste

buds telling her the soufflé was a dream and her mind screaming at her that she had to get out of here.

Something had changed and shifted in the last few minutes, something intangible but very real and infinitely dangerous. And she didn't mind admitting she didn't know how to handle it—or perhaps she should say she didn't know how to handle Mitchell Grey. Whatever, it was time to put her original idea into action.

She had finished the soufflé and now she put the last portion of delicious home-made bread into her mouth, swallowing it quickly before she said, 'Excuse me a moment; I need to powder my nose,' and she reached for her handbag.

'Sure.' As she rose to her feet he stood too and Kay acknowledged that the old-fashioned courtesy surprised her. 'The cloakrooms are over the far side of the room,' he said quietly.

'Thank you.' She gave him a brief smile and then forced herself not to hurry as she walked in the direction he had indicated. Just before she went through the door to the ladies' cloakroom she glanced back towards their table. He was seated again, his eyes on her as he drank his champagne. There was a brooding quality to his stance and for a second Kay found it difficult to look away. Then she opened the door to the cloakroom and stepped into the scented interior.

For a moment after the door had closed behind her she stood quite still, her heart thumping so hard it was painful. There was no one else with her, and she glanced round the ultra-deluxe room with its beautifully tiled white and gold walls and granite surfaces in which three washbasins were set, before making her way to the window.

Thank goodness the cloakroom wasn't an inner room, but did the windows open, and, if so, onto what? The modern frame had one large fixed pane of glass with two top-hung smaller windows either side of it, all with heavily opaque privacy glass.

Kay glanced at the locks on the smaller windows; there was no key that she could see. Please open, she prayed, please, *please* open. Her heart in her mouth, she tried the one nearest to her and felt a flood of relief as it swung outwards. It opened onto what appeared to be a small yard containing several large plastic dustbins in one corner and various other containers dotted about the limited space.

Directly below the window the area was clear, but it looked to be something like a six- or seven-foot drop to the ground. That wouldn't have mattered if she had been in jeans or trousers, but her short, slimline skirt didn't lend itself easily to mountaineering.

So, what were the options? Kay stepped back from the open window and turned to face the room as she ran things over in her mind. Did she let Mitchell Grey get away with tricking her here and all but forcing her to eat with him? No, not *all* but forcing her, she corrected herself in the next moment. He *had* forced her. She had decided to teach him a lesson in the car and she still intended to go through with it...didn't she? The moment of doubt was enough to put steel in her backbone. He had been trying to charm her out there but he had picked the wrong girl and she wasn't fooled for a minute. She wouldn't *let* herself be fooled. Not ever again. Perry had had the sweet talk and beguilement down to a fine art and could be Mr Irresistible himself—when he was getting his own way.

Kay bent down, slipping off her high-heeled shoes and holding them in one hand as she mentally prepared herself. She was going to look pretty silly if anyone came into the cloakroom in the next few minutes but that couldn't be helped. Better that than letting Mitchell Grey think he could bully her into submission!

There was a small upholstered chair in one corner of the cloakroom and now she lifted it over to below the window, taking a long deep breath before stepping up on it. She dropped her shoes out of the window onto the ground below, hearing them thud with a dart of fatalism. She was committed to the escape now; she could hardly pad back out there with bare feet.

She moved her shoulder bag so it was hanging on her back and clambered from the chair onto the window sill, her skirt riding almost up to her waist. She had never felt so silly in all her life. What *must* she look like from the rear? she asked herself with a little giggle of near hysteria. So much for the cool, collected businesswoman image.

The aperture was just about big enough for her to squeeze through although once or twice in all her wriggling and squirming she thought she was stuck. Only the thought of just how much Mitchell Grey would relish such a predicament kept her from giving up.

She had twisted round on the sill before worming her way out of the window backwards, which was just as well, because suddenly she emerged like a cork out of a bottle onto the ground below, grazing her knees on the wall on her way down. The air turned a delicate shade of blue as she picked herself up, examining her torn tights and bloody knees. Great. Just great.

Picking up her bag from where it had fallen in the rapid descent, she opened it, extracting a tissue and dabbing at her knees. Ow... She'd forgotten the pain of grazed knees but now she was transported back into childhood again. She must remember to give the twins due sympathy next time one of them fell off their bicycles, a fairly regular occurrence.

After dusting herself down and bundling as much of her hair as she could back into the pony-tail, Kay pulled on her shoes and limped off to the gate set in the high brick wall that surrounded the yard. It was bolted in two places but the bolts slid easily beneath her fingers; obviously the gate was in regular use. She stepped out from the yard into the side street, glancing about her rather like a fugitive from the law who expected a Bonnie and Clyde ambush any moment. Apart from a fat tabby cat busily eating something disgusting from an overturned dustbin some yards away, all was quiet, but the main street was just a little way along the pavement.

As she emerged into the busier road she saw the welcome sight of a taxi approaching and all but threw herself into its path, but it wasn't until she had given her home address and the vehicle was on its way again that it dawned on her she had actually *done* it. She had left Mitchell Grey sitting waiting for her in that swish restaurant with his grand bottle of champagne slowly losing its bubbles. It wouldn't be long before their main course would be brought to the table; how long would he continue to wait after that before he asked for someone, a waitress maybe, to find her? He was going to look such a fool...

She stared out of the window at the shops and buildings flashing by, and wondered why there was none of the pleasure she had anticipated in her victory, but only a feeling of consuming flatness.

CHAPTER THREE

'GOOD grief, child, whatever will you do next?'

Her mother had spoken as if she were a little girl again, and to be truthful that was exactly how Kay felt as she stood in the kitchen, clutching her torn tights and with her bruised and bloody knees on show. She had just given Leonora the bare outline of what had occurred, and the older woman had sat down with a sudden plump before she'd spoken.

'He deserved it.' There was more than a touch of defensiveness in Kay's voice.

'I'm not saying he didn't, although there are worse crimes than abducting someone to the sort of restaurant he took you to.' Leonora shook her head slowly, her still lovely face unable to hide her amazement.

'That's what he said.' Kay surveyed her mother with guarded eyes. 'But I don't appreciate being lied to or forced into accompanying someone somewhere when I'd made it clear I wanted to leave.'

'No, I can understand that.' Leonora rose from the stool. 'I'll make us both a coffee, shall I, while you have a shower and change? Are you going back to the office today?'

'No. Peter and Tom are both out and the answer machine can deal with any calls. People will have to try elsewhere if it's urgent. I thought I might meet the girls out of school. They'd like that.'

'They'd love it,' Leonora agreed softly. She was well aware of the real reason her daughter was doing the unheard of and taking an afternoon off, but thought it advisable not to refer to it. If Mitchell Grey should go to the office she wouldn't like Kay to be there alone, the sort of rage he would probably be in. No...a man like that—proud, ruthless—would almost certainly just cut his losses, Leonora assured herself hopefully as she watched her daughter leave the room.

Once upstairs in the minute but pretty lemon and blue bathroom, which was just big enough to hold a shower, toilet and hand basin, Kay undressed quickly. She was feeling a bit shaky, she admitted reluctantly, but it was just reaction, added to which she'd had that enormous cocktail and eaten very little. She wasn't in the least bothered about how Mitchell Grey would view her unceremonious departure from the restaurant and his life—she *wasn't*.

Just let him try any intimidation of any kind or turn nasty and she would— Well, she didn't know what she'd do, she confessed weakly, stepping under the warm water and letting the silky flow caress her. But she was not going to be bullied—that much was for sure.

After a minute or two she stirred herself to begin washing her hair, massaging her scalp with unnecessary vigour as though she could wash the thoughts tumbling about her head away with the perfumed suds. Once dry again, she daubed a liberal amount of antiseptic cream on her knees—gritting her teeth when it stung like sulphuric acid—before covering the raw patches with two enormous plasters.

After pulling on a pair of jeans and a big fluffy cream jumper, she conditioned and dried her hair but couldn't be bothered to engage in the normal fight to tame it. She let it fall about her face and shoulders in a mass of riotous red-brown silky curls and waves, aware it made her look about sixteen but uncaring. Her wild mop was the least of her problems.

It wasn't until she was ready to go downstairs just after her mother had called her to say the coffee was ready that Kay admitted to herself she'd behaved incredibly badly.

She paused on the small landing, shutting her eyes for a moment. Not that he'd acted any better, she told herself in the next moment—lying to her and forcing her to enter the restaurant—but it wasn't like her to be unkind. Oh, hell... She groaned softly, sitting down on the top stair and kneading the back of her neck, which was as taut as piano wire. But it was done now and he *had* asked for it—or some sort of retaliation at least. Sweet Revenge... She was sure it was that lethal cocktail that had given her the mother and father of a headache.

Kay walked the half-mile or so to the twins' school. The mild sunny day was mellowing into the sort of late October evening when woodsmoke and falling leaves provided a touch of pure English magic. It was usually at times like this that she reflected how lucky she was. She had her precious girls, a lovely home and the sort of job that made the nine-to-five slog interesting and absorbing. Tonight, however, was different.

She was unsettled, she admitted irritably. All at odds with herself. And Mitchell Grey was to blame. Not only had he tried to kidnap her but he now had her almost apologising for resisting it! She must be mad. She wasn't going to give him or the day's events another thought.

'If you can't take the heat stay out of the kitchen,' she muttered to herself aggressively as she reached the school gates. 'And that's for you, Mitchell Grey.'

After seeing the neighbour whose turn it had been to take the twins home, Kay waited for the two little girls to come out into the playground. She wasn't disappointed by their reaction when they caught sight of her and—as always at times like this—she felt the stab of guilt that she couldn't meet them more often. But—and it was a big but—they still needed every penny the company could bring in to pay a living wage to herself, Peter and Tom. They all had families to support, and, although the company had proved itself to be a growing and successful one, the next step—that of taking on more employees and expanding—was a gamble. They'd all seen firms that had grown too quickly, and enlarged into disaster and liquidation, and with the girls and her mother depending on her she couldn't take any chances.

'Hard work, determination, wealth, success. The first two giving rise to the latter when combined with that magical element called luck.' Mitchell Grey's words rang in Kay's ears as she and the twins made their way home through the dusky air. Well, unlike Mr Grey who only answered to himself if things went wrong, she had people depending on her, Kay told herself crabbily. She couldn't afford the sort of Russian roulette speculation that could take a relative nobody to millionaire status in business. Of course someone like him, a self-confessed autonomist who had no time for long-term personal relationships, would have no such qualms.

'We're home!' As she opened the front door Kay called to her mother in the kitchen before standing aside for Georgia and Emily to precede her. They raced across the sitting room, flinging open the door into the kitchen.

As Kay closed the door behind her she became aware of two things in the same instant. The girls had skidded to an abrupt halt in the doorway and her mother was saying something, her words high and rushed, which indicated she was nervous. And then she heard the deep, smoky male voice, and she knew...

By the time she reached the doorway she had herself under control again, only the whiteness of her skin betraying that she was scared to death. Mitchell Grey was sitting at the table with her mother, a cup of coffee and an enormous wedge of Leonora's carrot cake in front of him.

Kay stared at him, knowing she had to say something but utterly bereft of words to meet the occasion. He stared back silently with unfathomable eyes.

'Kay, darling, there you are.' Leonora rose hastily from the table, all fluster, and moved round the long breakfast bar that divided the dining area from the kitchen. 'Mitchell called by to have a word. I'll take the girls into the sitting room, shall I?'

'Not on my account, please, Leonora.' He smiled at her as he spoke before glancing at the two little girls who were shyly clutching Kay's legs. 'Your grandmother has told me about you two. Now, which is which?'

Mitchell and Leonora? She had only been gone for just under an hour and in that time her mother and Mitchell Grey had become best buddies?

'I'm Georgia and she's Emily.' Georgia, always the least shy spoke up as she looked curiously at the big dark man dominating the tiny dining area. 'What's your name?'

'Mitchell.' He smiled at the two small figures who were like peas in a pod. 'But you can call me Mitch if you like.'

Georgia nodded, her red-brown curls dancing. Always a child of instant decisions, she now walked over to the figure sitting at the table before Kay could stop her, her voice loud as she said, 'Do you want to know how you can tell us apart so you don't get mixed up?'

Mitchell stared into the earnest little face. The child's tone had suggested she was doing him a great honour and his reflected he was fully aware of this when he said, 'Very much, please, Georgia.'

'I'm an inch taller than Emily and she has got some green in her eyes but mine are all brown, like Mummy's.'

'Right.' He nodded. 'Thank you, I'll remember that.'

Emily, not to be outdone, had now joined her sister at Mitchell's knee. 'My grandma has got some green in her eyes too,' she said importantly, 'and my Uncle Peter.'

'Have they?' Mitchell glanced at the two women for a moment before his gaze returned to the twins. All four faces were so alike it was almost comical, like three stages of life in one person. 'Well, you've both got very pretty eyes, your grandma and mummy too.'

The girls beamed at him and Kay realised she had to get a handle on this, and fast. 'Georgia, Emily, you go up with Grandma now and get changed out of your school uniform,' she said briskly. 'When you're washed and changed you can come down and have a glass of milk and a biscuit, okay?'

'Will you still be here?' Georgia asked Mitchell, without glancing in Kay's direction.

'I'm not sure.' The silver eyes passed over Kay's face, which now, far from being drained of colour, was burning hot. 'You'd better ask your mummy that.'

'Mummy—'

'Georgia.'

It was obvious the tone was one the twins recognised because they turned from Mitchell without another word, walking over to Leonora who had her hands outstretched for them and leaving the room with just a wave at Mitchell.

'They're delightful.' As the door closed he pre-empted what Kay had been about to say, following the statement by taking a huge bite of the carrot cake.

Kay stared at him, aware her face was on fire but unable to do anything about it as she said, 'Mr Grey, why are you here?'

'Mitchell, please.' It was soft, but carried a warning in the lazy tone. 'Unless you prefer Mitch, of course?'

'I don't prefer anything.'

He nodded, taking another bite of cake as though he had every right to sit at her dining table.

He was angry, furiously angry with her. Kay didn't know how she came by this knowledge because the hard, handsome face was to all intents and purposes relaxed and sociable, the unusual ice-blue eyes clear and inscrutable. She decided to take the bull by the horns. 'You're angry.' It was a statement, not a question. 'And I can understand that but it doesn't give you the right to come to my home like this.'

'I disagree,' he said, the conversational tone not fooling her for a minute.

She decided to try another tack. 'How did you get my address, anyway?' she asked hotly, forcing the aggression into her voice when really she was having a job to hide the trembling in her stomach.

Did she have any idea how young and vulnerable she looked standing like that, her whole stance one of hostility but her mouth and eyes betraying her panic and alarm? Damn it, she was looking at him as though he were some sort of monster. The thought increased Mitchell's fury rather than diffusing it. 'Obtaining your address was not difficult,' he said evenly. 'I had your name and telephone number, after all.'

'I don't want you here, distressing my mother and frightening the girls.' Even to Kay's own ears it sounded ridiculous. Her mother had clearly taken to him and he'd had the twins eating out of his hand.

'Then you shouldn't have bolted like a scared rabbit, should you?' he drawled with insufferable detachment. 'Surprising though it may seem, I didn't appreciate the position you put me in this lunchtime. Neither do I countenance the waste of good food,' he added indolently.

'You left me with no other choice,' she shot back.

'Forgive me if I don't see it that way.'

'I don't like bullies.'

'Neither do I,' he agreed, as though it had been an objective statement.

Kay glared at him even as she asked herself exactly what it was about this man that made her react with such uncharacteristic antagonism. She had no illusions about the male of the species, not any more, but until Mitchell Grey had come on the scene she had been able to handle them just fine. If nothing else, the last few years—when she had carved out a life and a career for herself, and become sole provider for her mother and the girls—had taught her she was more than capable of surviving without a man. And with that knowledge had come confidence and self-respect.

Mitchell finished the last of the cake, smacking his lips appreciatively as he said, 'Your mother's an excellent cook. It's been years since I had carrot cake, and I was starving.'

She didn't miss the innuendo in the last words but chose to ignore it. She had to get him out of here, *now*, and if an apology was what he'd come for it was a small price to pay to end this fiasco. Nevertheless, she found the words stuck in her throat. She swallowed, glancing at him as she searched for the right tone—cool, collected and not too penitent.

The blue eyes were tight on her, silver-bright and unblinking, the corners of his mouth curved just enough in a cynical twist to tell her he knew exactly what she was thinking and what had motivated the forthcoming apology. It immediately withered and died. 'I'd like you to leave right now, Mr Grey,' she said crisply, her heart thumping painfully.

He folded his arms over his chest, settling more comfortably on the chair as he studied her interestedly—much as he'd done in the restaurant. 'I'm sure you would, *Mrs* Sherwood,' he said softly, the quiet emphasis on her name telling Kay her formal approach had been noted and was not appreciated. 'Tell me,' he continued, as though her demand had not been voiced, 'how did you leave the restaurant without my seeing you? I know it wasn't through the kitchens.'

Kay blinked. She'd half expected whoever had been sent to look for her would click onto what she'd done, but if he didn't know already there was no way she was telling him of her ignominious exit. She shrugged carefully. 'Does it matter?' she asked, forcing boredom into her voice.

'Do you know, I rather think it does—to me, that is.' His voice was low and rough now and for the first time Kay caught a glimpse of his outrage. It was immensely satisfying.

It was also an entirely inappropriate moment to feel amused but she couldn't help it, and although she kept her face straight it was clear he had sensed something when he said, 'Well? I'm not leaving until I receive the courtesy of an answer.'

Oh, to blazes with it! 'I climbed out of the washroom window,' she admitted expressionlessly.

There was a long moment of silence and then Mitchell began to laugh. Not a snigger or a sarcastic chortle, but a bust-a-gut roar of laughter that took Kay completely by surprise. She tried unsuccessfully to stifle her own amusement but his hilarity was infectious, albeit he was laughing at her, and she was still grinning when the silver-blue gaze swept her face again. 'I bet Harringtons had never seen anything like it before, and in that skirt,' he said, his voice still vibrating. 'You were fortunate not to do yourself an injury.'

She thought of her lacerated knees. 'Possibly.'

'And you would really rather dive out of a window than endure a lunch with me?' He'd stopped laughing now and something in his voice made the colour flare in her face.

'I... I don't like to be tricked,' she managed falteringly.

'And if you weren't tricked, what then?' he asked very softly, his voice oozing something that sent a tingle down her spine. He stood up as he spoke and she felt her body tense as he walked over to her, the overall height and breadth of him making her feel as small as the twins.

'I...told you, I don't date.' She wanted to take a step backwards but as he wasn't touching her it seemed silly, besides which she was worried it would give the wrong signals. She wasn't frightened of him, no way, she assured herself silently.

'Never?'

'Never,' she said firmly. 'There's the twins to take care of.'

'Your mother wouldn't babysit for one evening while

you go out?' he asked gently. 'I find that hard to believe. She seems a very nice woman.'

'She is,' Kay said hotly, 'and of course she'd babysit if I asked her but I choose not to. I prefer not to get involved...' Her voice trailed away as the faint seductive fragrance of his body warmth surrounded her. Kay's stomach clenched in protest at the tingles it was invoking. He wasn't even holding her so how come she felt hot and weak? she asked herself helplessly, a shiver of excitement dancing over her skin.

'So do I.' He looked down at her, the black of his hair throwing his tanned skin and mercurial eyes into even more prominence. 'I thought we'd already established earlier we're two of a kind? Free, self-determining, autonomous.'

Kay stared into the strongly chiselled features. Men were not to be trusted. They said one thing and meant another, and when the another led to a desire to control and subjugate the woman was fighting an uphill battle to retain her individuality. Why, even her father—good as he had been—had gambled with her mother's peace of mind and security for the future and lost everything without even telling her what he'd been doing. Men were a different species.

'I like women,' Mitchell said softly, 'but that doesn't mean I'm prepared to walk into a snare or set one for someone else. Fairy tales—one man, one woman and a lifetime of for ever—are for children.'

'I don't—' She stopped, her cheeks burning. 'I don't sleep around.'

'Good. Neither do I.'

'I meant—'

'I know what you meant, Kay.' He reached out and ran one finger gently down her cheek, his touch feather-light.

She felt it in every fibre of her body. 'And I have no expectations, okay? I'm not a green callow youth who can only enjoy a woman's company if the end of the evening results in animal mating. Sex is more than that, it requires mental as well as physical stimulation and this is always better when a couple know each other and have built up a level of trust. One-night stands are not my idea of a good time.'

She didn't believe she was having this conversation. She had only ever slept with one man—Perry—in the whole of her life, and she had given him her body because he'd had her heart too. Mitchell was talking about something else entirely.

'I'm sorry.' Now she did take a step away from him, willing herself to puncture the seductive bubble he'd woven round them in the last minute or two. 'I meant what I said earlier. I don't want a relationship in any shape or form. I'm not ready to start dating again.'

He took her into his arms before she realised what he was doing, kissing her firmly but without undue force or roughness. She was rigid for a moment but, before she could struggle or object to the nearness of him, the delicious scent she'd smelt earlier and the feel of his body, hard and sure, wove a spell. She didn't actively respond, not at first; the sensations she was experiencing were too new and amazing for that, but as his mouth continued to caress hers, demanding greater and greater access, her body curved into his in unconscious pleasure.

She had never imagined in all her wildest dreams that a man could kiss like this, she thought dazedly. It was intoxicating, a sexual experience all in itself and as unlike anything Perry had ever done as chalk to cheese. Perry had kissed her only as a necessary preliminary to lovemaking, something to be moved on from swiftly to the real crux of the matter, but this...

His tongue rippled along her teeth before probing the inner sweetness of her mouth and her eyes opened wide in startled pleasure at the sensation it created, little needles of desire beginning to jab in her lower stomach. Her hands had been clenched stiffly against his chest but now they moved almost of their own volition to the broad shoulders, her eyelids closing in drugged enjoyment.

Her breasts were crushed against the wall of his chest, the slightest movement between them creating waves of pleasure radiating from their hard peaks, and she had to restrain herself from arching against him like a hungry cat.

'Kay?' As he moved her away from him to arm's length she opened bewildered eyes, staring at him as he murmured softly, 'I think the twins are on their way down.'

It was a drenching shock to realise she had been blind and deaf to the girls' approach when they burst into the kitchen a moment or two later, but in her customary inspection of two pairs of small hands before the milk and biscuits were served Kay pulled herself together.

'I'm glad you're still here.' Georgia's first words were for Mitchell. 'Have you finished talking to Mummy yet?'

'Yes, we're finished.' Kay answered her daughter before Mitchell could, her voice amazingly controlled considering how she was feeling inside. 'Now go and sit at the table, please.'

'Grandma says you're a friend of Mummy's,' Emily put in as she bounded across to the dining table after Georgia. 'Does that mean you'll come again?'

'Would you like me to come again?' Mitchell prevaricated, smiling into the two little faces that were so like their mother's.

'Yes!' They answered in unison.

'Then we'll have to see.'

Over her dead body. Kay smiled a tight smile before she said, 'Say goodbye to Mr Grey,' as she placed the two glasses and biscuits in front of the twins. 'I'll be back in a minute.'

She walked across to the kitchen door, opening it and waiting for Mitchell to precede her into the sitting room, which he did after one cryptic glance at her set face. Leonora was just descending the stairs, and as the older woman's eyes flew from her daughter's face to Mitchell's, and then back to Kay's, Kay said, 'Could you watch the girls a moment while I see Mr Grey out?'

'Certainly.' Leonora didn't remark that the twins were more than capable of drinking their milk and eating the biscuits without supervision, but what she did say was, and warmly—much to Kay's annoyance—'It was very nice to meet you, Mitch.'

'Likewise, and the carrot cake was wonderful.'

'Thank you.' Leonora dimpled and Kay felt like shaking her.

As Mitchell opened the front door and stepped outside Kay heard her mother shut the kitchen door with a very deliberate click, which spoke of her disapproval of her daughter's attitude. She gritted her teeth and then, as he turned to face her, said firmly, 'Goodbye,' before spoiling the curtness by adding—as the thought struck—'Where's your car?'

'Worried I might have to thumb a lift?' It was mocking. 'My chauffeur is parked round the corner and no doubt taking the opportunity to have a little nap,' Mitchell said softly. 'And before you ask, yes, I did make sure you wouldn't see the car when you came home. I thought you might bolt again.'

He made her sound like a temperamental pony. She glared at him, trying not to notice how daunting his height was.

'I'll pick you up at eight, by the way.' He had turned on his heel and was halfway down the garden path before her shriek made him noticeably wince.

'I'm not going anywhere with you tonight!'

He turned, a cool smile twisting his lips. 'Wrong,' he said silkily.

Was he mad or was it her? Because one of them must be. 'I thought I had made myself perfectly clear,' she said tightly.

'What you made clear, Kay, was that you need to be kissed,' he said with outrageous equanimity. She had also revealed—unwittingly but absolutely—that this ex-husband of hers had been the sort of man who took rather than gave. She might have the twins as proof that she was not unaccustomed as to what transpired between a man and a woman, but he would bet his bottom dollar that she was sexually unawakened.

He felt his body leap in response to the thought, hardening as it had done when he had held her. Was she freckled all over? he asked himself. He intended to find out. But he wouldn't rush her; she was as nervous as a cat on a hot tin roof as it was.

'I do *not* need to be kissed!' She had followed him halfway down the path, her voice a low hiss. 'And I especially do not want to be kissed by you.' Her voice was all the more adamant because she was lying to herself as well as him.

'Then I'll have to work on that,' Mitchell murmured thoughtfully. 'Every woman should want to be kissed.'

For goodness' sake! His skin must be inches thick, or perhaps it was just a giant ego that couldn't take no for an answer? 'That's such a typical male comment,' she said as scathingly as she could.

'There is nothing typical about me, Kay, as I intend to show you, but all in good time. For now I'm suggesting nothing more threatening than a good meal and a relaxed evening where you can unwind a little. You've obviously forgotten how to have fun but fortunately I know how to remedy that.' He smiled as if his words were perfectly innocent but she had seen the gleam in the back of his eyes. 'I'll pick you up later and don't bother to dress up, this place is very low-key. And before you object again—' he had seen her open her mouth in protest '—I'm not above using force to get my own way. Would you really like to upset the twins by letting them see their mother carried off kicking and screaming?'

'That's blackmail.'

'Dead right it is, and very useful at times.'

She glared at him, the last of the evening sunlight catching the red in her hair and turning it to living flame. 'You're despicable,' she ground out through clenched teeth.

'Like the song, ''Baby, You Ain't Seen Nothing Yet''.' He grinned at her, totally unabashed, and turned, striding off down the path and out of the gate without a backward glance.

Kay stood for some moments in the quiet of the evening, but apart from a dog barking in the distance somewhere and the sound of children calling to each other she heard nothing. Wherever he had stationed his car it wasn't close enough to hear the engine start.

She walked to the end of the path, leaning on the gate as she glanced up and down the quiet tree-lined street in which they lived. She had loved this street as soon as she had seen it; it was a higgledy-piggledy hotchpotch of houses, some small and some large, detached, semi-detached and even a small row of terraced Victorian houses at the very end of the road, and her tiny detached property sat right in the middle of it all.

Bruised and heartsore as she had been when she'd first come here, she had known instantly that the minute house was meant to be hers. It was tranquil, the whole street was tranquil and that was rare in this modern age. And now the tranquillity had been shattered! She frowned as the image of a hard, handsome face with eyes as cold as a moonlit sea flashed onto the screen of her mind. He'd had no right to come here, no right at all, but then she suspected Mitchell Grey was a man who took no account of right if it suited his purpose not to.

She moved restlessly as her heartbeat quickened at the thought. Why had she gone to his offices that day? Why couldn't it have been Peter or Tom who'd delivered the wretched document? She didn't want this, not any of it. He had said they were two of a kind but that was so untrue. He was as free as a bird but she had her precious babies to consider, and Georgia and Emily would always come first.

The dusk was thick now, the birds in residence in the trees overlooking the road jabbering in annoyance when a latecomer disturbed their bedtime. She stood for a moment more, trying to capture the feeling of peace and contentment she normally felt on such sojourns, but it was no good.

Sighing irritably, she turned back towards the house, glancing at her watch as she did so. Five o'clock. In three hours he would be here again, expecting her to go out with him. In spite of herself her pulse quickened. Well, she would go with him but she'd make sure she spelt out where she stood even more plainly than she'd done already. She was a mother, with commitments—not one of the carefree, sophisticated women of the world men like him favoured. And she didn't want to have 'fun', as he'd put it. She wanted...

Oh, she didn't know what she wanted, she admitted crossly as she pushed open the front door, but it wasn't Mitchell Grey.

If Kay had but known it, Mitchell's thoughts were very similar to her own as he sat in the back of his car, staring moodily out at the shadowed scene beyond the window as the big vehicle ate up the miles.

Why on earth had he pursued this thing once the mother had told him Kay had children? This just wasn't his scene at all. When had he ever had contact with tiny people? Never. He should have got out of there before she'd returned, but somehow he hadn't been able to bring himself to do that. But this was crazy—*he* was crazy. Damn it, she'd made it clear she wanted nothing to do with him.

He leant back in the seat, stretching his legs and shutting his eyes. What a fiasco of a day! He'd rescheduled the meeting with Jennings and postponed the visit to the docks at Southampton, which made the rest of the week damn awkward, and for what? A little slip of a redhead who wasn't even particularly arresting and came with the baggage of two offspring and a mother to boot.

But there was something about her... He shifted in the seat, opening his eyes again. He couldn't put his finger on it, but there was definitely something about her that was affecting him in a way he hadn't felt in a long, long time.

He shook his head, reaching for his briefcase and switching on the interior light as he pulled out a wad of papers that needed immediate attention. He would see her tonight and then make an end of it—decision made. He had an address book full of the numbers of women who would be only too pleased to spend an evening with him; Kay Sherwood was a complication he could do without. By this time next week he wouldn't even be able to remember what she looked like.

But he knew he was lying to himself...

CHAPTER FOUR

'YOU'RE not going out to dinner with Mitch dressed like that?'

Kay looked at her mother and sighed. The older woman had said very little about Mitchell's visit since he'd left, but her silence had spoken volumes, not to mention her enthusiastic conversation with the twins about 'the nice friend of Mummy's'. Now Kay said mildly, 'I'm *twenty*-six, not six, Mum, and more than capable of deciding what to wear. Okay?'

Leonora sniffed, gazing at Kay who had dressed after settling the twins in bed and had therefore just entered the sitting room. The black jeans and long-sleeved cashmere jumper in a pale shade of violet were obviously not to the older woman's taste.

'He said casual, remember?' Kay reminded her. 'We're probably dining at the local fast-food place for all I know.'

'Mitch would never take a date there.'

'How on earth do you know?' She was losing patience, Kay thought irritably, she really was. 'You've met the man for a few minutes, that's all. He could be a serial killer or died-in-the-wool bigamist or whatever—'

'Now you're being silly,' Leonora interrupted with another sniff.

'Mum, at the risk of destroying your illusions about the white knight on a charger you've apparently decided he is, the man is interested in one thing and one thing only,' Kay said vehemently. 'And as he's not going to get it from me this is going to be a short and probably unpleasant evening. Let's leave it at that, shall we?'

'Oh, Kay.' Leonora walked across to take her hands, looking into her daughter's troubled face as she said, 'I just want you to be happy, that's all. You've had such a rough deal the last few years and a man like Mitch—rich, successful—'

'Single,' Kay put in mockingly.

'Yes, and single.' Leonora wasn't about to be put off by her daughter's sarcasm. 'A man like that only comes along once in a blue moon. Give him a chance, that's all I'm saying. See how it goes. Have some fun.'

'What is it about me that everyone wants me to have fun suddenly?' Kay smiled at her mother, her face rueful. 'Look, Mitchell Grey is just a ship that passes in the night, and by the end of this evening the term will be passed, I assure you. We have got absolutely nothing in common, for a start. He's rich, successful and single as you've just pointed out; we watch the pennies and come as a package or not at all. Not exactly the sort of bargain a man in Mitchell's position wants to strike. He could have his pick of any woman.'

'It's you he's asked out tonight,' Leonora pointed out swiftly.

'Maybe, but not in the way you think. More to prove a point after the episode at lunch.'

'Ah, but he asked you out to lunch, though, didn't he, in the first place?' It was triumphant. 'That must mean he's interested.'

'Don't hold your breath, Mum, that's all I'm saying, besides which I don't *want* a man. I'm perfectly contented with my life as it is.'

Leonora let go of Kay's hands without saying anything more but another eloquent sniff spoke for her.

'I'll leave my mobile on so you can contact me if you need me,' Kay said, glancing at the clock on the mantelpiece, which said five to eight. 'And if Emily starts coughing again her linctus is on the bedside cabinet. And no juice, if they ask for a drink—only water. I don't want sugar coating their teeth all night.'

'For goodness' sake just go and enjoy yourself, Kay,' Leonora snapped irritably. 'I'm more than capable of babysitting for one evening without you around, I do it often enough if you have to work a late delivery. You are supposed to have a life beyond that of mother to the twins, you know, dear as they are. You're young, you've still got your whole life in front of you. Stop acting as though you were my age.'

'Mum!' Kay was truly shocked and hurt and it showed.

Immediately Leonora retraced her steps, putting her arms round the younger woman and hugging Kay for a moment as she said, 'I didn't mean that the way it sounded, darling, really. I'm only thinking of you. You're a wonderful mother and daughter, the best there is, but it's time to put the past behind you.'

'I have,' Kay said firmly.

'I wish I could believe that.' Leonora had spoken pensively but then, as a knock on the front door announced Mitchell's arrival, the older woman started violently. 'He's here!'

Kay was amused to see there was something bordering on panic in her mother's face as she'd spoken, and it went some way to combating the butterflies in her own stomach. She breathed deeply before walking across the room and opening the door, and then her stomach turned right over as she looked into the dark face staring down at her. He looked sensational. The business suit had been replaced by a chunky black leather jacket and black jeans, which accentuated the brooding quality to his good looks even more, and she noticed he had shaved again, the five-o'clock shadow that had been evident earlier having vanished. For some reason the thought of him shaving because he was going to see her was so intimate it made her shiver—which only showed how dangerous it was to be around him, she warned herself silently.

'Hi.' He brought a big bunch of pale peach roses and freesias out from behind his back. 'These are for your mother.'

'Oh, right.' She was taken aback and it showed. He laughed softly, the silver eyes brilliant with mocking humour, and then she flushed pink as he delved in his pocket and produced a small transparent box in which reposed one delicate, beautiful white orchid.

'And this is for you,' he murmured, placing the box in her hands.

'Thank you,' she said uneasily. She didn't want him buying her anything. 'Come in for a moment while I get my coat.'

She left her mother gushing over the roses while she slipped upstairs for her jacket and took the opportunity to fix the dainty corsage on her jumper in front of the bedroom mirror, rather than give Mitchell the opportunity to suggest he do it for her. It had the most exquisite perfume, something resembling magnolia but slightly more exotic, and the smell was wafting under her nose as she went downstairs again.

Her mother and Mitchell were laughing about something or other as Kay descended, the atmosphere between them relaxed and friendly, and for a moment Kay felt thoroughly put out. It was almost as though he had inveigled his way into her life and home already, and she didn't like it. This was her refuge, her own tiny castle, but Mitchell seemed able to lower the drawbridge at will.

She smiled a brittle smile as they both turned to look at her, her voice tight as she said, 'Shall we go?'

'Sure.'

She noticed him raise his eyebrows at her mother in silent comment at the crispness of her voice but she pretended not to see. However, she did make a mental note to point out to her mother later that she had been right about the jeans. Mitchell was wearing them too. Admittedly his looked to be nothing short of Gucci or Armani, and hers were off the peg from one of the stores, but that wasn't the point.

'Where are you going?'

The three of them turned to see two small figures in teddy-bear pyjamas sitting halfway down the stairs, both sucking their thumbs and both with a rag doll tucked under one arm.

'Hey...' Kay's voice softened by several hundred degrees. 'What are you two doing up? You should have been asleep half an hour ago.'

'I'll see to the girls, you go.' It was clear Leonora was worried the best laid plans of mice and men were going askew.

However it was Mitchell who walked over to the foot of the stairs, smiling broadly at the two little girls as he said, 'I'm taking your mummy out for something to eat. Is that all right with you?'

They looked at each other and then turned back to him, nodding. 'We knew you were coming,' Georgia volunteered. 'We heard Mummy and Grandma talking about you.'

'Well, now you've said hallo I want you straight back into bed,' Leonora cut in hastily, moving past Mitchell as she added, 'Go on, right now, and I'll come and tuck you in.'

Kay glanced at Mitchell and saw his lips were twitching. He had obviously guessed whatever had been said wasn't particularly complimentary, but how could she have known the girls were listening? They had ears on them like donkeys, those two.

'Night night, darlings.' She called her goodbye as Mitchell turned and opened the door, but her mother was so intent on whisking the girls away before they said any more that she doubted they heard her.

'Was it that bad?' His deep, smoky voice didn't try to hide his amusement as they walked down the path.

'I'm sorry?' Kay prevaricated warily, although she knew exactly what he was asking. 'Was what bad?'

He glanced at her as he opened the garden gate and stood aside for her to precede him. 'I'm sure your mother is a wonderful woman,' he drawled lazily, 'but I doubt if tact is one of her strong points. Those poor kids' feet didn't touch the ground, she moved them so fast.'

'I'm sure I don't know what you mean,' she said primly, her voice a little weak as she stared at the magnificent sports car parked in front of the house. She didn't ask him if it was his car because it couldn't be anyone else's, but she was mentally blessing the fact she had decided to wear jeans and not a skirt as she looked at the low-slung monster.

He opened the passenger door and Kay slid into the leather-clad interior fairly gracefully, although she felt as though she were sitting on the floor, but when Mitchell joined her a moment later she felt every nerve in her body twang and vibrate.

'Put your seat belt on.'

'What?' She glanced at him and then wished she hadn't

because he was close, very close, and she was all of a dither as it was.

'Your seat belt?' He reached across her, the seductive and delicious smell of him adding to the sensations spiralling inside her and causing her heart to gallop. 'There.' Once she was strapped in he fixed his own seat belt before starting the engine, which purred into obedient life.

'Nice car.' She felt she had to say something to diffuse the electric atmosphere.

'Thank you.'

As the car leapt off with a low growl Kay just managed to stifle the squeak of fright, taking a deep breath before she said, 'What...what sort is it?'

'It's an Aston Martin sort,' he said softly.

'Oh.' She clearly should have known. 'I don't know much about cars.'

'There's no reason why you should.'

She *did* know that a car like this was a sex machine on wheels though, Kay thought desperately, and definitely a seduction tool in the hands of someone like Mitchell. She also knew from the one brief glance he was so close she only had to turn her head and move a little to caress that hard, square jaw with her lips... 'It...it must be quite expensive,' she managed weakly.

'Quite.' He spared her one piercing moment before his eyes returned to the windscreen. 'Boys' toys, is that what you're thinking?' he asked drily.

Boys' toys? There was nothing, absolutely and utterly nothing of the boy about Mitchell Grey. Kay tried to ignore the muscled legs and thighs clothed in black denim at the side of her. 'Not at all,' she said truthfully. 'Why? Is that how you view this?'

He smiled. 'Very cleverly sidestepped, Mrs Sherwood.'

Kay blinked. Had she been clever? She hadn't known she was being.

'Actually you might be right at that,' he continued quietly. 'I like fast cars with all the refinements, the thrill of speed and so on. I race at a private circuit now and then; you must come and watch some time.'

She couldn't think of anything she'd like less. 'Dicing with death?' she said coolly. 'I don't think I'd care to watch that. I think the gift of life is too valuable to be gambled on the turn of a card played by fickle fate.'

'Skill does play a small part in the proceedings.' It was very dry.

'Perhaps.' She shrugged. 'But if life is precious and happy enough, risking it in such a pointless way is not an option.'

His face didn't alter apart from his mouth tightening a little, but she knew he hadn't liked it. 'There are millions of people who would disagree with such a damning indictment.'

'That's their privilege,' she said shortly. 'It still doesn't alter what I think.'

'Are you seriously telling me that my participation in a sport in which I've been involved for many years is due to some kind of death wish?'

'I didn't say that.' She cast a sidelong glance at his grim profile. Wow, she'd *really* hit a nerve here. 'But I do think if you were utterly fulfilled in normal life you wouldn't need to take such unnecessary risks.'

'Spare me the amateur psychology.'

'Excuse me, but it was you who started this,' she said hotly.

Silence reigned for a few minutes as the car zoomed through the night at a speed Kay was sure was illegal.

'Why do you do that?' he asked suddenly, his voice rough.

'What?' She didn't have a clue what he was talking about.

'Argue, disagree, make waves,' he said irritably. 'No other woman I know is so damn opinionated.'

She bit down on the sharp answer that had sprung to mind and schooled her voice into order before she said evenly, 'If you want a dinner companion who will tell you exactly what you want to hear and agree with everything you say, as well as indicating she thinks you are a demigod who can do no wrong, you picked the wrong woman. I do have opinions and ideas of my own because I use the mind God gave me, and if you expect me to apologise for that or tread carefully in fear I might offend some precept of yours—tough. I've been in a state of mind where life lost its lustre and I know I could have taken chances then. Now is different. Life is precious now.'

'You're lucky,' he said drily.

'Perhaps. But luck is the flip side to misfortune and if you spin the coin fast enough both sides look the same. There were people who thought it was a calamity when I was left pregnant after Perry left—the final nail in the coffin—but it was the one thing in my life which proved a blessing and gave me strength to fight for the future.'

'Perry was your husband?' he asked softly, his swift glance taking in her intense expression.

'Yes.' She suddenly realised what she'd said and how much she had revealed, and to Mitchell Grey of all people.

'Don't freeze up on me again, Kay.'

Her eyes shot to the hard profile as his eyes turned to the windscreen again. 'I...I'm not,' she said shakily, dismayed at the ease with which he'd sensed her thoughts.

'So why did he leave?' he asked quietly.

He was aware she'd stiffened in the seat, but her voice came steadily when she said, 'I threw him out, actually. Her name was Tracy. But the marriage had been in trouble long before that. She...she was just the grand finale.'

'Do you still see much of him? What about the twins?'

'He's never seen them or been in contact since before the divorce.' When he made a sound deep in his throat she said fiercely, 'I like it that way, believe me. Look, can we change the subject?'

'Classical, rock or jazz?'

'What?'

'What type of music do you want on?' he asked patiently, making sure his voice revealed none of the anger that had gripped him towards this unknown husband who had let her down so monumentally.

There was a moment's pause, and her voice was a little shaky when she said, 'Jazz, please.'

Once the music was playing Mitchell concentrated on his driving and Kay sat quietly, her head whirling. She had been mad to tell him so much, she told herself bitterly. She should have kept the conversation light and easy, not spilled out everything barring her bra size! What must he be thinking? She stole a look sideways under her eyelashes but the granite profile was giving nothing away. Her throat felt locked and she couldn't think of a thing to say anyway, but the atmosphere inside the car was bordering on painful.

It was another ten minutes before he spoke, and then it was to say, 'We're nearly there, okay?'

She cleared her throat. 'Where's there?'

'Like I said, I thought we'd eat casual.'

Kay sat up straighter. There had been something in his

voice... ‘Where’s there?’ she asked again, her voice firmer.

‘My place,’ he said evenly.

‘Your place?’

‘But don’t worry, you won’t be all alone with the big bad wolf,’ he said mockingly. ‘I have a housekeeper who’s second to none and who provides a gourmet feast at the drop of a hat.’

Kay stared at him. ‘Is she residential?’ she asked at last.

‘Of course.’ His mouth twisted in the way she was beginning to recognise. ‘I’m offering dinner, Kay, not bed and breakfast. I told you, I don’t operate like that.’

She wasn’t so naive as to believe there weren’t men who said one thing and meant another; she’d married one, hadn’t she? But it was too late now, she would have to make the best of this evening, besides which she didn’t think Mitchell Grey was the kind of man who would force his attentions on a woman. He wouldn’t have to, for one thing, she thought ruefully. They were probably queueing for the privilege.

It was just a minute or so before they turned off the main road they’d been travelling on and into a more dimly lit avenue, one where large houses were set in spacious grounds from what Kay could see, and it was right at the end of this road that Mitchell pulled up in front of two big iron gates set in a high stone wall. He opened the gates from the car by remote control, closing them again once they’d passed through, and now the beautifully landscaped gardens were lit here and there by means of small lights laced in the trees and larger ones discreetly hidden in flowerbeds and ornamental bushes.

The drive was a long one, and by the time Kay caught sight of the house some moments later she had realised it was set in the sort of lovely woodland setting most people would give their eye-teeth for.

She swallowed hard before she said carefully, 'What a lovely place. Have you lived here long?'

'Eight years.' He drew to a halt on the gravel drive in front of the house, turning to face her in the car as he draped one arm along the back of her seat. 'I got it for what the estate agent described as a 'song' at the time because it was filthy inside and neglected, and the grounds were just an impassable thicket beyond a boggy field. It had belonged to folk whose ancestors had once been the lord-of-the-manor type aristocrats, but for decades there'd been no money. The 'song' cost me every spare penny along with a hefty mortgage at the time,' he added wryly, 'but I gambled that the business was taking off and that within twelve months I'd be sitting pretty.'

Kay nodded. Narrow-waisted and lean-hipped as he was, his broad shoulders and considerable height made his presence all encompassing in the confines of the sports car, the dark magnetism at the heart of his attractiveness intensified a hundredfold. 'It clearly paid off,' she managed breathlessly.

Mitchell smiled. 'All that was needed was imagination, creativity, bags of energy and some tender loving care,' he said quietly, the last few words causing a fallout in her already jangling nerves. 'I did some of the work myself but it was the army of carpenters, builders, plumbers, gardeners and others who really made the difference. I decided I wanted to start off by enlarging the kitchen and adding bedrooms and bathrooms and went from there. Come and have a look round.'

Immediately Kay stood on the drive she was struck by the mellow silence. They could have been in the middle of the country for the lack of traffic noise.

They were only on the bottom of the circular stone steps leading from the drive to the front door when it opened to reveal a tall and distinguished-looking man, his white hair gleaming in the shaft of light from the hallway at the back of him.

'Mr Grey, I thought I heard the car.'

Mitchell didn't reply to this but what he did say was, 'Henry, this is the young lady I was telling you about, Kay Sherwood. Kay, meet my housekeeper, Henry.'

His housekeeper? She'd expected a buxom, bustling little woman for some reason, but the man in front of her was the epitome of an upper-class butler. And then this image was shattered somewhat when Henry said, his top-drawer voice holding a touch of glee, 'I'm very pleased to meet you, Mrs Sherwood. I've been waiting a long time to see a woman put Mr Grey in his place but I think you accomplished it magnificently this afternoon, if I may say so.'

'No, you may not, Henry.' In spite of the words Mitchell sounded mildly amused. 'Mrs Sherwood needs no encouragement from you, believe me.'

Kay hoped she didn't look as surprised as she felt. She wanted to glance at Mitchell standing at the side of her but resisted the impulse; instead, stretching out her hand to the housekeeper who was clearly a friend too, she said, 'Thank you for the vote of confidence, Henry. I'll try to live up to it.'

'I have no doubt you will, Mrs Sherwood.' Blue eyes were twinkling at her and as Kay stared into the good-looking face she saw Henry wasn't as old as the shock of white hair would have led her to believe. His face suggested he was somewhere around fifty or so, maybe fifty-five, but not much older, and his handshake was firm and dry. She decided she liked Mitchell's housekeeper.

'I'm going to show Mrs Sherwood round first, Henry, then we'd like cocktails in the drawing room.' Mitchell had obviously decided the tête-à-tête had gone on long enough because now he took her elbow, pressing her forward into the house.

Kay found herself in a high ceilinged entrance hall, the fine ash and oak panelling on the walls and light timber floor creating an immediate feel of light and spaciousness. And it was this same airy, stylish look, enhanced by strategically placed mirror and glass, gleaming timber and clean lines, that she found all over the large eight-bedroomed house.

The gracious drawing room with its muted background colours and clever use of texture and Indian wall hangings, the family sitting room, breakfast room, dining room and huge kitchen were all both graceful and modern, with strong richness of colour and warmth married to wood and aluminium.

All eight bedrooms were *ensuite* and each with their own individual colour scheme, but it was the enormous master bedroom in coffee and cream that caused Kay to feel distinctly uncomfortable. It was unashamedly masculine, the huge billowy water-bed the biggest she'd ever seen and clearly custom-made, and the stunning bathroom with its corner shower and whirlpool hydrotherapy bath unit, separate sauna and steam room, a sensual experience all in itself. Pictures of Mitchell lounging on the bed with some naked, voluptuous beauty or indulging in sinfully enjoyable skirmishes in the shower or bath positively cavorted in her head, and she was hot and breathless by the time he escorted her down to the drawing room again. And it made her thoughts all the worse, somehow, because Mitchell had behaved circumspectly throughout, his voice mild and pleasant as he'd shown her around, and his attitude cool and even distant. Whereas she...

Kay forced herself to breathe deeply and steadily as Henry served them cocktails in the drawing room, but she knew from his moment-too-long glance at her face that her cheeks were still burning, even before he said in an undertone to Mitchell, 'I'll turn the heating down a little, Mr Grey. And dinner will be served in twenty minutes.'

'Fine, Henry.' Mitchell sat back in his chair opposite Kay's, utterly relaxed and apparently at ease with the world. He seemed to feel no pressure to make conversation, Kay thought as she searched for a safe topic to take her mind off the big, lean body in front of her. He had discarded the leather jacket to reveal a midnight-blue shirt undone at the neck and open to reveal the first hint of a hairy chest, the blueness of his piercing eyes accentuated by the rich colour. He looked tough, brooding and infinitely male.

'You didn't say that Henry was a man.' As soon as she'd spoken she realised how silly it sounded, adding quickly, 'What I mean is, I thought your housekeeper would be a woman.'

He raised mocking eyebrows. 'In this day and age of sexual equality? Shame on you, Kay.'

She smiled stiffly in answer to the warm amusement in his eyes, utterly unable to relax. 'It seems as if you've known each other for a long time,' she tried again when he simply continued to lazily contemplate her without speaking.

'Ten years,' he agreed quietly. 'He was one of the best chefs in London then and earning a small fortune.'

She frowned slightly. 'Then why—?' She stopped abruptly, aware that he might misconstrue what she'd been about to voice.

'Why is he here working for me?' Mitchell finished for her, apparently not in the least put out. 'Long story.'

'We've got twenty minutes,' she persisted, suddenly immensely curious.

He surveyed her through narrowed eyes. 'The story's not mine to tell.' It wasn't unkind but very definite.

'You're friends.'

It was a statement not a question, but he answered her as though it were the latter. 'Yes, we're friends. Henry's an honourable man and I haven't met too many of those.'

Kay finished her cocktail. It was every bit as good as the Sweet Revenge. She looked over to the full-length windows, the drapes either side of them as yet not drawn. Beyond the windows a floodlit courtyard garden had been constructed, a timber platform having a section cut out to accommodate an overhanging magnolia. Stone slabs set in gravel, large rocks, wisteria, azaleas, together with a screen of weeping cherry trees and simple garden furniture completed the scene, which Kay thought must be wonderful at the height of summer.

Mitchell followed her eyes. 'It's very sheltered,' he said softly. 'I can often eat breakfast out there from early May to the end of October. Next time you must come in daylight; there's a tranquil spot by the lake you'd like, complete with resident ducks.'

'You have a lake?' she asked, ignoring the 'next time'.

'A small one,' he qualified lazily. 'We often barbecue down there in the summer, it's a sunny spot.'

'You really are the man with everything,' she said lightly, and she wasn't even sure herself if she was being nasty or just aiming to needle him.

'You disapprove of enjoying the fruits of your labour?'

'Of course not.' She might have known her attempt would fail, Kay thought as she stared at the faint amusement curling his mouth. 'But some people work hard all their lives and never have two pennies to rub together.'

'True.' He flexed his long legs, settling more comfortably into his seat, and her senses went haywire. 'But it's not in my power to rectify that,' he said logically.

He was making her feel like a recalcitrant child, the more so because he was reason itself.

'I enjoy having a base, somewhere that's totally mine,' he continued conversationally, 'probably because I never experienced that as a child. Even now I'm forever travelling here and there and spending the night in some damn hotel or other. This place is my citadel, my fortress.'

'It's a very lush fortress,' she said with a small smile.

'Whatever I do, I like to do well, Kay.'

She knew full well his words had a double meaning, but even if she had been fooled by his innocent voice the gleam in his eyes would have told her what he was thinking about. She refused to blush, however, her voice perfectly even when she said, 'A worthy attribute.'

'Isn't it?' he agreed gently.

'You didn't stay in one place for long, then, as a boy?' Kay had decided she couldn't win in open confrontation. That razor-sharp mind of his was always one step ahead.

'My father was an army man,' he said evenly, his whole persona undertaking a subtle transformation. He hadn't moved a muscle but suddenly the relaxed, easygoing soul had vanished and in his place was a hard individual with ice-cold eyes.

'And you and your mother travelled around with him?' She could see she shouldn't persist along this line—a blind man would have been able to see it—but she couldn't help herself. She had a burning and quite illogical—considering she was determined not to see him again—desire to know more about what made Mitchell Grey tick.

He nodded slowly. 'It made it difficult generally,' he said, a curious lack of expression in his voice. 'We never stayed for more than a couple of years in one place so putting down roots wasn't an option. New schools, new friends, new house, new district...' He shrugged. 'My sister and I didn't really have a sense of identity, I guess.'

'Your sister? You have a sister?' He hadn't mentioned her before; she'd thought he was an only child.

'Did have.' He stood up, reaching for her empty glass before walking across the room. 'She died in the car with my parents.'

'Oh, I'm so sorry, Mitchell.' He'd lost his whole family in one fell swoop and when he was still just a boy. Kay couldn't think of anything worse and her voice reflected her genuine horror and sympathy as well as her embarrassment that she'd pressed him. 'I shouldn't have asked.'

'Don't be silly, it was a long time ago, Kay.'

His voice was too controlled, almost flat, and revealed far more about how he really felt than she knew he would have liked. The accident might have occurred a long time ago but he wasn't over it, not by a long chalk. He had kept his back to her as he had spoken and as Kay stared at the tall, broad figure the urge to comfort him was so strong it shocked her. He was hurting, he'd been hurting for a long while but he'd never let anyone see, she realised with sudden intuition. She followed through on this last thought when she said softly, 'Did you have counselling after it had happened?'

'Counselling?' He had poured them both another cocktail and now he turned to face her, and she saw immediately his face was closed against her. 'I didn't need any mumbo-jumbo of that kind,' he said evenly. 'The accident had happened, they'd gone, and at times like that you can only rely on yourself to get through.'

'But you were just a boy—'

'I was fifteen years old, Kay, not a small child, and more than able to look after myself.' He had reached her side and now handed her the glass, adding, 'As it seemed you did after your marriage breakup.'

'That was different; I was a grown woman.'

'Oh, believe me, I'd been a man for years—' He broke off but not before Kay had glimpsed something raw in his face, something that stopped her breath. What on earth had gone on in his home for him to look like that? she asked herself silently. Whatever it had been it had affected the child Mitchell so badly it had crippled the man. One thing was for sure, the façade of cool, successful man of the world who had everything he wanted and who controlled himself and everyone else was just that—a façade.

She took a sip of her drink, her stomach trembling. She didn't want to go down this road, she told herself shakily, not with Mitchell Grey. While she could think of him as robot man—someone cold and ruthless and detached from normal life—she could keep him at a distance. This growing conflict within herself was not good. It was not good at all.

'Your mother told me how she came to be living with you and your children.' He'd reseated himself and it was clear he was changing the subject. 'It couldn't have been an easy time for you, your father dying so soon after the twins were born, but she said you were her rock.'

'Did she?' She hoped that was all her mother had said.

'You look too delicate and slender to be anyone's rock, but I'm beginning to understand that appearances are deceptive where you're concerned,' he murmured thoughtfully, his voice smoky rich again.

She could say she'd just been thinking the same about him, Kay thought wryly, but she wouldn't.

'It was a brave decision, to leave your job and flat and come back to take care of Leonora.'

Kay looked him in the eye. 'She'd have your guts for garters if she heard you put it like that,' she said drily, 'besides which it isn't really true. She went through a bad patch, admittedly, but there was no taking care of in any physical sense. She just needed us around and having to look after the twins while I worked was therapeutic. She's not weak,' she added as though he'd intimated it. 'She's a very strong woman at heart.'

'You must love her very much.'

'Of course I do.' She looked at him in surprise. 'She's my mother.'

'The two things aren't necessarily synonymous.' He stared at her with shuttered eyes as he drank.

There had been no inflexion in his voice to make her suspect he wasn't speaking generally, but she knew he was referring to his own mother. She swallowed hard. 'No, I guess not,' she said quietly before glancing round the drawing room and purposely making her voice light as she said, 'Do you know, I think the whole of the downstairs of my cottage would fit into this one room. You must be able to give some wild parties here.'

'Frenzied,' he agreed with a sexy grin, which made her breathing decidedly disjointed. 'Fancy coming to one?'

'When?'

'We could start right now, if you like. Two can party just fine.'

'That wasn't the sort of party I was referring to,' she reproved him firmly.

'Pity. They're by far the best kind.'

He slanted a wicked look at her under half-closed lids,

which was so hammed up Kay just had to laugh, even as she thought, He's like a chameleon, this man, with more personalities than I've had hot dinners.

'So, what do you normally do for relaxation?' he asked lazily, his eyes moving from the burnished curls tumbling about her shoulders, over creamy smooth skin before becoming fixed on her mouth.

Relaxation? Was that the few brief minutes between giving a hundred and ten per cent to her job, the twins, her mother and a hundred and one things besides? Moments that occurred rarely and usually when she was so tired all she wanted was a hot bath and an early night? Kay smiled coolly, pretending not to notice the way his eyes were stroking her mouth. 'This and that,' she said airily.

'Leonora said you don't go out nearly enough.'

She'd have a word with her mother when she got home! 'Really?' It was frosty.

'In fact she said you don't go out at all,' he said silkily.

'I told you before, I haven't got the time or the desire for romance,' she said, much too quickly.

'But the odd evening with a girlfriend at the cinema or the theatre isn't romance and you don't even do that,' he pointed out gently. 'All work and no play...'

Kay glared at him. How *dared* he lecture her on what she should do and what she shouldn't! What business was it of his anyway? 'Being a mother as well as the sole breadwinner does carry certain responsibilities,' she said starchily. 'Not that you'd know anything about that, of course. We can't all please ourselves and burn the candles at both ends.'

'You don't even get a light near the wick,' he said relentlessly, 'and it's really very bad for you, Kay. You owe it to the twins to be a well-balanced and rounded person.'

She couldn't believe her ears. 'You...you hypocrite!' To use little children in emotional blackmail.

'That's a harsh word,' he said sorrowfully, rising to his feet and placing his empty glass on the mantelpiece before walking over to her. 'Come here,' he said very softly, stopping just in front of her chair and holding out his hand to pull her up.

Her panicky heartbeat caused her breathing to become quick and shallow but she managed to sound reasonably firm when she said, 'No.'

He bent down, taking her half-full glass from her nerveless fingers and placing it on a small table at the side of the chair. She stared up at him, her eyes deep brown pools. He was going to kiss her again and it was only in this very instant that she admitted to herself how much she wanted him to. Nevertheless she made no movement when he held out his hand again.

'Kay,' he said, his tone steady but carrying the thread of warm amusement that made his voice sexier than ever, 'I'm only going to take you in to dinner.'

CHAPTER FIVE

'How did it go?'

Kay had hoped her mother would be asleep, considering it was one in the morning, but the moment she had gingerly opened the bedroom door Leonora's bedside lamp had been switched on. She glanced at the older woman as she walked across to her own bed, half amused and half exasperated by the bright anticipation in her mother's eyes.

'Okay.' She had undressed and washed in the bathroom where she'd had the foresight to leave her nightie before she went out, so now she slid under the covers, deliberately turning her face to the wall as she said, 'Goodnight.'

'Goodnight?' It was a low whisper in view of the twins asleep in the bedroom next door, but none the less intense because of it. 'Is that all you're going to say?'

'Mum, I've got to be up at six in the morning and my work schedule is manic. I've had a nice evening and now I'm home. All right?' Kay waited but the bedside lamp remained on. She pulled her pillow over her head with a low groan.

'Just one thing.' Her mother's voice was a subtle mixture of bribery and entreaty.

'What?' Kay didn't take the pillow away, her voice muffled.

'Are you seeing him again?'

The sixty-four dollar question. She wrinkled her face against it under the soft down, taking a deep breath before she said, 'No.'

'Why?' It was anguished.

'Because he didn't ask me, and that's two things,' Kay pointed out. 'Goodnight, Mum.'

She knew the effort it must have taken for her mother to say nothing more than a subdued, 'Goodnight, dear' as she switched off the lamp, but for the life of her Kay couldn't hold a post-mortem about the evening out loud. However, as she lay there in the darkness her mind was dissecting every moment from the second he had arrived to pick her up.

It had been a wonderful dinner. As she progressed to the meal her eyes opened in the blackness. And Mitchell had been an amusing and fascinating companion—as she was sure he had set out to be. She forced herself to lie still, aware her mother was still awake, but every nerve in her body was jangling as she recalled how he'd looked, what he'd said, the way he'd made her laugh in spite of her determination not to be charmed.

Each of the five courses—served by a smiling and courteous Henry—had been more delicious than the one before it, and the pièce de résistance in the form of a torrone mousse with oranges and strawberries had been the most spectacular dessert she had ever seen and tasted. She could see it now, decorated with a curl of chocolate, slices of strawberry and oranges, torrone and crystallised orange rind, and hear Mitchell's deep voice saying, 'Your eyes are as round as a child's in a candy store,' his tone soft and almost—her mind hesitated on the word—tender.

Oh... She turned over cautiously, colour flooding into her cheeks much the same as it had earlier.

They had lingered over coffee and brandy, talking about all sorts of things, and she'd had to keep reminding herself that this was Mitchell Grey, enemy, because it had been...what? She stared into the darkness. Great. Wonderful. Magical.

When he had called the taxi she'd known it was because he had been drinking, but at the back of her mind she'd thought he would make the most of the opportunity too. Right up until the minute she'd climbed into the back seat with him she'd told herself she wasn't going to let him kiss her again, but the second he'd reached for her she had melted against him like...like the flipping torrone mousse! Her hands clenched as she willed herself not to toss and turn.

She was an idiot, an absolute idiot, she belaboured herself miserably, her frustration at her own weakness compounded tenfold by the fact he hadn't asked to see her again.

The trouble was he was so *good* at the seduction game. The warm, masculine scent of him as he'd held her, his clean, warm skin and firm lips... She let herself drift into the recollection, her pulse quickening. He had kissed her as though he were delicately sampling something very sweet and costly at first, their lips touching and drawing apart, touching and drawing apart as he'd tentatively tasted and stroked her mouth into eager submission. When his kiss had gathered force she had been there with him every inch of the way, enchanted by the desire he'd been calling forth with consummate ease.

The caress of his mouth had become sensual, his lips and tongue invoking ripples of sensation into every nerve and sinew in her body, drawing her on to a place she had never been before. The shadowed darkness had enclosed them in their own little world of touch and taste and smell and he had pulled her into him so she'd been half lying across him, his mouth doing wonderful things to the sensitive flesh of her ears, her throat, the soft, silky skin over her collar-bone above the cashmere jumper.

She had known her control had been paper-thin and she didn't doubt he'd picked up the signs her body had been giving, so why hadn't he tried for more intimacy? Desire had dampened her skin and brought a throbbing ache in the core of her, but he had done no more than kiss and caress her. Of course they *had* been in the back of the taxi, but he hadn't so much as brushed her breasts on top of her clothes. Not that she wanted him to, of course, she lied vehemently. And she definitely did not want to see him again either, so it was just as well he hadn't suggested it. They had parted on relatively good terms—her skin burnt as she recalled the last lingering caress just before the taxi had drawn up outside Ivy Cottage—so that was a civilised ending to what had not been a civilised day in parts. One hand moved to her knees, which were tight and sore.

And now she had to get some sleep. She breathed slowly and deeply, consciously shutting off her whirling thoughts as she employed a technique she'd perfected during the last caustic months with Perry and the ensuing aftermath. It took longer than usual but eventually she fell into a deep and dreamless slumber, curled under the duvet like a small, solitary animal.

The next morning bedlam reigned, as it so often did in the mad rush to get the twins dressed, fed and ready for school and herself out of the house by eight o'clock, but when Peter pipped his horn outside the cottage gate Kay was ready.

'Hi.' Her brother's greeting was distracted but that wasn't unusual; he'd never been much good in the mornings. Kay welcomed this today, it meant he'd probably forgotten all about her lunch with Mitchell the previous day and so she needn't go into the whole wretched story. She normally rode to work on her motorbike and Peter and Tom had a van each, but the bike had needed an overhaul and so she was picking it up at the garage near the office first thing.

'Hi yourself.' She settled herself into the seat beside him. She was already dressed in her leathers and intended to go straight to the first job from the garage. 'I'm out all day but there are a couple of breaks for both you and Tom in the schedule; make sure you check the answer machine as soon as you get back to the office, won't you? And of course any new deliveries you can fit in today take on, and don't forget to write everything down.'

'Sure thing, boss.' Peter spared her a fleeting grin before pulling away into the traffic.

'We're going to have to get someone in to man the phone if nothing else,' Kay mused out loud as the van sped along. 'With all the work we've got I'm rarely in the office these days, and it would be great for someone to be in charge in there and do some of the day-to-day paperwork. I'm so behind with it.'

Peter nodded. 'Talking of all the work we've got, how did your meeting with Mitchell Grey go?' he asked casually. Too casually.

Kay stared at him. 'Mum phoned you,' she said flatly.

'Well, not exactly, it was more... Yes, she did,' he admitted wryly, keeping his eyes on the traffic ahead.

She might have known! There were times when she felt she was living her life in a goldfish bowl. 'So? What exactly did she say?' She tried, and failed, to keep the annoyance out of her voice.

'Just that the lunch hadn't gone too well—something about you having jumped out of a window,' Peter said, as though such an occurrence were perfectly normal—and that he'd turned up at the house and you were seeing him last night.'

'That about sums it up,' Kay said shortly.

'Any business coming our way from him?' It was hopeful.

'No.'

'Right.'

The rest of the journey to the garage was conducted in silence.

By the time Kay drew up outside Ivy Cottage at six in the evening she was bone-tired. The day had gone well without any hitches, the weather had been kindness itself—mild, sunny with a positively warm breeze—and she'd had plenty of time for a snack at lunch time plus a couple of coffee breaks during the day. So why, she asked herself as she wearily parked the bike at the side of the house and pulled off her crash helmet, did she feel as if everything was wrong? It wasn't like her.

She flexed her aching neck muscles, looking up into the dark evening sky as she did so. It was Halloween in a day or two, then Guy Fawkes night and before you knew it Christmas would be upon them and the end of another year would be fast approaching. And it had been a good year. The business had grown, the twins were well and happy and had taken to big school like ducks to water. Her mother was settled and comfortable in her mind again, and Peter and his family were financially secure after finally paying off the last of the debts that had accumulated during the time her brother had been out of work, before she'd started Sherwood Delivery.

So—everything positive and nothing negative. Moonlight lay in silver pools in the garden and someone somewhere had lit a bonfire earlier, the smell of wood smoke drifting in the breeze and adding to the perfection of an English autumn evening. Stars sparkled above, the last of the dying leaves on the trees whispered below—*and she couldn't stop thinking of Mitchell Grey*. It was a relief to finally admit it to herself.

Kay lowered her head, staring blindly into the sleeping garden as the faint sounds of a television and children's laughter from within the house brushed over her.

What was it about him that had so got under her skin? she asked herself silently. She knew there wasn't one single thing going for any sort of relationship between them, and they were as far apart as east was to west, so why had he been there in her head for every second of every minute of the day?

Was it just the dizzying and lethal combination of fascination and danger? Or the sexual magnetism he exuded like no other man she had ever come into contact with? Or the potent aphrodisiac of wealth and success and power?

She leant back against the wall of the house, taking a deep lungful of sweet smoky air. Whatever, she was in a spin and she had never felt like this before, alive from the top of her head to the soles of her feet—tinglingly, frighteningly, thrillingly alive.

'Stop it.' She actually spoke the words out loud, needing to hear them. 'Stop this right now. It's over, finished, not that it ever really began. You were just an irritating hiccup in his busy life, that's all. He didn't ask to see you again, which is just as well. You are a mother of two children, not exactly the sort of woman Mitchell Grey would go for.'

She took a few more lungfuls of air before straightening her shoulders and raising her chin.

It would be dangerous to get mixed up with him, very, very dangerous; every instinct in her body was telling her so. And with Georgia and Emily relying on her to be both mother and father, danger was not an option. Everything had worked out for the best and these ridiculous feelings would soon shrivel and die. They would have to.

She marched round the side of the house to the front door, opening it and stepping into warm light and the delicious smell of one of her mother's pot roasts—that and the sweet perfume emanating from the most gigantic basket of flowers set at an angle on the coffee-table to catch her eye as soon as she came in.

'Kay! Hallo, darling.' Her mother appeared from the direction of the kitchen at the same time as the twins jumped up from the sitting-room carpet where they had been lying in their pyjamas playing a board game together.

'Mummy, Mummy, look!'

'Mummy, we've been waiting for you to come home for *ages*.'

They had seized her hands, pulling her over to the basket of flowers, their small faces alight, and over their heads her mother mouthed silently, Mitch?

'There's a card, Mummy, but Grandma wouldn't let us open it.' Georgia was hopping from one foot to another in an agony of anticipation. 'Look, there.'

Kay obediently extracted the small envelope from the profusion of cream and yellow rosebuds, carnations, orchids, daisies and freesias, hoping her mother wouldn't notice her hands were trembling. It was addressed, 'Mrs Kay Sherwood, Ivy Cottage, 24 Bishops Road'. She stared at it for a moment before turning it over and carefully slitting the top open. The small card inside read, 'I enjoyed last night. Can we do it again some time? M.'

She read it twice and then handed it to her mother who was at her elbow, before turning to the twins and saying, 'It's a present to all of us from Mr Grey, the gentleman you met last night? Isn't that kind of him?'

'For us too?' Georgia and Emily were enchanted.

'For all of us,' Kay repeated firmly. *'Can we do it again some time?'* What did that mean? Was this an extravagant brush-off or did he really mean to contact her? And if he did, what was she going to do? It would be utter folly to see him again; it would give all the wrong signals. But perhaps this was how he always gently let a woman down? She had no idea of how men in his position of wealth and influence behaved.

She glanced at her mother and the older woman's eyes were waiting for her. 'They're beautiful flowers,' Leonora said impassively, handing Kay back the card as she spoke.

'Yes, they are.'

'And there's so many of them,' Leonora pointed out.

'Yes.' She stared at her mother and Leonora stared back.

'I'll see to our dinner while you shower and change. The girls have already eaten but I said they could stay up a while, okay?'

'Yes, fine,' Kay agreed quickly. Anything to prevent a cosy chat over dinner.

She asked the twins about their day and admired some paintings they had brought home from school for her before going upstairs, angry with herself for the excitement bubbling in her veins. She had to get a handle on this, she told herself, stripping off her clothes in the bedroom and padding through to the bathroom in her robe. She hardly recognised herself any more.

Once in the shower she let the warm water wash the tension away, standing under the flow for longer than usual. She thought she heard the telephone ring at one point but, when no one called her, assumed the call was one of her mother's friends.

By the time she had dressed in a light jumper and old jeans she felt more like herself again. She stared at the face in the mirror. Her freckles seemed to stand out even more tonight and she was sure she was getting a pimple on her chin. Mitchell Grey interested in her, indeed! She must have been mad. But no more, she was quite sane again. The flowers were his way of saying goodbye. He could have asked to see her again last night if he'd been interested, or written something specific on the card.

Her mother called to her from the kitchen as Kay walked downstairs. 'There's a sherry by the sofa for you, and one for me. I'll come and join you in a minute.'

'Thanks.' Kay sat down and immediately Georgia and Emily climbed either side of her, snuggling into her like two small puppies. She stroked their curls, still damp from their evening shower and smelling of baby shampoo. Her precious babies, how could she want more from life than having them close to her? she asked herself guiltily. And she didn't, not really. *She didn't.*

The phone rang and her mother appeared like the genie from the lamp. 'That'll be Mitch,' Leonora said casually. 'He called earlier when you were in the shower. I told him to call back in a few minutes.' She didn't meet Kay's eyes as she spoke.

Georgia had already lifted the receiver, speaking the number as Kay muttered, 'Mum!'

Then the little girl said brightly, 'Yes, Mummy's downstairs now,' holding out the phone as she called, 'Mummy!'

Kay's heart had begun a wild hammering, the palms of her hands suddenly damp. She stood up, walking over to

Georgia and taking the phone from the little girl as though the receiver were red hot. 'Hallo,' she said weakly.

'Kay? This is Mitchell.' It was soft, darkly seductive, and she shivered.

'Mitchell?' She hoped her voice sounded stronger than she felt. 'Thank you so much for the flowers; they were a lovely surprise but you really shouldn't have.'

'My pleasure.'

His cool, easy tone made a mockery of her racing pulse and Kay made a huge effort to pull herself together.

'I was wondering if you're free at the weekend?'

'I...um...' She had never felt so confused in her life. If she said no he probably wouldn't bother again; if she said yes...

'I thought maybe dinner and a film on Saturday evening? Or we could just go for a drink somewhere if you prefer?' His voice gentled still further as he added, 'No big deal, Kay, that's what I'm saying. You said you're not ready for a relationship; I think you need to be let out of the steel box you've put round yourself and start testing life again. So we start as friends with no strings attached and go nice and slow. Any time either of us wants out, that's fine. Any time either of us wants to take it a step forward we discuss it. How's that?'

Cold-blooded in the extreme. Kay stared blankly across the room. He was talking with about as much emotion as he would when suggesting a business deal. She didn't know whether to be pleased by his reasonableness or offended by the lack of ardour.

'Kay?'

His quiet voice reminded her she couldn't hesitate any longer. She took a deep breath. She had to admit he couldn't have been fairer and this way she had nothing to lose. 'A meal and a film sounds great,' she said carefully.

'Good. I'll pick you up at seven and book tickets for a late performance. Anything in particular you'd like to see?'

It dawned on Kay afresh just how much of a rut she was in when she realised she didn't have a clue what films were out. She hadn't been to the cinema since the twins were born. She'd hardly been *anywhere* since the twins were born! 'You choose,' she said hastily.

'I'll surprise you,' he said softly.

Kay swallowed. 'Fine.'

She was sure his voice was redolent with amusement when he made his goodbyes, but as her mother was positioned in front of her now she didn't prolong the farewell.

'You're seeing him again.' Leonora spoke as though Kay had won a gold medal at the Olympics.

'Calm down, Mum. It's strictly on a friends-only basis,' Kay warned softly, vitally aware of her daughters' little faces as they stared up at her.

Leonora smiled benignly. 'Of course it is.'

Kay stifled the words hovering on her tongue, instead saying, 'I'll talk to you later, okay? Once we've eaten.'

'As you like, dear.' Leonora sailed off back into the kitchen, every inch of her still-slim body registering satisfaction.

Wonderful. Kay stared after her mother, frustration paramount. What was it about Mitchell Grey that could charm any female within a ten-mile radius? she asked herself irritably.

'Was that the man who sent those?'

Emily had spoken, her dimpled hand pointing to the basket of flowers as she stared at her mother.

Kay nodded. 'Yes, it was, sweet pea.'

'I like him.'

'So do I,' Georgia agreed earnestly.

Kay plumped down on the sofa, her hand reaching for the sherry glass. Three against one wasn't really fair, was it?

CHAPTER SIX

THE next few weeks were ones of change. Kay found herself seeing Mitchell every day; they ate lunch or dinner together, sometimes in one of the plush restaurants Mitchell frequented or at his home, they danced in nightclubs, visited the cinema and theatre, went bowling, ice-skating and even scoured one or two antique fairs and auctions. As he had promised they had fun—lots of fun. But it wasn't really *real*, it wasn't everyday life. Not her life, at least, Kay reflected.

She was standing in the kitchen on the Saturday morning before Christmas, up to her elbows in suds, idly watching the garden's resident robin as he militantly sent off one or two marauding sparrows who had thought to plunder the bird table of pieces of bacon fat.

If she thought about it, they hadn't had one no-holds-barred conversation since that first evening at his home. Oh, he had entertained her all right, and, yes, if she was totally honest, the more she saw him, the more she liked him, but... She frowned at the window. She didn't know him at all. He was tough, formidably in control of himself and those around him, but she could never penetrate that invisible barrier even in the slightest. And the ironical thing, the really *ridiculous* thing was that he'd accused her the night before of the self-same thing.

'What will it take before that barricade is smashed?'

She had glanced at him as he'd spoken, his voice soft and his eyes faintly amused as they'd driven home after a night at the theatre.

'Sorry?'

'You know what I mean, Kay.'

His tone had still been easy, even lazy, but perhaps—in hindsight—there had been something more, anger even, behind the indolent posture.

'I don't.' She'd tightened instinctively.

He had said nothing for a mile or two, handling the car with his normal expertise, and then he had made some fatuous remark about the play they'd just seen, one that hadn't necessitated an answer but that had made a reluctant smile come to her lips. And so the moment had passed.

His goodnight kiss had left her aching for more, as his kisses always did, but again—analysed in the cold light of morning without the normal unbearable sexual tension sending her into a spin—she felt he had been playing a part. So far but no further, mentally, emotionally and physically, that was how she felt it was. But then, was she really any different?

She shut her eyes tightly, biting on her lip as she washed a breakfast plate with unnecessary vigour. He unnerved her more now than when she had first met him, that was the truth of the matter. The more she was with him, the more she wanted to be with him, and that wasn't how it was supposed to have been.

Maybe if they had gone to bed, if they'd become lovers in the full sense of the word, this crazy attraction would have burnt itself out? And then she curled her lip at the stupidity of the thought. It might well have on his side, in fact she didn't doubt it for a minute, but she wasn't built like that. The reason she had tried and tried for her marriage to work even when logic had said it was doomed was because she'd committed her body as well as her heart. The two were inseparable where she was concerned. It might not be the prevailing fashion but she couldn't help that. She couldn't bear the thought of being just another notch on his bedpost, figuratively speaking of course, she added, thinking of the massive water-bed as she smiled wryly.

Kay flexed her shoulders, which had become tense with the nature of her thoughts.

Had she been wrong in keeping any contact between Mitchell and the twins to an absolute minimum? she asked herself soberly. Had that added to the contrived, meretricious nature of it all? One minute she was being dined and wined in the most fabulous of places or being whisked off to goodness knew where with money no object, the next she was back home changing the girls' beds in the middle of the night when they'd succumbed to the stomach bug playing havoc at their school, or checking their thick curls in response to a letter from the nurse who'd warned parents a child in their class had been found to be lousy.

The thing was, she hadn't wanted Georgia and Emily to get used to Mitchell, to get fond of him, she admitted reluctantly. It wasn't fair on them. He had made it plain on that first date that long-term fidelity wasn't an option, and she'd known that this friendship that wasn't a friendship but defied any label she could think of wouldn't last. But how could you explain that to two little girls who had been determined to like him from the first?

She sighed heavily, finishing the washing-up and drying her hands on a towel before she boiled a kettle for the lemon drink she was making for her mother. Leonora had been suffering from what she'd insisted was a cold the last couple of days, but this morning the older woman had been too ill to get out of bed and Kay had called the doctor. She suspected her mother had fallen foul of the vicious flu bug that was sweeping the country, but the hacking cough that had become much worse during the night spoke of a chest infection on top of the virus.

Kay was just at the bottom of the stairs with the mug of hot lemon when a knock at the front door announced Dr Galbraith.

The doctor was cheerful enough as he examined Leonora, but once downstairs in the sitting room he lowered his voice after glancing at the twins—snuggled together watching a Christmas cartoon in front of the fire—and said quietly, 'We need to watch that chest infection. I don't want it developing into anything more serious, so don't take any nonsense from her about getting out of bed. A side effect of this particular virus is inflammation of the lungs in my more elderly patients, not that your mother would appreciate being referred to in that regard,' he added with a wry smile. 'Plenty of liquids along with the antibiotics and paracetamol, all right?'

'Thank you, Doctor.' Kay nodded and then wished she hadn't as the headache she'd woken up with made itself known.

'You look a bit peaky yourself,' Dr Galbraith said as he took in her pale face, the whiteness of her skin in sharp contrast to her red curls. 'You might be going down with it—it does tend to run through a whole household. Get plenty of paracetamol in and call the surgery if you need to. Frankly, if you'd got anything planned over Christmas I'd cancel it now.'

Great. And a happy Christmas to you too! 'Thank you, Doctor,' Kay repeated, and saw him out into the frosty morning, shutting the door quickly as the icy chill made her shiver.

'Shoes, coats and hats, girls,' she said with deliberate brightness, knowing the twins wouldn't appreciate being pulled away from their Saturday morning programmes on the TV. 'We've got to go and get some medicine for Grandma, and if you're good we might call in the cake shop and buy two of those gingerbread men you like so much.'

Fortunately the row of shops comprising a small supermarket, chemist, cake shop, butcher's and grocer's was only a couple of streets away, but nevertheless Kay was regretting she hadn't had one of the vans for the weekend by the time she and the girls got home later that morning. She was feeling worse by the minute and now Emily was complaining her head hurt her, and refused to eat her gingerbread man, which she normally loved.

After remaking her mother's bed and giving Leonora the antibiotics and paracetamol with another hot lemon drink, Kay went downstairs to find Emily lying listlessly on the sofa with her teddy bear. When her daughter refused a chocolate off the little Christmas tree standing next to the TV, Kay knew she was ill, although Georgia was bouncing around as usual.

She felt the small forehead, alarmed to find it was far too hot, and in bending over nearly landed on top of Emily when she went all giddy. Darn it, they were dropping like flies and Christmas was only three days away, and the girls had so been looking forward to it.

Emily tucked up in a blanket in her pyjamas on the sofa after a dose of paracetamol for her temperature, Kay made herself a fortifying cup of tea and took stock. Fortunately she'd made the decision to close the office all the following week as Christmas day was on the Tuesday, so work wasn't a problem. They had enough food to last them for a while, although she had been going to do the big Christmas shop on Monday—still, she might feel better by then, and she could perhaps call Peter in to sit with the girls while she went out. No, that wouldn't do. She didn't want to infect Peter and his family for Christmas. Oh, she would manage somehow; she couldn't think of that now with her head aching so badly.

Mitchell. She sat up straighter in the kitchen chair. She had been going to go out with him this evening; she must call him and explain.

It was Henry who answered the telephone, but within moments Mitchell's deep rich voice said, 'Kay? Henry said your mother isn't well?'

'It's the flu along with a chest infection, and now Emily is feeling poorly. I'm sorry but I can't make tonight.'

There was a pause, and then he said, 'How would it be if I hired a babysitter? I know a couple of my friends swear by a certain—'

'No.' She didn't let him finish. She would no more have let a stranger—however well recommended—babysit her girls than fly to the moon. 'I'm not feeling too good myself, actually, so we'd better leave it.'

Another pause, and then he said evenly, 'This isn't because of last night, is it?'

'What?' She didn't have a clue what he was talking about.

'I have a feeling the drawbridge is being raised,' he said softly, 'rather than the barriers coming down.'

Why did men think everything was about *them* all the time? If she had been feeling better she would have let rip; as it was she just said quietly, 'Mitchell, my mother is ill in bed, my daughter has a temperature and I don't feel great myself. Those are the facts, okay? I'll ring you.' And she put the telephone down. She couldn't argue with him, not today. He'd have to think what he liked.

The telephone rang almost immediately and she breathed deeply and braced herself before picking it up.

''Kay, if you need anything give me a call.' It was

Mitchell, his voice holding a quality that suddenly—ridiculously—made her want to cry.

'Thank you.' She managed to keep the wobble from sounding. 'We'll be all right, but thank you.' And then, as Emily chose that moment to reach out for her glass of orange juice on the small table Kay had pulled close to the sofa, catching it with the teddy bear's foot as she did so and sending the glass and its contents cascading onto the floor, she said, 'I have to go. Goodbye, Mitchell,' and she put down the phone on his soft 'Goodbye.'

That night Kay was up and down to Emily several times as well as helping her mother to the bathroom twice, Leonora being too weak to stand by herself. Kay knew she was going down with the flu now—her headache was blinding, she was cold and shivery but her skin was clammy to the touch, and everything was a huge effort. By morning she felt so ill she didn't know how she was going to cope, and she just prayed Georgia wouldn't get sick.

The morning passed in a haze of fixing hot drinks, dispensing medicines and checking Emily's temperature, and when the telephone rang downstairs as she was staggering to the bathroom with Emily in her arms Kay felt too exhausted to even call and ask who it was when she heard Georgia talking to someone.

She was tucking Emily back in bed when Georgia appeared at her side. 'That was Mitchell,' Georgia said importantly. 'I said everyone was poorly except me, and he said I've got to help you. What shall I do?'

Kay lay down on Georgia's bed, next to Emily's, for a moment or two as the room spun. 'Just be a good girl,' she whispered weakly, 'and play with your toys until I get your lunch in a minute.'

She was aware of Georgia nodding and then scampering out of the room, and she shut her eyes, willing the dizziness to pass. It seemed like the next second when she heard voices downstairs but she knew she must have been dozing. She forced her leaden limbs to obey her, sitting up and then swinging her legs over the side of the narrow bed before she rose and tottered towards the door. She was hanging onto the door knob like grim death, the landing a kaleidoscope of rotating colour when a deep voice said, 'What the...?' a moment before she felt herself lifted right off her feet.

'Mitchell.' Kay was aware she was clutching at him but the dark face above hers was barely in focus. 'I feel so ill.'

Leonora was calling from the other bedroom, obviously wondering what was going on, and now Kay said frantically, 'She mustn't get out of bed; she'll fall and hurt herself.'

Mitchell didn't answer this except to shout, 'Henry! Get up here,' making Kay wince as the sound reverberated in her brain and made it rattle.

She heard Mitchell tell Henry to go and reassure her mother everything was all right—although what her mother would make of a strange man entering her bedroom, Kay didn't know—but with Mitchell here taking charge she suddenly felt so utterly helpless, so weak and drained, it was too much effort to keep her eyes open. He was holding her next to his chest, his strength and vitality tiring in itself, and then she felt herself placed on Georgia's bed again and he said, 'Lie there, Kay, and don't move. I'm going to have a word with Leonora,' just before he added, 'It's okay, little one, Mummy's just a little sick like you,' as Emily began to cry.

Kay struggled into a sitting position, holding out her arms as she said, 'Pass her to me, Mitchell, please.'

She sat cradling Emily to her as she heard voices in the bedroom next door but it was too much effort to try and distinguish what was being said. If Mitchell would be prepared to stay for just an hour or two so she could sleep a while she would be all right, Kay told herself. It was the combination of a sleepless night on top of the flu that had knocked her for six.

She came to with a start a little while later, staring bleary-eyed at Mitchell, who had just marched into the room. 'Everything's settled,' he said briskly, reaching down for Emily who was fast asleep on Kay's lap. 'You're coming home with me.'

'What?' She was still in one of the weird catnap dreams she'd been having since the flu hit; she had to be. He couldn't really have said what she'd thought he'd said.

She saw him hand the still-sleeping Emily to Henry, who had appeared in the doorway, and then he turned back to her, saying, 'Georgia and Emily will need a couple of changes of clothing and their night things. Where are they?'

'Mitchell.' She struggled to get the words past the cotton wool in her head. 'I'm not going anywhere. What are you talking about?'

'I'm taking you all to my place.' It was not an invitation, more of a decree.

'No way.' She wasn't *that* ill. 'I've far too much to do here for Christmas.'

'Christmas has been moved.' He eyed her impatiently. 'All the presents you and your mother had hidden from the twins are in the back of my car concealed under a blanket. There's also some of their toys from their toy boxes so they've got something to play with over the next couple of days. Once we've packed their clothes we're done.'

Done? *Done?* Was he mad? 'My mother, our clothes...' she said weakly.

'All in the car.'

'You've put my mother in your car?' she said faintly.

'Not in the boot with the other things,' he qualified with dry amusement at her horrified tone.

If she hadn't have felt so rotten she would have glared at him. 'Her pills—'

'I've told you, all taken care of,' he said with the touch of irritation she'd noticed on other occasions when he considered she was labouring a point. He had walked across to the twins' wardrobe as they'd been speaking, opening it and taking various clothes, underwear and night attire from the hanging space and shelves inside. 'That'll do.' He put the mound on Emily's bed. 'Where's a suitcase?'

'There's a big sports bag on top of the wardrobe,' she answered in a whisper, her throat hurting badly. She couldn't argue with him, she didn't have the strength, but she couldn't believe this was happening, and with her mother's consent too. Consent? She dared bet her mother nearly bit his hand off, so quickly did she agree to Mitchell's offer. They'd certainly tied it all up tight while she'd been dozing.

'I'll take this bag to the car and come back for you,' he said quietly, looking down at her with unfathomable eyes once the clothes were packed.

'We...we surely can't all fit in,' she murmured.

'I came in the Voyager,' he said briefly.

'Oh, right.' She didn't know he had one. He seemed to have a vehicle for every occasion, she thought with a slight touch of flu hysteria as he left the room.

It was only when she heard his footsteps going down the stairs that it dawned on Kay he must have planned to take them back to his place all along if he'd brought the huge people carrier. She wasn't quite sure how that made her feel but now was not the time to explore her emotions, she told herself muzzily. She made a great effort and got to her feet, her legs feeling as if they didn't belong to her.

She was halfway down the stairs when he came in the front door and he swore, softly but a very rude word, she thought primly.

'What are you trying to do, Kay? Prove a point by breaking your neck?' he grated out angrily, glaring at her as she wobbled on the last step.

'Don't shout at me,' she muttered weakly. 'I'm not one of your female slaves who only live to do your bidding.'

'I wish.' He shook his head at her as she clung to the post at the bottom of the stairs. 'Look at you, dead on your feet and still determined not to give an inch. Superwoman is allowed to be ill, you know. Even the most magnificent of the species have off-days.'

'Probably.' The room was swimming again and she was forced to acknowledge the brief few steps had taken all her strength. 'But if I don't look after Georgia and Emily and my mother no one else will.'

'Wrong.' He picked her up as though she weighed nothing at all, his tone terse. 'For the next few days you are all under *my* protection and you'll damn well do as you're told, woman. Why can't you be more like Leonora? She doesn't argue and fight over the simplest thing.'

Much as Kay loved her mother, she was hugely insulted. 'I hate you,' she said hotly, wincing at the pain in her head.

'Perhaps.' He stared down at her steadily, his silver-blue gaze so piercing she shut her eyes against it. 'But hate is the sister of love.'

'Huh.' It was the most she could manage and she kept her eyes tightly shut.

'I must be mad,' he said softly, amusement warming his voice as he walked across the room to the front door, bending down and picking up a blanket he'd placed there and wrapping it round her, ignoring her protests. 'I've got not just one redhead but four of them under my roof for Christmas.'

'But the others don't argue and fight over the simplest thing,' she reminded him bitterly, still furious.

'True.'

And he actually had the gall to chuckle as he stepped out into the icy afternoon, hooking the door shut behind him before striding down the path to the handsome vehicle waiting at the roadside, Henry at the wheel and her mother and the girls staring anxiously out of the windows, wrapped up like Eskimos.

Over the next couple of days Kay slept most of the time away, her mind more at rest when Emily threw off the worst of the bug overnight.

Mitchell insisted on calling in his own doctor to examine the houseful of patients, but he merely confirmed what had already been said and repeated the advice of rest, hot lemon and paracetamol.

Late Christmas Eve afternoon it started to snow, and for the first time since the flu had manifested itself Kay found she could lie and gaze out of the window without feeling as though her brain were going to break into pieces. She could hear sounds from downstairs; they had permeated her dreams once or twice over the last twenty-four hours, but she hadn't been able to make herself respond. Now her lips twitched as she heard the unmistakable sound of children's laughter. The girls were all right, thank goodness. And Henry had said her mother was feeling a little better when he'd brought her some soup earlier.

She couldn't miss being with the girls Christmas Eve. Kay forced herself to sit up, although it had been very pleasant lying in the warm cocoon with the aches and pains that had racked her body beginning to subside a little, and the big fat flakes of snow drifting past the window.

The room was luxurious—all the bedrooms were—the colour scheme one of soft golds and cream, and the carpet ankle-deep. Kay knew the twins' room was to the right of hers and her mother's on the left, but, apart from several very brief visits from Georgia and Emily, she had seen nothing of them. Henry had kept up a steady supply of light nourishing 'invalid' food, and Mitchell had made the odd appearance, but she had felt too out of it to do more than open her eyes for a few minutes at a time.

Kay flung back the duvet and swung her legs over the side of the bed, making her way slowly to the bathroom. It was a great effort and she had to rest several times before her toilette was finished, but eventually she was washed and dressed, her hair free of tangles and tied back from her face. She sat on the bed for a few minutes after she was ready, amazed at how tired she felt. In the past she'd had the occasional heavy cold and labelled it the flu. She now made a mental note never to do that again. The real thing was so different.

Once she was on the landing she could hear children's laughter and followed the sound. She noticed the staircase had been decorated with fresh garlands of holly and ivy and there were more in the hall once she reached the bottom of the stairs, but it was as she pushed open the drawing-room door and stood quietly surveying the scene within that she had her biggest surprise.

The room had been transformed into a glittering festive pageant, tinsel and ornamentation decorating the walls and every available surface or so it seemed to Kay's dazed eyes, but it was the eight-foot Christmas tree that really drew the eye. It stood in regal splendour at the far end of the room, its branches bedecked with glittering trinkets, baubles and tinsel and the huge tub that held it surrounded with gaily wrapped parcels.

Emily was lying on one of the sofas, which had been pulled close to the blazing fire, busily threading a paper chain with Henry, her mother was lying on another sofa close by in her dressing gown with a blanket over her legs, and Mitchell and Georgia were sitting together on the floor wrapping a parcel.

It was a charming scene, a homely and comfortable one, which suggested the five of them were totally at ease in each other's company, and as Kay watched she felt suddenly cold. She was the one on the outside looking in. Ridiculous, maybe, but that was how she felt.

And then Emily looked up and saw her, her shriek of delight causing the others to glance towards the door. Within a moment Georgia was at Kay's side, taking her hand and leading her over to sit beside Emily—Henry having moved—as both little girls began talking nineteen to the dozen.

'Do you like the Christmas tree and everything, Mummy? We did it as a surprise for you.'

'And there are presents for you and Grandma under the tree but we're not allowed to say what they are.'

'Ours are with Father Christmas. Uncle Mitch has written to tell him we're here for Christmas so he can bring our sacks here.'

'It's taken us ages to get everything nice, Mummy.'

This last from Georgia was a little uncertain. Kay realised her face must be betraying her, but the 'Uncle Mitch' had hit her like a savage punch in the solar plexus. This was exactly what she'd feared, the reason she'd made it a policy not to date while the children were small, why she'd hesitated particularly with regards to Mitchell Grey. She didn't want her girls to be made conversant with 'uncles'. She knew friends in a similar situation to herself and no sooner had their children got used to one uncle than he disappeared and another took his place. Uncles were transient. It stood to reason, didn't it, that if the fathers of the children weren't prepared to stick around, uncles were going to be even less reliable? And Mitchell had already laid out the ground rules well in advance.

She had been foolish to think she could keep the two lives separate—that of having a light 'friendship' with Mitchell, and that of her real life with her babies. But it would have been all right, it would, if she hadn't got sick.

She forced a bright smile to her face as she pulled Emily onto her lap, and put an arm round Georgia, who was standing at her knee. *Pretend; don't spoil their Christmas.* 'It's absolutely beautiful, my darlings. You must have been so busy. I can't believe it.'

Her gushing must have worked because both children's faces became animated again, their chattering washing over her as she met Mitchell's eyes. They were narrowed on her face, the ice-blue depths glinting as though he had read her mind.

She stared at him, knowing she ought to say something but her mind registering only the dark attractiveness at the root of his maleness. He was in a light shirt and jeans, his feet bare, and his hair looked ruffled. She had never seen it like that before. Usually it was ruthlessly sleek and impeccable, like him. This was another Mitchell; she was seeing yet one more facet of his complex persona and, if anything, although this being was more casual and laid-back than any so far, it disturbed her the most. It was the most human, seemingly the most approachable, and it was an illusion.

'Darling, how are you feeling?' Her mother's voice from the sofa some feet away brought Kay's head turning. 'We looked in on you an hour or so ago when I came down, but you were fast asleep.'

Kay forced another smile as she said, 'A bit shaky but much better.'

'This is my first time up too.' Whether Leonora had guessed how she'd felt when she had watched them all from the doorway, Kay didn't know, but her mother continued, 'Not that you could really call it that when I was all but carried down here and then tucked up and forbidden to move. All this work has been done over the last day, apparently.'

'The girls needed something to take their minds off missing their mother,' Mitchell said softly, speaking to Leonora but with his eyes on Kay's pale face.

Kay nerved herself to meet his gaze again. 'You've been very kind to us, thank you,' she said stiffly. 'I can't believe all the trouble we've put you to.'

'No trouble.' He had risen to his feet when Georgia had rushed to meet her, his hands thrust in his pockets and his dark face inscrutable. 'That's what friends are for, after all.'

Colour flooded into her pale face. He *had* sensed her thoughts earlier.

'Besides which, it's given Henry and myself the chance to act like boys again, eh, Henry?' His voice was mocking. 'We might even be persuaded to build a snowman if the snow falls thickly enough over Christmas.'

'I've never made a snowman.' Georgia had left Kay's

side before she could stop her, walking across and tugging on Mitchell's jean-clad leg to get his attention. 'There was only a teeny weeny bit of snow last year and it melted.'

'It did? That's a shame, munchkin.' Mitchell put out a hand and ruffled the child's curls. 'I tell you what, I'll put in an order with Father Christmas to leave enough snow for a snowman this year. How about that? Then we can make one with big coal eyes and a carrot nose.'

'Emily can't go out into the cold.' Georgia looked artlessly up at her hero. 'She'll have to stay inside and watch.'

'No, I won't.' Emily's lower lip began to tremble. 'I want to build a snowman too.'

Four years old and they were fighting over him already, Kay thought helplessly. What was it about Mitchell Grey and the female race? Even her mother had a glow about her that wasn't due to the heat from the huge coal fire burning in the hearth.

'Emily will be fine all wrapped up in a day or two,' Mitchell said firmly, his tweak of Georgia's nose letting the tot know he wasn't falling for it. 'Building a snowman is a job for everyone to do together or not at all. Okay?'

Georgia nodded adoringly and Kay groaned silently. He had her feisty little Georgia eating out of the palm of his hand. They were going to hear nothing but 'Uncle Mitchell' for months after this.

'Now, there just happens to be two early Christmas presents for two little girls I know on the Christmas tree.' Mitchell grinned at the twins. 'See if you can find them. Not under the tree, mind. On it.'

Emily was off Kay's lap and across to the tree only seconds after her sister, and they found the parcels without any trouble. On opening, the boxes revealed two beautifully dressed, long-haired dolls, complete with muffs and capes and other accessories, identical but for the fact one doll was dressed in silver and the other in gold.

Kay watched as the girls came dancing back to thank Mitchell without any prompting, and when he said the dolls were from both himself and Henry they immediately went to Henry and hugged him too, before settling down on the rug in front of the fire and beginning to play with their new babies.

'They're two lovely little girls, Kay. You're bringing them up very well.'

Henry was sitting with her mother now and as Mitchell joined her on the sofa Kay felt herself tense. 'Thank you.'

'How are you feeling?' he asked softly.

He was sitting close but not too close. Nevertheless every nerve in her body had twanged and now she found herself utterly unable to break the hold of his eyes. 'I...I'm surprised how weak I feel.' She hadn't meant to be so honest but the nearness of him had totally thrown her.

'You haven't eaten anything but mush for twenty-four hours,' he said just as softly, his delineation of Henry's superb homemade soups and soufflés grossly unfair, 'besides which the news has been full of how this particular strain of influenza has young and old and everyone between off their feet. It's nasty.'

'Georgia still seems okay.' She glanced towards the girls, their curls like living flames in the glow of the fire. 'Right from a tiny baby, bugs just seem to bounce off her somehow, whereas poor Emily catches everything that's going.'

'It must have been tough being sole parent, especially when they were first born.'

Her hands twisted in her lap. 'Sometimes.' She kept her eyes on the two small heads. 'But they more than made up for any difficulties,' she said defensively, 'and they've always been very happy children. They haven't wanted for anything.'

'I wasn't criticising,' he said soothingly, 'and I can see what a great mother you've been and are.'

'Perry would have been a terrible father. He only ever thought of himself and would have made their lives miserable. The fact that he has never even tried to see them proves that.'

'Kay, for what it's worth I think you did the only thing you could when you threw him out.' He stared at her. 'Were there people who said you should have stayed with him regardless?' he asked quietly. 'For the sake of the children?'

'A few.' And it had hurt, terribly, even though she'd told herself they had no idea what had gone on behind closed doors.

Anger thickened his voice. 'Fools are always the first to give an opinion. I was brought up in a home that resembled a war zone for a great deal of the time. Believe me, the twins are very fortunate. You have two normal, well-adjusted and happy little girls; they're a testimony to the fact that you were right in the course of action you followed. Don't ever doubt that, not for a minute.'

Funny, but she hadn't expected such understanding and comfort from him, not from Mitchell. She hadn't spoken of how she felt to a living soul before this, not even her mother, but he had seemed instinctively to guess the doubts and fears she managed to keep under lock and key most of the time. With her father having died when he did, the girls had never really had a male figure in their lives, apart from her brother, and Peter was too busy with his own family to spend much time with them.

'Better no father at all than one who would have put them through hell, Kay.'

He took her hand, feeling it flutter in his before it became still.

The sky was dark outside the warmth of the house, but with the snow steadily falling a winter wonderland was forming in the garden, its glow luminescent in the light from the windows. Her mother and Henry were still talking quietly together, their voices too low to be overheard, and the twins were busy with their dolls, and it just seemed the moment to say, 'It's affected you deeply, the way your father was, hasn't it.'

She saw his jaw clench and for a moment she thought he was going to draw away. Instead his hand tightened on hers. 'It was my mother who was a serial adulteress.' It was bald and flat. 'It got in the end so it was any man, any time, but long before that I knew she didn't love my father or my sister and I. I don't think she was capable of love in any form.'

'You...you knew she was having affairs, even though you were just a boy?' Kay whispered.

'I can't remember a time I didn't know,' he said bitterly. 'They would row—no, that's too mild a word for what went on. They would fight, quite literally, at times. She'd fly at him and he'd try and hold her off for a while, but she always pushed him too far. She broke his arm once; I was about nine at the time and I can remember his scream when she brought a poker down on him. He said he was leaving then, but of course he didn't. Don't ask me why because I don't think he loved her any more.'

'Oh, Mitchell.' Pain streaked through her. Pain for him now, and for the small, bewildered little boy he had once been. For the sister who had also been embroiled in the madness. 'Your sister? Was she younger than you?'

He nodded. 'I used to look after her as much as I could; she was a sweet kid, timid. Scared to death of our mother.

Most times when we'd get home from school the house would be empty. Dad would get home from work, sometimes before she got back and other times after. She never tried to deny where she had been or with whom. She was very honest.' His mouth twisted bitterly.

'I got a couple of paper rounds, one before school and one after. I think I'd got some crazy idea of saving enough to take Kathleen, my sister, and I away somewhere. Normally I was back long before Dad got in but this particular night my bike got a puncture. From what the neighbours said, Dad was waiting for my mother when she got home and when he found out she was seeing a man he worked with, he dragged her to the car to go and confront him at his home in front of his wife and family. Why he took Kathleen with him I don't know—perhaps it was to make this guy feel bad, or because he didn't want to leave her alone in the house. There was a head-on collision with a lorry anyway. End of story.'

Kay put her other hand on top of his, pressing it as she said, 'It wasn't your fault, Mitchell. You weren't to know he would do that, that he'd take Kathleen with him.'

He shrugged powerful shoulders. 'I was all Kathleen had; she trusted me. I should have been there. I wouldn't have let her go with them.' His voice was so raw she blinked against it.

'Perhaps your father would have made you go too and you'd all have been killed. Four lives lost instead of three.'

'For a long time I wished it had been that way.' He looked her full in the face, his mouth twisting. 'I was an angry young man, Kay. Very angry, very bitter, very foolhardy. I did some things I'm not proud of and it was more by luck than judgement I didn't end up in prison. Then one day a group of us were racing each other on motorbikes. One of my friends was killed in front of my eyes. It brought me up short. I realised I wanted to live after all.'

'I'm glad you did,' she said softly. She hadn't meant to say it the way it had sounded. Her voice hadn't been nearly as matter-of-fact or prosaic enough. But what really scared her half to death was the consuming urge to comfort him, to take the look of bleakness out of his eyes and to kiss the hard set of his mouth until it relaxed beneath her lips. Friends. The word mocked her. The feelings she had for Mitchell were not ones of friendship, they never had been, and they didn't remotely resemble the starry-eyed infatuation and girlish love that had led her to marry Perry either.

A CD of Christmas carols had been playing in the background and now, as it finished, Mitchell rose to his feet. 'There's a cartoon called *Santa's Special Christmas* starting about now. Fancy watching it, girls?' he asked Georgia and Emily.

Kay stared at him as he walked across to the huge television set and switched it on. Was it her imagination—part of the shock of acknowledging how she felt about him—or had his action been a deliberate withdrawal? Did he feel he'd said too much, revealed too much? How did she handle this?

As the twins positioned themselves at a suitable distance in front of the TV clutching their dolls, Kay lay back against the sofa and shut her eyes. She was aware of Mitchell walking across the room again but when she opened her eyes she saw he had picked up the blanket that had been wrapped round Emily, and was now tucking it round the small child as she sat with Georgia on the floor. The action was so poignant for some reason that Kay wanted to cry.

'Do you think you ladies could manage a sherry now you're in the land of the living again?' Mitchell included Leonora in the smile he gave, and when Kay and her mother both accepted and Henry made a move to rise he waved the older man down, saying, 'Stay where you are, Henry, I'll get them. A drop of your usual?'

Kay had to admit she thoroughly enjoyed the rest of the evening, even though she dozed off twice before dinner.

Georgia and Emily were so excited it was no use insisting on their normal bedtime, and so the little girls ate dinner at the elaborately festive dining table with the grown-ups, beside themselves with delight. They were almost asleep over their dessert, and when Mitchell picked them up, one on each arm, Kay went with him to tuck her daughters into bed. She was aware it was all too cosy, too intimate, but she couldn't do a thing about it for the time being, she told herself helplessly. It wasn't as though she had chosen to inflict them all on him, it had just...happened.

Both children were asleep as their heads touched the pillows, so worn out by all the excitement of the day and the anticipation of the morrow that they didn't need a reminder to go straight to sleep if they wanted Father Christmas to come.

Mitchell didn't hurry her to leave, standing with her as she watched the sleeping children for a couple of minutes. 'You love them very much, don't you?' he said softly.

It was on the tip of her tongue to say, Of course I do, they are my children, but, remembering all he had said downstairs, she answered simply, 'They're my world.'

Mitchell expelled a quiet breath. 'I know.' He turned his head, lifting her face up to his with one finger in the slumbering stillness as he murmured, his tone rueful, 'I thought it was going to be all so simple, dating you.'

'And it isn't?'

'No, it damn well isn't and you know it. You do know it, don't you, Kay? I want you, need you.' He drew her out of the room as he spoke, shutting the door quietly behind them and then taking her into his arms on the shadowed landing. He didn't have to tell her what he wanted, the desire was there to read in his eyes, his mouth hungry as it took hers.

Kay clung to him, her head whirling less with the after effects of the flu and more with the feel of his hard body against hers. She kissed him back; she couldn't help it. She always kissed him back—that was the effect Mitchell Grey had on her, she thought with a thread of bitterness for just a second before it was burnt up in the liquid heat coursing through her body.

His hand was in the small of her back to steady her and she gasped as the other cupped one of her breasts, his fingers beginning a languorous rhythm on its sensitive peak that had her stifling a moan of pleasure.

Something had happened, she told herself bewilderedly. There was a release of the restraint he had shown thus far. This gentle eroticism was as deliberate as it was powerful; he was forcing her to acknowledge her own need of him in the age-old way. Little did he know she'd got there before him...

His mouth and hands had complete mastery over her quivering senses, her body melting against his as he kept up the barrage of sweet sensation, fuelling her own passion with his. She thought briefly of the times Perry had made love to her, taking her with barely a kiss beforehand and thinking only of his own pleasure. What would it be like to *really* be loved by Mitchell? she asked herself dazedly. To lie with him all night, to explore and stroke and kiss every inch of that hard-muscled male body and to let him do the same to her. Because he would want to; she knew he would want to. Not for Mitchell a quick, brief coupling.

He had moved, pressing her back against the wall of the landing, and she could feel his thighs hard against hers, her softness stamped with the rock-hard power of his arousal. It was heady, intoxicating, to know how much he wanted her; it made her alive to the potency of her femininity in a way she had never experienced before.

There were sounds in the hall below them, then Henry's voice saying something to her mother as he opened the dining-room door and a faint whiff of coffee in the air. She felt Mitchell slowly draw away with a low groan of regret, his chest rising and falling with the force of his need as he straightened. 'We have to go,' he said huskily. 'Unfortunately.'

'Yes.' She was breathing hard, her cheeks flushed and her hands trembling at the tumult of desire he had released. She hadn't known she was capable of feeling like that, not in a hundred years, and now he wasn't holding her any more she felt dizzily adrift.

She raised a shaking hand to her hair, stumbling slightly, and immediately his hands came out to steady her, his voice rueful as he said, 'Damn it, I forgot you're still far from well. You've only been up five minutes and I've practically eaten you alive. Why can't I keep my hands off you?'

'I don't know.'

'I do. It's because you're enticing, mouth-watering—'

'Me?' In spite of herself Kay smiled. 'I'm not one of your gorgeous model-type females, Mitchell, as I'm only too aware. I do have mirrors in the house, you know.'

He let go of her, stepping back a pace and surveying her through eyes that were brilliantly clear in the darkness of his face. 'One, I don't have a harem of gorgeous model types, Kay,' he said quietly, his voice holding the edge of irony. 'Two, whatever you see when you look in the mirror, I see a warm and beautiful woman who is yet to be fully awakened to the power of her charm. And three, I never say anything I don't mean.'

She stared at him, her eyes locked with his, and then he moved closer again, his thumb stroking her cheek in a caressing gesture that brought a lump to her throat. 'Red hair that glows like fire when the light catches it, brown eyes as deep and soft as velvet, skin so delicate and fine it's like porcelain. How can you not see all that, Kay?'

She didn't dare believe this meant anything beyond what was for him a tried and tested seduction technique. He had *told* her he didn't want commitment or anything lasting; he had been totally up front about it. Maybe if she didn't have the twins, if she were answerable only to herself without any responsibilities, it would be different. Maybe then she would take a chance and give herself to him, hoping he would come to love her eventually, that when the time came to say goodbye he wouldn't be able to let her go.

But she did have the twins. She couldn't mess with their security or stability, neither did she have the luxury of being able to flirt with emotional suicide. And whatever he said, she still couldn't quite bring herself to believe that a man like Mitchell Grey—a man who could have any woman he wanted—would be interested in someone like her for long. She was five feet five of ordinary womanhood. She had freckles, her breasts were too small and her bottom was too big, and at that certain time of the month her skin could erupt like Mount Vesuvius. Whereas he... He was perfect.

Perry had hurt her but she had picked herself up, dusted herself down and got on with life. But if Mitchell betrayed her, if she gave herself to him and then he tired of her...

She turned her head from his intent gaze, shrugging her shoulders and making her voice as light as she could. 'Beauty is in the eye of the beholder, isn't that what they say? And hadn't we better go down now?'

'Sure.' He made no attempt to touch her. 'But it's only fair to let you know I never give up, Kay. I always get what I want.'

She felt more vulnerable than she'd ever felt in her life. Even after Perry had gone and she'd realised she had a pregnancy and then single parenthood to face, she hadn't felt such a sense of desperation, but she couldn't let him see how he had affected her. She forced herself to start walking towards the top of the stairs, tossing over her shoulder, 'Ah, but do you always get what you deserve, Mr Grey?'

She heard him chuckle. '*Touché*, Mrs Sherwood.'

This was still just a game to him. As they began to descend the stairs she felt exhaustion sweep over her in a great wave. Thank goodness she hadn't done what she'd wanted to do a few minutes ago and thrown herself into his arms, telling him she was his for as long as he wanted her. Madness. That was what he created in her: madness.

As they entered the dining room Kay saw her mother glance at her, and then Leonora said, consternation in her voice, 'Darling, you're as white as a sheet. You've done far too much on your first day up.'

'I am tired.' Kay seized the opportunity, but it was the truth anyway. She suddenly didn't know how she was going to put one foot in front of the other to climb the stairs again. 'I'm going to go to bed, if you don't mind?' She included the three of them in her swift glance. 'Goodnight, and happy Christmas.'

'I'll see you up the stairs—we don't want you falling headlong, do we?' Mitchell said silkily, ignoring her protests as he took her arm, saying to the other two, 'I'll be back in a second, and I'll have my coffee black, Henry, with a brandy.'

'I can manage perfectly well, thank you,' Kay muttered once they were at the foot of the stairs. 'Go back and have your coffee.'

'Bossy little wench, aren't you?' He grinned down at her but his eyes were thoughtful as they took in her pale face and the shadows under her eyes. 'Your mother's right, damn it, you have done too much. I shall have to watch that in the future.'

She couldn't take much more of this. For some reason she felt as though every single nerve end was exposed tonight.

'Right, let's get you into bed.' It was deliberately wicked and she opened her mouth to make a tart retort that never got voiced, Mitchell cutting it off by the simple expedient of whisking her up into his arms.

'Put me down, Mitchell. I can walk.'

'Perhaps, but this is nicer.' He looked down at her as he mounted the stairs, taking her mouth in a hard, swift kiss that took Kay's breath away.

He was too strong to fight, too powerful. She sagged against the hard wall of his chest, willing the moment to go on for ever. She wished she were a tall, stunning blonde with the sort of vital statistics to drive a man wild; she wished *he* hadn't been hurt so badly by the one woman in his life he should have been able to trust, and who had shaped the young boy Mitchell into the man he now was; she wished—oh, she wished for all sorts of things and all of them pipe dreams.

He was holding her closely, securely, as they reached the bedroom. He set her down outside the door, looking down at her quizzically as he said, 'I presume you want me to leave you here?'

No. No, she didn't. 'Yes, please. Mitchell, the girls' presents? We usually leave them in a pillowcase under the tree at home.'

'All taken care of. Henry and I have got them ready and we'll leave them there before we retire. Leonora said there's also a small matter of a glass of sherry and mince pie? We'll make sure the glass is suitably sooty and most of the mince pie's eaten, of course. Santa has to keep his strength up.'

'Thank you.'

'My pleasure,' he said softly. 'It's been fun.'

'Your home being turned upside down with a houseful of invalids?' Kay said disbelievingly.

He smiled as he lowered his head, his kiss tender and painfully sweet this time. His body was bent over her but no part was touching except his mouth fused to hers. 'You're here,' he said huskily as he straightened. 'That makes it fun.'

'Goodnight, Mitchell. Happy Christmas.' It was a whisper and she opened the door as she spoke, stepping inside the room quickly and closing the door without looking at him again. She stood leaning against the wood for several moments, however, her heart beating fast and her legs trembling.

Christmas Eve, a magical time.

Tired as she was, she levered herself off the door and

walked across to the window, looking down into the snow-covered garden for a minute or two before she drew the curtains.

But it was no good wishing for the moon.

CHAPTER SEVEN

THE twins must have been tired out with all the excitement and anticipation of Christmas Eve, because it was after seven o'clock when Kay's bedroom door was flung open and two tiny pyjama-clad little figures hurled themselves onto the bed.

'Mummy! It's Christmas morning!'

'The baby Jesus is born, Mummy.'

This last exclamation was from Emily, the ever practical Georgia adding, 'Has Father Christmas been? Has he left our presents?'

'I don't know, my darlings.' Kay had slept deeply and dreamlessly and now, as she struggled up in bed, brushing her hair out of her eyes and hugging each little wriggling girl, she added, 'Shall we go and see what's under the tree?'

'What a good idea.'

The deep male voice from the doorway brought the twins bouncing round and Kay hastily pulling the duvet up to her chin. Mitchell was leaning against the door post, his hair ruffled and his face unshaven, and Kay's heart gave a kick like a mule. He was dressed in a black silk robe and matching pyjama bottoms, and he looked more sexy than any man had the right to first thing in the morning.

'I presume Grandma will want to come and join in the proceedings?' Mitchell asked Kay, his eyebrows raised. And at her nod, added, 'Go and get her, girls, but gently, okay? Wake her gently.'

As the twins scampered past him he ruffled each head of curls and then, to Kay's horror, came further into the room, walking across to the bed. 'What do you think you're doing?' she yelped weakly.

'Saying good morning.' He bent and kissed her, hard. 'Good morning,' he said softly.

'You shouldn't be here.' She hadn't even brushed her hair or cleaned her teeth, and with the twins and her mother next door...

Mitchell raised mocking eyebrows. 'Excuse me, but I was under the impression I live here?' he said lazily, purposely misunderstanding. 'Besides, it's not the first time I've seen you in bed. You've been here three days.'

'I was ill before.'

'Don't be so school-marmish,' he reproved her sternly.

'Mitchell, *please*.'

'I'm going to have to work on those inhibitions of yours.' He gave her one last swift kiss on the tip of her nose and walked over to the door, saying, 'You were more fun when you were ill, tossing and turning quite deliciously at times, I might add. Are you wearing that nightie with the very thin straps that's almost transparent?'

'You...you peeping Tom!' She was blushing crimson and furious with herself for doing so.

'Could I help it if you kept throwing off your covers in gay abandon?' he protested innocently.

'You, you...'

'Get your dressing gown on and make yourself decent, woman. There's children around.'

He grinned at her and she glared at him.

'Tut-tut.' He shook his head sorrowfully. 'Where's your Christmas spirit, Kay? Goodwill to all men and so on.' He shut the door on her splutterings but not before he added, 'And you'd better be quick; Georgia and Emily are raring to go.'

They all went down together in the end, even Henry joining them on the landing and looking very distinguished in a pair of dark aubergine cotton pyjamas and a striped dressing gown.

Once the twins had indulged in an orgy of unwrapping, delving into their pillowcases until they were empty, Mitchell nodded to Henry and the older man left the room briefly to return with the most enormous brightly wrapped package.

'This is from Henry and myself, girls,' Mitchell said softly. 'Happy Christmas.'

It was a doll's house, complete with beautifully fashioned furniture and a little family of dolls right down to a baby in a crib. The twins were ecstatic.

The adults then exchanged gifts, and Kay was thankful she had bought something for Mitchell, and a little present for Henry, before she'd fallen ill. However, the leather driving gloves and cashmere scarf that Mitchell seemed to receive with genuine pleasure paled into insignificance beside the dainty white-gold and diamond watch he presented her with.

'Oh, Mitchell, it's beautiful.' As he fastened it on her wrist she stared down in wonder. She had never thought to own anything so exquisite, but it must have cost a *fortune*. And gloves and a scarf... 'But I didn't get you anything nearly so nice.'

He shushed her by putting a finger on her lips. 'I needed new gloves and the scarf is perfect,' he said softly. 'You needed a new watch. I noticed your present one was always stopping or told the wrong time.'

Kay thought it was very nice of him not to mention at this point that her old one also had the gilt flaking off. It had been a quick buy off a market stall the year before but all she could afford at the time, the twins just having needed new shoes and a winter coat each. She looked at him, her eyes enormous. 'Thank you,' she said tremblingly, wondering why—after such a marvellous gift—she should want to cry.

'Tea, toast and croissants everyone?' Henry cut across the moment, suddenly reverting to housekeeper and cook. 'I'm not going to cook a full English breakfast because I want you to do justice to Christmas dinner, which will be served promptly at one o'clock. And woe betide anyone who says they're not hungry. No excuses about post-flu appetites either,' he added warningly.

'Can I come and help you?'

This was from Leonora, and when Henry said, 'That would be most welcome, thank you,' in his old-fashioned way, Kay caught Mitchell staring at his friend in open astonishment.

'What is it?' she whispered when the other two had disappeared in the direction of the kitchen, and only the girls remained, playing contentedly with the doll's house. 'Why did you look at Henry like that?'

Mitchell smiled, a curiously satisfied smile. 'Because in all my years of knowing Henry he's never allowed anyone to storm the bastion of his kitchen,' he said thoughtfully, 'and I mean no one, full stop.'

Kay stared at him as the import of his words dawned. 'You don't mean...'

'I think Henry rather likes your mother.' He watched her for a minute, seeing her absorb the idea. 'Would you mind?' he asked quietly.

Would she? It might make things a little difficult when she and Mitchell stopped seeing each other, but if her mother liked Henry and the feeling was reciprocated, that was wonderful. If nothing else it would give her mother an interest beyond that of her own family. 'No,' she said firmly. 'I wouldn't mind at all.'

It started to snow again as they were having breakfast, but when Kay said she wanted Emily to wait another day before she went outside to build the snowman the twins didn't object too much, content to play with all their new toys. Hence the morning was a lazy one of sitting by the roaring fire watching the children play while they listened to carols on the radio, the four adults talking of this and that as the smell of roasting turkey began to permeate the air.

After Henry served particularly wicked elevenses of coffee laced with Tia Maria and spices and topped with whipped cream, along with a plateful of his delicious home-made shortbread, Kay settled back on the sofa next to Mitchell in a haze of festive well being. She awoke some time later with the embarrassing realisation that she must have dozed off, her head now lodged comfortably on his chest and his arm holding her close as she curled into him.

She stiffened, raising her head cautiously only to stare into a pair of bright blue eyes. 'You don't snore when you're asleep,' he said conversationally, 'but you do make the most enchanting little sniffles now and again, like a small animal making itself more cosy.'

Kay could feel heat flooding her cheeks and now Mitchell laughed softly, straightening as he said, 'You're not the only one who had a nap. Look over there.' She looked and saw her mother was dead to the world too, stretched out on another sofa with a blanket over her lower half. 'It'll do you both good; you still look peaky.'

Peaky? What did that mean? A mess? Something the

cat wouldn't deign to drag in? 'Where are the girls?' she asked, more to change the subject than anything else.

'Helping Henry make a batch of muffins for tea. Apparently he was brought up with muffins for tea on Christmas Day afternoon, and as this Christmas seems to have turned into a family affair...' He shrugged.

Did he mind? There had been an inflexion in his voice Kay couldn't quite fathom. He must have had other plans for Christmas after all. A man like Mitchell Grey didn't sit at home twiddling his thumbs.

He had bent to nuzzle her curls with his chin, murmuring almost to himself, 'You smell wonderful. What is it you're wearing?'

'Baby powder.'

'Baby powder?' He leaned back to stare at her. 'You're joking.'

She shook her head. 'When you carried me off I wasn't in a fit state to think of perfume or cosmetics,' she reminded him. 'The twins had some baby lotion and powder in their toiletries so I'm using that.'

He shook his head, his eyes bright with laughter. 'Do you mean to tell me that I've spent a fortune over the years on expensive perfume as gifts, and all the time I could have got away with baby powder?'

She stared at him. It was unintentional—probably—but suddenly she was reminded yet again that he was a 'love 'em and leave 'em' type. She breathed deeply. 'I don't think the sort of women you date would appreciate baby powder, Mitchell,' she said evenly. 'Do you? I'm a mother; that smell has been second nature to me for years.'

He wasn't smiling any longer. 'Meaning?'

'Meaning nothing,' she said carefully, 'except that they're used to Chanel and Gucci, and I'm used to baby powder and off the peg, that's all. They could be ready to fly off round the world or attend an elegant function at the drop of the hat; I have to make sure my mother can babysit and even then half my mind is on the girls if one of them is poorly or upset about something. Two very different worlds.'

They both knew what she was saying. 'Unbridgeable?' he asked softly.

No, not unbridgeable. In fact if there was even the prospect he could offer something beyond a brief affair, she would build the bridge herself, brick by brick. She gave a brittle smile. 'I think so. It's a case of butterflies and moths, I suppose.'

'You're not a moth,' he said roughly, a hardness entering his tone. 'Not unless you choose to be.'

'My option to choose ended four years ago.' She eyed him bravely, inwardly shaking and outwardly composed. 'And I wouldn't have it any other way. All the Chanel and Gucci in the world couldn't begin to compare with my children's smiles. Cartier diamonds are nothing compared to a gaudy plastic ring and bracelet I have at home, things they got from some crackers that they think are wonderful but which they gave to me.'

He nodded. 'I can buy that.'

'But you can't buy it, don't you see? They give me their unconditional love and trust and I have to do everything I can to make sure their world is not shaken or disturbed,' she said, deliberately misunderstanding his words. 'They're little children, Mitchell. They don't understand about moving on, and temporary liaisons, and being replaced, and I don't want them to, not yet. Time enough for all that when they're grown up and making their own way in the world. They'll probably experience rejection and loss then. For now stability and a solid foundation is what is important. They'll make lots of mistakes of their own; they're bound to. That's life. But I don't ever want them to suffer through a mistake I make, no more than they have already by not having a father.'

There was a vibrating silence for a moment. She hadn't meant to say that last bit, Kay thought distractedly; in fact she hadn't even been aware it was there, buried deep in her subconscious. But she *had* made a mistake in marrying a rat like Perry, and her babies *were* paying for it in not having a father figure.

'You can't blame yourself because Perry turned out like he did, Kay,' Mitchell said at last. 'Nothing in life comes with a cast-iron guarantee.'

Her mother was beginning to stir, and now Kay said quickly and dismissively, 'I know that.'

'Do you? I don't think so.'

She couldn't do this. She really couldn't do this. In a small voice she said, 'Can we talk about this some other time?'

He nodded, lifting her chin, which had drooped, before he murmured, 'It strikes me we've got a lot of talking to do. That wall you built to repel intruders is still steel-clad, isn't it?'

The wall *she* had built? What about the one he'd constructed? She stared at him. 'You were the one who said we're two of a kind,' she reminded him quietly. 'You've done some building work of your own, Mitchell.'

There was no time to say anything more before the twins returned, flushed and proud from their cooking efforts, and woke Leonora fully. But all through Henry's delicious Christmas lunch and the afternoon that followed Kay found herself going over what she'd said time and time again until her head was spinning. Had she said too much? Probably. Very probably, she admitted. But it was too late now.

They had muffins with the twins at five o'clock and it was obvious the two little girls were tired out even then. By six they'd had their bath and were in their pyjamas snuggled down in bed, looking impossibly angelic as Kay kissed them goodnight.

'Where's Uncle Mitchell?' Georgia asked sleepily as Kay dimmed the light. 'Isn't he going to kiss us goodnight?'

'Not tonight, darling, he's talking to Grandma and Henry.' Kay had made it clear—not so much by what she'd said as what she hadn't—that she intended to settle the children down herself without any help before she had left the drawing room. She had seen Mitchell look at her intently, his eyes searching her face, but he hadn't objected or attempted to follow her.

It had only been a few days but already Georgia and Emily were far too fond of Mitchell, Kay told herself as she walked slowly down the stairs to join the others. She had to calm things down, put an emotional brake on the proceedings. She had been so determined to prevent anything but the most fleeting of exchanges between Mitchell and her children in the last two months, and now here they all were actually living in his house! It was ironic in the extreme. But it couldn't continue. *They* couldn't continue.

The thought hit her hard and she bit her lip. He had been very kind to her, to all of them, and she appreciated it, she did really, but it didn't alter the facts. She had been crazy to start seeing him in the first place and now suddenly it had mushroomed into a giant tangle. The bottom line was he wanted her in his bed with no involvement other than a sexual one. She knew that, she had always known it, so all this was no one's fault but hers.

He had tried to seduce her in a hundred little ways, in fact just being with him was a seduction all in itself, but he hadn't lied to her. He had laid it on the line from the beginning; he'd been positively barefaced about his intentions. It wasn't comforting at all.

As she reached the drawing-room door she heard her mother laugh from within, a warm, carefree laugh that was almost a giggle. Kay stopped, her heart thumping. It had been years since she'd heard that laugh—the last time had been when her father was still alive, in fact.

In spite of her father's foolishness with money and his last disastrous run of speculating, which had resulted in her mother being left virtually destitute, Kay knew her parents had loved each other deeply. They had shared the sort of 'till death do us part' type of love she'd imagined she and Perry had got, but with her parents it had been real.

Now her mother was laughing with Henry. Kay's brow wrinkled. Did it mean...? And then she caught her racing thoughts, which had galloped ahead to picture them walking down the aisle.

For goodness' sake, she told herself sternly, her mother and Mitchell's housekeeper had only known each other for a few days; she mustn't read too much into something as unimportant as a laugh. She had been speaking the truth when she'd told Mitchell she was glad they liked each other, and if it did develop into something more she would still be glad. But only time would tell.

Nevertheless, Kay found she had to stand for a full minute composing herself before she felt able to open the door and join the others.

Why was life so complicated and up in the air? she

asked herself, stitching a bright smile on her face as she entered the warmth of the drawing room. And then she glanced across and met Mitchell's darkly brooding gaze from the other side of the room, and she had her answer,

CHAPTER EIGHT

WITH Henry and her mother present, Kay found it wasn't difficult to act a part for the rest of the evening. She managed to mention, fairly casually, that the twins had an invitation to a friend's birthday party in a day or two, so she felt it best they return home the day after Boxing Day. They were all *so* grateful for Mitchell's open-handed kindness, she emphasised carefully, but they must have inconvenienced him dreadfully, and now everyone was back on their feet it was better to get back to normal.

Mitchell had smiled an easy reply with his mouth but his features had been as flint-hard as his eyes, and she had tried to avoid meeting his gaze for the rest of the evening.

At eleven o'clock, when her mother had yawned for the hundredth time and had made noises about going to bed, Kay had leapt to join her, sticking to Leonora like glue as they said their goodnights to the men and then climbed the stairs to the bedrooms.

'Okay, what's wrong?' As they reached the landing Leonora took her daughter's arm, pulling her up short when Kay would have just said goodnight and entered her room. 'Have you two had a row or something?'

'More a something.'

'Why? When?' Leonora whispered. 'I thought we'd all been together today. When did you fit a row in?'

'I told you, we haven't rowed. It's just...' Kay didn't know how to put it but she knew with absolute certainty her mother would favour Mitchell whatever she said. 'Mitchell's not looking for any sort of ongoing relationship,' she hissed quietly, glancing back down the shadowed landing as though he were going to leap out any moment. 'And I don't want the twins confused and upset when he's not on the scene any more. They're growing too fond of him.'

'Who says he's planning not to be on the scene any more?' her mother asked, reasonably enough, Kay supposed.

'Me. Him. Oh...' Kay gazed at her mother irritably. 'He's made it clear his intentions are strictly *dis*honourable, okay? A few weeks or months or whatever of warming his sheets and having 'fun'—' she was beginning to really loathe that word '—and then bye-bye with no regrets on either side. That's how he operates. He spelled it out to me when we first started seeing each other, if you want to know.'

'And you still agreed to see him?' Leonora asked expressionlessly.

'Not exactly.' Kay bit on her lower lip. 'It wasn't like that. He just wouldn't take no for an answer and insisted we could date as friends. I said it was a mad idea, but—'

'He talked you round.'

'Yes.' Kay shrugged her shoulders helplessly.

'Are you sleeping with him?'

It wasn't like Leonora to ask personal questions of such a nature. Kay stared at her mother for a few moments before she said, 'No, I am not sleeping with him.'

'But you want to,' Leonora blithely stated.

'Mum.'

'It's a perfectly natural desire, Kay, and you are a grown woman of twenty-six.'

'I know how old I am, Mum.' She didn't believe this!

Leonora looked at her daughter's troubled face and her own softened as she put a hand on Kay's arm. 'Come into my room a moment, love. I want to talk to you properly.'

For a second it was on Kay's lips to refuse. She felt so battered and bruised emotionally she didn't feel like talking, and especially not on the Mitchell subject with his most ardent fan.

'Please, Kay?'

She nodded grumpily, and once inside Leonora's bedroom walked across to one of the two easy chairs positioned under the window and sat down. 'Well?' Her tone wasn't conducive to a heart-to-heart and she knew it. She just hoped her mother would take the hint.

Leonora seated herself in the other chair before she spoke, and then her voice was more matter-of-fact than persuasive when she said, 'Speaking as a third party, this is how I see it. You meet, he chases after you—' as Kay went to interrupt, Leonora held up her hand '—let me finish, Kay, please. I repeat, he chases after you, even after he discovered you have a family. He makes it clear he wants you and then, when you don't want to see him, he suggests you date as friends.' Her mother arched her eyebrow at this point. 'Kissing-cousin type of friends, I'm sure, but, nevertheless, he doesn't press his cause. Right?'

Kay nodded. She didn't need this. She really, *really* didn't need this.

'You get ill and he removes the whole lot of us to his home for Christmas, and, I might add, makes an enormous effort to give the children as good a Christmas as is possible in the circumstances. Right again?'

Her mother could be the most irritating person on

planet earth when she wanted to be. 'So, what's your point?'

'My *point* is, whatever he said to you in the beginning, I think he's a different man to the one you think he is.'

'Oh, *Mother*. For goodness' sake.' Kay shut her eyes, putting a hand to her brow. 'It's your most endearing quality, but also one that makes me want to scream at times like this, that you always insist on seeing the best in someone you like. Look, I know you mean well, but I think I know Mitchell better than you.'

'Has he told you how Henry came to be working for him?'

'Henry? No—no, he hasn't. I did ask once but he said it was Henry's story to tell,' Kay said flatly, wondering why on earth her mother had brought it up now.

'Well, Henry told me his story,' Leonora said, 'and I know he wouldn't mind me telling you.'

Kay wasn't so sure about this but with her mother in full flow there was no stopping her. Besides which, she admitted contritely, she was curious.

'Henry used to be one of the best-paid chefs in the country,' Leonora said with such pride that it made Kay wonder again how deeply her mother liked the tall, aristocratic housekeeper. 'He has worked in Italy, France, America—all over the world, in fact, and because he remained single he indulged in a lavish lifestyle: wine, women and song. Twelve years ago he was contacted by one of his old girlfriends. It appeared she'd had a child, a son. Henry's son. She'd never told him, they had only been together a few weeks and it was just one of those things that burnt out very quickly. She was wealthy in her own right and hadn't seen the need to inform him he was a father because she didn't need anything from him.'

Leonora sniffed here, one of her more eloquent sniffs, and Kay surmised her mother hadn't agreed with the girlfriend's decision.

'Only she did need something,' Leonora continued. 'Something it appeared only Henry might be able to give. The child was ill, very ill, and needed a bone-marrow transplant, but in spite of this woman and her family's wealth no matching donor had been found. Henry agreed to see if he could help and in so doing met the child, his son. He was a lovely boy apparently, eight years old and the image of his father. Henry's bone marrow matched but before they could do the operation the boy died.'

'Oh, Mum.' Kay was horrified, her mother's heart instantly putting herself and one of the twins in that position.

'It broke him, Kay.' Leonora stared at her daughter and they both had tears in their eyes. 'He came back to England from America where the boy had been and resumed his life, but he felt it was like his spring had snapped. He started to drink, had days off work, generally fell apart. He lost his job; got another and then lost that, and then the word went out and he was unemployable. His so-called friends didn't want to know. He'd got as low as he could go, when Mitchell saw him one day and recognised him as a chef he'd once known. Mitchell picked him up out of the gutter—literally—and took him home.'

Kay was sitting forward in her seat now, hardly breathing, transfixed as she was by the unfolding drama.

'Henry said Mitchell gave him shelter, clothes, food, but most of all friendship, even when he was at his worst. Mitchell's doctor diagnosed a breakdown and the recovery was slow, but one day Henry found he wanted to live instead of wanting to die.'

'Like Mitchell,' Kay breathed softly. And then, as her mother raised questioning eyebrows, she said, 'It doesn't matter. Go on.'

'There's not much more to tell. Henry didn't want to go back to his old life—even if he could have found places to hire him, which he probably could have done with Mitchell backing him—and as his recovery coincided with the purchase of this place Mitchell offered him a home and a job for as long as he wanted to stay.'

'You've fallen for Henry, haven't you?' Kay said gently.

Leonora blushed, an answer in itself. 'He's a good man at heart, Kay. Like Mitchell.'

They were back to Mitchell again. Kay sat back in her seat, trying to assess what was nagging at her now Henry's heartbreaking story had come to a conclusion. And then it dawned on her.

'I'm not denying he has the capacity to be amazingly kind on occasions,' she said very slowly, trying to formulate her thoughts as she spoke. 'Like he was with Henry, and with us this Christmas. But don't you see? The fact that he was so good to Henry negates your argument that I'm in some way special to him, different to the rest, and that was what you were trying to say, wasn't it?'

'Kay—'

'No, it's my turn now,' Kay said firmly. 'What he did for Henry was great, it really was, and for all we know he might have done a million and one good Samaritan deeds in his time, but that still doesn't change the way he looks at women and commitment. There are things in his past that have shaped him, things that happened when he was a boy, and it would take someone very special to help him get rid of his hang-ups. I'm—'

'Lovely,' Leonora put in quickly.

'Ordinary,' Kay said, smiling faintly. 'Face it, Mum. I am.'

'You care about him, though.'

If her mother's voice hadn't been so sad Kay might have been able to bluff her way out of it. As it was she swallowed hard, tears pricking at the back of her eyes as she fiercely told herself she couldn't cry. 'Then that's my misfortune, isn't it? I walked into this with my eyes open and I suppose I was hoping...'

'Hoping?' Leonora prompted gently.

'Hoping he might fall madly in love with me, like I have with him, the more time we've spent together over the last couple of months. Stupid.'

'Not stupid, just human.' They sat together in silence for a few moments, Leonora taking Kay's cold hands in her own warm ones. 'What will you do?'

Kay didn't answer for a little while, and then she roused herself, straightening her shoulders. 'End it. Not in a big, dramatic way because, Mitchell being Mitchell, he'll look on that as a challenge. I think that's why he was interested in the first place, because I didn't fall at his feet and worship like most women. I was different, that's all it was,' she added with a shred of bitterness. 'No, I'll do it carefully. Cut down on the dates I can keep, put up obstacles, that kind of thing.'

'And you think that will work?' Leonora asked doubtfully.

'Eventually. He's a proud man, Mum.'

They talked for a few more minutes and then Kay kissed her mother, hugging her tight for a moment before she left. Once outside on the landing she stood listening but she could hear nothing from downstairs. She walked along to the twins' room, opening the door very quietly and tiptoeing across to the little girls asleep in their beds. She stood there for some time and it wasn't until she felt the salt at the edges of her mouth that she realised she was crying. After rubbing her eyes with the back of her hand she tucked the duvets more securely around the two tiny figures, positioning their teddy bears under their arms, before leaving as silently as she had come.

On opening the door to her room Kay nearly jumped out of her skin, smothering her yelp of alarm with the palm of her hand as she realised the big dark figure sitting in one of the easy chairs was Mitchell. 'Where was the party?' he asked sarcastically, not moving a muscle as she closed the door before taking one or two steps into the room.

'I'm sorry?'

'You've been—' he consulted the Rolex on his tanned wrist '—thirty-five minutes, and this from a woman who was allegedly so tired she couldn't keep her eyes open downstairs.'

The shock of seeing him sitting there had died and healthy anger was taking its place. 'I *was* tired,' she said shortly, 'but I had a chat with my mother. That isn't a crime, is it? I looked in on the twins too,' she added crisply. 'That's what I do, Mitchell. I'm a mother.'

'So you reminded me today—exhaustively.' The crystal eyes in the handsome face were cold. 'Which brings me on to why I'm here.'

'Which you shouldn't be.' She glared at him. 'It's twenty to twelve. I'm tired.'

'Tough.' He spoke with a softness that carried true menace.

'Charming,' Kay said sharply. 'Very host-like.'

'And you needn't take that tone. You've frozen me out all this afternoon and evening and I want to know why. Is it still this ''two different worlds'' thing? Because if it is that's bull. Half the world's population wouldn't be with their partner right now if their past and present had to match perfectly, and you know it.'

'It's not a question of being the same in that sense, of course it's not,' she snapped hotly, the tension of the afternoon and the emotionally wearing chat with her mother stretching her nerves to breaking-point.

'Then what?' He levered himself up from the chair and Kay forced herself not to move or react as he walked across to her, her eyes wide and steady as she met his angry gaze. 'What is it? All this talk of you being a mother? Damn it, Kay, you've been a mother since I met you; Georgia and Emily haven't suddenly arrived on the scene. You must know I wouldn't ask you to upset them in any way, disrupt their routine or security. Don't make me out to be some sort of self-centred, mercenary dictator because I don't like it.'

'I didn't say you were a monster,' she fired back quickly, her heart thumping.

'Well, that's the way you've made me feel all afternoon.' He raked a hand through his short hair, the gesture one of extreme frustration and fury. 'Damn it, I've trodden on eggshells with you for the last couple of months. I've had so many cold showers it's not true, cautioned myself to go slowly until I'm half out of my mind, and for what? To be looked at as thought you're scared stiff of me one minute or that I'm something that's just crawled out of the slime the next.'

'That is so unfair! Hugely unfair.'

'No, it is not, Kay.' He was standing so close she could see where he'd nicked himself shaving, the warm, faintly delicious smell of him teasing her nostrils.

'Well, if you feel like that why have you bothered?' she said feverishly. 'Us dating was your idea, if you remember.'

'Oh, I remember, all right,' he said with more than a touch of sarcasm. 'I remember everything about that first lunch with you, believe me. It will be engrained on my memory till my dying day.' He pulled her towards him suddenly, wrapping his arms round her as if to bind her to him. 'A defiant scrap of nothing with flashing eyes and a skirt so short I was rock-hard for a week just thinking about it.' He shook her slightly, his voice holding a faint note of self-derision. 'I knew when they came and told me you'd flown the coop I should cut my losses. I didn't need aggravation in the form of a red-haired siren who was intent on telling me to go to blazes. But you'd got under my skin, even then.'

She stared up at him, unable to say a word. His eyes were very silvery in the light of the one bedside lamp he had clicked on, the blue almost non-existent. She knew what was happening; the dark magnetism that was at the heart of his charm had reached out yet again to convince her black was white and white was black. She *knew* the sensible thing would be to end this right now, but standing here locked in his arms, with his anger dying and being replaced by something very different, logic and reason went out of the window.

But she had to try. She tensed, pulling back a little.

'This is crazy,' she whispered. 'It can't work, you must see that. We're too different, Mitchell.'

'I'm getting too close. That's the real problem, isn't it?' he said softly.

She took a deep breath. 'Yes,' she said bravely, 'in a way. It...it wasn't part of the deal that you'd get to know my family. And I am grateful, really,' she rushed on, 'for all you've done, but...'

Anything else she might have said was swallowed up as his mouth descended on hers, his kiss fierce and hungry. Kay found herself clinging to him with desperate urgency, pressing closer into the hard male body as he kissed her with a raging passion that sent the blood rushing through her veins more warmly than the hot mulled wine they'd had earlier.

The thought came that she had to stop this, that it went against everything she had been thinking and talking about, but she couldn't bear to move away. She wanted him, she needed him, and if it had to finish soon, so be it, but she could have this one night in his arms, couldn't she?

She felt weightless and light-headed, enchanted and quivering with the sensations spiralling through her body. She was barely aware he had moved them over to the bed, but then she was lying down on the soft covers and he was bent over her, his hands and his mouth creating a yearning she felt she'd die from if it wasn't properly assuaged.

'You're so beautiful, Kay. Far more beautiful than you realise, my darling.' He was kissing her eyelids, her cheeks, her lips, her throat, his mouth moving over the delicate freckled skin at the swell of her breasts and then lower. She was lost in whirling desire, the ache in her body needing his to appease it.

She hadn't felt her blouse being undone, and even when his mouth and touch registered on bare skin the sensation was too sweet to stop. Right from when she'd met him her nights had been invaded by torturous longings and wild dreams, too erotic to dwell on in the cold light of day. But now her imaginings were coming true and he was everything she'd known he would be, knowing exactly where to touch, to kiss...

Why hadn't she known it was possible to feel like this, that the mediocre sex life she had experienced with Perry wasn't the real thing? She had read in novels about a woman's body becoming a warm, pulsating, mindless energy but she had thought that it was fiction, clever writing to titillate. But this wasn't fiction, this was real.

He was stroking the silky skin of her abdomen and as her hands clasped him to her, her fingers moving under his shirt and finding the hard range of planes and muscles beneath, he groaned softly. She could feel the hard pulse of his desire and it created such a fierce excitement she didn't recognise herself.

She opened drugged eyes to see him bending over her, his face harsh and dark with passion and different from the Mitchell she knew. There was no trace of the cool, controlled entrepreneur or wry, mordacious man about town now. He wanted her, badly. She reached out to fumble with the belt in his jeans, desire making her all fingers and thumbs, and it came as a drenching shock when his hands moved over hers, stilling them.

'No, Kay.'

'No?' It was the barest of whispers, all she could manage.

He groaned, the sound wrenched from the depths of him. 'Don't look like that,' he growled huskily. 'Don't you think I want to? Hell, I'm going insane and it gets worse every time we're together, but I don't want it to be like this. That bozo you were married to; I only had to touch you once to know he had never awakened you. You responded to me like a virgin, unsure, overwhelmed by your feelings—'

'Mitchell, I have two children.' She had gone white then scarlet before hauling herself into a sitting position on the bed, desperately aware of the state of her clothing and feeling more humiliated than she'd ever felt in her life. She had thrown herself at him and he had refused her. It was the one refrain beating in her head. 'I'm no virgin.'

'Not physically maybe.' He watched her as she groped with the buttons of her blouse, her frantic haste adding to her clumsiness. 'Kay, when we make love—and we will—it will be a decision of your mind and not just your body. You will know exactly what you are doing.'

'How civilised,' she said with an attempt at derision that didn't come off at all.

'If you want to put it like that.' His voice was cold now, contained. 'Whatever, you won't have any regrets because you were swept away by emotion or curiosity or anything else. It will be your first time—in everything that counts it *will* be your first time,' he added as Kay went to protest again, 'and you will make a conscious decision as a grown woman to let me love you.'

Kay's eyes jerked to meet his at the last words. If only, *if only* he had meant that in the real sense of the word. But he was talking about sex, not love. 'And if I don't?'

she said shortly, forcing iron into her voice to combat the trembling she was trying to hide.

'You will.' It was supremely confident, and for a moment she actually hated him. 'You will come to me of your own volition and I will make you into the woman you were always meant to be. It's fate, kismet.'

'It's wishful thinking.' She didn't know where she was finding the strength to act as though her heart hadn't been just torn out by the roots, but she was grateful for it.

'Still fighting,' he said softly.

His eyes had gone to her hair and now Kay snapped, her fragile cool deserting her. 'Don't you dare mention the colour of my hair or, so help me, I'll hit you. And could you please leave my room? I was brought up to think that when one was a guest in someone's home it didn't automatically mean the host had visiting rights.'

He ignored the slur but she had seen his eyes narrow momentarily and knew he hadn't liked it. It was a poor comfort in view of all that had gone on, but better than nothing.

'Goodnight, Kay.' He walked over to the door, his tall, lean body more relaxed than it had the right to be, she thought tightly. Here was she burning up inside and knowing she would toss and turn for hours in an agony of sexual frustration, whereas he looked as cool as a cucumber. 'Dream of me.'

She glared at him. 'A very remote possibility,' she lied icily.

'"Satire should, like a polished razor keen, Wound with a touch that's scarcely felt or seen." That was written by a woman over two hundred and fifty years ago,' he said silkily. 'Do you think Lady Mary Wortley Montagu had such as you in mind?'

Kay raised her chin haughtily, two spots of bright colour still burning on her cheekbones. 'If there were men like you around, very probably.'

'Ow.' He pretended to wince as he opened the door, turning on the threshold one last time as he surveyed her, rumpled and flushed, still sitting on the bed. 'Don't forget we're building a snowman tomorrow,' he said softly. 'I want you up bright and early or else I'll have to come and fetch you.'

How *dared* he talk in that sexy, smoky voice when he had just refused her? Kay asked herself furiously. She hated him; she really *really* hated him.

She was still trying to think of an adequately scathing retort when Mitchell closed the door.

CHAPTER NINE

BOXING DAY dawned crystal-bright, the blue sky and pearly cold sunlight turning the thick snow to a carpet of shimmering white and sending the twins mad with delight.

Leonora and Henry opted for staying in the warm, so it was left to Kay and Mitchell to build the snowman with the two little girls.

The acute embarrassment Kay had felt at breakfast when she had first set eyes on Mitchell faded somewhat in the general mayhem, which involved much shrieking and rolling in the snow by Georgia, a great deal of serious and careful building by Emily and a bit of both by Mitchell, much to the delight of the twins.

When Frosty—christened so by Georgia and Emily—was finally finished, Mitchell lifted both little girls in his arms so they could put the snowman's hat and scarf in place along with his coal eyes, carrot nose and pebbled teeth.

'He's just lovely, isn't he, Mummy?' Georgia breathed reverently, turning in Mitchell's arm to hold out her hand to Kay, which immediately prompted Emily to do the same. As Kay took the mittened paws in her hands she was aware of Mitchell's eyes tight on her face, the four of them joined together in what could have been a family unit. It hurt. Unbearably.

'He's wonderful, darling,' she said brightly, her smile brittle. 'The best snowman in the world.'

Whether Mitchell had noticed the tell-tale glitter in her eyes Kay didn't know, but she felt his gaze brush over her face before he said, 'Now Frosty's all wrapped up in his hat and scarf, how about we go and feed the ducks on the lake, eh? Why don't you two go and ask Henry for some bread?'

'Can we? Really?' The twins didn't need any prompting after Kay had nodded her permission, racing off as fast as their little red wellington boots would take them.

When they had disappeared into the house there was a vibrant silence for a moment or two, and then Mitchell said softly, 'How were the dreams?'

Trust him not to pretend last night hadn't happened! The dart of anger produced enough adrenalin for Kay to be able to answer stiffly, as though he had just made a polite enquiry, 'I slept very well, thank you.'

'I didn't.' He wasn't smiling as he looked into her eyes.

Your fault. 'Really?' She raised superior eyebrows, refusing to meet his gaze as she turned to survey the winter wonderland in front of them. 'You should try warm milk with a spot of honey. It always works for the twins.'

'I know what the cure for my disturbed sleep pattern is, Kay,' he said drily, 'and it sure as hell isn't warm milk.'

There were a hundred and one answers she could make to that, but, as she might betray herself with every one, Kay contented herself with turning her back on him and pretending to adjust Frosty's nose until Georgia and Emily reappeared two seconds later.

'Henry let us have a great big bag of bread, Mummy, and some cake too,' Georgia shouted as she hurtled towards them, Emily in her wake. 'Won't the ducks be pleased?'

The little family of ducks on Mitchell's small but charming lake were pleased, delighting the twins by coming up out of the water and taking the bread right out of the girls' fingers.

'They're virtually tame,' Mitchell said quietly, 'thanks to Henry. He went to see his sister in Kent in the spring—she keeps a smallholding, nothing grand—and while he was there a fox took the mother. He brought the eggs home still in the nest but enclosed in a polystyrene box with a hot-water bottle, so the kitchen became a duckling nursery. They all hatched and he didn't lose one of them. Would you believe the utility room off the kitchen had a paddling pool in it for weeks?'

'Really?' Kay was fascinated. She decided she thoroughly approved of Henry.

'It was a bit difficult as they grew to convince them that Henry wasn't their mother,' Mitchell said with a wry smile. 'For weeks there was the patter of tiny feet about the house if the utility-room door was left ajar. There would be Henry going to answer the door with a perfectly straight line of seven balls of fluff with webbed feet behind him.'

He grinned at her and her heart turned right over.

'Do you know that ducks have got personalities?' He turned to look at Georgia and Emily kneeling in the snow with the ducks all about them, bills opening and shutting. 'That one there in the front, the little bruiser, is called Charlie and he's the boss. And the little brown one hanging at the back is Matilda. She's the most timid one among them and yet Charlie and her are inseparable. It's like he knows she needs looking after.'

He turned to look straight at her, his gaze intensifying and the silver eyes holding hers in such a way she couldn't have spoken to save her life. Kay began to feel she were drowning in the mercurial blue orbs, which seemed to be reflecting the vivid azure of the sky; she couldn't breathe, couldn't move. There was just Mitchell in all the world.

'Have...have the others got names?' she managed at last, her voice breathless.

He smiled, a beautiful smile. 'Oh, yes.' He moved closer, taking her hand and slipping it through his arm as he pointed them out. 'That's Clarence, Lolita, Nessie, Percival and Agnes. Although Nessie might be Agnes and Agnes might be Lolita, if you get my meaning. Henry's the one who can pick them out as though they're his grandchildren.'

If she could just stand here for ever, with the blue sky above and the twins giggling and laughing as they fed Henry's little tribe, and the feel of Mitchell's hard body next to her, she would be happy. She slanted a glance at him from under her eyelashes, the big charcoal overcoat he was wearing making him even more dark and male in the white fairy-tale world surrounding them.

He must have sensed her gaze, his head turning as he looked down at her. Slowly his mouth came closer and she made no move to turn her face away. The kiss was light, sweet and warm in the frozen air and lasted no more than a breath or two, but afterwards his other hand came across hers where it rested in his arm.

'Why is it I want to lay you down in the snow and ravish you until you're moaning my name?' he asked, shockingly, a moment later, his voice a low murmur audible only to her ears.

Her eyes opened wide and she saw his mouth twist in the lopsided smile that spoke of self-derision. 'And now I've lost all the brownie points I'd gained with the account of Charlie and his tribe,' he said sadly.

She laughed, she couldn't help it, but at the same time an inner voice said despairingly, Why did he have to be so drop-dead gorgeous? She would have been satisfied with average, she really would, if Cupid could have shot his arrow into an appropriate male. But instead she had to go and fall for Mitchell. An impossible situation. An impossible man.

He kept her arm in his on the walk back to the house, the twins dancing in front of them like a pair of tiny winter sprites. Their last full day here. As they entered the house by the kitchen door Kay's heart was suddenly as heavy as lead. They would never come again; she would make sure of that. It was too sweet, too intoxicating, too dangerous. It gave her a taste of what could have been if Mitchell had felt differently.

Her mother and Henry were sitting at the kitchen table, close together, the fragrant aroma of percolating coffee scenting the air. Kay watched as Georgia and Emily ran to them, the children's faces glowing as they recounted the adventure with the ducks, and the older couple's expressions benevolent.

What would she do if this affection she could sense between her mother and Henry grew? Kay asked herself as she divested herself of her outdoor clothes. It would mean Mitchell would for ever be on the fringe of her family, even when he had someone new and she was just another of his exes. The thought stung like a scorpion.

Lunch was a cold buffet but none the less delicious for it. Henry had the enviable knack of making even the most ordinary food taste sublime, and Kay thought it showed the strength of Mitchell's will-power that he wasn't showing any signs of surplus fat on his altogether perfectly honed body.

Leonora must have had similar thoughts, because they had just finished the last of a wickedly calorie-loaded chocolate mousse when she said, 'Henry, that was wonderful but in spite of the flu I know I've put on a good few pounds. I'm amazed you and Mitchell are so slim.'

'Men are built differently to women,' Henry said factually. 'Different fat cells and so on. Besides, what does it matter?'

'Plenty when you get to my age and middle-aged spread starts showing its ugly face,' Leonora said ruefully.

'You're perfect.' Henry was looking straight into Leonora's eyes and Kay thought he'd forgotten the rest of them for a moment. 'Fat, thin, it wouldn't matter to me. *You* are perfect.'

Oh, wow! Kay glanced across at Mitchell, who raised laconic eyebrows. There was definitely something going on here all right.

Leonora had gone pink and fluttery and by unspoken mutual consent the conversation moved to safer channels, but the look in Henry's eyes and the emotion in the older man's voice stayed with Kay for the rest of the day.

It was much later, when Kay was lying in bed, that she dissected the events of the day. Building the snowman, the episode with the ducks, the way Georgia and Emily had utterly insisted Mitchell read them a story after their bath once they were tucked up in bed, the wonderful candlelit dinner Henry had cooked for the four adults and the easy laughter and camaraderie between Mitchell, Henry and her mother—it was all too beguiling. She could deceive herself very easily here—pretend it was the start of a for-ever story. But it wasn't.

'Reality check, Kay,' she whispered in the darkness. Tomorrow morning Mitchell was going to take them back to Ivy Cottage and real life would resume again. The strange cat-and-mouse game he seemed determined to play would begin once more, but this time she had to start making a few changes. Cooling things down, refusing the odd date, cutting out any contact between Mitchell and the twins so the little girls could gradually forget him. It was all for the best, it *was*, she assured herself desperately, so why did she feel she was being unfair to everyone?

She turned over onto her stomach with a sigh, angry with Mitchell, herself and the whole world.

As it happened, the return to Ivy Cottage went far easier than Kay had anticipated, mainly due to the fact that there was an emergency with Mitchell's branch in Southampton, which necessitated a personal visit from the man himself. Nevertheless, he insisted on taking Kay, her mother and the girls home even when Henry offered to do it with Kay backing the older man enthusiastically.

'Holden and his inefficient workforce can wait,' Mitchell said grimly after the call during breakfast from the manager in Southampton. 'An hour or two either way is not going to make any difference. I'm taking you back, okay?' He glared at Kay as though she had contrived the situation herself. 'And we'll call in at the supermarket on the way as planned. No argument.'

Kay nodded, said thank you and left it at that then. At least, with Mitchell having to dash off, the farewell should be brief and short-lived, no need to offer coffee or anything else that might have delayed his departure. A quick, clean and concise end to what had been a vitally disturbing and—she had to admit—wonderful Christmas.

It happened exactly as she had envisaged, and within a couple of minutes of their return to their tiny home Kay, her mother and the girls were standing waving Mitchell off from the doorstep.

'Such a shame,' Leonora murmured at the side of her as Georgia and Emily jumped up and down, waving wildly to their hero. 'It would have been nice for us to offer Henry and Mitchell a meal tonight after all they've done for us.'

Oh, no, no. She wasn't starting that. No cosy foursomes. 'We haven't got the room to entertain here, Mum.' It was firm and brooked no argument. 'Besides which, you know how I feel about things.'

Leonora pursed her lips disapprovingly. 'Darling, I wish you'd think again,' she said quietly. 'Henry is sure Mitchell is very fond of you.'

'I've no doubt he has been very fond of plenty of women in the past,' Kay said just as quietly as, the Voyager having driven out of sight, the twins disappeared up to their bedroom to reacquaint themselves with their room and toys as though they had been away for several months instead of several days.

'But how do you know this isn't different?'

'Because I face facts.' Kay turned to look at her mother once they had walked through into the kitchen to unpack the shopping Mitchell had insisted on paying for. 'For example, has Mitchell had other women back to the house for romantic dinners and so on in the past?'

Leonora wriggled uncomfortably. 'I guess so,' she admitted unhappily.

'You know so, and so do I. Probably quite a few stayed over too, and on a regular basis. They got to know Mitchell and be part of his life—but only for as long as he wanted them in it. That's the sort of man he is, Mum. He's head of a large and successful business, he works hard and plays hard, and enjoys the bachelor lifestyle with no ties and no commitments. All his loyalty and commitment is to his business.'

'That doesn't mean he couldn't give it to a woman if he fell in love,' Leonora argued stubbornly.

'That's a bigger "if" than you'll ever know where

Mitchell is concerned.' Leonora stared at her unhappily and Kay's voice softened as she said, 'Look, Mitchell doesn't understand about family. His own was disfunctional and violent, and he has never wanted to settle down. Why would he take on a ready-made family, for goodness' sake? And I come as a package, Mum. Those are the facts. Face them. I have.'

And then she surprised them both by bursting into tears.

Some time later, after a mopping-up session followed by a hot, milky mug of chocolate, Leonora said apologetically, 'No more talking about you know who, I promise. Okay?'

Kay smiled. Until the next time. 'Okay. But don't let how things are with Mitchell and I affect your relationship with Henry, all right? He's lovely, I mean it, and I want you to see him as much as you want to. I think Mitchell and I will begin to tail off now, anyway, and it's all for the best. Really.' *Really.*

At ten o'clock Kay sat toasting her toes in front of the fire, a glass of wine at her elbow. Her mother had gone to bed early and she was all alone in the small sitting room, the Christmas tree lights twinkling and the beginnings of a storm howling outside, if the wind was anything to go by. It was cosy and snug, she was warm and safe with all her family around her—and she felt more miserable than she had ever felt in her life.

When the telephone rang she nearly jumped out of her skin, the book on her lap falling to the floor as she hastily reached for the receiver. 'Hallo?'

'Missing me?'

She nearly dropped the phone, her heart beginning to thunder. 'Mitchell?' she said weakly.

'I hope there's not another man in your life with the

right to ask you if you're missing him,' he said softly, his voice full of laughter. 'So, are you?'

'What?' Her brain wouldn't function.

'Missing me.'

'Are you missing me?' she prevaricated.

'Like hell.' There was no hesitation.

'Well, I'm missing you too.' What else could she say? she asked herself helplessly. Besides, it was the truth.

'Good.' She could tell he was smiling. 'Very good.'

There was a pause while Kay tried to steady her breathing and gain control of her rapid heartbeat. 'Where are you phoning from?' she asked quietly, hoping the trembling in her stomach didn't communicate itself to her voice.

'A hotel I use when I'm down here.' It was offhand and stated he didn't want to talk about his bed for the night.

'How were things when you arrived? As bad as you expected?'

'Worse.' She could hear the irritation in his voice as he thought of it and didn't envy the unfortunate Holden one little bit. 'Looks like I'll be a day or two at least trying to sort out the damn mess.' His voice changed. 'Think you can manage without me that long?' he asked softly.

'I'll just have to try, won't I?' she said lightly, having gained control of her equilibrium after the shock of hearing his voice.

'Don't try too hard.'

It wouldn't matter how hard she tried, she thought ruefully. He was the most fascinating man she had ever met—exciting, sexy, funny, handsome and she loved him to bits. She had never dreamt it was possible to be so captivated by another human being. So, all that being the case, what chance did she have of trying to squeeze him out of her life in a couple of days? It was going to take far, far longer than that, and buckets full of tears. 'You should be pleased I can manage without you,' she said levelly. 'No snares, no promises, right?'

'Modern woman.' There was a note in his voice she couldn't quite place and she wrinkled her nose as she tried to discern it.

'Exactly,' she agreed.

There was another pause. A second passed, then another and another. 'You can be too modern, you know,' he said with faint emphasis.

'I didn't know,' she said, still in a light tone. Keep it nice and easy, Kay, she thought as her heart raced.

'Neither did I until recently.'

She didn't know what to say or how to interpret the meaning of his words. Riddles, things half said, it was always the same. She never knew if she was on foot or horseback.

'How are the twins?' he asked in a different tone of voice entirely.

'Fine. Tired out. They spent ages arranging all the furniture in the doll's house after they'd decided where they wanted it in their bedroom. Big decision between on the floor next to the bookcase so they could lie on the carpet and play with it, or on the dressing table so they could sit on the stool. Georgia wanted the floor, Emily wanted the dressing table. I let them sort it out.'

'I bet I know who won,' he said wryly.

'No prizes, it was Georgia,' Kay admitted.

'She's nearly as strong-willed as her mother.' The smile in his voice softened any sting in the words.

Nevertheless, Kay felt compelled to protest, 'Strong will isn't a bad thing, surely?'

'No, unless...'

'Unless what?'

'It stops someone seeing what's under their nose.'

She blinked, completely taken aback.

'Goodnight, Kay,' he said smokily. 'Dream of me.'

This time she couldn't come back with the sarcasm she'd used the last time he had said the same words. She swallowed hard. 'Goodnight, Mitchell.'

She stood staring across the room with the telephone in her hands for some time after the line had gone dead, until it bleeped loudly at her. She replaced it slowly, her head spinning, and then reached for the glass of wine and drank the whole glassful straight down, whereupon she walked into the kitchen and poured herself another.

After reseating herself in front of the fire with the book on her lap again, she took another hefty sip of wine. If ever she needed a drink it was tonight, she thought ruefully. What was she going to do? Every time she made a conscious decision to withdraw it was as though he reached out and pulled her closer to him.

What did he want? Really want? With his strange, grim background and meteoric success, which had brought him wealth and power, what did he really want? Did he know himself? He had set the boundaries of their relationship in concrete at the beginning of it all, and he hadn't said anything specific to indicate he had changed. She would be crazy to hope that a few shrouded words and the odd glance might suggest she meant more to him than all the others. It wasn't even as if she had the sexual skills, the worldly knowledge, the sheer 'it' factor of his exes—not to mention the women he met socially and in business all the time.

Jealousy streaked through her and she clenched her stomach against it, telling herself not to be so stupid. She shut her eyes, relaxing into the plumpy back of the sofa.

He was in some anonymous hotel room right now—probably very luxurious, with everything he wanted at his fingertips, but characterless none the less. She wished she were with him; she wished it so much it was a physical ache in the essence of her.

CHAPTER TEN

MITCHELL wasn't due back until Monday some time, but he phoned Kay on Friday and Saturday night. Not for anything would she have admitted to a living soul that she was on tenterhooks all day long, every nerve and fibre in her body longing to hear his voice.

She'd got it bad, she told herself helplessly when, at three o'clock on Sunday morning, she still hadn't been able to drift off to sleep. And it scared her to death. Scared her witless, in fact. Which was what she was—witless, crazy, off her trolley, stark, staring and completely mad.

She sat up in bed, brushing her hair out of her eyes before throwing the duvet to one side and swinging her legs onto the floor. After reaching for her robe she slid her feet into her slippers and silently left the bedroom. Her mother was fast asleep; Leonora had spent the day with Henry and hadn't arrived home until gone eleven o'clock, whereupon Kay had noticed she was flushed and happy with the kind of rosy glow that suggested the day had gone extremely well.

Once downstairs she fixed herself a mug of hot milk sweetened with honey and carried it through into the sitting room, not bothering to turn on the light. There was a full moon slanting in through the windows and, with the glow of the dying fire in the grate, she could see enough.

She curled up on the sofa, cradling the warm mug as she sipped at the drink, and when it was finished she snuggled down, pulling her robe about her. Maybe she could sleep down here? she thought drowsily. She *was* tired, exhausted in fact, but for some reason the bedroom she had shared with her mother for the last few years had become claustrophobic the last day or two. Or perhaps it was just the fact that she had always been asleep as soon as her head touched the pillow in the past?

She must have fallen asleep because when the noise awoke her she was conscious of spiralling up from a deep, warm place where she'd been dreaming of Mitchell.

She was curled up in a little ball on the sofa in front of the now-dead fire and it still wasn't light, the moonlight causing dancing shadows to flicker across the room from the bare branches of the tree outside. Kay raised her head, peering over the back of the sofa towards the window as the noise—a kind of scratchy, fumbling sound—came again.

Afterwards she could never explain why she hadn't been frightened up to that point, but she hadn't. Maybe because the cat from across the way often prowled into their garden at night, or because she was still more asleep than awake, she didn't know, but in the same moment that a swirl of icy cold air met her face she saw the outlines of two men at the now-open window.

In the few seconds that she remained frozen with fear one of the men levered himself up onto the window sill, putting one leg into the room, and all the movements as silent as a cat.

The shrillness of Kay's scream, when it came, surprised even her, and after that several things seemed to happen all at the same time. She was aware of ducking down on the sofa and reaching for the poker in the grate, at the same time as she heard one of the men—the one inside the room, she thought—swear profusely and the other one say something urgently, although she couldn't work out what it was.

There was the sound of breaking glass, noise and scurry, but as the landing light went on and Leonora called, 'Kay? Kay, what's happening?' in a voice filled with terror, Kay knew they had gone.

'Stay with the girls,' she called urgently to her mother, rushing across to the light switch. 'I'm going to call the police. We've had some intruders.'

'Intruders? Oh, Kay, Kay! Are you hurt?' It sounded as though her mother was going into hysterics, but when the twins called from their bedroom Leonora's voice was more controlled as she answered, 'I'm coming, dears, don't worry. Everything's all right.'

'Keep them up there,' Kay warned as she dialled. 'I don't want them down here.' She was still gripping the poker and she knew she would have no compunction about using it should the men come back. 'I'm perfectly all right; they didn't touch me.'

In the few minutes in which it took the two young policemen to arrive, Kay stood by the phone without moving. She could see now the burglar who had been inside must have broken the window in his haste to escape, along with a heavy glass vase that had been on the window sill. She was shaking, her teeth chattering, as much from reaction as the freezing air swirling into the room.

They had been trying to invade her house, and with her babies asleep upstairs. She felt such a sickening mixture of shock and rage it made her legs tremble. *How dared they?*

When she heard the car draw up outside, she forced herself to walk to the front door and open it, her face ashen. The two policemen were wonderful, another car—this time with a female police officer—arriving moments later. While one of the policemen took a statement, the other searched the garden outside, but Kay had already told them she was sure the men had gone.

The woman police officer went upstairs to talk to Leonora, returning shortly and smiling at Kay as she said, 'You've got two lovely little girls.'

Yes, she had, and those men would have been here, in the same house with her precious babies. By rights she should have been asleep upstairs, Kay thought sickly. That was what they'd expected.

The police woman must have seen in her face what she was thinking because now she said briskly, 'A cup of tea, I think.'

It was a long night, but by the time a weak and windy dawn began to banish the darkness the police had gone through the wreckage with a fine-tooth comb, dusting and sorting and even finding a piece of glass with some blood on it.

'One of 'em cut themselves,' the policeman said with a great deal of satisfaction. 'Nice of 'em to leave a calling card. We might well find we've got this one on file.'

Her mother and the twins had come downstairs at some point, the children's curiosity overwhelming, but Kay was pleased and relieved to find both Georgia and Emily didn't really seem aware of the significance of what had happened. They had clung to her a while at first, and neat, tidy little Emily had been indignant about all the mess, but there had been no tears. It had been too cold for them to remain downstairs, and her mother had reported both girls were asleep within ten minutes or so once they'd been tucked up back in bed.

'Are you sure we can't call your brother or someone else, a friend maybe, before we leave, Mrs Sherwood?' the woman police officer had asked, once they had done all they could. One of the policemen had stuck a large piece of cardboard across the hole in the window, but the room was still icy.

Kay shook her head. 'No need to disturb anyone now,' she said quietly. It was still only seven o'clock. 'Time enough for that later.'

'I'm ringing Henry.' The police officers were hardly out of the door when Leonora picked up the telephone. 'He always rises at six and he'd want to know.'

More like her mother was longing to tell him, Kay thought indulgently. But she didn't mind. If she was honest her first coherent thought when she'd been waiting for the police to arrive had been an intense desire to be able to talk to Mitchell.

Her mother was a little deflated when the answer machine cut in after she had dialled the number, but, assuming Henry was down at the lake feeding the ducks their normal hearty breakfast, she left a message and hung up.

Once Kay had showered and dressed she felt better, although the white face staring back at her from the mirror still looked like death warmed up. Coffee. Lots of strong, sweet coffee before the girls woke up, she thought practically. Those men, whoever they were, weren't going to get the better of her. She wouldn't let them frighten her, not in her own house.

She put the coffee on to percolate while her mother went upstairs to wash and dress, and was just checking every tiny piece of glass had gone when she heard a car screech to a halt outside. Henry, bless him. He'd obviously heard her mother's message and come flying over in person, rather than ringing back.

She got up from her knees and walked to the front door. They had closed the curtains earlier, hoping it would help to warm the room a little, but it was still icy cold, despite the heating being on. She didn't wait for Henry to knock, opening the door with a smile of welcome, which remained fixed in surprise when she found herself looking into a pair of silver-blue eyes set in an ominously dark face as Mitchell strode up the path, Henry following some yards behind.

'Are you all right?' He didn't wait for her to speak, taking her into his arms as he reached her and holding her so tight she couldn't breathe. 'I'll tear them limb from limb, I swear it.'

'Mitchell, *Mitchell.*' She had to struggle to become free, but when she saw the look on his face her voice gentled. 'I'm fine, I am,' she said quickly. 'No one was hurt—no one but one of the burglars, anyway.'

She had stepped backwards into the sitting room as she'd spoken, the two men following her, but as Henry shut the door Mitchell pulled her to him again, his voice hoarse as he murmured, 'I'd have killed them if they'd hurt a hair on your head. Damn it, I should have *been* here.'

She understood immediately. Her hand lifted to his face and he grabbed it and held it there as she said, 'No, you shouldn't, of course you shouldn't. You can't be everywhere,' knowing that old ghosts had been resurrected and the torment of his sister's death was heavy on his shoulders.

Henry was standing silently behind them, his face grim, and now Kay said, 'Mum's getting dressed, Henry, but there's coffee on the go in the kitchen if you'd like to take charge. And don't you look like that either—we really are all right.'

'Kay, Kay...' As Henry disappeared into the other room Mitchell's hands moved to cradle her face, his lips desperate as they bruised hers in an agony of fear at what might have been. 'Are the twins okay? How badly were they frightened?'

She loved that he'd thought of the girls. 'They're too young to really realise what's happened,' she said softly, her lips tingling and burning. 'I'm not sure how they'll be today, but they're still asleep so that's a good sign.'

'When I think what could have happened—'

'Don't.' She cut off his voice by putting a finger to his lips. 'The police think they are just two petty thieves who have been working this area, apparently. They break in at night and go for things like the TV and video, but they're not violent. One of them cut themselves on the window, they were so desperate to get away when I screamed.'

'You screamed?' His face went greyer. 'Damn it, Kay, I want to do murder.'

Kay thought he needed a cup of coffee more than she did. She pulled him over to the sofa and when they were both sitting down, his arm enclosing her, she said, after they had kissed again, 'What are you doing here? I didn't think you got back until this afternoon?'

'I worked through the night and made the others do the same,' he said grimly, 'and caught the early train this morning. Henry was collecting me from the station when your mother called.'

'You worked through the night? Why?'

'Because I wanted to see you as soon as possible,' he said simply.

Her heart leapt and then began to pound.

'We need to talk, Kay. I can't go on like this,' he said softly, 'but now is not the time. Later.'

She stared at him, doubt mixing with exhilaration. Was this his way of telling her she had to make a decision about the future? Accept his terms or else? The 'iron fist in the velvet glove' approach? She didn't know; she just didn't know. How could you ever read Mitchell's mind?

'Tell me exactly what happened here, Kay,' he said quietly as Henry appeared from the kitchen with a tray holding the coffee. 'Minute by minute.'

Her mother appeared at the top of the stairs just as she began to relate the story, and Kay was left in no doubt as to Henry's feelings for her mother—or her mother's for Henry, come to that—by the exchange between the couple.

Once they were all sitting down, Kay told the two men everything that had happened before they transferred to the kitchen for toast and marmalade and more coffee.

Kay was beginning to feel panicky about what was to come. Mitchell was thoroughly in control of himself again, his brief glitch when he'd first arrived gone as completely as if it had never happened at all. He was attentive, considerate, but his eyes were veiled against her and his face was giving nothing away. She knew all over again that she just didn't understand what made him tick. But he had come, she told herself feverishly. He had rushed here to her side when he'd thought she needed him. That had to mean something, didn't it?

Guilt? a nasty little voice in her head said tauntingly. Could it mean guilt? He had never got over the way he felt he had let his sister down; perhaps this morning hadn't really been about her, Kay Sherwood, so much as demons from the past?

The four of them were still sitting talking when Georgia and Emily came padding downstairs, the little girls' transparent delight at seeing Mitchell causing Kay further misgivings. They adored him, she told herself helplessly as she watched the girls clamber onto his lap. And he was so good with them.

It was mid-morning when Mitchell rose to his feet and took Kay's hand. 'Go and get your coat,' he said quietly. 'We're going for a drive and lunch somewhere after I've phoned a guy I know to come and fix the window.'

'It's a Sunday.' Kay stared at him in surprise. 'No one works on a Sunday.'

'He'll come.' Mitchell turned to Henry and Leonora. 'You two okay to hold the fort for a while?'

'Of course,' said Leonora eagerly, too eagerly, clearly delighted by events.

'Can we come?' Georgia asked immediately.

'Not this time, honey, okay? But I promise we'll go somewhere nice soon,' Mitchell said gently.

'Can we see the ducks again?'

This was obviously considered the ultimate in nice. Mitchell smiled, ruffling the small head of curls as he said, 'I don't see why not.'

Oh, please, God, make all this turn out right, Kay prayed as she fetched her coat, not even stopping to check her hair or put any make-up on. If I'm not what he wants, if he can't break free of the past, don't let my girls be hurt.

As they walked towards the car Mitchell took her hand and Kay found she couldn't speak at all, but her fingers wound themselves round his. She felt in her bones what he was going to say would either make or break them, and she didn't have any idea which way it would go.

'I've finished racing at the circuit.'

It was the very last thing in all the world she had expected him to say, and now, as she slid into the car, she stared up at him as he stood holding the door open for her.

'For good?' she asked after a moment or two.

'Oh, yes, Kay, for good.'

She nodded, her heart beginning to thud harder. 'I'm glad.'

'I'm glad you're glad.'

'Mitchell—'

'Not yet, Kay. I want to talk to you, really talk to you somewhere quiet where there's just the two of us.' He shut the door, walking round the bonnet and climbing into the driver's seat. 'There's a pub I know that serves excellent Sunday lunch not too far from here and you don't have to book.' He glanced at her, his eyes crystal-clear. 'We can be there by twelve after I've said what I need to say first.'

Kay nodded. 'Fine.' Fine? What a stupid thing to say when she was so nervous she knew she would never be able to eat again in the whole of her life.

He drove out of the town and into the country and he didn't say a word as the powerful car ate up the miles. They had been travelling for about twenty minutes when he pulled off the road and into a gateway that overlooked a valley still white with snow. It was beautiful, tranquil and sweepingly majestic, the trees stark and bare against the pale world surrounding them. A few lone birds were flying overhead but otherwise everything was still, a frozen world captured in time.

She sat staring straight ahead for a moment as the engine died, and then she forced herself to turn her head and look at him, knowing he was staring intently at her.

She saw a muscle clench in his jaw as he looked into her eyes. 'We both said a lot of things when we first met.' He said quietly. 'Do you remember?'

Did she remember? They had haunted her ever since. 'What sort of things?' she murmured warily, still terribly unsure of where he was coming from.

He gave a short, mirthless laugh. 'Stupid things.' He

raked back his hair, the action impatient but at the same time carrying a hint of nervousness. 'And yet not so stupid because I thought that was how I felt at the time, that I would never—' He stopped abruptly. 'What I mean is, until then—'

He paused again and Kay stared at him in disbelief. Mitchell, controlled, concise Mitchell, ruthless and focused and as to the point as a sharp blade, struggling for words? Somehow it was more illuminating than anything that had happened that morning.

'What are you trying to say?' she whispered weakly, knowing it had to come from him. If what she was daring to hope was true, it had to start now, properly, for it to have any chance at all.

'I love you, Kay,' he said grimly.

She looked at him, a tiny part of her mind that seemed to be working separately from the rest of her pointing out that even in declaring himself Mitchell had to be different from other men. He had spoken more as though he were pronouncing a death sentence on her, rather than giving her the one thing in all the world she really wanted.

'I know you don't feel the same, not yet, and I can understand that,' he said quickly as she remained stock-still just staring at him, her mind racing as she still didn't dare let the hope run free. 'But one of the things we said when we first met was that if either party wanted the situation to change, one way or the other, they had to say. Well, I'm saying, Kay. I've had a bellyful of going softly, softly, and this last episode with those ba—' he stopped short, taking a deep breath before he continued '—with those men this morning was the final straw. I need you to know how I feel. I need to be able to have the right to strangle scum like those two because they dared to come anywhere near the woman of my heart,' he finished angrily.

Kay stared at his dark, furious face and thought she had never loved him so much as in this moment.

'Kay, I want a future for us,' he continued with barely a pause, his chest rising and falling with the force of his emotion. 'I want—oh, I want the lot, I guess. But I won't rush you, I'll keep to that—' And then, as though to disprove the last words, he said, 'Say something, damn it.'

Oh, Mitchell. She swallowed, fighting back the tears as she said, 'You...you're sure? I mean, really sure? There's the girls...'

'More sure than I've ever been of anything in the whole of my life.' He was looking at her intently now, his face changing as he took in her trembling mouth. 'I want you in my life for ever, I want a ring on your finger to keep the other wolves off and to let them know that you are mine. Is that chauvinistic?'

'Probably.' Tears had spilled out of her eyes now but she smiled tremulously.

He reached out a wondering hand and touched a glittering tear as it hung on an eyelash. 'Does this mean you care a little?' he asked shakily.

He looked big and dark and handsome as he sat looking at her uncertainly, his jet-black hair in stark contrast to the piercing silvery-blue eyes, and she wondered what she had ever done to deserve the love of this man. Because it was there, shining in his eyes. He was letting her see it and it filled her heart with such joy she could hardly breathe.

'I've loved you for the whole of my life,' she whispered, 'long before I knew you. When I first saw you, something happened inside and it scared me to death. I tried to tell myself it was all sorts of things but it grew and grew and finally I had to admit it was love. A forever love. But you didn't want me like that...'

'Oh, my love, my love.' His voice was thick as he took her into his arms, pulling her against the wall of his chest as he nuzzled into her hair.

'I tried not to fall in love with you, so hard, but it happened right from the first,' she said, her voice muffled against his overcoat. 'But you had had so many women, beautiful women.'

'I never loved one of them.' His voice was soft above her head. 'I liked some more than others but they never stirred my heart. If I'm honest, until I met you I didn't want to acknowledge there could be anything beyond sexual attraction between a man and a woman and I didn't have to. Then you came along, and...'

He hesitated, and she said, 'Yes? Tell me,' as she raised her head, kissing the corner of his hard mouth, still unable to believe she could do that freely now.

'I had always told myself that my father didn't love my mother towards the end, that she had burnt his love out,' he said huskily, the words being forced up from some dark place within him. 'It was the only way I could come to terms with an essentially good man like he was loving a woman like her. I told myself he stayed with her because he believed in family, that misguidedly he thought having a father *and* mother was more important than splitting us up. But deep down I knew it wasn't true, and that's what I've been fighting ever since the accident. He still loved her, Kay. He sacrificed my sister—he would have sacrificed anyone—to be with her, to hang onto her. I never wanted any woman to have that sort of power over me. It filled me with abhorrence, with disgust, but mostly blind fear.'

He looked down at her, his mouth twisting. 'Great, eh? I'm a mess, I admit it.'

'I'll sort you out.' She smiled up at him, her arms going tight round his neck. 'I promise.'

'I believe you can.' His voice held a note of wonder.

'We can do anything, the two of us,' she said, happy tears still squeezing themselves out of her eyes. 'We can take on the whole world and win.'

'I only want you,' he said huskily. 'When you told me how badly you'd been let down, how you'd fought back, taking on the responsibility of your mother and the business, even sorting your brother's life out, I couldn't believe that a tiny, slim little scrap like you could have that sort of fire and will-power in her. Boy, did I learn fast,' he added wryly. 'And more surprises were in store. I met your daughters. *Daughters.* And you not looking old enough to be out of pigtails at times.'

He pulled her into him again, kissing away the tears and then taking her mouth in a kiss that shook her to her very roots. His breathing was heavy when at last he lifted his head, his lips slowly leaving hers.

'The twins, Mitchell. You don't mind that they come with me?' she whispered, feeling she knew the answer but needing to hear it all the same.

'Mind?' He kissed her again. 'Oh, my darling, how could I mind? They're wonderful, amazing, two miniature Kays. Georgia has all of your determination and fire, and little Emily is your other side, the vulnerable, needing reassurance, unsure part of you. Two little individual clones from one beautiful lady.'

'They love you already.' Her hand moved gently to his mouth again, her fingers tracing his lips. 'Children see so much more clearly than us at times. They recognised the real Mitchell long before you let me see him.'

'I think your mother is for me too,' he said with some satisfaction, grinning down at her suddenly. 'I sensed an ally in her from the very beginning.'

'As well you might.' She met his eyes in amusement.

'Marry me, Kay.'

His voice was soft with a catch in it and her heart soared with the birds overhead. 'Yes,' she said shakily, 'but not straight away. First we'll get the twins used to the idea and just have some time...'

She didn't know how to put it, and he finished for her, his face understanding, 'Getting used to it ourselves?'

Did he know there was still just the tiniest doubt, the merest smidgen that he might find he couldn't do the whole family thing? She didn't know, but she was grateful he had put it the way he had. She nodded. 'I love you, Mitchell, with all my heart,' she said before she pulled his head down to hers.

Just so that he knew.

CHAPTER ELEVEN

'Do I look all right, Kay? Are you sure this suit is my colour?'

'Mum, you look fantastic. When you walk up the aisle Henry is going to be knocked sideways,' Kay said reassuringly as she looked into her mother's flushed, anxious face.

It was true—Leonora did look amazing in the pale cream suit and huge bridal hat with pale blue feathers waving gently over the rim.

'Is the car here yet?'

Leonora was flapping, but then every bride had the right to be nervous on her wedding day. Kay smiled at her mother, putting out a hand and touching Leonora's dear face before she said gently, 'Everything's under control, Mum. And if I hear correctly, I think the car's just arrived.'

She hung out of the bedroom window of Ivy Cottage and, sure enough, an elegant cream Rolls complete with ribbons and driver was waiting outside, its paintwork shining in the mild December sunshine.

Leonora turned to her daughter, her voice trembling as she said, 'The end of an era, Kay.'

'And a great new one about to start.'

'Your father wouldn't have minded me marrying again, would he?'

'Of course he wouldn't.' Kay took her mother into her arms, mindful of the new hat. 'And it isn't as if you've exactly rushed into it, is it? Two years you've kept that poor man waiting; it's about time you made an honest man of him.'

'Oh, Kay.' Leonora giggled and then took a deep breath. 'Right, I'm ready.'

The drive to the church through the slanting sunshine was very pleasant, but Leonora kept tight hold of Kay's hand all the time. Kay could understand why. Her mother had had her own gremlins to come to terms with before she had felt she could finally commit to Henry. Kay's father had been a good man and they had been happy most of the time, but it wasn't until Henry had proposed to her mother some months after Mitchell had popped the question that Kay had realised how the past had affected Leonora. The uncertainty about money, which had been a constant thorn in Leonora's flesh when she had been married before, the final catastrophic finale when she had been left with nothing due to Kay's father's speculating, had all taken its toll.

But Henry's persistence had finally paid off. He wanted her as his wife, he had insisted firmly. Not as his companion or his partner or any other of the modern terms bandied about these days. He was old-fashioned, he admitted it, but he wanted a gold ring on the third finger of Leonora's left hand and that was that.

'I've never really said thank you for saving me after your father died,' Leonora said quietly as the church came in sight.

'Saving you?' Kay stared at her mother. 'I didn't save you.'

'Oh, yes, you did, darling.' Leonora squeezed her daughter's hand. 'I was in a state, more of a state than I was willing to admit to anyone at the time. You left a secure job, a flat, all that you'd worked for for yourself and the twins after Perry left, and you came home to be with me. And you did it so sweetly. Never once did you make me feel as if you didn't want to be there.'

'I did want to be there, that's why,' Kay said softly, smiling at her mother as she added, 'And don't cry, not now, not when I've done your make-up so well.'

'Even my meeting Henry was through you.' Leonora gave a loud sniff and then put down the little winter posy she was carrying. 'Have you got a tissue, darling?'

'Oh, Mum.' Kay grinned at her mother. 'I do love you.'

'And I love you.'

Then the car stopped at the little wicker gate in front of the long, winding path leading to the church door, and it was all flurry and movement for a minute as Kay helped her mother out, adjusting her hat and handing her the posy once she was on the pavement.

'Grandma! Grandma!' The twins had been waiting just inside the gate, holding Mitchell's hands, and now they came dancing out, small faces aglow as they caught sight of Leonora and their mother.

Kay smiled at her husband.

They had married within six months of his proposal, a quiet summer wedding with just family present and the girls as bridesmaids, dressed in fairy-tale dresses of white muslin and pink rosebuds. It had been wonderful, magical.

Now the twins were being bridesmaids again, but this time they were in blue satin with fake fur muffs and little warm cloaks. Her mother—the most conventional of women normally—had cut with protocol and insisted she wanted Kay to give her away, and with Mitchell being Henry's best man it was a real family affair.

Kay looked at her husband now as he hurried up the church path to take his place beside Henry, ready for when they came in. She touched the round mound of her stomach briefly wherein their first child, a little boy with strong, healthy limbs, from what the scan had revealed, lay.

Mitchell had cried with joy when he had seen his son on the monitor; in fact he'd had them all crying—the doctor and herself as much with the look on his face as the wonder of the new little life growing inside her.

And it had happened at just the right time. With Henry now leaving their house to live with her mother in Ivy Cottage, and Kay just having finished work completely after making the delivery business over to Peter, lock, stock and barrel, she felt ready to become a housewife again.

It had taken a little time for her to be comfortable with the idea after she had fought so hard for a measure of independence with Perry, but life was so different with Mitchell, so absolutely wonderful and perfect and glorious, that all her faint doubts had disappeared. He loved her in a way she had never dreamt of being loved, only desiring the best for her, and she felt more treasured and cherished than any woman on earth.

'"Perfect love casteth out fear."' She murmured the words the minister had spoken on her wedding day, and which had stayed with her ever since.

'What was that, dear?'

Her mother had turned to her, and now Kay said as she pushed open the gate, 'Nothing, Mum. Come on, he's waiting.'

They walked up the long path hand in hand, and when the wedding march sounded and Kay had ushered Georgia and Emily in front of them they still walked hand in hand to Henry and Mitchell, waiting at the end of the aisle.

The sunlight had turned the stained-glass window overlooking the altar into a spectacular backdrop, and as Kay delivered her mother into Henry's care and took her place in the front pew her heart was full.

She loved the most wonderful man in all the world and he loved her. Their days were filled with warmth and closeness, Mitchell hungry for all that real family life meant, but it was the nights, when it was just the two of them in their huge, soft bed, that she felt she really became the woman she'd always been destined to be.

In the warm afterglow of their lovemaking, lovemaking that was so wonderful and incredible that sometimes she thought she would die from the pleasure he induced, he would tell her how much he loved her. She was his woman, his treasure, his reason for breathing, the only woman in the world for him—beautiful, perfect and incomparably precious.

And in the soft darkness she would hold him close, her body moulded into his as she laid her heart and her soul bare before him. She kept nothing back; she didn't have to. He was Mitchell, her husband, and she could trust him completely, and she wanted to give him the reassurance she knew he would always need. The world saw a strong, powerful, ruthless man, but that was only a part of him. The real part, *her part*, was so much more than that.

As he joined her in the pew Mitchell smiled at her. 'Happy, love?' he asked softly, his fingers brushing over his child briefly as his eyes devoured her in a most unchurchlike way.

'More than I can say,' she answered mistily as joy and gratitude for all that life held flooded her heart. Life was rich and filled with love. She had Mitchell, she had her family and there was new, strong life growing inside her.

She was blessed.